For Jen. I'm risking it.

Tell Me Everything

Also by Laura Kay

The Split

Tell Me Everything

LAURA KAY

QUERCUS

First published in Great Britain in 2022 by

QUERCUS

Quercus Editions Ltd
Carmelite House
50 Victoria Embankment
London EC4Y 0DZ

An Hachette UK company

A CIP catalogue record for this book is available
from the British Library

HB ISBN 978 1 52940 985 7
TPB ISBN 978 1 52940 986 4

10 9 8 7 6 5 4 3 2 1

Typeset by Jouve (UK), Milton Keynes

Printed and bound in Great Britain by Clays Ltd, Elcograf S.p.A.

Papers used by Quercus are from well-managed forests and other responsible sources.

Prologue

'See,' Georgia says, 'it was worth the walk, wasn't it?'

She picks up a peach from the picnic basket in front of us and takes a bite. The juice dribbles down her chin.

I might lean forward and wipe it off but instead I sit back and watch her, pink from our walk in the sun, sleeves rolled up on her white T-shirt, cross-legged with her trainers kicked off. I smile despite not really believing it was worth the three hours and severe sunburn it took for us to get here.

'It was,' I say.

She sticks out a foot and nudges me gently in the thigh.

'You're not even looking at the view.'

I take my sunglasses off my head and make a show of putting them on, as though they're my actual glasses and I need them in order to properly see. I plan to say something silly but, actually, the view is spectacular. Green rolling hills and far in the distance, sparkling under the blue skies, the sea.

'It's lovely, George. Honestly.'

'Has it made up for a weekend with my family?'

We've been staying with Georgia's parents for the long weekend and though they've been nothing but lovely to me, it has felt like the longest weekend of all time. Despite being in the countryside with nothing but miles and miles of fields between us and the rest of civilisation, I've spent the past few days feeling increasingly claustrophobic, longing to be back in Brighton.

This weekend away was something I agreed to months ago when we were lying in bed together and Georgia was propped up on one arm leaning over me. In that moment I'd have said yes to anything she asked. My vague feeling of unease was so quickly dismissed, went so easily unanalysed. This trip was something someone else would have to deal with in the future. But here I am.

Georgia lobs her peach stone into the distance and comes to lie beside me. She smells like sun cream. I think she's developed a hundred more freckles since we left the house this morning.

'That might take some more making-up actually,' I say.

'Really?'

Georgia turns onto her side so she's facing me and slips her hand under my T-shirt, tracing lines on my stomach. I can feel that I'm sticky with sweat around my waistband but I don't stop her.

'Can you believe it's been a year?' Georgia says.

'No,' I say, 'I can't.'

Us having been together for a year is Georgia's favourite topic of conversation recently. It's the longest relationship I've had and she sees it as a personal accomplishment.

'A year of us,' Georgia says. I turn to look at her.

'I hate those sunglasses,' she says, 'I can't see your eyes.'

I sit up a bit, resting on my elbows. I leave my sunglasses on.

'Shall we open the wine?' I say.

I set about attempting to dislodge the cork while Georgia screws stems to the plastic wine glasses her parents insisted we brought with us.

'Cheers,' I say, tapping my glass to hers.

'To a year together,' Georgia says. Just as I've taken a sip, she adds, 'And to many more!'

The wine sticks in my throat. It tastes sour. I pick up a bottle of water and take a few large gulps. Georgia doesn't appear to notice my discomfort.

'We won't be with my parents for our anniversary next year, I promise,' Georgia says. 'But this was the only weekend we were all free. And they so wanted to finally spend some time with you.'

I nod, an agreement that we won't be here next year, that we have indeed spent some time with her parents. We sit for a while side by side, blinking into the sun. I can practically feel her contentment, a gentle hum vibrating next to me. My stomach churns, the feeling that's been festering for the past few weeks finally coming to the surface. I close my eyes, its predictable familiarity is almost a relief.

Georgia sighs.

'Couldn't you just stay here forever?'

I don't reply. I just put a hand on her knee and squeeze it, trying to impress as much meaning as I can into my fingertips. To say I wish I could. I wish I could tell you that.

Georgia picks up my hand and presses her fingers into my palm.

'You're all clammy.' She peers at me. 'Are you all right? You look a bit funny.'

I nod and wipe cold sweat from my forehead with the back of my hand.

'A bit too long in the sun, maybe.'

Without hesitation she takes her baseball cap off her head and places it on mine.

'Are you sure?' I say.

'What's mine is yours,' she says. 'Always.'

1

Two years later

It is not even 9 a.m. and our flat is already hotter than the sun. I stand by the coffee machine inserting capsules and stabbing at buttons until something happens. Georgia is bashing ice cubes out of a tray. She swears as half of them land on the floor but the ones she manages to salvage she picks up in fistfuls and piles into our coffee mugs. She walks over to the fridge and passes me the oat milk, I put a splash in her mug and fill mine up to the top. I stir hers, pass it to her and then add sugar to mine. She grabs two paper straws from the drawer where we keep all the miscellaneous things that don't have homes and places one in each of our cups. We both lean against the counter, take a sip at the same time and grimace slightly. We don't like this flavour. It's too strong. Ours is a very well-rehearsed morning coffee dance. This is the last time we'll do it.

'Want some?' Georgia says as she spoons Greek yoghurt over a bowl of blueberries.

'No thanks,' I say, 'I'm going to buy a smoothie on the way into work.'

'A smoothie?' Georgia raises her eyebrows but doesn't comment further. She licks her spoon and puts the yoghurt back in the fridge.

'Sure.'

A smoothie, a croissant, a bacon sandwich. Who's to say?

'So what time are you going to be home later, do you think?'

I glance at my phone, as if knowing the time now will provide some sort of answer to her question.

'Erm, realistically? Like . . . seven?'

'Natty!'

'What?'

I take a sip of my coffee. I know what.

'You still have to pack!'

'I will, I will.'

'Have you even started?'

'Obviously!'

'Natasha.'

She looks at me seriously.

'Look, have I physically started packing? No. But mentally I am fully on top of it. Don't worry. I'm going to have it done in minutes.'

Georgia rolls her eyes at me but ends up smiling. She's extra chipper this morning.

'Right, I'm off,' she says decisively without actually making any moves to go. 'I'm having a quick drink with Zara after work and then I'll be home to help you, OK?'

'Oh, Zara's not coming this evening?'

Georgia smiles patiently.

'She'll be here first thing in the morning.'

'Of course, to escort me out.'

Georgia ignores me, puts her bowl in the sink, takes the straw out of her coffee and downs the dregs, crunching on a couple of ice cubes. I shudder.

'OK, have a great day,' she breezes past me, pausing to give me a swift kiss on the cheek on her way out. She smells nice, clean hair and perfume.

'You too,' I shout after her.

I stand in the kitchen alone for a moment, savouring the last drops of my horrible coffee for the final time.

In the end I swerve the smoothie and eat a croissant so flaky I end up inspecting myself for stray crumbs all day. The therapy room I rent is no cooler than the flat. It's on the top floor of a converted town house. I have the window open and an ancient fan whirring away but I'm pretty sure it's making things worse by pushing the thick air around the room. I've had three clients this morning – one midlife crisis, one quarter-life crisis and, finally, a terrible boyfriend. He's the kind of client where instead of saying, 'Hmm, and how does that make you feel?' I want to put down my notebook, grab him by the shoulders and say, 'Dump him! Dump him now!' Instead I power through, nod in all the right places and privately count down the hours until I can have a very cold glass of wine.

'The thing is,' David is saying, 'the thing is he's had such a hard time with relationships in the past, and that's not his fault. It's just that now when it comes to commitment he really struggles, you know?'

'Mmm,' I nod, not a yes, not a no. I wait for him to keep talking.

'So when he says it's not the right time for him to come to my mum's sixtieth birthday party, like he's too overwhelmed to do that, even though I told him that it would mean a lot, and like, even though he cancelled on the day and was going to drive us and I had to buy a train ticket and it was really expensive, that's really because of his deeper trust issues and I should respect that. Like maybe . . . maybe the issue is that I should have more empathy.'

'Remind me,' I say, 'just refresh my memory so I'm clear. How long have you and Will been dating?'

David sits back in his chair and wipes some sweaty hair from his forehead. He knows I don't need reminding.

'Three and a half years.'

I let that hang in the air for a moment.

'It's a long time,' he says eventually.

'So you consider three years a long time. I think that's valid. A lot of people would consider three years a significant amount of time. I wonder if it might be worth reflecting on just how many years you want to wait for someone to commit to you.

And what that commitment might look like. And whether that's something Will can offer you.'

He nods, tired. I'm tired too. This is perhaps too much for one person to reflect on in thirty-five-degree heat.

'He's not a bad person,' he says. 'I don't want you to think . . . I wouldn't want you to think badly of him.'

I nod.

'What do you think you've said to me that would make him seem like a bad person?'

I do actually think he's a bad person, a bad boyfriend anyway. This sixtieth birthday party was important. Just go and drink an Aperol Spritz with Margaret, Will. It's one afternoon!

'Just, I don't know. I talk about him letting me down a lot but none of the good stuff.'

'Do you feel let down?'

He looks at me, surprised at his own words echoed back at him.

'I do feel let down. I just want him to be . . . I want him to be . . .'

He shakes his head.

'I want him to be different.'

I nod. We're out of time.

As soon as David leaves (to catch his train to go glamping with terrible Will and terrible Will's friends) I grab my phone, order an Uber and race across town to make it in time to teach my class. Sometimes on Friday afternoons I run an Introduction to Therapy taster session. I've never committed to teaching the whole course. I don't particularly like teaching but I do particularly love regular income.

I arrive at the nondescript office building with twenty minutes to spare, enough time for me to drag some plastic chairs into two semicircles, one behind the other, and stick a sign on the door which reads, 'Please wait outside until class begins at 2pm'. Good to enforce boundaries early on. Boundaries are the bedrock of therapy. Also I don't want to make small talk with all the very keen people who arrive early. But mainly the boundaries thing. Very important.

I had hoped the temperamental air conditioning might have kicked in but, if it has, I can't feel it. I try to open the windows but they're locked shut. A safety measure. I wonder if it is possible to boil alive in an office block. It smells of old carpet and microwaved lunches. It's eerily quiet.

I decide, since I have a few minutes to myself, to eat the Twix that's been melting in my bag all day and read the news, by which of course I mean, scroll through Twitter. I have a message from Georgia asking me for the thousandth time if I'll definitely be home at seven. My stomach flips at the prospect of the evening. How long can packing really take?

I've just finished the first stick of my Twix when the door opens.

'Excuse me? Natasha?'

I wipe my mouth on the back of my hand and quickly fold the wrapper around the second stick.

A woman is standing in the doorway clutching a takeaway

coffee cup in one hand and her phone in the other. She's wearing skinny jeans. Super tight and black. I don't know how she's coping with the heat. She smiles and makes to step into the room, assuming she's found the correct one.

I stand up.

'There's a waiting area outside. Please go and take a seat and I'll call you all in at two. There's actually a sign on the door.'

It comes out much harsher than I intend it to. She stands completely still for a moment. It happens too quickly to be sure but I could swear I see a flicker of a smile play on her lips, just for a second.

'Got it,' she says as she backs out and down the hall.

I eat the rest of my chocolate hurriedly and watch the clock, waiting until it's exactly 2 p.m. to go and fetch them all. My own voice, shrill and officious, rings in my ears: *There's actually a sign on the door.*

When I pull the door open to let them in, I lean against it, making room for them all to file in past me.

'Welcome,' I say. 'You can all come in now and find a seat.'

The girl in skinny jeans is the first to make her way towards me.

I reach out my hand to shake hers and she shoves her phone in the back pocket of her jeans in order to do so.

'I'm Natasha.'

'Margot.' She says, 'Sorry about before.'

Margot. A childhood friend had a dog named Margot. 'If you catch her in the wrong mood she'll have your arm off,' my friend's mum used to say, lovingly.

'It's OK,' I say, feeling guilty about admonishing her. Should I apologise? Really it was more about Twix time getting interrupted than anything else.

'I just like to set clear boundaries right from the start,' I say. She nods.

'Of course, that makes sense.'

She brushes past me. I carry on holding the door open for everyone else but, instead of greeting them properly, I can't help but watch her as she makes her way into the room. She sits down in the seat directly in the middle of the front row and puts her bag under her chair.

I wait for everyone else to file in and find a seat. They all mumble introductions to each other as they pull brand-new notebooks and pens out of backpacks and sip from identical reusable water bottles. There's fifteen of them all together. A fairly typical bunch. Becoming a therapist is an expensive business so these courses attract a pretty homogenous crowd. Most of the women are older than me, a couple by decades. All but one are white. There are two men, perhaps in their forties. Margot is an exception to the rule. I wonder if she's rich and being funded by family or whether she plans to take my path – two jobs, no sleep, mercifully low rent.

I introduce myself and do my usual spiel about the afternoon taster session, what we'll cover and what we should hope to achieve but it's hot and it's the end of the week and I can tell I've lost some of them before I've even begun. It's a shame because I know what this taster session is costing them.

'I need a volunteer,' I say and before anyone else can even lift a finger, let alone raise a hand, Margot stands up and walks over to the empty chair next to mine, set slightly apart from the rest of the group. She takes her coffee and a bottle of water with her and places them by her feet.

'Happy to help,' she says. I can't quite identify her accent but I think it's Australian. Or maybe New Zealand. The way she says 'help', *hilp.*

I look at the rest of the group. I wonder if they're expecting me to admonish her for just walking up here and not waiting for me to choose someone or let anyone else get a look in. Should I assert my authority somehow? Set another bloody boundary? They just look weary but I can tell their interest is somewhat piqued. No one looks too put out to still be in their seats.

'Thank you for volunteering,' I say to her and then I turn to the group. 'OK so . . .'

I look at Margot as if I need her to remind me of her name. Apparently I'm going to assert my authority like I'm in high school. It's pathetic but I feel briefly back in control.

'It's Margot,' she says kindly, not breaking eye contact with me. She smiles slightly. She knows my game.

'Margot and I are going to demonstrate what an initial therapy session might look like between a client and a therapist. Now,' I turn to address Margot again, 'you obviously don't have to tell me anything you don't want to – in fact, for the purposes of this session, you don't even have to tell me anything that's true.'

Margot shrugs.

'I'm happy to tell the truth.'

I nod.

'OK then. During this exercise I am your therapist and you are my prospective client.'

She widens her eyes at me, indicating she gets it. She nods impatiently.

'And it goes without saying,' I say, 'that this is a safe space and anything you share here stays within these four walls.'

I glance around the group and everyone nods. They're all sitting up a bit straighter, pens poised. They're hoping for something juicy.

'So Margot,' I smile at her, 'how are you doing today?'

'I'm good,' she says brightly.

There's a ripple of laughter throughout the room and Margot smiles at me, not acknowledging it.

'Good.' I smile serenely back at her and then around the room, refusing to be put off. 'And how do you feel about today's assessment?'

'Fine, thanks.'

More laughter, quieter this time.

'OK, so what brings you here?'

She shrugs and takes a sip from her cup. It smells sweet, like vanilla syrup. I don't think she's being deliberately obtuse. I think she's waiting for my questions to become interesting.

'Maybe you can just start by telling me a bit about yourself?'

'Like what?'

'Like where you're from? What you do? Single? In a relationship?

Are you close with your family? The basics. If you're comfortable with that, of course.'

She looks at me warily.

Christ this is going to be difficult.

'I'm from New Zealand originally but I've lived in the UK for like . . . twelve years now. My parents are still together. I love them but we're not close. I mean, we're literally eleven thousand miles apart. I'm a barista but I'm also a writer and a comic. I'm . . . dating.'

She looks at me, trying to convey some sort of meaning. It seems important to her that I know the last part. Maybe it's for the sake of our captive audience. I remain impassive.

'A writer?'

'Yep.'

'What, like, books?'

She rolls her eyes at me. They're green and almost comically expressive. Underneath them are deep, dark circles.

'I write stories, poems. Sometimes I perform them, sometimes they're in books. That kind of thing.'

'Great. And a comic? So that's like . . .'

'Jokes,' she says. 'I stand on stage and tell jokes.'

She stares at me, looking for clues of recognition or, perhaps, judgement. I hope there are no traces of my natural repulsion to performance of basically any kind on my face.

'And did you want to talk about your work in these sessions?'

'Not particularly.'

'Dating?'

A smile plays on her lips and she pushes some hair from her face. It's dark and glossy and she has a fringe that looks to be in the awkward stages of being grown out.

'No.'

'OK, well what would you like to discuss?'

She pauses. I think she's trying to decide whether to tell me something real or make something up. In the moment it's very difficult to be open in front of a group of strangers, no matter how confident you are.

'I can't sleep.'

Ah, the truth.

'Talk about that a little.'

'What is there to say? I go to bed, I read, I listen to some podcast that's meant to send you to sleep, I close my eyes, I stay awake.'

She kicks her sliders off and goes to tuck her feet underneath her on the chair but she stops with one foot still on the floor.

'Is this OK?'

'Would you be more comfortable?'

'I guess I would.'

'Then it's OK.'

She tucks the other foot underneath her. I glance around the room, the whole lot of them are taking notes. *Tucks foot under self.*

'So yeah, I've tried everything. I took sleeping pills for a while but it wasn't for me. I've been hypnotised. Yoga. Crystals. Everything you can think of. My mother thinks it's something deeper. That there's something in my psyche keeping me awake.'

'Like anxiety?'

She nods. 'Or guilt.'

'Guilt. Why guilt?'

'I guess it would keep you awake.'

'What would you have to feel guilty about?'

She shrugs.

'Everyone's guilty of something, aren't they?'

I'm aware that the room is suddenly completely silent, no one's even scribbling.

'Do you think everyone's guilty of something?'

She smiles again.

'Yes.'

I write 'intense' in my notebook and nod like I'm mulling over what she's said.

'So what would you be hoping to achieve in our sessions if we worked together?'

She sighs heavily.

'I don't think we're going to achieve anything. But what's the harm in trying? Plus . . .' she grins, she's about to put a shield up, our moment of clarity dissolving in front of us, 'it'll make my mother happy.'

'Tell me about your mother.'

She laughs and everyone else does too, relieved, the tension broken by this classic therapy line of questioning.

'Are you going to tell me that I can't sleep because I hate my mother and want to have sex with my father, is that it?'

I smile and there are more titters around the room.

'We don't have to talk about your mother if you'd prefer not to.'

She nods, shakes her coffee cup, decides it's empty and places it on the floor next to her feet.

'So what about you?'

I feel my whole body tense.

'What about me?'

'Where are you from? Single? In a relationship? The basics.'

I put my notebook down.

'We're not here to talk about me.'

This is good, I tell myself, despite my cheeks flushing. This is good because this is something I can point out later to the group. An example of setting boundaries.

'You don't tell your patients anything?'

'You're not my patient. I'm not a doctor.'

'Aha! So we know you're not a doctor.'

She looks at me hopefully, trying to make me laugh. Not uncommon for real new clients. And especially not uncommon for performers.

'That's right.'

'Are you from Essex?'

I'm temporarily thrown. Not many people can detect my accent after many years of being ironed out at university, and by spending time with people who my twin sister Natalie would describe as 'annoyingly posh'.

'I am.'

I immediately regret answering. She's thrilled, which confirms it was the wrong thing to do. I glance around the room and unbelievably they're still taking notes. *From Essex originally . . .*

'I knew it. I've been watching *Love Island*. I can recognise all the accents now. Before I moved here I thought you all – *talked like this.*' She does an impression that lands somewhere between the Queen and Dick Van Dyke.

'It seems to me that maybe you don't particularly want to be here.'

She looks straight at me, unblinking.

'Why would you think that?'

'It seems like you'd rather not talk and that you're quite sure I won't be able to help. I wonder what brought you here.'

'Um, curiosity, mainly.'

'Curiosity to see whether it would help you sleep?'

'No. More like . . . curiosity about the process. About you. Therapy in general. I'm writing something so this is like . . .'

She waves her hand around in the air, looking for the word.

'Research?' I suggest.

'Yes! Exactly that. And if it helps my sleep, then . . . bonus.'

'Right.'

I draw a big question mark in my notebook. I can't tell who I'm speaking to now, real Margot or fake client Margot.

I thank her and turn to the group to ask if they have any questions. No one raises a hand, which is ridiculous. None of them have ever done any therapy training before and they've just witnessed a car crash of a 'session'. I have questions and I'm meant to be teaching the class. They're all too hot and tired or too shy. Maybe they're nervous around Margot too.

'OK, well now we're going to have everyone split into pairs for a few minutes and have a go themselves. Remember the focus at this point is practising active listening with your partner. One person should play the role of therapist, one the prospective client, and you should interact using what you've just seen as a blueprint.'

A blueprint for a deeply dysfunctional session.

There's an odd number so there's going to have to be one group of three. Normally I'd just make the odd one out join another group. Come on, Natasha. Group of three. I open my mouth to allocate someone to join another couple but instead I find myself turning to Margot.

'There's an odd number,' I say, frowning at my notebook as if it contains some sort of complicated calculation about how to split the fifteen students in the room. 'So you stay with me.'

'Yes, ma'am.'

I look up at her and she's leaning back in her chair, seemingly utterly relaxed. She reaches up to push her hair out of her face and I see she has a couple of tattoos on her upper arm that I didn't notice when she came in. A simple line drawing of a flower and a tiny anchor.

There's a low rumble of noise as the rest of the students get started around the room but it feels oddly intimate now that we're without our audience.

'Do you want to have a go at playing the therapist?' I ask her. She shakes her head immediately.

'No. I want to see more of you in action.'

I nod. I wonder if I should insist on switching roles but instead I say, 'For your research?'

She grins and reaches up to her forehead to move the hair that's fallen in her eyes.

'Ugh, this thing is driving me insane!' She blows up at her not-quite-grown-out fringe.

I look at her and smile, trying to convey calm, to conceal my heart thudding in my chest. I scold myself. This is ridiculous. I am the one in charge here. I'm a professional woman. Be professional!

'You should clip it back.'

She waves her hand dismissively.

'I can't be bothered. I just feel like one morning I'm going to wake up and I'll be able to tuck it behind my ears. I've been growing it out for fucking ever. I feel like it's got to be over soon.'

'I'm not sure it just happens overnight.'

I find myself wanting to tell her about the time in primary school when my sister cut my fringe off right to the hairline and how I had a spiky visor growing over my face for months.

'You'll see.' She flashes me a grin and I find myself smiling dopily back.

Oh god. I look around the room at everyone diligently working. Am I really going to sit at the front of the class flirting with this incredibly annoying girl? I mean, yes? No. No. I'm going to get a grip.

'OK, so let's just pick up where we left off since we're . . . slightly more advanced than everyone else.'

I'm fully winging it now, having never role-played twice with a student and never having role-played with a student without an audience.

'Tell me, how has your week been?'

I settle back into my chair, gripping my notebook tightly.

She picks up her bottle of water and takes a sip.

'My week, my week. What have I done this week? Had a few gigs. They were fine, nothing special. I'm working on some new stuff but there's something missing at the moment. It's fine though. I'll get there. It sometimes just takes a while to click.'

She pauses to take another sip of water.

'What else? What else? I've had the flat to myself. So it's been nice to watch whatever I want on TV, leave the kitchen in a state, that kind of thing. Work is fine. I've sold a lot of iced coffee. I've been drinking a lot of iced coffee. Erm, I was going to go on a date but then I literally was too tired. Too. Tired. So that's tragic, isn't it?'

She pauses, checking to see if there's anything she's missed out. 'Yeah that's it, I think. Pretty standard week.'

She takes another sip of water.

'You?'

I ignore her.

'How's your sleep been?'

22

She smiles broadly.

'I'm sorry to have to tell you, Natasha, that your assessment approximately seven minutes ago did not cure me of my insomnia. I am still very much awake, much of the time.'

'I didn't mean that! I meant, do you experience any different patterns? Is there anything, now you've had time to reflect, that you'd like to tell me about?'

She opens her mouth to reply immediately but then closes it again. As though she's decided to actually think about what I'm saying instead of firing off some smart-arse response.

'I'm tired all the time.'

'And what does that feel like?'

'Being tired?'

'Describe it.'

She pauses again. Leans forward and puts her bottle of water down as if she can't properly think and hold it at the same time.

'It feels like wading through treacle. I'm almost used to the slow thoughts, you know? I'm always slightly foggy but it's the heaviness of my limbs. It's like I'm weighed down with rocks some days. And my eyes.'

She gently touches under her eyes with her fingers. Purple.

'My eyes sometimes feel like they're being dragged halfway down my face. They feel like that all the time. At night too and I think, this is it. I can't feel like this and stay awake, it's impossible. But I close them and my brain is just like . . . ding! It comes alive. It's like turning on an engine. It just fires up.'

She looks at me desperately then. It's so fleeting if I'd blinked I would have missed it.

'What do you mean when you say it fires up?'

'It's like a movie I can't switch off. Replaying highlights. Playing trailers. Every scenario I've ever been in, every scenario I ever could be in. Every song I've heard, person I've met, dream I've had, food I've tasted, feeling I've experienced, sensation I've felt. It's like a live action replay.'

She's tense. She has shifted in her chair now to sit upright. She has one leg crossed over the other and she's jiggling it, holding onto her knee. Her knuckles are white.

I nod. I want to convey to her that I understand. I wish I could reach over and prise her hand away from her knee and hold it until she relaxes.

'Do you go back to anything in particular?'

She's quiet for a moment.

'It's a lot. It's all different things.'

I wait. She's going to say yes. If I'm quiet.

'It's everything I've ever done wrong. No. That's not even it. It's everything I've ever worried about being wrong. Things I've said to people, the way I've looked at someone. Choices I've made that might have offended someone.'

'Do you often do things to offend people?'

'No. I don't think so. Well, I don't know. I hope not.'

'Don't you think you'd know? If you were always upsetting everyone?'

'I'm worried that I don't notice. I just think . . . what if I haven't noticed that I've said something awful and all of a sudden there are consequences?'

'Can you tell me a bit more about what you mean?'

'Oh you know . . . I've accidentally been rude to my neighbour so they throw a brick through my bedroom window. Or I bump into someone on the train and they push me onto the tracks. Or I look at someone the wrong way at work and they throw their coffee in my face.'

She reels off these scenarios as if they're off the top of her head. As if they've just come to her now in this moment. She is very good at saying them as if they're ridiculous and she knows they're ridiculous. Her eyes are so tired.

'Those are very violent ends for such minor transgressions.'

She nods.

'I'm interested about why you think the people you encounter would be so quick to be violent.'

'I don't think that really. That's what I'm saying. I don't walk around all day terrified of everyone. I'm saying this is what keeps me awake. This is what comes to me when I should be asleep. They're almost like subconscious thoughts, aren't they? Dreamlike?'

She looks at me earnestly. She's vulnerable now and I sense the shield is about to go back up. She wants me to tell her something scientific. Something concrete. I can't do it. Again I feel the urge to reach out to her.

'You were too tired to go on a date this week.'

She laughs and looks up to the ceiling. I'm worried briefly

that she's irritated with me for changing the subject but she looks relieved. She visibly relaxes.

'Yeah, I couldn't face it. I wanted to lie in bed and think about meeting a violent end for a . . . how did you so eloquently describe it?'

'A minor transgression.' I can't help but smile at her.

'Yes. I honestly decided I'd rather do that.'

'Do you often choose that over dating?'

'I often do, Natasha.'

The shield is well and truly back up. She says my name like she relishes it. Before I can ask my next question she interrupts.

'Can I call you Tash?'

'No.'

'Why? Because you love boundaries?'

'It's not . . . I don't *love* boundaries. I require them in a professional setting to have meaningful and useful relationships with clients and students.'

'So, what, you just hate the name?'

'Yes. I hate it.'

'Interesting.'

'It's not particularly interesting.'

'It is because you're an enigma. You know I'll spend a lot of time trying to figure you out.'

I can feel colour rising in my cheeks. I click the end of my pen a few times. I lift it to the page as if to note something down but I just draw a deep line down the middle of the page.

'That's common.'

'People thinking about you?'

'No. People trying to figure out their therapists.'

'Oh it's a thing, is it?'

'Yes.'

'Not just about you?'

'No.'

'I'd spend a lot of time thinking about any therapist?'

'Yes. I expect you would.'

She nods, clearly enjoying this exchange. I look around the room to see if anyone can hear us. They're all focused on their own work.

'So . . .' I say, trying to get us back on an appropriate track, 'you turn down social events because you feel too tired . . .'

'Do you know how exhausting it is to date?'

I know I shouldn't answer. It's not about me. She looks me directly in the eye.

Eventually, I nod.

'All the small talk and the same stories over and over again. And you know immediately if it's not going to work but then you have to spend at least an hour in the company of someone who is best-case scenario just incredibly boring. And it's so expensive.'

She pauses to take a breath. She's on a roll as if she's doing 'a bit' about dating. 'And then even if it does go well, then what? I have to kiss someone? I have to have sex with them? Ugh, my god it's exhausting. Do you know what it's like to have sex with a stranger?'

I stare at her and then look down at my notebook, refusing to answer that one.

'It can be fun, don't get me wrong. It's just there's so much to it. What do they like? What are they expecting? What are they into? What if they do something you're not expecting? What if you do something to embarrass yourself? You know? Sometimes I would just like the comfort of having sex with someone who knows me. For it to feel familiar and easy, you know?'

'Is that something you want in general?'

'What?'

'Comfort.'

'Oof.' She sits back like I've winded her. 'You're good. You're very good. I did not see that one coming. I didn't even know I'd said it.'

'Do you want comfort, Margot?'

'I'll have to think about that one.'

She's still joking but I can tell that she really will think about it. Very satisfying. I feel as though I have the upper hand again and then immediately catch myself. This is not meant to be a power struggle.

'We've got a couple more minutes. Is there anything else you'd like to talk about? Are you sure you don't want to swap places?'

She sits forward in her chair again and rearranges herself, crossing her legs the other way.

'No,' she says. 'I like having you tell me all about myself.'

She smiles and I find that I'm smiling back. I catch myself again and close my notebook. I glance up at the rest of the group and clear my throat to get their attention. It's an adjustment when they go quiet and look at me, it feels like an intrusion on Margot and me when, just moments ago, we were the only people in the world.

The rest of the session flies by. I think everyone is relieved when I start talking through a PowerPoint and they can just relax and take notes and dream about whatever their Friday night plans are. When it reaches six o'clock I stand at the door and see everyone out, thanking them for putting up with the heat and wishing them a great weekend. Margot is the last to leave. She stops when she gets to the door, standing between me and the frame. I press my back hard against it trying to create some space between us.

'Thank you for coming,' I say. 'I hope you found it useful for your book.'

'I did. Thank you.' She smiles and makes to head out of the door but then turns back.

'You're different to how I thought you'd be.'

'Excuse me?'

'You're not what I thought a therapist would be like. What I thought you'd be like from your website. On there you look kind of like . . . I don't know. A primary school teacher or like . . . someone who teaches yoga. But here you're . . .'

I wait for her to finish her sentence but she just smiles at me, head tilted to one side. I'm stunned. I've never been evaluated after a class before.

'You're colder than I thought you'd be. Kind of like . . . an ice queen rather than a cosy confidante.' She looks pleased with her alliteration. Bloody poets.

'OK. Well. I'm sorry you feel that way, Margot.'

'No. Don't be sorry.' She grins widely. 'I liked it. Good to meet you, Natasha.'

I stand in the doorway for a while after she leaves, dimly aware of making myself later and later for Georgia. My heart is beating so loudly I can feel it thudding in my ears. I feel something close to humiliation but it's not quite that. I feel like I'm exposed. That for whatever reason, Margot was able to see me.

The flat is still hotter than the sun and we've been packing my belongings into boxes for what feels like eternity. I'm only fifteen minutes late in the end but completely flustered by my afternoon with Margot. Moments keep popping up in my mind and replaying. My head is definitely not in the packing game. When I dashed through the door I very nearly told Georgia why I was late but something stopped me. I wanted to keep Margot for myself.

I'm desperate for a sit-down and a glass of wine but Georgia is in her stride and I can tell she won't let me rest until we've finished. I look at her. All that time and money spent at the cult she calls her gym has certainly paid off. She's wearing board-shorts, an item of clothing she has several pairs of despite never having been on any kind of board, and a tight, cropped vest top. She's recently had her hair cut into a pixie cut (although she hates when I call it that), the kind of thing that would make my face look like the moon. She looks good. Better than she ever did when we were together. It occurs to me that maybe that's because now she's actually happy.

'Who bought these?'

Georgia yanks two dark green velvet cushions off the sofa and waves them at me.

'You, I guess?'

Georgia paid for pretty much everything. Sometimes when I get home I can't believe that the flat belongs to us. Well, that it belongs to Georgia. But that I get to live in it. She always says that it's ours. *Ours*, she emphasises. *Our* money, *Our* things, *What's mine is yours*. Even now. Well up until now when we started splitting our things into boxes with our names on them. It was always hers really – when push came to shove.

Georgia looks at the cushions, examining them, trying to decide whether she actually wants them. After turning them over a couple of times she holds them out to me.

'You sure?' I say as I reach out to take them.

'Yeah, they're more your thing anyway.'

I take them off her and throw them in the general direction of my pile of boxes.

'I'm sure Zara will want to choose some new stuff anyway,' I say.

'Yeah.'

Georgia runs her fingers through her hair and surveys the room. It has barely changed. I really didn't realise how little I'd contributed to the household.

'I'm sure she will.'

Zara is Georgia's new girlfriend. Well, not new exactly. They've been together for five months. They met at the gym, of course. Bonded over protein or gains or something equally dull. Zara is a brand manager for cosmetics and candles and she always has a faint smell of something sickly sweet on her. I really want to like her but there's this big barrier between us. If we're hanging out at the house and Georgia leaves the room it's always intensely uncomfortable. Sometimes she looks at me like I'm from a different planet.

Zara was very 'cool, cool, everything's cool' when she and Georgia first got together but in the past couple of months Georgia and I still living together has become a bit of an issue so I'm getting the boot.

'You're not getting the boot!' Georgia said when she took me out for dinner to break the news. 'Didn't we always say you staying at the flat was bound to be temporary? One of us was always going to meet somebody who didn't love the arrangement.'

'But . . . it's my home. I've been there for nearly three years, Georgia! She knows I sleep in the spare room, right?'

'It's not about where we sleep. It's about the fact that while we live together, she and I can't . . .'

'So is she moving in then? It's only been ten minutes!'

'It's been months, and you moved in after three weeks.'

'And look how that ended up!'

Georgia laughs and despite myself I can't help laughing too.

'I just don't want you to end up repeating the same mistakes, George.'

'You don't want me to move in with Zara, then get dumped and be stuck with her for years afterwards?'

I open my mouth to protest but that's actually a fairly accurate assessment of what happened between us. Instead I sigh, resigned.

'Will Zara let me come and visit at least?'

'I'm sure we can arrange some visiting hours, yes.'

'Supervised of course. No funny business.'

Georgia rolls her eyes at me.

'I really like this girl, Natty.'

'I know,' I said. 'I'm sorry. I know.'

The kitchen is the easiest part of the house to pack up because I have only bought one pan and one spatula, both to replace Georgia's stuff which broke during my time living here.

'OK, are we done, done?' I ask, wiping sweat from my brow, dramatically.

'I think so, yeah.'

'So we can have a drink?'

Georgia opens the fridge and passes me a beer. She's being very patient with me, probably because she feels horribly guilty. As she should.

'We can have a drink. We've done good.'

I take a sip of beer and pull myself up to sit on the countertop. Georgia hates when I do this but she can't complain now. This might be the last time I ever sit on the countertop again.

'So how are we going to celebrate my last night in the flat? The end of an era!'

'Have a few drinks, maybe order some food . . .?'

Georgia stretches to grab her phone. She's got straight-up abs now. I make a mental note to google what paleo actually is.

'You don't eat fun food anymore.'

'I'll eat fun food tonight. Cheat night. What shall we do? Pizza?'

'Oh my god, I'm honoured. Yes, that sounds perfect.'

She taps her bottle against mine and squeezes my knee.

'End of an era, kid.'

'Don't call me kid,' I say but I grab her hand and squeeze it as she walks away.

We end up eating pizza on the floor of the living room, listening to Magic FM like we did when we first moved in. Georgia had been at the end of the process of buying the flat in Brighton (with a great big 'loan' from the bank of mum and dad) when we'd first got together. We decided it made sense if I just moved in with her. That first night we'd opened a bottle of champagne that Georgia's parents had sent and ate on the floor because we had no furniture. We'd slept on a blow-up mattress and thought that it was funny when it completely deflated in the night, which goes to show how absolutely batshit you are in the first month of a relationship.

I fell in love with our flat straight away. We have the top two floors. What was once our bedroom, but has been Georgia's bedroom for the past two years, is in the attic and has a tiny en-suite with just a toilet and a sink in it. That's where we would brush our teeth. When we first moved in, we did it together, side by side like they do in films. We used to get the giggles. We stopped pretty quickly. The appeal wears off once you've had your hand spat on a few times.

We don't have any champagne tonight but we do have several bottles of Chablis from a case that Georgia was given by her parents when they last came back from France, which drinks quite nicely with a veggie hot 'n' spicy stuffed crust.

'Do you remember that first night when we met Miriam?'

Our downstairs neighbours are an elderly lady named Miriam and her two Pomeranians who yap every time we open our front door. We share a front garden with her but it's like sharing a garden with a ghost. We never see her but occasionally something of ours has been moved ever so slightly. Or a plant has been watered. I think she is solely responsible for our lavender surviving.

Georgia leans back against the sofa and wipes her greasy pizza hands on her shorts.

'Oh my god, yeah.'

I pick my wine glass up from the coffee table and take a large gulp. I wonder if anyone would notice if a couple of bottles of Chablis went missing.

'And then we literally never saw her again and it was like – was that a ghost?'

Georgia laughs.

'Do those Pomeranians just live downstairs by themselves? When we hear the bins get taken out is it just them pushing it with their little paws?'

'They're out there in the night watering our plants and strimming the hedges.'

'Don't!' I squeal. 'That's too cute. I can't deal with mini dog gardeners.'

Georgia leans over to top up my wine glass; she waits for me to say 'When' and then just stops when she reaches the brim.

'We used to talk about getting a dog, didn't we? I'd have loved that.'

Georgia nods.

'If you want to, you could get one tomorrow, Natty. Nothing's stopping you.'

I lean over to take a sip of my wine without picking it up from the table, so as not to spill.

'I actually can't because Diane doesn't get along with other dogs.'

Georgia rolls her eyes dramatically.

'Of course she doesn't.'

'What? She doesn't. She's very sensitive.'

'Yeah, that sounds right. Like mother, like daughter.'

Diane is our friend Poppy's chihuahua. I actually met Georgia through Poppy at one of Poppy's birthday parties. Georgia's known Poppy since school and I met her at university. They are supposedly the best of friends although you wouldn't know it to hear Georgia talk about her.

'So how are you feeling about living with Poppy then?'

Georgia picks up her drink and looks at me. She is trying to pull off asking an innocent question but it doesn't work because she's chronically earnest. She's desperate to know all about it. I decide to answer as if I haven't noticed her being supremely annoying.

'I feel good about it! It makes sense. Her flatmate just moved out, her spare room is nice. I love Diane even if you don't.'

'Mmm, OK, you feel good about it?'

'Yeah, of course, she's my friend. Why wouldn't I?'

'Natasha!'

Georgia picks up a pizza crust and chucks it at me. It misses by quite a long way which I can see annoys her. She even takes the sport of pizza-throwing seriously.

'What?'

'You love her!'

'I do not *love* her.'

'Come on.'

'I don't.'

'OK.'

'I can tell you don't believe me that I don't!'

'Do you believe you?'

I am not in love with Poppy. Have I had complicated feelings for Poppy in the past? Yes. Have I occasionally daydreamed about her dumping her boyfriend Felix and falling into my arms? Perhaps. Do I sometimes gaze at her with her long hair and her full lips and her startling green eyes and think she

37

looks like a goddess or a mermaid or some other kind of mythical creature? Sure. But am I in *love* with her? No. The idea of actually being with Poppy is ridiculous. She'd drive me mad. I don't know why Georgia can't grasp that, has never been able to grasp that.

'I've known her for like,' I do some quick maths, working out how long it's been since I started university and wince when I realise how old I am, 'twelve years, Georgia.'

'I know, that's a long time for unrequited love to fester.'

I sigh. This is one of her favourite paths to go down. She knows it winds me up. I'm not sure if she'd find it as funny if she found out that Poppy and I hooked up several times while we were at university together. I suspect she would not. I keep my mouth shut.

'OK, sure. So you really believe that the whole time we were together, I was madly in love with Poppy?'

'Not madly in love with her. I was never threatened by her,' Georgia does a little obnoxious smile and gestures to herself, 'obviously.'

I roll my eyes. This relentless line of questioning makes it slightly less obvious, actually. I don't point that out.

'But yeah,' she looks down at her wine glass and swirls it around a bit before carrying on, 'you've always had a thing for her. I've always known it, even when we were together.'

I don't really know what to say to that, protesting seems useless and I'm suddenly tired from all the packing. And the drinking. I turn up the volume on the speaker and The Beach

Boys singing 'God Only Knows' fills the room. A classic. I find my mind wanders to Margot. My stomach flips just thinking about being pressed against the door as she left, that smile on her face.

'I'm not going to miss this.'

Georgia's voice pulls me back into the room.

'Miss what?' I say.

Georgia points at the radio.

I roll my eyes.

'Sure you will. You'll be listening to Mellow Magic every day.'

'I won't.'

'Well, I will. Tuning in with Poppy and Diane. And Felix, the whole crew.'

Georgia cannot even talk about Felix, she finds him too ridiculous. Felix and Poppy have been together for the past two years. He's exactly what you'd imagine someone called Felix to be like: he works in finance, he has ruddy cheeks, he used to shoot things for fun before he met Poppy but she's a vegan so he only talks longingly about shooting things for fun now. He calls everyone 'chaps' and 'ladies'. He can't figure out Poppy at all and is completely and utterly besotted with her.

'I'm sure you're all going to have a lovely time living together,' Georgia says.

She changes her tone suddenly, realising how sarcastic she sounds.

'You really will. And I'm probably just being bitter because I'm going to miss you.'

'You won't. It makes sense for you to live with Zara. You can share protein powder, spot each other when you're weight training . . .'

'Ha ha.'

'Seriously though, you two are great together.'

I'm not sure why I say that. I don't necessarily mean it but it certainly sounds like a nice thing to say. Georgia's face lights up, confirming it was the right thing to do.

'Thanks so much, Natty.'

She is one of the only people on the planet who can get away with calling me that.

'That means a lot coming from you. And you know we'll see each other all the time, right?'

'Of course!'

My head starts running through all the things we do together now and then what 'all the time means' when it comes to my other friends – coffees fortnightly, maybe the pub on a Friday night, texting each other saying that we 'absolutely must' do something soon.

'We really will,' she says gently. Always good at reading my mind.

'I mean,' she looks down at her phone and pauses for a moment – Zara, I suspect, 'we've literally got my birthday in two weeks.'

I groan and throw my hands up to my head and she smiles. We do this dance a lot about her family. Georgia comes from the kind of family where birthdays are sacred. They have these huge dinners for every single birthday where they book the private dining rooms at restaurants or throw massive dinner parties at their house and they always have these absurdly large cakes with sparklers. As well as her mum and dad, Georgia has a brother, Josh. That is four of these celebrations a year. Approximately three tonnes of cake.

'Do I still have to come to that now I won't be living with you?'

I'm kind of kidding but also kind of not. I'm not sure Zara will be thrilled about my going.

'Of course you'll come! It's at the house, isn't it? We've not booked anywhere. So it's more people than usual, friends too. My parents will be heartbroken if you don't come, you know they adore you.'

I'm not sure if it's quite right to say that they adore me. Georgia's parents are the kind of people who love to collect. Stories, anecdotes, people. They're loud and eccentric but not flashy – ridiculous birthday bashes aside. They wear the same clothes they've had for decades, their furniture is ancient. They have labradors. They know their place in the world and they're deeply comfortable. These aren't people who have had to worry about homes, careers, getting by or fitting in. They believe every room is for them and they can talk to and are liked by everyone. Georgia says I have a case of reverse snobbery, which is probably true, but actually I can't help but like her parents. Their joie de vivre is infectious. They don't *adore* me though, they're fascinated by me. I'm a great addition to their collection. They want to mine me for anecdotes. They love that I'm so different to Georgia. That my mother is a nurse. That I don't speak to my father. That I have a twin sister who has twins herself. That I don't quite fit into a box that they already have.

'Don't be daft, obviously I'll be there.'

'And we've got my little birthday trip.'

I nod and smile at her. She often gives the impression that she considers herself different to her clueless friends, and most of the time she is, but sometimes she slips up and describes something like a week in California for her and her friends as a 'little birthday trip'.

'We sure do. Thanks again.'

Georgia's early birthday present to me was my plane ticket. She insisted on paying given that we're going to be away over my birthday.

'No! Don't thank me. Thank *you* for coming. I feel like it's a bit much to be honest but you know what my parents are like about birthdays and this is my thirtieth so I think they just wanted to get me something extra special.'

'It's going to be great, George.'

Georgia nods, looks at her phone again and starts typing so I pick up mine. I find myself wishing I had Margot's number or that she had mine, that there was a chance her name would flash up on my screen. Instead I send a 'hey' to this girl I've been texting. We matched on Hinge, bonded over everyone's terrible chat and have been sending 'hey' and 'all right?' back and forth to each other ever since.

'Right!' I say decisively without making any move to get up. 'We should go to bed, shouldn't we?'

Georgia doesn't look up from her phone which she's smiling dopily at.

'Georgia.'

'Hmm?'

'Bed.'

'Right. Yeah, I'll be heading up in a minute. Big moving day tomorrow.'

She doesn't move and simply furiously types on her phone instead. I'm sure Zara is checking that every single trace of me is gone by the time she arrives tomorrow afternoon. Perhaps they're planning their celebratory workout.

Eventually I slide off the armchair and in standing up realise I'm a bit more drunk than I thought. As I stagger towards the door Georgia puts her phone down and lifts her arms up for me to help her stand. She looks at me pleadingly.

'No come on, you can get up.'

She makes a small noise, somewhere between a wail and a whimper.

'It's a reverse squat, isn't it? Standing up?'

She shakes her arms at me so I sigh and drag her to her feet. As soon as she's up she pulls me into a big hug, squeezing me so hard I feel my back click.

'Owww,' I squirm but instead of putting me down she lifts me up off the ground and squeezes even harder.

'I'm going to miss you, roomie!'

'Put me down, you're making me feel sick.'

She deposits me on the floor with a thud and steadies herself with her hands on my shoulders. She looks at me for a moment and then reaches across and ruffles my hair.

'It's gonna be weird without you here.'

'It's gonna be weird not living here. Remember when we first got together and you said that everything that's yours is mine? Well, I was thinking about that and isn't technically half of this flat . . .'

'Night, Natty.'

Georgia walks past me to head up the stairs to her room and grabs a phone charger on the way out. The good one with the long cable. Damn it, I am going to miss that charger.

'Night Georgia.'

I turn around to take in the discarded pizza boxes and wine bottles. The armchair I've watched hundreds of episodes of *Keeping Up with the Kardashians* on, the rug where I spilled a pint of Ribena. The sofa that Georgia and I used to curl up on, really believing it belonged to us both.

I switch off the lamp vowing to deal with the mess tomorrow and make my way to the bathroom, which I like to refer to as 'my en-suite' just to wind Georgia up. I stand in the shower and shiver underneath the tepid water, trying to get as cold as possible before getting into bed. It works and when I get to my room I pull on an oversized T-shirt that possibly once belonged to Georgia's brother but I've since claimed as my own and climb into bed.

I lie on my side and stare at my phone. I'm meant to be keeping it far away from me before moving it out of the room entirely as if I'm a dog learning how to sleep on my own. I tell myself it's Friday, I'm drunk, I can have my phone in bed as a treat. I scroll through Instagram and then quickly open Hinge before immediately closing it again. I feel restless. I don't know what it is that I'm looking for but whatever it is isn't in the blue light emanating from my clammy hand. When I eventually put my phone down, I turn over onto my back and stare into the darkness, little shapes where my eyes are adjusting from the screen darting in front of my eyes. I don't think about moving, about Georgia or Zara or Poppy. The only thing on my mind is Margot. I replay her over and over until I succumb to sleep when she becomes a blur and spills into my dreams.

2

'Hiya Natty! Bet you won't listen to this for hours. I've been up since six with the kids, they're driving me mad. I think I've actually forgotten what a lie-in is. Anyway, just wanted to say good luck with the move today, hope it's not too stressful . . . I . . . what? WHAT? I can't hear you, I'm trying to . . . no you can't you've only just had your . . . OK ONE, BUT ONLY ONE. Shit, Ella's asking if she can have a Wagon Wheel but I'm pretty sure I ate them all last night. Oops. Anyway, what was I saying? Look, are you still coming over tomorrow? I know the kids would love to see you. Maybe you could bring them something to do that'll keep them quiet? A game? Some Xanax? Literally the school holidays are endless. It's like a bottomless pit of children. Oh god, I think she's figured out I ate them all. I've got to go. Love you, ring me later.'

I groan, seeing that it's 9 a.m. already. Poppy is coming to pick me up at 11 a.m. and that doesn't feel like enough time to rally. I put my phone back down on the bedside table, patting it for a glass of water I might have had the foresight to put there last night. No such luck. Natalie is always acting like my life is so much more exciting than hers but honestly I wish I'd just been on the Wagon Wheels last night, maybe I wouldn't feel quite so grotty. I feel bad that I haven't been around as much as I should have been for her this summer. I've been 'typically self-involved', as my mum would say, or 'just really busy with work and everything', as Natalie would kindly correct her. The truth is somewhere in between.

I can hear Georgia in the kitchen already. I open my mouth to shout at her to bring me a cup of tea but there's no way she'll hear the feeble noise that comes out of my mouth over the sound of the terrible music she's got on. Georgia listens exclusively to EDM bangers and Spotify playlists with titles like 'YOLO' and 'Young, wild and free'. How dare she criticise Magic FM.

I lie in bed for a few more minutes trying to take in my room for the last time. My last ever hangover in this flat. I'm just about to make a move towards sitting upright when there's a faint knock on my door.

Georgia pops her head around and squints at me, her eyes adjusting to the darkness.

'Are you up?'

She walks over to my curtains and wrenches them open. I scream as though the light is burning my skin.

'I am now!'

I pull the duvet over my head and groan.

Georgia walks over to my bed, perches beside me and yanks

the duvet back down. She puts a cup of coffee on my bedside table. After all this time she still hasn't retained that when I'm hungover I need a cup of tea basically the moment my eyes open. Still, it's the thought that counts. I sniff it, inspecting it for signs that it's been tampered with.

'It's just a normal coffee, don't worry. Milk and one sugar. I know your specifications.'

She gets back up and stands in the middle of my room with her hands on her hips, surveying the boxes. She's wearing the kind of shorts you'd see Mr Motivator wearing in the eighties and a sports bra. She looks like she's about to run a marathon – I mean, for all I know she very well could be. She glances at me hesitating over my coffee.

'There's really no butter or coconut oil or god knows what else in here?' I ask.

'No! Although bullet coffee is really very good . . .'

'OK, OK. Thanks.'

She rolls her eyes at me.

'So Zara is coming over at ten so that she can help load your boxes into Poppy's car, which is nice, isn't it?'

She looks at me pointedly.

'Oh yes, very nice,' I say into my coffee cup.

'So if you could be up and,' she sniffs the air in my room, 'showered maybe, before then that would be great.'

'Yes, Mum, I will wash and dress myself this morning.'

She turns around and smiles at me on her way out of my room.

'Great, thanks!'

She's so excited, I almost feel bad for being such a grump. I don't know how she hasn't also got a raging hangover. Perhaps it's all the butter in the coffee or the muscle mass.

An hour later and I am just about ready, I'm wearing my selected 'moving outfit' – a cropped T-shirt and short dungarees. I admire myself in the mirror; I definitely look like I've just stepped out of a ladies-only removals van ready to lift boxes with ease. I do a tentative flex of a muscle and if I press really hard something is definitely there. Maybe not in an obvious 'gym' way but in a subtle 'I have a yoga mat somewhere in my house' way.

'You look like a toddler in those,' Georgia says immediately as I walk into the kitchen in search of food.

'No,' I say, lifting the lid of a pizza box to inspect it for leftovers. Empty. Damn it. 'I look very cool and capable like I work for a lesbian removals company.'

Georgia scoffs and then rearranges her face when I glare at her.

'OK. Yes. That's what you look like, not at all like you're about to go to nursery.'

I smile and smooth down the front of my dungarees.

'Thank you.'

Just as I've shovelled a huge spoonful of granola into my mouth, there's the sound of a key in the lock and Georgia runs to the top of the stairs. I follow her, bowl in hand, to observe from the kitchen doorway.

Zara runs up the stairs and squeals and Georgia squeals and

then they both squeal together and I realise I am witnessing a seminal moment in their relationship.

'First time with my own key, babe!'

Zara wiggles the key in Georgia's face and then jangles it at me where I'm hovering.

'First of many,' Georgia says which is, more than anything, just incredibly obvious unless Zara plans on staying indoors forever. She leans forward to kiss her, which makes Zara go all silly and say to me,

'She's so soppy, isn't she?'

'So soppy. It's disgusting really.'

Georgia shakes her head at me.

'So soppy,' Zara says again, stroking Georgia's face and pretending she hasn't heard me.

For the next hour, Zara 'helps' me stack all my boxes outside on the front step so that as soon as Poppy comes to get me I'll be completely ready to vacate the premises.

When we're done, Zara looks at all my stuff.

'Gosh, you don't have much, do you? Where's all your furniture?'

'I don't have any furniture.'

'What? Well where do you sit?'

'Natasha and I just shared furniture, babe.'

'Oh. Of course. I just assumed *some* of the stuff in the flat must have been yours.'

'Nope! I fully freeloaded.'

I squint into the sun and check my phone. Poppy is now

fifteen minutes late and Georgia and Zara are getting antsy. I've seen them both checking their fitness watches several times.

'Look guys, you don't have to wait here with me.'

Georgia starts to say, 'Of course we will' just as Zara says, 'Are you sure?'

'Really, it's fine. I mean, who knows how much longer she'll be. It's a gorgeous day, I've got my book,' by which of course I mean, my phone. 'I'll be fine. Just leave me on the doorstep.'

'OK, if you're absolutely sure,' Georgia eyes me suspiciously. 'It's just that we do have a class and then we're going for a little celebratory brunch.'

Zara squeezes her arm.

'I'm absolutely sure. Enjoy your gym. Enjoy your brunch.'

I reach into my pocket and produce my front door key with the little felt badger key ring on it. I once said to my mum that I'd never seen a badger in real life apart from dead at the side of the road and since then she's made it her mission to get me every bit of badger paraphernalia she can find. I twist it off the key ring and hand it to Georgia.

'You can keep it, Natasha,' she says. 'What if we go on holiday and need our plants watering?'

There is a barely perceptible shift in Zara's smile, frozen on her face. Her eyes widen ever so slightly.

'No, you know Miriam will do your plants. You keep it as a spare.'

'OK,' she reaches out and takes it from me. Zara immediately relaxes.

We all have a little hug and I wave them off to their gym class and settle down on one of the boxes to scroll through my phone. I'm restless scrolling through Instagram, it all feels so insipid, so boring. I can't seem to find what I'm looking for, which after a few minutes I realise is Margot. I start typing her name and delete it again. I don't ever look up people I work with on social media. Not even ones who are so mind-bendingly infuriating that I'm still thinking about them nearly twenty-four hours later.

It is another forty minutes before Poppy screeches up along-side me in Felix's Land Rover. She doesn't indicate and as she swerves in front of the house the car behind her beeps its horn several times. She waves out of the window at me, utterly serene as if she hasn't just nearly caused a crash, as if she is not even a minute late. Diane is perched on her lap quivering, as per usual. I don't even want to know if Poppy drove the whole way with her there.

'Hey roomie!' she yells out of the window and ruffles her hair, shaking it about, wanting me to notice something. It is impossible not to notice that she has cut most of it off. It now sits on her shoulders instead of cascading down her back. It looks great, obviously.

'Your hair!'

'I know! Isn't it crazy – I just woke up this morning and said to Felix, "I can't live like this anymore", so I got up super early and went to the hairdressers and just said, "Free me from this hair, it is *smothering* me", do you know what I mean?'

I nod gamely, having never felt particularly smothered by my hair.

'This feels so much better.' She shakes her head again dramatically, the diamond stud in her nose glinting in the sunlight.

'So is that where you've been this morning?'

'Yes!'

She notices my expression and claps her hand to her mouth.

'Oh my god, am I late? What time is it?'

She looks at the bangle on her wrist as if it might reveal something to her.

'It's nearly twelve!'

'And what time did we say?'

She really has no idea.

'Eleven.'

'Oh shitty, shit shit shit. Sorry! I am a HORRIBLE friend. HORRIBLE. Will you ever forgive me? I tell you what, I'll help you load some of those boxes into the car to make up for it.'

'I mean . . . were you not already going to . . .'

She puts Diane on the passenger seat and hops out of the car. She walks over to me, kisses me on both cheeks and then starts lifting one thing at a time and flinging it into the boot.

I wince as I hear a clatter, wondering what might have become of the few mugs I do actually own.

She claps her hands as I lift the final box into the boot.

'Well done team!'

She pulls me into a one-armed hug. Any irritation I might have had with her melts away and I briefly rest my head on her shoulder.

'I know it's weird, darling.' Poppy calls everyone darling, I've heard her call her own mother darling, but it still makes me feel special somehow. 'But moving is always weird, and we're going to have the most wonderful time living together, I can just feel it. And I'm always right about these things.'

She also thinks she is psychic and won't be told otherwise.

'I know. We will.'

I open the passenger seat door and Diane flinches like I'm about to attack her.

'Diane! You silly little sausage, it's Auntie Natasha! You love her!'

I pick her up gingerly and slide into the car before putting her on my knee and carefully patting her little head. I've been on the wrong side of Diane before and she's got a good nip on her. She's so tiny, I can pick her up one-handed. Honestly, these dogs should be illegal. Poppy 'rescued' Diane from a family friend. Georgia reckons that 'friend' is a breeder and that Poppy handed over money to 'rescue her'.

'So what are we doing tonight? Little celebration for my first night in the house?'

Poppy is humming along to the radio and paying little to no attention to the road. I double-check my seatbelt.

'Absolutely!'

She says it in a way that makes me think we *absolutely* won't be doing anything to celebrate.

'A hundred per cent, a hundred and fifty per cent. It's just one tiny thing, is that I've got to go out with some of Felix's work friends for some terrible birthday thing.'

'OK, what time is that on?'

'It's sort of a seven till late thing, I think, probably an all-nighter knowing us!'

She laughs to herself and sails through a light just as it turns red, to a chorus of beeping.

'So wait, if you're going to be out from seven until . . . all night . . . that's a no then on us celebrating tonight?'

'Oh, is it really a no? I don't know! I mean, if you think so then we can do something another night instead?'

Absolutely classic.

'It's fine, don't worry.'

I look out of the window and try to mentally calculate how long it takes to get to Poppy's flat to figure out how much longer I need to spend in the death seat.

I thought Felix might be waiting at Poppy's to help me move in, mainly because he's literally always there, but he's out getting a good spot in the pub for the rugby so Poppy and I unload the car ourselves. Fortunately her flat is on the ground floor so there are no stairs to tackle.

'Pops.'

'Mmm,' she says, frowning at her phone as she closes the door once we've got the last boxes inside. She flings the car keys in the direction of the table next to the front door. They skim over the top of it, falling with a clatter to the floor. She doesn't appear to notice.

'Obviously I'm so happy to be moving in here but . . .' I bend down to pick up the keys and place them gently in the plate she was aiming for, 'how come you didn't get Felix to move in? I mean, surely you've talked about it?'

She grimaces and steps over a box to go through to the living room. I follow and she chucks herself down on the sofa, flinging her feet up. I go and sit on the armchair opposite and put my feet up on the little footstool.

'You know I love Felix. But we've only been together five minutes.'

'Two years.'

She stares straight ahead, ignoring me.

'And I just feel like the moment he moves in there's no moving out, you know? Like, once he's here, it's a clear path and I know exactly what it looks like. He'll propose, we'll get married, we'll have a baby, we'll move into a bigger house somewhere out of the city, we'll have another baby. We'll die.'

'Christ. There's got to be something to look forward to between your second baby and death hasn't there?'

I think about my own mother. I am the second baby by a six-minute margin. Is it only death on the cards for her now? No wonder she resents me so much.

'I mean possibly,' she says as if it's the most far-fetched suggestion in the world, 'but I'm just not ready for that life to be mine yet. I want there to be twenty, fifty, a hundred different paths in front of me and I don't want to know for a fact which one I've chosen. I feel too . . .'

She waves her hands in the air looking for the right word.

'Young?' I suggest. 'Restless?'

'Restless! Yes, that's exactly it.'

She rolls over onto her side to face me instead of the ceiling.

'I feel restless. Like, I know I have a lovely life. I have a charmed life really, don't I?'

I nod, vigorously.

'But I feel like there's something just out of my reach that I can't quite . . .'

She screws up her eyes like she's trying to see something in the distance and reaches out in front of her.

'I can't quite get to it. But I know that it's there and I'm terrified if I make a decision that takes me in just one particular direction it'll just get further and further away.'

She sighs heavily.

'Does that make any sense at all?'

I nod again.

She smiles at me suddenly and wags her finger at me as if I've played a trick on her.

'You're very good, aren't you?'

'Good at what?'

'Look at this, I'm even lying down on a couch as I pour my heart out to you. So cliché! Is this what it's going to be like living with a therapist? You just analysing me all the time? Delving into my soul for my deepest, darkest secrets?'

I pick my feet off the footstool and sit up straighter, crossing my legs instead.

'I'm not analysing you! We're two friends having a conversation.'

She sits up too and shakes her head at me as if to say 'you can't fool me.'

'Yeah sure. I'll have to watch out for that, won't I? Naughty girl.'

'No! I wasn't trying to . . .'

'Listen, let's go and put all your things in your room and open a bottle of fizz, shall we? If we can't go out tonight, we'll have to have a little celebration now.'

She smiles at me, a real smile now that she's forgotten she's accusing me of underhanded therapy. Poppy has always had the ability to make you feel like the most important person in the world. Georgia would say she bewitches people.

'That sounds perfect, yes please,' I say, bewitched.

Fizz in my vocabulary means a bottle of frizzante, fizz in Poppy's world means champagne. I've never knowingly turned down a 'fizz' from her in my life.

We spend the afternoon organising my room and getting tipsy on a bottle of Bolly that Felix had bought for them to celebrate an anniversary. When I protested that it was too special to open just for me she said, 'Oh he celebrates the *minutes*, don't worry about it.'

My room here is smaller than my room at Georgia's but has a big window overlooking the garden and an antique dressing table that once belonged to Poppy's grandmother. The walls are painted white and Poppy gives me loads of different-sized picture frames that she's collected for me to hang on the wall. She's already put photographs in some of them. How she can veer from oblivious to thoughtful with such ease I'll never understand.

When we've got the room looking somewhere close to finished we collapse on the bed and lie back with the dregs of the champagne to admire our work.

'Thanks for letting me move in here. I appreciate it so much. The idea of moving in with strangers was just . . .'

'You don't have to thank me, darling.'

I take a deep breath.

'OK then but will you please let me pay . . .'

'Oh god, don't!' She covers one ear with her free hand and starts 'la la la' ing so she can't hear me.

I yank it away from her ear and hold onto it.

'You have to let me pay you rent! It's not a fair arrangement to just . . .'

She downs the rest of her champagne, puts her glass down on the side and clasps my hand with both of hers.

'I can't accept money from you when I'm not paying to live here. You know this flat was my grandmother's.'

I squeeze her hand.

'I can't live somewhere and not pay for it.'

'Why not?'

She looks at me wide-eyed. It occurs to me she has only ever lived in places she hasn't paid for.

'I just can't. I don't think I can explain it to you in a way that you'll understand. But we're just different people.'

She opens her mouth to interject but I carry on.

'Not that I'm saying it's a bad thing that you don't pay to live here but this isn't my flat, I can't live here for free.'

'Did you pay Georgia?'

'Of course I did. She has a mortgage to pay. I was renting the room from her.'

'OK, fine. So why don't you just pay me what you paid Georgia and I'll put it towards bills and . . .'

She looks around the room for inspiration.

'General . . . upkeep?'

'Well yeah. That's generally what rent is for.'

'Oh god, stop saying rent. I'm not your landlady.'

'You are, kind of.'

We hear the front door slam and Felix thunders down the hallway to my room. Felix thunders absolutely everywhere he goes, I don't think he has any concept of gentle or quiet or subtle. He's tall and even in places with high ceilings he always ducks a bit. He's obviously hit his head so many times he's on the constant lookout in case he's caught out by a beam or a doorframe.

The door of my bedroom swings open and Felix strides towards me with open arms.

'Natasha!'

He pulls me in to hug him and I nearly spill champagne down his back.

'Huge day! Huge! How totally brilliant, we're going to get to see you all the time. This is going to be epic.'

The thing about Felix is, as much as you might want to dislike him – and believe me, I do – he makes it very difficult.

He walks around to the other side of the bed, kisses Poppy and plonks himself down next to her on the bed, which sends us both bouncing up slightly into the air.

'Thanks Felix.' I say, 'And thanks so much for letting us borrow the car to move my stuff.'

'Oh god of course, of course. Anytime. You know I can just stick you on the insurance, Nat. It's no trouble.'

He gets out his phone as if he's going to do it this very minute.

'Um, thanks but . . .'

'Darling! You know Natasha can't drive,' Poppy loudly whispers as if it's a big secret.

'Stop.'

He looks at me like Poppy's just announced I'm from the moon.

'You are joking?'

'No, I really can't drive.'

'Why the bloody hell not?' He laughs. Like he's honestly never heard anything so ridiculous.

'Driving is just so terrible for the planet that we should *all* be like Natasha really, shouldn't we? And when you live somewhere so well connected there's really no need for any of us to . . .'

I interrupt Poppy.

'I can't drive because I couldn't afford to learn. And my mum couldn't afford to pay for me. And then I had to pay for uni and then my training and I suppose I could learn now but . . .'

I take a breath, this is a well-rehearsed speech and I always end it gently.

'What's the point when I have friends like you to chauffeur me around?'

Felix roars with laughter.

'Good point, fair play.' He's a bit pink, embarrassed to have asked, relieved everything's fine. 'You know, if you want lessons, I can always teach you.'

'Oh yes! What a good idea!' Poppy claps her hands together and looks at me expectantly.

Oh no. 'No, you don't have to do that, I couldn't . . .'

Felix is suddenly quite serious.

'Listen, actually. I insist. I'd love to do this for you. It's the very least I can do given everything I've got that, you know, I've taken for granted.'

Poppy puts a hand on his knee and nods, her eyes closed. Christ, he thinks he's giving back to the community. This is moments away from being a Comic Relief montage. Is one of them going to cry? Am I meant to cry?

'I, um.'

They both look at me, wide-eyed.

'OK, yes. Thanks. That's very nice of you to offer.'

'Amazing! Can't wait. We'll start ASAP. Tomorrow!' He points at me for confirmation.

'I can't tomorrow, I'm going to Natalie's.'

It would actually be very useful to be able to drive to Natalie's.

'Yeah and, to be fair, I am probably not going to be in any bloody state to drive tomorrow. Right, we'll do it after work next week then, you choose – just tell me and I'll be there.'

'Cheers, Felix.'

'My pleasure.' He reaches across Poppy and pats my leg. Well, I assume it was meant to be a pat, from him it's a slap so hard it stings.

'Now listen, Pops, we need to leave in an hour so maybe time to start . . .'

'Yes I'll be ready, don't worry!'

'We've all heard that before though, haven't we?'

Felix winks at me as he heads out of the room. Yuck.

'What are you going to do?' Poppy rolls over to face me, making absolutely no moves towards getting ready.

'I don't know, probably just stay in.'

A lie.

'That's a lie,' Poppy says and pokes me in the side of my stomach.

'Ow!'

'What are you really going to do? Go on a little date? Call up one of your little friends?'

'OK, why is everything little? And don't say "friends", you sound like my mum.'

I pause.

'Although, yes, I am just going to see a friend. Probably.'

Can you be friends with someone you've only met twice?

'She's just a friend!' Poppy does a terrible impression of me and honks with laughter.

'Whatever.'

Poppy finally heaves herself off the bed to go and get ready and I reach for my phone to text Alice. We'd vaguely said something about maybe seeing each other tonight. We'd met last weekend on a Hinge date which essentially involved drinking a bottle of wine each and having sex. We don't have a great deal in common but this is the beauty of 'the apps', which I discovered after Georgia and I broke up. You don't *need* to have a great deal in common to enjoy the company of someone for an evening, or two or even three. You just need to have the desire to get plastered and have sex with someone, which I do, a lot of the time. I half consider texting the 'hey, you all right?' girl to see if she fancies actually meeting up but settle on Alice. A safer bet.

Hey Alice, you free tonight?

She texts back immediately.

Maybe, why?

Drink?

Do you mean, 'would you like to go for a drink with me this evening, Alice? It would be lovely to see you.'

Yes!

Then yes. Could meet at the Seven Stars at 8?

See you there.

The drink with Alice is uneventful. It's fine. We sit in a corner of the pub and talk about our respective weeks. I tell her about moving out of Georgia's and in with Poppy. And about Poppy's new hair and how she won't ask Felix to move in. Alice tells me something or other about her new job in recruitment or sales or marketing and how her housemate did something to do with the boiler? Or didn't do something to do with the boiler? It's all a bit hazy and I'm not really paying attention. It's fine, I'm sure she isn't listening to me either. I mean, the thing is, not to be rude, but Alice is just *incredibly* dull.

My mum's voice pops into my head: *Only boring people get bored, Natasha.*

At one point, when Alice is at the bar getting drinks, I check my phone and see that Georgia has messaged me.

How's it going? Feels weird without you here . . . it's very quiet and none of my food is missing.

Ha ha ha. I'm actually on a date. I'm with that girl Alice from last weekend.

65

She reads the message straight away. Obviously they're having a wild one on their first night living together.

> *Boring Alice?! Why? Oh wait, no, don't tell me. Have*
> *fun . . .*

I shake my head and put my phone away just as Alice gets back. She's empty-handed and irritated.

'So the bar's rammed.'

She looks at her watch and then sort of up at the sky, as if seeking some guidance. She sighs heavily and watches me as I pick up my glass to drain the dregs of my wine.

'Shall we just go back to yours?'

She says this in exactly the same tone as you might ask, 'Shall we just get this over with?'

I raise my eyebrows and, in the brief moment I take to answer her, it seems I've accidentally said a thousand things.

'I mean, do you think there's any point me waiting around at the bar?' she says accusingly, waving her hand in the direction of a very small group of people waiting to be served. 'We can always stop off at the off-licence if you *need* another drink.'

Bloody hell, all right.

'Yeah, of course, let's go back to mine, that's fine!'

'Fine?'

'Good! Great! Let's do that.'

This is more work than it's worth. I start to plan a text to send her in the morning to let her know I've had fun but maybe we aren't quite on the same wave . . .

'Are you coming?'

'Yes!'

Christ.

We get home to an empty flat. Poppy and Felix will likely be out for hours yet.

'Nice place,' she says, taking off her jacket and chucking it onto the kitchen stool.

'Thanks.'

'Your old place was nice too.'

An image of drunkenly pouring Alice a glass of wine in the old kitchen flashes through my mind. On the way to my bedroom I'd bumped into Georgia in the hallway and couldn't quite meet her eye when she'd said goodnight. It never really did get easier, that part of living together.

'Yep.'

'So wait, this one is owned by . . .'

'My best friend.'

'Wow. You do all right for yourself, don't you.'

I decide not to ask what she means and instead tilt my head towards my bedroom, indicating she should follow me.

The thing about Alice, and the reason why I went on a second date with her, is that despite being very dull and quite judgemental she is very good at sex. Surprisingly good. I was so shocked last weekend that I nearly said something to her like 'It's always the quiet ones, isn't it?' but decided best not.

We don't bother to close the door behind us when we get into my bedroom, Poppy won't be home for hours. After a moment of hesitation, both of us standing in the dark, amidst the empty boxes, Alice reaches out and places her hand on my lower back. She pulls me towards her and kisses me.

I think I must really irritate her or remind her of somebody she doesn't like because the way she is kissing me, so aggressively, feels incredibly personal. Not like kissing someone who you've only exchanged boiler anecdotes with.

She bites my lip so hard it hurts. I instinctively pull away and bring my hand up to my mouth to see if it's bleeding. She looks at me, concerned, and opens her mouth to say something.

Oh god, no.

'It's good, I'm fine!' I say quickly before she has a chance to speak. She nods and presses me up against the wall, pushing my top up and kissing my breasts, and then with a sigh as if she's giving in, like she just can't wait any longer, she puts her hand up my skirt, roughly pushes my underwear to the side and fucks me. I grip onto her shoulders, the back of her neck, her arms, which I notice are very toned. I am briefly distracted thinking of my own arms and wondering if I remembered to steal a kettlebell from Georgia but it's not long before Alice brings me back into the room. I come quickly (standard) and I manoeuvre her to switch places with me, pull her jeans down, kneel in front of her and go down on her. She gasps and I'm worried she's going to talk to me but she doesn't, she just alternates between holding my head gently and pulling my hair. Shuddering, she pulls me closer, before eventually releasing me as her body relaxes.

After yanking up her jeans, she helps me up off the floor and we sit down on the edge of my bed. It feels weirdly more intimate than everything we've just done.

'Do you . . . want to stay?' I ask eventually, willing her to say no with every fibre of my being.

'No,' she says immediately. But then she smiles at me. She looks more chilled than I've ever seen her, like she's finally let something go. I find myself feeling tenderly towards her. I hope she's worked something out tonight.

I very nearly say, 'If you ever want to talk', but stop myself.

I see her out of the door and into her Uber and she kisses me on the forehead as she goes. An odd move. I feel confident we will not cross paths again.

As I get ready for bed, I realise I've left my toothbrush at Georgia's and decide I'd rather borrow Poppy's than not brush my teeth at all. She won't mind – if I asked she'd probably say something like 'Mi toothbrush es su toothbrush' very earnestly. I have a quick nose in Poppy's bathroom cabinet and decide she also won't mind if I use her posh face wash.

When I eventually get into bed I'm horrified to find that I feel an almost childlike homesickness. I look at Georgia's velvet cushions propped up on the other side of the bed and swallow a lump in my throat. I don't want to cry. The therapist in my head wants to explore my feelings – what am I homesick for?

Who am I homesick for? Why is a cushion making me cry? But the much more dominant drunk person in my head wants to go to sleep and put it down to post-sex sadness and not enough water. I briefly wonder about going to fetch Diane to keep me company but I'm worried her little heart would give out at the panic of being in bed with a stranger.

I message Georgia.

> *I left my toothbrush at yours! Please tell Zara she can personally bin it and I will buy a new one.*

I wait to see if she reads it straight away but it doesn't even deliver. Her phone's off for the night. She'll be fast asleep.

I lie awake staring at the ceiling, thinking I'll hear Poppy come in soon and that I can talk to her, maybe go and sleep in her bed. But she doesn't come and I fall asleep alone in a room full of empty boxes.

3

My sister loves the heat. She always has. If you look at photos of us from holidays or on our birthday when we were little, she's front and centre, top off, hands on hips, radiant in the sunshine – in her element. I'm a gremlin next to her, covered in sunscreen but burnt anyway, wearing some kind of long-sleeved swimming costume and a hat with a neck flap, suffering.

Because it's the run-up to our birthday, Natalie is bombarding me with photos of us asking my opinion on the best ones for an Instagram post. She is nothing if not prepared.

How cute is this one, Nat?

I hate being called Nat but I call her Nat too. The Nats. Honestly, what were our parents thinking?

Or this one? Oh my god look at your face!

The photo she's sent is from an album. I can see her iPhone reflected in it. She and I are sitting in a paddling pool in our matching swimming costumes. Pink and frilly. We can't be older than five or six and we're clutching ice creams that look freshly bought from the ice-cream van. They're enormous in our tiny, chubby hands and looking very likely to be dropped in the water at any moment. We're both grinning and I'm wearing huge sunglasses that are wonky on my face; they must be Mum's. I zoom in as much as I can to inspect our faces. We're not identical twins but we looked much more similar then than we do now. Dark hair cut into the same bowl shape, big brown eyes, little squishy noses. We were very cute. As adults you wouldn't be surprised to find out we're sisters but no one would guess we were twins. Natalie is bigger than I am, rounder. I'm more angular, sharper at the edges. She's more beautiful. People say, 'No don't be silly, you're *both* beautiful' when I say that but I'm not trying to be self-deprecating. It's just the truth. She's very beautiful. Her hair is long and thick and she just knows what to do with it. One of those hair people. I'm sure she was born knowing how to do a French plait. And she has the most perfect, glowing skin.

Acid! Get yourself some acid! she always tells me whenever I bemoan how mine still gets spots. Wrinkles and spots – the cursed skin of a thirty-something-year-old woman.

I'm on my way to Natalie's house for lunch. She still lives in Essex around the corner from my mum. It's a long way to go for a few hours – train into London, the tube and then another train back out the other side – but it's a Sunday and I don't have anywhere to be. When I leave, fairly early in the morning, Poppy's bedroom door is still closed. I suspect she'll be out of action for the day.

Although I've recently made myself some vague promises to no longer work on the weekends I can't resist getting through some emails on the train. It feels like if I do something useful it might in some way compensate for the hangover I have. There are a couple of new client enquiries, one student – never had therapy before but struggling to cope with their first big break-up – and one older woman who's questioning her sexuality. I send them both my availability and some forms to fill in. I also have some emails from my peer supervision group arranging our next session. Peer supervision is basically a group of therapists who all get together once a month to check in on each other, offer advice and make sure none of us are fucking up too badly. There are three other people in my group, Philippa and Louise, both of whom fit the exact description of what you might picture when you think about a therapist – linen trousers, long, flowing cardigans, alarmingly large necklaces. Then there's Charlie, who is my favourite therapist friend because they are also occasionally hungover in supervision and they also occasionally write 'fuck off Louise' in their notebook while she is talking.

I text Charlie to see if they want to get a drink later. I know they will want to hear all about Alice and I definitely want to hear all about whatever they got up to on Friday night. Plus I know Poppy is likely to be out at Felix's or he'll be at ours and

I'm not sure I can handle either being by myself or being their third wheel.

I manage to get to Natalie's house unscathed, by which I mean, without seeing anybody I know from school. It's a risk because it's a half-hour walk from the station. A mile of memories and potential meetings with former best friends, former enemies, former frenemies. I had a rich school life. Natalie is still friends with people from school and asks me at Christmas and Easter whether I'd like to go with her to meet them at the pub. I absolutely do not.

Natalie lives in a terraced house almost identical to the one we grew up in, on a street of similar terraced houses within streets of many other terraced houses. This town was built in the late 1940s – one of the original 'new towns' – by incredibly unimaginative people.

'Natasha's here!' my niece Ella shouts at no one in particular as she answers the door to me and then walks away without saying hello. She's suddenly twelve going on twenty-five. Very busy and important.

'Lovely to see you, El.' I step inside and follow her into the kitchen where she's getting a can of Coke out of the fridge.

'Mum's in the garden.' She cracks it open, takes a sip and then, after a pause, hands it to me so I can have some.

'Thanks.' I take it from her and start to drink; she watches me for a moment before realising what's happening.

'No!' she shrieks, part furious, part delighted. 'No, you're going to finish it all!'

She runs towards me but I twist away from her, tipping the can up so I can get it all before she wrestles it off me.

'Oh my god I hate you,' she screams, hysterical now, not able to stop herself from laughing.

'No, you love me,' I say, grabbing her and pinning her arms down by her side to pull her into a big, unwanted hug.

'I do not.'

'You do, you love me so much. Let me sniff you.' I take a deep breath into her beautiful curls, which she's wearing loose today.

'You're so weird.' She's still wriggling but with much less passion. She reluctantly puts her arms loosely around my waist.

'Mmm, you still smell like a little baby.'

'No I don't! I don't. I smell like perfume. I've got perfume on!'

'Nope, a teeny, tiny baby. I love it.' I'm winding her up but I could stand there all day in the kitchen with my nose buried in her hair.

Eventually I let her go and she pats at her hair like my sniffing might have really messed it up. She goes to the freezer and gets out a box of ice lollies. She offers the box and before I can say, 'Yes please' she snatches it back and shoves it in the freezer. Revenge.

We go out into the garden where Natalie is sprawled on a sunlounger. She's in a swimming costume and shorts and holding her phone above her face. She waves at me but doesn't take her eyes away from her phone; she points at it to indicate she's talking. I go and sit on the sunlounger next to her and shout hello to Daniel, who is lying flat out in the middle of the grass with headphones on. He half-heartedly lifts an arm at me by way of greeting. I vow to grab him for a good head sniff later.

I settle in next to Natalie who turns her head to me. I think she's going to whisper, 'Sorry' for being on the phone but instead she loudly says,

'Sorry Natty that I'm having to be *so rude* but my boyfriend is incapable of going to the shop for BBQ things without me even though I *gave him a list* so now I'm having to walk him through it.'

I don't respond since she is not really talking to me and since I don't want to get involved. I like Luke. He puts up with a lot.

'Babe, your list literally says, "Get BBQ things!" What am I meant to do with that? Hi Natasha.'

I jerk my head over her sunlounger to wave at him.

'Hiya Luke, listen, sorry to be a pain but can you get some halloumi? I've got a real craving for it and also some Doritos and some Fanta and maybe some Magnums?'

'Hangover?'

'Yeah. Cheers Luke!'

Luke and Natalie have been together forever. Since we were sixteen. She brought him home at the same time I brought home one of my most terrible girlfriends – played acoustic guitar at parties, wore a bandana, called people 'dude'. We're all very grateful that theirs is the relationship that ended up lasting.

Eventually Natalie gets off the phone, once she's confident Luke can complete his mission.

'Sorry babe!' She rolls her eyes.

'Don't worry. Poor Luke.'

'Don't get me started with *poor Luke*. I can't even talk about him.'

Now it's my turn to roll my eyes. She loves to do this dramatic, 'is my relationship in peril?' stuff. She's just craving a bit of excitement from watching too many reality-TV dating shows – her favourite genre of TV.

'Why are you hanging then?'

'Because I was drinking last night.'

'Ughh, you know what I mean, what were you doing? Getting drunk with Poppy and Felix?'

She puts on a special high voice to say Poppy and Felix. She actually loves Poppy, they both have a natural affinity for bypassing small talk in favour of deep and meaningfuls.

'No, they were out.'

'Who were you with then?'

'Just someone off Hinge.'

'Did you have a little sleepover?'

'Maybe.'

I can't help but smile.

'Oooh, give me all the details. Who strapped on?'

'Neither of us!'

'Boo,' she rolls onto her back again, disinterested. Natalie is really into the lesbian accoutrements but not bothered about hearing about what she describes as 'a lot of fingering basically'.

'Sorry. Maybe if your own sex life wasn't so boring you wouldn't need to hear so much about mine.'

She doesn't even bother to protest.

'Yeah, maybe. Listen, did I tell you Mum's coming round to join us later?'

I groan and slide further down the sunlounger.

'Natty! It'll be nice. You haven't seen her in ages.'

'I know, I know. It's fine. I just can't deal when I'm hungover.'

'You won't be by the time she gets here. She told me that she didn't know you were moving . . . I think she was surprised you hadn't told her.'

'I told her!'

But even as I say it, I realise I probably hadn't. Why would I, when Mum finds mine and Georgia's relationship so strange? She doesn't understand how I could live with an ex. She can barely get her head around my dating women, let alone dating them and then continuing to live with them once the relationship has ended. I think she thinks I live in some lesbian commune filled with interchangeable partners, singing folk songs and wearing hemp. I mean, I wish.

When Luke arrives with the food and he and Natalie start bickering by the BBQ, I spend some time lying next to Daniel trying to get him to talk to me but I stopped being interesting to him about a year ago. Natalie assures me he'll come back to us in a few years' time, but I'm sure there are glimmers of the old Daniel in there underneath the grumpy adolescent exterior. The little boy who would sit on my knee and have me read to him or who would very patiently try and teach me his video games, speaking to me like you would an incredibly elderly person.

I know I'm trying too hard, I may as well lie next to him and scream 'Love me!' in his face but I can't get enough of him. I cried for ages when I first met the twins, a few hours after they were born. Natalie was totally out of it, full of fantastic drugs, and Mum was running around checking on things, completely unable to sit down and enjoy the moment. Luke and I just sat next to each other in silence passing these babies back and forth. They were barely babies, more like aliens. Their little hands squirming, their heads too small for the hats Mum had knitted. They had long eyelashes like Luke (who has the eyelashes of a Disney princess) and a few wispy strands of soft black hair and I couldn't take my eyes off them. It is hard to explain being a twin but I had thought I couldn't love someone more than I love Natalie and then I met the babies and they ruined my life. I am completely obsessed with them.

'You're obsessed with me.' Daniel removes one earbud and studies me.

'I am not.'

'Then why are you staring at me?'

'Ugh, fine. I'm obsessed. Just talk to me, tell me what's going on, give me something and then I'll leave you alone.'

'Like what?'

'Anything! How's school? Have you gone to any fun parties? Have you got a girlfriend?'

He sighs heavily at my boring questions.

'Have *you* got a girlfriend?' He smiles at me.

'Ha, fair play. No, not at the moment.'

'Why?'

Damn it. This is the last thing I need to think about with my mum on her way and a severe hangover. Ella wanders over and plonks herself at my feet. She's eating another ice pop and red juice is sliding down her arm. I resist the urge to lean over and wipe it off her, she'll just bat me away.

'What are we talking about?' she says.

'Why Auntie Natty doesn't have a girlfriend.'

'Oooh,' Ella's eyes widen, 'why don't you?'

'Oh well, um.' Christ. 'I think that's a very complicated question and there's a lot of different . . .'

'Mum says you can't commit to anyone.'

'Does she now?'

'She says you always leave before it gets serious.'

'Right.'

They both look at me, expectantly. Waiting for me to elaborate.

'I guess . . .' I sit up, trying to catch Natalie's eye but she looks deep in thought, eating a tablespoon of the coleslaw that she's decanting into a bowl. 'I guess I just haven't met the right person yet.'

Ella opens her mouth to ask a question but I bellow over her head, 'Do you need a hand over there?'

And before Nat can answer I jump up and walk briskly towards the table. I wonder if anyone's going to start drinking soon.

I'm set to work putting up the umbrella that goes through the middle of their outdoor table. It seems unnecessarily complicated. A series of strings that you have to pull and tie like you're sailing a ship. Just as I'm at a crucial point, my head buried in umbrella folds, my mum walks out into the garden carrying a large tray wrapped in foil.

'Nan's here!' Ella announces but doesn't get up to greet her, which I get a pathetic, petty kick out of.

When I'm satisfied the umbrella is not going to collapse into our plates, I duck out from under it and turn to my mum, who is hovering, still clutching her tray.

'All right Mum?' I say and lean forward to give her an awkward little kiss on the cheek. I don't recognise the smell of her; she must have started wearing a different perfume.

'I'd like to put this down,' she says and then looks down at the table now covered in plates and napkins and bowls of crisps and mayonnaise-covered salads, 'but I see there's nowhere to put it.'

I take a deep breath and resist rolling my eyes. She has only been here thirty seconds. Instead I pick up two bowls of crisps and gesture with my head for her to put her tray down in the space I've made.

As she puts it down she says, 'But where are those going to go?'

'In my mouth,' I manage to say through a mouthful of chilli heatwave.

My mum does not bother to resist rolling her eyes at me. Perfect.

After what feels like a lifetime of faffing about and the kids taking hours to do their one job of setting the table and managing to argue about it the whole time, we eventually all sit down. I sit in between Daniel and Luke on the opposite side of the table from Mum, who picks up her napkin and starts wiping her cutlery. I grit my teeth and tell myself she doesn't even realise she's doing it. I try to catch Natalie's eye but she is resolutely avoiding looking at me.

Just as I've taken an enormous bite of my burger, my mum asks, 'So how's work, Natasha?'

I spend longer than is necessary chewing and swallowing, making a point of being extremely put out about it.

'It's fine, Mum.'

'Right.'

She looks down at her plate and starts picking at lettuce with her fork. My mum has refused to eat anything cooked on the BBQ. She doesn't trust it.

'Anything good?' Natalie asks.

For some reason Margot flashes through my mind, her taking her shoes off, taking a sip of water and seeing right through me.

'No, nothing in particular.'

There's a lull and Mum's hard stare makes me realise I'm meant to elaborate or at least somewhat participate in this conversation.

'How's work for you, Mum?' I take another bite of my burger and add, 'Anything good?'

I immediately regret asking in case she tells me someone came into A&E having eaten a poisoned burger or that someone died from simply being too hungover.

She sighs.

'Well no, there isn't anything good, we're even more short-staffed than ever. I did a run of nights last week and I'm still not quite recovered. You know, on my shift yesterday I was there for twelve hours, and I didn't sit down *once*. For lunch I managed to grab a biscuit that I ate walking down a corridor.'

I look at her properly while she's talking. She's taken off her sunglasses now she's under the umbrella and she suddenly looks so much older than I think of her as being. Although she's been a nurse all my life, I suddenly can't stand the idea of her working all night, unable to eat or drink or sit down.

I'm just about to say something. To tell her that sounds awful, that I'm sorry, when she interrupts.

'And how is Georgia?'

I nod, acknowledging that on her precious day off she doesn't want to dwell on A&E.

'She's good! Although you know I literally just moved out yesterday. She seems happy to be moving in with Zara.'

'Mmm, I'm sure,' Mum says.

I shoot Natalie a 'what is that supposed to mean' look and she just widens her eyes at me as if to say, 'leave it.'

Fortunately for me, Ella and Daniel start to chatter about their friends and holidays and what they're going to have for pudding and all we're required to do is listen. My mum softens around them in a way she never has around us. She is sitting next to Ella, who at one point sends a fork clattering onto the patio. Mum doesn't even flinch, she just calmly leans over, picks it up and hands Ella her own fork to use instead.

Once we've finished eating, Natalie and I say we'll clear up while Luke and the kids set up the ridiculous paddling pool they've bought. One of those ones that's about three metres tall and you need a ladder to climb into.

I begin to get up from the table but Natalie motions for me to sit back down.

'Actually . . .' she says and shoots a look at Luke, who nods at her. 'If we can all just hang on a minute, Luke and I have got something we want to tell you.'

She takes a deep breath and Luke nods at her again. He's got his hands clasped together in front of his face. He looks nervous.

Mum and I go completely silent. I look at Ella and Daniel to see if I can gauge what it might be from their reaction but they're just on the edge of their seats, itching to be able to go and set up the pool.

'So, it's good news,' Natalie says, breaking into a smile, and I immediately know what she's going to say. My mum's hand flies up to her mouth when Natalie places a hand on her stomach. 'We're having a baby.'

I scream and burst into tears all at once and run around the table to hug her.

'Wait,' I say, pulling back and holding her by the shoulders, 'just one, right?'

'Yes!' Luke answers for her quickly. 'Just one this time.'

'Thank God. No offence,' I say to the twins, who are still twitching about in their chairs, massively underwhelmed by the whole situation.

I move out of the way so that my mum who is waiting patiently behind me can get her turn to hug Natalie.

'Wait, did you know?' I say to the twins.

'Yeah we've known for ages,' Daniel says.

'Well, what do you think about it?' I ask.

Ella shrugs.

'Good?' she says. 'If it's a girl that'd be cute.'

'Oh yes,' I say, turning to Natalie again. 'Do we know if it's a . . .'

She shakes her head.

'We're keeping it a surprise. It doesn't matter. We just want a happy, healthy baby.'

'We want a boy,' Luke mouths at me and Natalie smacks him on the arm.

'When's the due date?' Mum asks. She's sitting back in her seat now, dabbing the corners of her eyes with a piece of kitchen roll.

'December twenty-third.'

'Hmm,' I say.

'What?'

'Capricorn.'

My mum rolls her eyes but Natalie nods at me, knowingly.

'I know. If it's a couple of days early, it'll be a Sagittarius,' she says and crosses her fingers.

'Much better.'

'So you're four months pregnant,' Mum says, ignoring us both.

'Yes,' Natalie says. 'We just wanted to be, you know . . .'

She looks at Luke.

'To just be sure everything was really happening.' He finishes her sentence for her and they smile at each other. Sadly maybe, or is that just the way you smile at someone when you're saying a thousand things at once? I'm suddenly painfully aware of a whole world that she lives in that I'm not a part of.

'Come on!' Daniel says, finally losing his patience with the baby chat. 'You said we'd do the pool *today!*'

Natalie and I get up from the table and start clearing plates. I'm hoping this will be a chance for us to chat properly but Mum insists on helping us. She comes into the kitchen and absent-mindedly switches the radio on, it's adverts but she leaves the station on. She's so comfortable in Natalie's house. I think about what it would be like to have Mum in my kitchen and I can't even picture her there.

We scrape plates and rinse glasses in silence for a minute, taking in the news. I have a big grin plastered on my face as I scrape uneaten salad into the bin. The Magic FM jingle plays and Fleetwood Mac, 'Go Your Own Way' blares out of the speakers. Natalie groans and goes to switch it off.

'No, leave it!' Mum and I both say at the same time. She looks at me and then quickly looks away. The corner of her mouth is slightly turned up but I can't tell if she was going to smile.

'You two have the worst taste in music.'

We carry on in silence for a while before Mum says to me, 'So Natalie tells me you won't be in the country for your birthday.'

'Yeah that's right, I'm going on holiday with Georgia and everyone.'

'To Los Angeles?'

'Right, yes. And a couple of days out in the desert, I think. She, um, she paid for my ticket.'

I don't know why I say that.

'Hmm.'

'What?'

She looks into the dishwasher so intensely it's like she's speaking to someone in there.

'You should see your dad while you're out there.'

Natalie is rooting around in the fridge but abruptly stops what she's doing and spins around.

'What?' she says quietly.

'Your *dad*,' Mum says, as if the concept of a dad is what we didn't understand.

'What do you mean, I should go and see him? I thought he was in France?'

'No, California,' Mum says. 'He hasn't been in France for a few years.'

'How do you know that?' I ask.

'I get a Christmas card from your Auntie Linda every year. She fills me in. I did send you both the newsletter she does on email. It had that picture of her dog dressed up as an elf.'

Mum says this with some measure of judgement – animals dressed up is one of the many things she finds distasteful.

Natalie and I both look at each other blankly. I vaguely remember an email from Mum and distinctly remember not reading it.

'So what's he doing in California?'

'Oh, you know. What he always does. Following around his new . . . partner.'

My dad left my mum, and us when we were in our second year of high school. It was not entirely unexpected. They argued a lot. Mum had once been more fun than she is now and Dad had once been more attentive and kind. Oh and, also, my dad is gay. I think that probably had quite a lot to do with it. He left us for a man named Carl. Carl lived in London in a flat and for the first few months Natalie and I would go up to this flat every other weekend and sleep on a futon on the floor. It was fun at first. Carl was a nice man, he would make us pancakes and let us have as much syrup as we wanted on them and he didn't care if we ate fruit or not. He was a nice man but he didn't sign up for kids. And my dad was a nice man but he didn't know what to do with us without Mum and nor did he know how we fitted into his new life. After a while our visits became monthly and then every few months and then my dad and Carl moved to France into a big, run-down farmhouse that they were going to do up and turn into a guest house. Eventually we stopped visiting altogether.

'So he's not with Carl anymore?'

Mum shakes her head. Tight-lipped. She still can't bear to talk about it.

I stay for a couple more hours, long enough to drink a gin and tonic in the sun and watch the kids realise with crushing disappointment just how long it takes to fill up a giant paddling pool. By the time I'm saying goodbye the water comes up to their ankles.

When I get up to leave, I squeeze Natalie as tightly as I can.

'So you *are* still having sex,' I whisper in her ear.

'Who says it's his?' she whispers back.

Mum sees me out at the door, insisting she needs to get something out of the car. She wants to give me a lift to the station but I need the time to think.

Standing by the open car boot she says, 'Wonderful news about the baby, isn't it.'

'It is wonderful, Mum,' I say.

'Natasha.'

'Mum.'

She twists her keys around in her fingers and looks at the ground.

'You will think about seeing your dad, won't you?'

'Why do you care?'

'I just . . . I think you two will get along, that's all, and I don't want you to miss out on that.'

'Why do you think we'll get along?'

Mum is suddenly flustered. I know the answer she doesn't want to say is: 'Because you're just like him.'

'You're his daughter!' she says eventually.

'OK.'

'You'll think about it?'

'Yes. I'll think about it.'

She reaches into the boot of her car and stuffs a small paper gift bag into my hand.

'I saw these and thought of you. You can open it on the train if you're running late.'

I nod and shove the gift bag into my backpack. She kisses me stiffly on the cheek, slams the boot shut and heads back into Natalie's house.

Charlie does want to meet for a drink so we agree, since it's a beautiful evening and we're both attempting to spend less money, to meet on the beach and drink some cocktails courtesy of Marks and Spencer. I'm extremely grateful to earlier me for making plans this evening. I feel like I might go mad if I have to sit with the events of today by myself. I spend most of the train journey home sending voice notes back and forth with Natalie.

'What the fuck? OK wait, first of all. I'm so happy for you. Like, the main takeaway from today is you're having another baby and I'm so, so happy about it. Maybe this kid will let me give it cuddles and not find me super embarrassing? At least for a few years anyways. But Natalie, can we please also talk about DAD?! Is Mum serious? I don't . . . I mean . . . would he even want to see me? Do I even want to see him? What the hell is he doing in LA? We really should start reading Linda's newsletters. Like . . . what else have we missed?'

'Awww no sorry, the baby will definitely find you super embarrassing. I know, mate. I can't believe it. Yeah I don't know, like if he wanted to see us would he not have . . . I don't know . . . been in touch? Made some effort? But then like, why is Mum pushing for it? She must think he wants to see us for whatever reason. Maybe he said something to Linda? God, I don't know. It's too much info to be honest. Yeah, what the bloody hell is he doing there? Are we going to find out he's some big famous person now? I tell you what, if he's hit the big time he's bloody giving us every penny he's got. I'll take that child support now thank you very much!'

I arrive at the packed beach before Charlie and spot them way before they spot me. They're wearing a sarong, the likes of which I haven't seen since the nineties, and a tie-dye crop top. Charlie has the kind of figure, straight up and down, where they could pull off basically anything and make it look fashionable. Their hair is tied back in a high ponytail and they have a huge straw beach bag which I assume is filled with tins of cocktails. I met Charlie when I was a volunteer therapist at a charity when I was still training. Charlie had already been qualified for a year but was still volunteering to build up the hours to gain accreditation. They took me under their wing and also got me a part-time job at the pub they were working in to tide me over while I was trying to set up my practice. Charlie turned out to be simultaneously one of the wisest and silliest people I have ever met. Whenever I get a case of imposter syndrome I think of Charlie – insightful, empathetic, professional – absolutely out of their tree at 3 a.m. trying to get literally any ex on the phone, smoking like a chimney and then getting tucked up on my sofa for the night.

When they reach me Charlie plonks down next to me and gives me a huge hug, which nearly knocks me backwards.

'Are we the only people on the beach not BBQ-ing?'

We are surrounded by loud groups of people, plumes of smoke and the smell of burnt sausages.

'I think so,' I say. 'Though I'm actually all BBQ-ed out.'

I fill Charlie in on my day and they nod and groan and roll their eyes in all the right places while downing a can of Porn Star Martini.

'I can't believe she's going to have another baby,' I say, shaking my head.

'How does it feel to be becoming an auntie again?' Charlie asks.

'So good,' I say. 'The twins are everything. I can't believe there's going to be another one.'

'Does it not make you broody?'

I shake my head immediately, an auto-response to anyone asking about children.

'No. It doesn't make me broody. I don't think I'm in that place. I don't think I'll ever be in that place. It's definitely made me feel . . .' I search my mind for the words to describe what exactly it is that's sitting on my chest and manage to come up with, 'something.'

Charlie rolls their eyes.

'Ever in touch with your feelings.'

I smile sarcastically at them.

When I get to the part of the day about my dad, Charlie's eyes widen. Their jaw actually drops.

'Hang on, what?'

I pause.

'What?'

'Why didn't I know about your dad being *gay*?' Charlie says, scandalised.

I shrug.

'I don't know. We've just never really talked about it. I don't really talk about him at all.'

'All this time I thought he was just a deadbeat.'

'He is.'

'Natasha.'

'What?'

Charlie looks at me, waiting for me to acknowledge that meeting with my dad could be a breakthrough moment for me. I hate therapists.

'What? Why would I talk about my dad? I don't even know him anymore. I don't even know why I told you that. I'm not going to see him.'

'Really? Why not?'

'Ugh, because! Because, Charlie.'

We're both quiet for a moment. Charlie looks at me steadily and takes a final sip of their drink before digging the can into the pebbles.

'Because it's just easier to pretend he doesn't exist.'

Charlie nods and thankfully decides to leave it. I know that I haven't heard the end of it. *You told Charlie for a reason*, the therapist in my head says. *You want their input.* I push the thoughts away. Have a day off.

'So are you going to ask about my day?' Charlie says reaching into their bag, throwing me a drink and opening their own second can.

'Sorry, yes. I've just been going on and on about myself. Please tell me all about your day.'

Charlie beams.

'Aaron texted me.'

I groan as Charlie shoves their phone in my face, showing me the evidence.

'Wait, I thought we didn't like Aaron anymore?'

'We didn't because he didn't text me. But now he has.'

'High standards there, Charl.'

They ignore me.

I tip my head back to drink the final sip of my mojito before diving right into the next one. The dull ache in my head that's been lingering all day has finally disappeared.

We lie back on the pebbles, leaning on our elbows, enjoying the slight breeze that makes the heat briefly more bearable. We're quiet for a minute watching a couple of boys (of the 'lads lads lads' variety), who are clearly daytrippers, strip down to their pants and run into the sea.

'Have you heard much from Georgia since she kicked you out?' Charlie asks.

'Um, a bit,' I say, tearing my eyes away from the sight of the friends of the 'lads lads lads' running up the beach with their clothes. 'I only moved out yesterday. I mean, how much would we normally talk in a day?'

It's meant to be a rhetorical question but Charlie looks at me pointedly. They are a fully paid up member of the Georgia fan club. They think I'm a fool for ever breaking up with her. They also think she's a fool for letting me carry on living with her. Charlie stays quiet. They're doing that thing where therapists wait for you to fill the silence. Of course, that's exactly what I do.

'I mean, they're probably too busy having sex in all the rooms, aren't they. Zara needs to make her mark.'

I mean to sound funny or at the very least glib, but I actually just sound bitter. I take a sip of my drink. It's too warm now and starting to coat my teeth in fuzz.

'Could be that,' Charlie says. 'Could be unpacking, eating dinner, setting up the home gym in your old room.'

I can't help but smile at them.

'I have her birthday party soon though so at least I'll see her then.'

We lie down for a while, properly so that we're staring up at the changing colours of the sky. I tell Charlie about the introduction to therapy class, ostensibly so I can discuss how it went but actually, I realise, it's so I can talk about Margot. I've not spoken about her to anyone else.

'She sounds very intense.'

'She was really intense.'

I feel that Charlie hasn't grasped what I'm trying to say about her. But then what am I trying to say? I spent a very strange couple of hours with someone and I haven't stopped thinking about her since?

'You'll have to look out for her book. See if you're featured.'

Charlie tells me about the two-week holiday they've booked for themselves at the end of November in Thailand. How they're looking forward to spending time alone. I tell them I can't think of anything worse.

'Than Thailand?'

'No, Thailand's lovely. I can't think of anything worse than being by myself for two weeks.'

I feel Charlie shift beside me, turning their head to face me. I don't move, my hand up over my eyes, shielding them from the light.

'I think it would be good for you. Some time to reflect, maybe to confront . . .'

'No thank you!'

'Natasha, it'll be amazing, I'm going to do yoga every day.'

'Even worse.'

They roll their eyes.

Eventually Charlie looks at their phone and sighs.

'I'd better head off in a minute, I'm going to Aaron's tonight, he's going to cook me dinner.'

I grin and raise my eyebrows.

'Sure. Dinner. That's what they're calling it these days.'

'He is! A romantic dinner. That's all. Very classy.'

'OK. Enjoy your classy, chaste dinner.'

Charlie stands up and dusts off their sarong. Ridiculous. It looks so good.

'See you soon? Shall we do a drink? Next Friday?'

'Yes please.'

I blow Charlie a kiss and watch them hop quickly over the pebbles, carrying their sandals in one hand and an Aperitivo Spritz in the other.

I sit on the beach staring at the sea for a little longer after Charlie leaves. I can't quite face going home yet, well, to Poppy's. The wind has picked up and it's finally starting to cool down. I reach into my bag for my phone so I can take a picture of the sunset for Instagram and find the paper bag from Mum. I pull the Sellotape off the top and slide out a pair of socks – grey and covered with badgers. I roll my eyes. I don't know where she finds these things. It's like she has a sixth sense for badger paraphernalia. I've never seen badger socks in my life. I pull them on, digging my badger-clad feet into the warm pebbles.

I don't know how Mum and I got to the stage where we can only communicate through paper bags with socks in them. Although, this is a major improvement for us. I was a difficult teenager – well I guess through most of my twenties, too, so maybe that just makes me a difficult person. I don't know whose word difficult is. Someone must have told me that once.

My mum isn't the yelling type so when I'd come home drunk or high or with a different person every weekend she responded with silence. The quieter she got the louder I became until it felt like I was screaming all the time. It never seemed to affect her. Some years I'm sure we barely spoke at all. I screamed into the void.

She'd probably say I'm still difficult now. She's probably right.

I take a photo of the socks instead of the sunset and send it to Natalie.

Bloody badgers. She's mad.

I send the same photo to Mum.

Thanks. They're great.

She reads it immediately and types for ages before eventually sending a single thumbs up.

I get a message from the girl who only texts me 'hey' saying, predictably, *hey*, and I text her back saying *you OK?*

Yeah, you? she messages back immediately.

Yeah, I say. *Fine.*

And then on a whim I write,

Do you fancy getting a drink soon? I wait for a few minutes pretending to look out at the sea but really looking at my phone out of the corner of my eye. She reads it but she doesn't reply.

4

'Why are you looking so peaky, Natasha?'

Felix slaps me on the back as we make our way out of the flat. It is my first driving lesson this evening and I am not excited. I had planned on cancelling but I put him off all of last week and tonight he was waiting for me at the kitchen table when I got home from work, eager to do his community service.

I have had some driving lessons before. I once saved up money from my supermarket Saturday job to buy a bundle of ten lessons. But the thing with driving is that ten lessons really doesn't get you very far. And those ten lessons were about fifteen years ago in a car where the passenger has access to a brake pedal.

'Take care of her! Very precious cargo!' Poppy calls after us. Diane is barking ferociously, the kind of bark she does when she senses danger on the other side of the front door. I try not to read too much into it.

I go to get in the passenger seat of the car and realise that Felix has the same idea.

I glare at him.

'Aren't you going to take us somewhere where there aren't any other cars? So I can get the hang of it?'

When we first discussed these driving lessons I had pictured us driving around an empty car park in the dead of night.

'Absolutely not,' he says, gleefully. 'In at the deep end. It's the only way to learn. Sink or swim, baby.'

'Right. It's just that in this case if I sink I'll actually crash the . . .'

Felix's phone rings and he holds his finger up to cut me off. He answers it by saying, 'Hola amigo! Can't talk now brother, I'm with my student!'

I roll my eyes and make my way very slowly to the driver's side.

'Shouldn't we have an L plate?' I ask as I slam the door behind me. It feels indescribably weird to be sitting in the driving seat. I look out of the window, not wanting anyone to see me in case they, what? Call the police on a thirty-year-old woman getting behind the wheel?

'No need, no need. You're going to smash it,' says Felix buckling his seatbelt and then checking it again. Reassuring.

I nod and try to familiarise myself with the car. I adjust the mirror because it feels like the kind of thing I should be doing. Felix is furiously tapping away on his phone and only looks up when I say,

'Um, Felix. How do I start the car?'

'Right, right, right.'

He puts his phone away.

'So lesson numero uno, starting the car.'

He pauses to grin at me and I stare straight ahead.

'You just press "start",' he says, like it's the most obvious thing in the world.

I look to the left-hand side of the steering wheel and see a big 'start' button. OK, seems easy enough.

'And then,' he says, patronisingly, as if we've been through it all before. 'And then you just move the stick into drive.'

I look at him and then down at the gear stick. I can't believe I didn't notice when Poppy was driving me on moving day that this is an automatic. Clearly too busy clinging on for dear life.

'You just put it into drive?'

'Yeah! And then if you want to stop just take your foot off the pedal and put it on the brake. If you want to park, into park, if you want to reverse, into reverse. You get it, Nat? It's super, super easy!'

'What if I stall?'

'Oh, you literally can't stall this car. The engine just starts again automatically.'

I realise that my problem may not have been the fact I was learning in a Fiat 500, or that I only had ten lessons, it was that I hadn't learned to drive in what is, essentially, a giant go-kart.

Felix directs me up the road and I drive at approximately ten miles an hour around all the streets near the flat. I scream every time I see another car or a person or a bird but after about twenty minutes of turning up one street, indicating and then turning back down another, I'm feeling slightly more confident. I can drive down three streets very slowly as long as no one else is driving, walking or flying near me, which feels like a success. Felix is extremely encouraging and, actually, a very good teacher.

'Are you all right with parallel parking, Nat?' Felix says as we turn down our road.

'No. Definitely not,' I say as I stop in the middle of the road outside our flat.

'Oh, it's super easy. Super easy,' he says as if he hasn't heard me and points forward to indicate that I should keep going. I slam the brakes on a few metres down the road and put the car in reverse. A video of the road behind me pops up on the dashboard.

Turns out that super, super easy is not the correct description of parallel parking. After about fifteen minutes of trying Poppy comes outside and starts cheerleading from the front step. Diane is in her arms, barking hysterically. It is not helpful.

'That's it!'

'You just have to get behind that car and in front of the other one!'

'So close! Actually . . . not that close.'

After what feels like forever, I admit defeat and Felix takes over. When I reach her Poppy pulls me in for a hug and I exhale properly for the first time since I got in the car.

'You're so tense!'

'Yeah I know, I just *drove*. A car. On the road.'

We head inside and Felix joins us for post-lesson gin and tonics. I pick my glass up and realise my hands are shaking.

'She did so well,' Felix says to Poppy as if I'm not sitting there. I feel a little rush of pride, despite myself.

'Amazing! Maybe she can drive us to Georgia's party at the weekend.'

'I think not.' I say, 'I mean unless we can go at snail's pace and you can guarantee that there'll be no one else on the road?'

'Maybe next time,' Felix says.

'So what's the vibe at Georgia's?' Poppy says. She's standing with her back to us straining something over the sink. There is always something earthy and milky going on in this kitchen – homemade oat milk or tempeh or cashew butter. I don't know when any of it ever gets used given the number of times a week Poppy gets Deliveroo.

'The vibe?'

'Mmm. Is it like smart casual? Smart, smart? Are there loads of people going? Or is it more intimate? Are we doing a big present from all of us? Cake? Wine? Are we staying over? Is there a dinner?'

She switches on the NutriBullet and turns to face us, totally serene as if she simply can't hear the noise of hundreds of nuts being obliterated.

I realise I actually have no idea what the vibe is.

'I'll find out. But I've already got her a present. You two will have to sort something out yourselves,' I yell over the racket of the blender.

'Oh, Felix isn't coming,' she says, switching it off and sticking her finger into the beige mixture.

Despite myself, my heart leaps.

'Really? Oh no, what a shame.'

'Yep, already had plans to watch the rugby with the boys. Been in the books for yonks, can't miss it.'

Felix wanders into the garden with his phone in one hand, his gin in the other and Diane tucked under his arm. He is always on the phone. He takes it into the garden now ever since Poppy told him when he's with her he needs to be more present.

I message Georgia.

George, what should we wear on Friday? Is it posh posh? Like a stand up in heels and eat tiny food thing or a sit down in jeans and eat proper food thing?

Poppy sits down next to me; she has a little spot of whatever the concoction is on her chin, which I instinctively reach out and wipe off for her with my thumb. It's so intimate that I'm almost embarrassed. She barely notices, instead she sticks a spoon out and holds it millimetres away from my mouth.

'Open!' she says brightly and I obey.

The mixture is thick and oily and tastes predominantly, in fact overwhelmingly, of cinnamon.

She smiles at me expectantly while I try to swallow the paste, which is stuck in every single crevice of my mouth. I reach for my drink and try to wash it down with gin.

'Wow!' I say eventually. 'It really tastes of cinnamon . . . a lot.'

'Thank you!' She says, 'Yes I invented it, it's loads of different nuts whizzed together and then I just put a load of cinnamon in there. Is it enough?'

'Yes,' I say, firmly.

'Ooh,' she says as she begins to dump large spoonfuls of the stuff into various jars. 'You know, I could give some to George for her birthday. Everyone loves a homemade gift, don't they?'

'Oh yes, do that.'

I smile as I watch her carefully writing labels for her jars of disgusting mush. I hope no one ever tells her.

Tonight I've got a date with the 'hey, you all right?' girl. She eventually replied saying,

I thought you'd never ask

Poppy and Felix are cooking dinner together, which I know will take hours because they're also getting incredibly high. Poppy has a smoke-out-of-the-window rule but it gets forgotten after a couple of drinks. They have a friend of the family who grows it on their farm so it's 'like, super organic'.

I potter into the kitchen before I head out. I pick up Poppy's bottle of beer and take a large gulp.

'You're not nervous, are you darling?' Poppy is holding a carrot in one hand and a really badly rolled joint in the other. She's lolling against the sink, her hand vaguely in the direction of the window which is not open.

'No, I'm not nervous,' I say, taking another sip. It's a lie. I'm always nervous before a date.

'Of course she's not nervous,' Felix says. He's lying down on the couch also holding a carrot. I wonder what they're planning to make. 'She's not nervous, she's done this a hundred times.'

'All right,' I say, holding up a hand to stop him.

'A thousand times!' he says gleefully.

'OK. I'm off.'

'Have fun, Natasha!' Poppy yells after me. 'Be safe!'

I leave them to their carrots and decide to walk into town. It's a beautiful evening and I'm going to be early. We've chosen a very generic, chain pub but I like it because they have a massive beer garden in which you can always find a patch of grass to sit on, even when it's rammed. I have a denim jacket with me specifically so that I can casually say, 'Oh I guess I can sit on this!' should that situation arise. Dating level: expert.

I arrive early as predicted and see that she's messaged me to say she's running a few minutes late but that she'll take a large glass of Pinot Grigio.

Opting for a bottle of wine, I make my way outside and actually manage to find an unoccupied table. I wish, like I always do, that I smoked just so I could have something to do while I wait. I pour two enormous glasses of wine and I'm just getting out my phone to tell her where I am when I hear a voice that makes my heart leap.

'Natasha!'

I look up and take in Margot standing in front of me. Her cheeks are flushed pink, maybe from the heat or maybe from the fact she is clearly, absolutely thrilled.

'I . . . uh . . . fuck.'

I look behind her and down at my phone, trying to figure out when my date might arrive and how I can stop the two of them bumping into each other. It takes me a couple of moments longer to realise. She stands and grins in front of me the entire time.

'No.'

'Oh, yes!'

'No. No! The girl I'm meeting is named Mara. You're not called Mara . . . you're called . . .'

'Right. I'm Margot and everyone calls me Mara. Is this for me?'

She gestures at one of the glasses of wine, picks it up and takes a sip.

'This is so . . . this is so . . .'

I find myself lost for words.

'Crazy, right?'

'Did you know?'

'No I didn't know! We've been talking for ages and you never once mentioned you were a therapist.'

I put my hands to my temples and close my eyes.

I can't help but feel that she's playing with me.

'Right, sorry, I'm just surprised. I didn't recognise you from your . . .'

'I didn't recognise you either,' she says. 'But we've been on WhatsApp for ages and, no offence, but I haven't been back onto your profile to pine over pictures of you.'

She seems sincere but I'm not certain I believe her.

'Have you got a fringe in your photos?' I squint at her, trying to recall if I'd seen her. If subconsciously I recognised her in class.

'You're obsessed with my fringe!' she says, smiling. ' I think it's just some old photos. One of me and my friend's dog. Dogs are really popular on dating apps, you know. Women just love a dog.'

A photo of a woman in sunglasses with a pug on her lap flashes in front of my eyes. Must pay more attention to people, less attention to pets.

'OK look. I'm sorry, this feels a bit off. I feel like I should go.'

I get up to leave.

'Hey, hold on.' Margot gently puts her hand on my forearm as I pull myself up from the table and I snatch it back.

'Sorry. Sorry!' She holds her hands up and takes a step back from me. 'It's just . . . we already have the drinks, please don't leave me here to drink all this alone. It's Thursday night. It's been a rough time for me . . . as you well know.'

I groan and cover my mouth with my hand. An image of us

sitting opposite each other in class flashes through my mind, my notebook open, her knowing smile.

I open my mouth to tell her that this probably isn't the best idea, that I'm going to go, but she puts her hand up to stop me talking.

'Look, you're not my teacher, and you're definitely not my therapist,' she says. 'I'm not going to take the course and, even if I was, you don't run it, do you?'

'Well, no I don't, but . . .'

My heart is pounding, I stand still next to the table trying to work out exactly what my reservations are. Why I'm not just laughing about the coincidence.

'OK? So you were my teacher for, like, an hour. Plus you were terrible! I still can't sleep at all. Or give anyone therapy. Honestly, I got absolutely nothing out of it. So now we're just two people having a drink together.'

I hesitate just for a moment and she smiles broadly, like that hesitation was an enthusiastic agreement to stay.

'Come on,' she says, picking up a glass of wine and holding it near my hand. I automatically reach out and take it. I realise my hands are shaking. I look down at the wine, cold and crisp and numbing. I've never wanted a drink more in my life.

'Look,' she says, holding her hands up as if to show me she doesn't mean me any harm. 'We've been chatting for ages. It's just, like . . . a miscommunication. A case of mistaken identity! Plus . . .' She leans forward conspiratorially, 'I'm twenty-nine. I think I'm allowed to date my teacher?'

Her eyes are wide with excitement. I close mine and take a deep breath, not allowing the frisson of excitement to take hold.

'OK, fine. Just this one. Since we're here.'

'Sure.'

'I mean it.'

I try to convey how serious I am but I can't help but smile back at her. Her buoyancy about the fates pushing us together is infectious. Even though I'm still not sure how much fate had to do with it.

I sit back down and she sits down opposite me. Her knee brushes mine and I flinch, swinging my legs around to the side, trying to keep all my limbs very far away from hers.

We're quiet for a moment. I stare into my drink but I can feel her looking straight at me. I take a few gulps of wine and immediately feel calmer.

'So,' I say, 'how was your day, Margot? Or Mara? Are we doing Margot or Mara?'

'No one calls me Margot apart from you. I was going to tell you but you were already mad at me for barging in.'

I smile, despite myself.

'I wasn't *mad* at you, I was setting a boundary.'

'Well whatever, you seemed mad and then you called me Margot and I liked it, it was like you were telling me off.'

'Jesus Christ.'

'What?'

'Nothing.'

She picks up her wine and takes a sip.

'No, what? Tell me.'

'Nothing! I'm just . . . it's a really good thing we're not going to work together.'

'Why?'

'Because you'd have tried to conquer me and that would never have ended well.'

Margot's face lights up.

'Ooh really? How would it have ended?'

'Well, your research would have been really off for a start.'

'Oh. Not as fun as what I was thinking.'

She reaches into her bag and pulls out a pouch of tobacco.

'Do you mind if I smoke?'

'Not at all.'

'Do you want one?'

'No thanks.'

Margot raises her eyebrows and tilts her head back as if to get a better look at me.

'Aha, so she doesn't smoke . . .'

'Oh god, stop it.'

'What?'

'Trying to figure me out.'

My cheeks flush as I say it, it sounds so ridiculous. I touch one with the back of my hand. On fire. Margot looks completely cool.

'Well tell me about yourself then. Remember you know my deepest, darkest secrets. You've plunged into the depths of my soul, you've reached into . . .'

'Fucking hell, OK. I forgot you were a poet.'

'Tell me everything,' she says, her cigarette between her lips, rummaging in her pockets for a lighter.

'OK, well. I'm from Essex originally, as you know.'

Margot nods as she rolls her cigarette, she makes a motion with her hand like, hurry along, get to the good stuff.

'I have a twin sister.'

'Identical?'

'No.'

'Shame.'

'Don't be gross.'

'OK.' She takes a drag on her cigarette and immediately relights it. She fumbles slightly with the lighter. I wonder if her hands are shaking too.

'More.'

I pick up my drink and take a sip.

'I live with my friend Poppy and her dog.'

'Keep going.'

'I've lived in Brighton for a few years now, since I finished uni.'

She nods.

'Where did you go to uni?'

'Durham.'

Margot raises her eyebrows.

'Long way from home,' she says.

'About as far away as you can get, yeah.'

I chose Durham on a whim. I knew it was a good university. I knew it had colleges and weird banquet-style dinners but it wasn't as terrifying to me as Oxbridge, which I didn't even bother to apply for. I also chose it because it was miles away from home in every possible sense. I didn't actually realise how far away it was though, having never been further north than one very cold, very wet week in the Peak District with Mum and Natalie when we were thirteen. *Jesus, Natty*, Natalie had said, *It's practically Scotland.* I missed home constantly.

'And what did you study?'

'History. I did my therapy training down here after I'd finished.'

'So you moved here with Poppy and the dog?'

'No, I actually only just moved in with them.'

She nods, taking it all in.

'So who did you live with before then?'

'Well when I first moved here I was in a house share but then I moved in with someone called Georgia.'

'A girlfriend?'

'Yes.'

'The love of your life?'

She says that without a hint of irony. She's not making fun of me. Or the concept of someone being the love of your life.

'Well, I hope not because she just kicked me out so that she could move her new girlfriend in.'

I smile because I really mean for that to come across light-heartedly, but unexpectedly something about it sticks in my throat. Margot spots it immediately.

'So, she left you for this new woman?'

'No, no, no. She would never . . . we've been broken up for years.'

She frowns.

'We just carried on living together after we broke up.'

She raises her eyebrows.

'Healthy.'

'It was! We are. It worked very well.'

'Really? So there are no feelings left?'

'I . . . how can I . . .'

The idea of saying I have no feelings for Georgia feels preposterous. It's Georgia, I want to say to her. You know, *Georgia*. But of course that means nothing to her. And of course, to an outsider, it doesn't make a whole lot of sense.

'We're very good friends.'

Margot laughs.

'You sound like a celebrity being interviewed.'

She lights a new cigarette and takes a deep drag. She waves her free hand, theatrically.

'The woman behind the curtain.'

'It's not very interesting.'

'It is. I always thought therapists really had their shit together, you know.'

'Erm, excuse me, I actually do have my . . .'

'But here you are doling out advice to everyone . . .'

'I don't give out advice I . . .'

'And you're a mess!'

'Sorry, what?'

'Not a mess. I mean, romantically, things are messy. Sorry, I was being dramatic.'

'Right.'

I take another large gulp of wine, suddenly feeling exhausted but Margot shows no signs of letting up on the inquisition.

'So wait, why did you and Georgia break up?'

'It's very complicated,' I tell her. I say it in such a way that she doesn't ask any more about it. It's actually not especially complicated. Georgia and I had known each other for a while through Poppy before we got together but we weren't close. Then once we did eventually get together (wine, drunken confessions of always secretly fancying each other) everything moved so quickly that I don't know that we ever had the chance to properly get to know each other. I shouldn't have moved in. That was a big mistake. A year later she asked me if I was OK. *You feel distant*, she'd said to me, *in a way you never did before. I feel like you're somewhere else.* I told her that I didn't think we were on the same page anymore, that we wanted different things. That I couldn't give her what she wanted. *I don't want to lose you though, George. I can't bear for you to not be in my life. I know that isn't fair.* She had every right to kick me out and never speak to me again but she was gracious enough to let me stay and gracious enough to become my best friend.

'OK, and this Poppy who you live with now.'

'Yes.'

'Is she . . .'

'She has a boyfriend.'

'Don't they all,' Margot says, blowing smoke almost directly at me.

I smile at her and roll my eyes.

'Right, same again?' she says, gesturing at the now empty bottle of wine.

I hesitate for a second before saying no. I really do mean to say no. There's something in my stomach that feels off even though my head is telling me I want to sit opposite her drinking wine with our knees touching forever. Go with your gut instinct, I often tell my clients. Listen to that feeling, what's it telling you?

'Hey,' I say, 'tell me something.'

'Something in particular?' Margot says.

'You knew who I was when you came today. And you knew who I was at the training day.'

Margot looks at me, her face giving nothing away. If she's at all flustered you wouldn't know it.

'Are you asking me?'

'I'm asking you.'

'What makes you think that?'

'You're just so . . . there's something so . . . I can't put my finger on it.'

I pause for a moment, wading through my slightly hazy, boozy mind for the right way to describe it.

'I can't help but feel that nothing is accidental with you.'

Margot raises her eyebrows.

'Nothing is accidental,' she repeats.

I shake my head, I can't tell if I'm right or if I've offended her or both.

She takes a deep breath and then breaks out into a grin.

'Fine. I knew who you were.'

'Oh my god!'

I'm still surprised somehow, even though I'm not sure I ever really believed it was just coincidence.

'I'm sorry. I actually did mean to say something at the training day. To introduce myself. I didn't, like, specifically seek you out, but when I found that course and I saw your website . . . I was honestly going to come in and say, "Hey, you all right?" But it was all so interesting and we had such a great dynamic going on, I didn't want to ruin it. I don't think you would have talked to me the same way you did if I'd have said, "I'm that girl off Hinge." '

'But why didn't you say just now? Or when I asked you out for a drink even?'

'I don't know! You were so shocked by it. It made me feel so . . . calculating. In the moment it was easier just to pretend.'

'Bloody hell.'

'Oh god, do you think I'm a creep?'

Margot's eyebrows are narrowed. She looks concerned. I don't think I've seen this on her yet.

'I don't know you well enough to think that.'

'Huh,' she nods. 'You don't hate me though?'

'Well, as I say . . . I don't know you well enough.' I try to look serious but I can't quite manage to keep the smile off my face.

'You don't,' she says, relieved, grinning back at me.

'I don't.'

'So just one more,' she says and gestures up at the sky, 'now that we've established I'm not a creep. It's such a beautiful evening and we've got a lovely spot. I even promise I won't grill you anymore.'

I sigh, as if she's persuaded me, as if I was really going to leave. 'OK, one more. And only if you really mean it. No more interrogation.'

'I mean it. Sorry, I'm coming on so strong. I'm just excited to be out with you.'

She says it so sincerely. I'm lost for words. I just watch her walk away and slip inside the pub. The second she's out of sight I grab my phone from my bag to message Charlie.

Charlie, I'm out on a date with that girl from the training day!!!

Charlie writes back immediately.

WHAT?

I didn't know it was her before I came, OBVIOUSLY.

Mad!

I know.

Charlie doesn't read my final message. I go to type something else but stop, not knowing quite what it is I want to say. I still can't shake the feeling I shouldn't be here but the idea of not spending the rest of the evening with Margot feels impossible, ludicrous even. But it's just meeting someone for a drink. It's just a drink.

'Are you texting all your friends telling them you're on a nightmare date?'

Margot plonks a bottle of wine down on the table and two glasses with ice cubes in.

'Actually, yes.'

She grins and pours me a glass of wine that reaches the brim.

The rest of the evening is a lot less like being in a particularly personal and gruelling job interview and a lot more like the kind of date I was expecting. Margot is fun and funny and tells me all about the novel she's writing about an expat from New Zealand living in Brighton.

'You have a wild imagination.'

'Thank you.'

I tell her all about Ella and Daniel. I tell her about my mum.

'Mummy issues,' she says, pretending to write down a note on her tobacco and I smile sarcastically.

I tell her a bit about my dad. I'm surprised by the ease with which I find myself mentioning him to her. Perhaps because she divulged so much to me at the training day, I feel I owe her. Perhaps, the therapist in my head suggests, it's because it's low stakes and she doesn't care about you. She's not going to follow this up.

Or challenge you. I leave out the information about Dad now living in California, which still feels too new and unprocessed to be sharing with people who up until this evening I would barely have considered an acquaintance.

'Daddy issues,' she says, grinning. I pick up a beer mat and aim it at her. She puts her hands up in surrender.

At one point, deep into the second bottle of wine, I reach over without even thinking about it and brush her stupid, long fringe away from her eyes. She's leaning forward animatedly, in the middle of telling me a story about the time she and her ex-boyfriend went travelling to South America and fought the whole time, but, when I move her fringe, she freezes.

'Sorry,' I say. Immediately embarrassed. 'I don't know why I . . . your bloody fringe, you just need to clip it back.'

'No, it's fine,' she says, and touches the hair I just moved. 'And I don't need to, it's grown out practically.'

She carries on telling the story but I can tell she's flustered.

By the time we've finished our drinks it's properly dark and approaching closing time.

'I really am going to go now,' I say and push myself up from the table before Margot can object.

'Yes. You make a stand,' she says. 'Three hours and six glasses of wine later. I simply *cannot* stay, it's not right.'

I laugh and gesture at her to walk in front of me as we weave our way out of the pub. On standing up, I realise I am considerably drunker than I'd like to be.

We stop outside the pub.

'Which way are you heading?' she asks.

'I'm not telling you.'

She rolls her eyes.

'Just in case we could share an Uber, that's all! I'm not going to stalk you.'

'I don't believe you. Anyway I don't need an Uber, I'm going to walk.'

Margot frowns and glances up the road ahead, dark and empty.

'Can I at least walk you?'

'No.'

'Some of the way. Just to the end of that street.'

She points vaguely up the road.

'No.'

'How will I know if you got home safe?'

I sigh.

'I'll let you know when I get home safely. It is literally a ten-minute walk. I'll be fine.'

'Promise you will.'

I pause before replying and she rolls her eyes at me.

'Come on. We WhatsApp all the time.'

'Yes, I promise.'

'OK, good.'

She looks at me and for a moment I'm sure she's going to kiss me. My stomach flips. Damn it. She leans forward and gently kisses my cheek. Dangerously close to my lips. She lingers and

I think about tilting my head slightly but then a group of shrieking girls walk past and instead I pull back.

I raise a hand, awkwardly, a half wave, and then turn to walk home.

'Natasha.'

I turn back around. She looks up from her phone as if I'm the one who called after her, which for some reason, like a lot of things about her, is absolutely maddening

'When are we meeting again?'

She's so sure of herself that it makes me laugh. She smiles but holds my gaze.

I shake my head slightly, meaning to say something cool and non-committal but actually come out with, 'Soon.'

She nods.

'Goodnight, Natasha.'

Shit.

5

'Thank god it's Friday, eh?'

I smile at the woman opposite me.

'Long week?' I say, my notebook still closed. This is just the preamble.

'Oh, you know how it is,' the woman says. 'The kids are off school so it's all a . . .' she gives me a look, what she considers a quick and subtle assessment of whether I'm a parent or not; she decides not and waves away the rest of the sentence.

'And it's been so hot,' she says.

'It has,' I say. 'Far too hot.'

We share a smile about our new-found common ground. We both feel heat.

Claire is the woman who emailed a couple of weeks ago asking for an assessment. Married, mid-forties and having an identity crisis. She is so nervous she can barely sit still.

She talks extensively about her marriage, her children who

she adores, her career in physiotherapy which she used to enjoy and now feels stuck in. Sometimes I immediately warm to a client but this isn't one of those times. There's something about this woman that grates slightly. I can't quite put my finger on it.

After she's been talking for more than half of our session, it becomes clear she is not going to mention the reason she told me she was here unless prompted.

'I wonder, Claire, if we could touch on the email you sent me. I'd like to explore that a little bit just so I can get a sense of what you'd like to get out of these sessions.'

She nods vigorously.

'Absolutely. Absolutely.'

Her mouth remains slightly open but she's lost for words. Even after all these years of practice it's so tempting to jump in and rescue her. Instead I pick up my glass of water, take a sip and smile at her encouragingly.

'I, um, it's not a new thing,' she says eventually.

I nod.

'I've always, ah . . .' Her hair is already tucked behind her ears but she goes through the motions of doing it anyway. She glances at the window, as if she might be considering climbing out. 'I've always had these . . . feelings. But I've never actually . . . I met my husband when I was twenty-five and that was it.'

I open my mouth to speak but she interrupts,

'I really love him,' she says, a wobble in her voice. 'That's important. That's important for you to know.'

I nod.

125

'Of course.'

She seems relieved. That she's said it. That I believe her. She sits back in her chair, not relaxing exactly but she does take a deep breath.

'It's just that recently these feelings . . . they've been harder to ignore.'

'What's changed recently?'

She looks at the window again and sighs.

'There's a woman. She works at my son's school.'

I nod seriously, not letting any sign of intrigue or excitement pass across my face. This is going to be *good*.

'At first I didn't even realise there was anything more than . . . I just thought I liked her in a . . . in a *normal* way, you know?'

'And what made you realise that your feelings for her weren't normal?'

Claire winces at hearing her own words repeated back at her.

'Not . . . I don't mean normal. I mean . . . platonic. I mean like a friend. But I wasn't thinking of her like a friend, I was thinking of her more as a . . .'

She leaves the end of the sentence hanging, blushing furiously. I don't finish it for her.

'Do you have any kind of relationship with this woman?'

'Oh no, I mean . . . we text a bit back and forth.'

I wait for a moment and just when I'm about to ask my next question she corrects herself.

'Well, I'm not sure . . . we probably text a bit more than I text other people, it's a lot. It's nothing . . . nothing's happened.'

She looks at her feet, her shoes suddenly fascinating.

'I'm not ever going to judge you in here,' I say gently. I gesture around my head, at the four walls surrounding us. 'It's a safe space.'

People laugh about the phrase 'safe space', about what it implies and who it's for. But in my experience, it really means something.

She looks up at me.

'Thank you,' she says quietly.

'You're welcome.'

Claire decides she would like to come back next week if I think we'll work well together. I assure her that I think we will. Despite finding her somewhat challenging, I know that I have the experience to help her, plus now I'm invested in Teacher-gate. She takes her time gathering up her bag and checking she has everything, while I wait for whatever question she wants to ask me but is trying to figure out the words for.

It's only when she reaches the door that she speaks up.

'I hope you don't mind me asking . . .'

I look up at her. My notebook is closed again for the day.

'It's just on your website you talk a lot about LGBTQIA . . .'

She over-pronounces the letters, wanting to get them right, like they're new in her mouth.

'And I wanted to know, are you . . . Are you? Do you identify as, um . . . one of those?'

One of those! She's so uncomfortable. I want to tell her to take a few deep breaths.

'Would it help you to know that you're talking to someone who understands?'

She nods quickly.

'I can assure you, I really do understand, Claire.'

She breaks into a wide smile, relieved at the answer and that the interaction is over. I feel a rush of sympathy for her.

'Oh . . . good! Good! OK, have a lovely weekend!'

'You too,' I say to the back of her head as she finally makes her escape.

I'm meeting Charlie for a quick drink after work before heading home to get ready for Georgia's birthday party. One perk of working for ourselves, which somewhat makes up for the precariousness of self-employment, is that we have the luxury of choosing not to book in clients for Friday afternoons, which means we can make it to the pub at 2 p.m. and pretty much always get a table. We sit in the corner of a quiet beer garden, sunglasses on and a glass of wine each, which we swear is all we're drinking. Charlie is incandescent with rage while telling me the latest on Aaron.

'So I turn up for dinner and there are *other people there*.'

'No!'

Charlie takes a sip of their wine and shakes their head, momentarily speechless at the horror of their own story.

'I managed to get him alone in the kitchen and I was like, *You invited me over for dinner, I bought a bottle of £15 wine, I left drinks with Natasha early for this*, and he was just like, *Erm, I don't remember saying it was just dinner for us. Anyway why do you care . . . I thought we were cool?'*

'Oh no,' I say, grimacing. 'Cool? What does that even mean?'

'Thank you!' Charlie says, banging their hand on the table. 'What does that even mean?'

'So, what did you do?'

Charlie takes another sip of wine and then looks at me sheepishly.

'I stayed.'

'For the dinner?'

'For the night.'

They bury their face in their hands and then peek out at me. 'Charlie!'

I can't help but laugh at them.

'I know, really bad. But I can't help it.'

'You're not seeing him again, are you?'

'No definitely not. Well, after this weekend. After that we're done.'

'Why, what's this weekend?'

Charlie shrugs.

'One last hurrah?'

Before I can interrogate them any more they point at me accusingly.

'Anyway, what's going on with you? You're going out with this annoying girl who ruined your workshop?'

'I'm not *going out* with her.'

'But you literally went out with her, didn't you? Last night?'

'Yeah but we're not *going out.* It was a one-time thing.'

'Really?'

'Yes.'

I sound much surer than I am.

Charlie raises their eyebrows at me but doesn't ask any more questions. I have a feeling they have something else that's even more annoying that they'd rather talk about.

'So, your dad.'

I groan and gulp down some wine.

'What about him?'

Charlie just stares at me from behind their sunglasses.

'What? I don't know what you want me to say.'

'I don't want you to say anything. I was just interested to know how you're feeling about it all.'

I look down at my phone on the table, willing it to light up telling me there's a minor but pressing emergency I need to attend to. It stays black.

'I feel fine. I don't know, I haven't thought about it.'

'How is that possible?' Charlie says.

'I just haven't! I've had other stuff on my mind.'

This sounds like an excuse or a lie but truly I haven't thought about it. Or I've hardly thought about it. I've happened upon a really great distraction.

'How old were you when your dad left?' Charlie says.

'Year eight.'

'What was that like?'

'It was shit, Charl. Look, I really don't want to get into it. I know you mean well but we've managed fine without him up until now.'

'I know, I'm just interested in him, you know? He sounds like he might be an interesting person. Someone you might like to meet up with for a couple of hours say . . . on an upcoming holiday.'

I roll my eyes but I find myself softening.

'It's not that I don't think it would be interesting to see him.'

'What's he like?'

I want to answer but I'm not sure where to begin.

'Complicated.'

Charlie nods.

'I've got to go,' I say. 'I need to get party-ready.'

We both finish our drinks and make our way out of the side gate of the beer garden.

'I'm not trying to put you on the spot, you know. Or make you uncomfortable,' Charlie says as we pause on the street before we part ways. 'I just don't want you to miss something special because you're afraid of what will happen.'

I hug them a little longer than usual.

'When have I ever done that?' I say into their neck and they laugh and give me a kiss on the cheek.

I make my way home without thinking about my dad even once.

Poppy and I arrive at Georgia's parents' house on time despite the Friday night traffic. It's a beautiful evening, not as brutally hot as it has been recently. Poppy is wearing a white dress, super high heels and bright red lipstick. Her earrings look like they might be diamonds but are probably made of something that's been recycled. I don't want to ask lest I get a short history of blood diamonds and the human and environmental cost of the jewellery industry. I've been burned before.

'Do you think she'll mind?' she'd asked me before we left the house.

'Mind what?'

'That I'm wearing white, Natasha!'

'It's not her *wedding*.'

'Right, right.'

I'm wearing a pink suit that I have mixed feelings about. I bought it online after a couple of drinks when I emotionally decided that I *am* the kind of person who can wear pink suits and 'get away with it', whatever that means. When it arrived, I was concerned that it was a bit Mr Blobby but paired with bright red stilettos and a white shirt I feel OK. Good even. The moment I step out of the car I hear someone yelling.

'Pink suit!'

I look up at the house and Georgia's younger brother Josh is standing at the door, leaning against the frame. Josh is outrageously good-looking, almost too good-looking. He's all blond hair and stubble and teeth. Sort of past the point of attractive and all the way back around to unattractive. Like a Ken doll.

'Well done, Josh!' I say to him as we get closer. 'You know colours now!'

'I know bright fucking pink when I see it.' He grins.

I roll my eyes and let him kiss me on the cheek.

'Poppy, always a pleasure,' he says as she offers him her face. 'Can I take that off you?'

He goes to take the bottle of champagne she's carrying but I put a protective arm in front of her.

'Don't give it to him. You'll never see it again.'

We slip past him and through the cool house.

'See you later, girls,' he calls after us.

We walk through the kitchen, past caterers arranging food on huge trays, and I suddenly realise I'm starving. I stop and grab a blini with smoked salmon on and pop it in my mouth.

'Want one?'

'Vegan!'

'Sorry. I'm sure this was a horrible fish. Really mean.'

We step out of the kitchen and into the garden where there must be a hundred people gathered on the terrace and the lawn drinking glasses of champagne and chattering loudly. There's music playing and I'm both surprised and somehow not surprised to see an actual DJ set up on one side of the garden.

I turn to Poppy to comment on it just as I hear someone screech, 'Pops!' and she screeches back, 'Megs!' and I lose her to a group of screaming girls, presumably childhood friends who I've never had the pleasure of meeting. I wonder if Georgia got any say over who came to this thing.

I wander down the steps onto the lawn, gratefully accepting a glass of champagne from someone walking by with a tray. I don't recognise anyone apart from Georgia's dad who doesn't see me, he's deep in conversation with a group of other dads. He's wearing a white shirt unbuttoned to reveal an alarming amount of hairy chest. He's also sporting a fedora.

Just as I'm deciding to do a lap and then see if Poppy's done screeching with the Megans I feel arms slip around my waist and Georgia's head rests on my shoulder. I spin around and she hugs me tightly.

'I thought it was you and then I was like, no surely that cannot be Natty the *model* strutting around in this insane suit.'

Georgia steps back and takes me in, shaking her head.

'Do you really like it? It's not a bit much?'

'It is a *lot* and I love it.'

Georgia is wearing an outfit not dissimilar to her dad's – or to Josh's, come to think of it. White shirt, chinos, thank goodness she's forsaken the fedora. She has little gold hoop earrings in her ears that I've never seen before.

I lean forward and grab her earlobe for a closer inspection.

'These are nice. Since when do you wear earrings?'

'Oh, thanks,' she says, touching the other lobe as if checking it is still there. 'Zara got them for me.' She looks around to make sure we're not about to be ambushed and then leans forward conspiratorially. 'I actually had to pretty much re-pierce my ears with them this morning. It was . . . not pretty.'

'Fuck.'

'Yeah.'

'Well, one hundred girlfriend points to you.'

She sips the last of her champagne in her glass and waves at someone behind me who is beckoning her over.

'You go, George. I'm fine.'

'You sure?' she says. She means it too. If I wanted her to stay with me, she'd stay.

'Positive. This is . . .' I wave around me. 'This is quite something.'

She groans.

'I know. Mum and Dad went totally mad. I don't know who half of these people are. This is really a party for them. You know what they're like.'

'I know.'

She squeezes my hand and darts off into the waiting arms of a family friend, and I head off in search of Poppy and more champagne.

The next couple of hours are increasingly more fun the more champagne I drink. Poppy is mostly on the mocktails, given she's our designated driver, but unlike me she doesn't need any alcohol to be the most sociable person at the party. We're having an animated conversation with Josh and his friends when suddenly the music turns off and everyone begins to sing 'Happy Birthday'.

Two caterers carry out a tray with an enormous two-tiered cake on it. It is covered in candles. They look very stressed. Eventually they make it to a table where Georgia is standing with her mum and dad and Zara. She doesn't even let go of Zara's hand while she blows the candles out which, for some reason, I find unbearably annoying.

People start shouting, 'Speech' at Georgia. These people love speeches. She waves her hand to quiet everyone down.

'This is so amazing,' she says, gesturing at the cake and then at all of us standing watching her. 'Thank you all so much for coming and for making my thirtieth birthday so special. Cheers!' She raises her glass and we all raise our glasses back. Just as I'm about to take a sip, grateful that she's kept it short and sweet, Zara steps forward and puts her arms out, gesturing for us all to hang on and to put our glasses down. My heart starts pounding. I glance at Poppy and she's already looking at me, wide-eyed.

'Thanks so much, everyone! I'm just going to take up a little more of your time. Sorry!'

Zara beams at us and then gazes back at Georgia who has a nervous smile fixed on her face. Zara looks really pretty, she's wearing a floral dress with a high neck and sort of puffy sleeves. It would make me look like a Victorian ghost but it really suits her.

'I just wanted to say that the past few months with you, Georgia, have been the best of my life.'

Everyone around me says, 'Aah.' I swallow, my mouth suddenly completely dry.

'They've been the best of my life and I can't imagine ever being without you.'

The crowd starts to murmur and then goes completely silent when Zara reaches into her pocket.

'Georgia,' she says, taking her hand. Georgia looks stunned. 'Will you marry me?'

Everyone inhales at the same time.

Georgia is quiet for a moment, her mouth open but no sound coming out. I reach out and grab Poppy's hand. She squeezes it hard.

'Yes!' Georgia says and breaks into a smile.

Everyone exhales and then starts cheering and whooping.

Zara slips the ring onto Georgia's finger and then kisses her hand and then pulls her closer and kisses her properly. Georgia's parents are crying their eyes out behind them. I turn to Poppy in complete disbelief. I try to smile and realise to my horror that I'm crying. I quickly wipe away my tears.

'I'm so happy for them!' I say loudly, to Poppy, to everyone around me, to myself.

'Do you want to go, darling?' Poppy whispers.

'No! Absolutely not. I'm fine! I'm happy!' I say.

I spend the rest of the evening celebrating Georgia and Zara's engagement without actually being able to get anywhere close to them. Every time I think there's an opportunity to go over and speak to them, somebody beats me to it until eventually it's midnight and it's time for us to drive home. We decide we'll text them after we've left rather than join the queue of people hugging them goodbye but when I get to the car I realise I've not given Georgia her present. There's a table with a huge pile of them just inside the door so I grab my gift, wrapped in brown paper and tied with a red string, and carry it inside. I lean it up against the others and turn to head back out when I hear my name being called.

'Natasha, wait!' Georgia is behind me with Zara in tow. They're now surgically attached by the hand, it seems.

'I wasn't trying to . . . I just wanted to drop off your gift and you were both so busy.' I slap my hand to my forehead. 'What am I even saying? Sorry guys. Congratulations! I can't believe I haven't said that yet!'

I lean forward and hug them both; it's horribly awkward because they won't bloody stop holding hands.

'Thank you, I'm so relieved it's over. And that she said yes!' Zara says. She's beaming. I don't know if I've ever seen anyone look so happy. I feel exhausted just looking at her.

'Look at all this,' Georgia says, gesturing at the presents. 'Way too much. Everyone is too generous.'

'They just love you,' I say. And then look down at the floor.

'Which one is from you?'

'Oh no, no. Don't open it now. You can just open them all tomorrow, can't you?'

'Yes,' Zara says, her smile still plastered on her face but starting to fade rapidly. 'You're going to open them tomorrow, aren't you darling?'

'I can open one, can't I? Let me guess.' She reaches forward and taps my present with her finger. 'This one?'

I nod.

'Always the same wrapping.'

'I just have that one roll of paper and it never runs out.'

She smiles, finally lets go of Zara's hand and starts to tear into it.

'It's not much, it's really just . . . I know you saw it and you said you liked it and . . .'

Georgia holds the picture frame at arm's length so she can inspect it. It's a painting of Brighton beach at sunset that she spotted in the window of a local artist's gallery a few months ago.

'It's like she painted your Instagram feed,' she'd said to me. 'Wow, it's really beautiful.'

'Natty, this is just . . .' she says now.

She holds it out for Zara to look at too. She doesn't say anything.

'You can put it up in your house,' I say to Zara. She looks up at me and nods.

'I will. Thank you.'

'Bye guys,' I say. 'I really have to go, Poppy's waiting in the car.'

I can't bear to hug them again so instead I just run out shouting behind me, 'Congratulations again!'

We get home quickly, the roads mostly empty and Poppy's driving the speed of light. I expect to feel exhausted but instead I feel wired. It is still somehow unbearably hot. The air is sticky.

Poppy picks up Diane and kisses me on the cheek before she heads to bed.

'Love you, darling,' she says. I briefly rest my head against hers.

Normally I'd try to keep her up, wanting the company, but tonight I can't bear to sit with her. To think that she might feel sorry for me is excruciating. I imagine her texting Felix to tell him the good news and speculating about whether I'm OK and shudder. I grab a glass of water, lie down on the sofa and pick up my phone, still half pretending to myself I might just go to bed in a minute. It's 12:30.

I type it out, just to see what it looks like.

Hey, are you awake?

God, am I really going to send her a 'you up?' I delete it quickly.

Hey, what are you up to?

I shake my head and delete that too.

Hey.

Absolutely rubbish. Completely embarrassing. We haven't sent each other messages like this since we agreed to meet for a drink. I press send anyway.

I am just about to throw my phone across the room and sink into the warm, familiar pit of drunken despair when my phone screen lights up. She's calling me.

I stare at the screen for a moment, frozen, before picking up.

'Hello,' I whisper.

'Hello,' she whispers back. 'Why are we whispering?'

'Because it's the middle of the night and Poppy's asleep.'

'The middle of the night!' She laughs.

'Why are you calling me?' I ask, rolling over onto my side. I wish I had a phone cord to twist around my finger.

'Why are you texting me in the middle of the night?'

'Um, to say, "hey", I guess.'

'Couldn't wait until the morning?'

'No.'

She's quiet for a moment, I hear her breathing.

'What do you want, Natasha?'

'I don't know.'

'Yes, you do. What do you want?'

'I want to see you.'

'OK.'

'OK?'

'Shall I come to you?'

'No!' I say quickly, the thought fills me with dread. 'No. You can't come here.'

'Right. In case I'm a stalker.'

'No, in case Poppy wakes up. I just . . . that won't work.'

She's quiet again and I realise I'm worried she'll give up on me if I don't say something.

'Let's go for a walk,' I say.

'OK. Where?'

'The beach? I'll text you where to meet me.'

'OK.'

'OK, see you soon.'

'Hey, Natasha?'

'Yes?'

'How romantic.'

I hang up and walk into the hall. Having been wearing heels all evening, it's a relief to slip my white Converse high-tops on. I catch a glimpse of myself in the mirror by the door as I'm fumbling about for my phone and keys. A pink blur. I can't quite meet my own eyes.

I arrive first. Outside a grotty hotel on the seafront, our agreed meeting point. It feels suitably seedy. Because it's summer and because it's still twenty-five degrees, there are people every-where, spilling out of bars and takeaways and B&Bs. It's as noisy as it would be in the middle of the afternoon. If it feels sketchy I don't notice. Perhaps tonight I just feel a part of the sketchiness. I stare out at the sea across the road, inky black illuminated by the lights on the promenade.

'Natasha?'

Margot's wearing a white T-shirt with the sleeves folded up and high-waisted denim shorts. She has a white jumper tied around her waist. I wonder if she was still dressed when I mes-saged her, or if these are clothes she chose for me to see.

We stand still for a moment, facing each other.

'Nice suit,' she says.

'Thank you.'

'Are we walking then? Or are we staying the night?' She ges-tures at the hotel behind us.

'Walking.'

We cross the road in silence, we don't even comment when a man shouts, 'Wheeey pink suit' at me and all his friends say,

'Wheeey' too. We make our way down onto the pebble beach where we are plunged into relative darkness. It is much quieter, there are only small huddles of people and others walking two by two like us far off in the distance, not wanting to be disturbed.

We walk right down so that we're toe to toe with the waves trickling over the pebbles. We instinctively turn right and start walking towards Hove but it's dark and hot and unpleasant sinking into and tripping over the pebbles. I only manage a minute or so before I stop – suddenly the swell of emotion that's been sitting in my chest all evening combined with the sticky heat is too much.

'Fuck!' I kick the pebbles. It's disappointingly undramatic. They scatter a few inches in front of me.

Margot doesn't say anything but when I turn to look at her she's smiling.

'Shall we sit down?' she says.

I cautiously lower myself down, aware suddenly of the tightness of my trousers. Once I get low enough I just let myself drop into the stones. I make a noise like a very elderly person plonking themselves down into a chair.

Margot sits down next to me all sprightly like a pixie in her shorts. She reaches into her backpack and produces a hip flask which she offers to me.

'Old school,' I say, taking it from her.

'What can I say?'

I take a sip and grimace.

'Oh my god, is this tequila? Who puts tequila in a hip flask?'

'I think you mean,' she says, taking it back from me, 'thank you very much for the drink, I really needed it.'

I laugh.

'Sorry, I am grateful. I just wasn't expecting it.'

We're quiet for a moment. We pass the hip flask back and forth a couple of times.

'So, rough night?' she says eventually.

I nod.

'A weird night. I, um . . .' I look at her, really taking her in and taking in the fact that we're sitting here on the beach together at what must be now one o'clock in the morning. 'I didn't expect to react like this.'

'React like . . .'

'Like freaking out, walking around town in the middle of the night and calling you to feed me tequila on the beach.'

'Oh right, yeah.'

She picks up a pebble and chucks it at the sea. The waves are too loud to hear it drop.

'So am I allowed to ask what happened?'

I nod.

'I was at Georgia's birthday party.'

'The ex who you lived with for years after you broke up but are definitely not still a thing?'

'Correct.' I pause. 'You know, I love the way you say ex. *Ix*.'

'My accent isn't that strong.'

'It is. *Iccent*.'

144

'Come on. You were at the birthday party . . .'

'And they were doing her birthday cake and speeches and stuff, it was a whole big thing. And then, her girlfriend, Zara . . .'

'Loves the gym, hates you.'

Margot passes me the hip flask and I drink from it. Every sip goes down a little easier.

'Very good. You're a great listener.'

'I know. Maybe I should become a therapist.'

'So anyway,' I say, ignoring her. 'Her girlfriend proposes to her. In front of everyone.'

'Fuck.'

'Yeah.'

'But wait, you don't care, right? You're just friends.'

'Well yes but . . .'

'Unless . . . you're not just friends . . .'

'No we are! We are!'

'But you do care?'

'Well,' I say, gesturing around me, at her, at the flask of tequila. 'Evidently.'

She nods.

'It's weird to see someone move on,' she says eventually. 'It's a little glimpse of what might have happened.'

'Yeah. It's like a door closing.'

She takes a sip of the tequila and then screws the cap back on and sets it down beside her. Probably a good idea.

I take my jacket off and roll it up to create a makeshift pillow. Margot winces.

'What?'

'Just looks like it was expensive, that's all.'

'It wasn't, don't worry. But thanks.'

'Is expensive a compliment?'

I don't answer and instead lie back and place the blazer under my head. Lying down, the sky above me starts to spin. It's not unpleasant yet, I'm newly drunk. Or re-drunk, I suppose. It'll be a while before the spinning shapes start to make me feel queasy. I pat the pebbles next to my head, indicating to her that she should lie down too. She unties the jumper from her waist, folds it under her head and lies down next to me. She's facing upwards but I'm suddenly very aware of how close we are. Her hand is touching mine.

'If there wasn't so much light pollution we'd be able to see the stars,' she says.

I squint up at the sky and point.

'There's a star.'

'That's a plane.'

I don't look at her but I can tell she's smiling.

'Oh.'

Her fingers, no longer just incidentally brushing against mine, have made their way into my upturned palm. She traces a line from my index finger down to my wrist and it sends a pulse of electricity through me. I stay completely still.

'What were you doing before you came to meet me?' I say to the sky. I hear someone shriek further along the beach but it still somehow feels like we're the only people for miles.

'Um, I was writing something. But it was going really badly. I was glad of the distraction to be honest.'

'On a Friday night? Wow. That's dedication.'

'Well, I'd only just got in so I was just jotting some ideas down really.'

She stops tracing my palm and I can barely concentrate on what she's saying with how much I'm willing her to start again.

'Only just got in from where?'

I pull my hand away rather than have it untouched and turn onto my side to face her. The sensation of turning is strange. My head takes a moment to catch up with my body. I knew tequila was a bad idea.

'From a date,' she says.

She turns her head to face me but doesn't twist her whole body around. Her hand stays in the same place by her side.

'Oh. Was it good?'

'Well. I got home at eleven p.m., wrote a terrible poem and now I'm lying on the beach with you.'

'So no?' I say.

'No,' she confirms.

She hesitates and then looks back up at the sky, facing away from me.

'No, it wasn't bad, that's not fair. It just wasn't . . . I'd rather be here.'

She takes a deep breath and without turning to face me says,

'I was being serious when I said I would spend a lot of time trying to work you out.'

'Oh, I know,' I say.

She turns and catches me grinning at her. Despite herself she grins back.

'It's not funny! It's been torture.'

'Oh please.'

I poke her gently on her arm and she grabs it like it really hurt.

'It has! You've been driving me mad,' she says.

'I haven't been around you enough to drive you mad.'

'The idea of you then.'

We're quiet for a moment.

'Sorry about that.'

'You're not sorry. You have a big smile plastered on your face.'

'I'm just happy to be here with you. I feel loads better.'

Oh God, tequila talking.

'Great! That'll be £60 please.'

'Ha ha ha.'

I smile at her sarcastically.

We've been incrementally moving closer towards each other. An inch with every adjustment, trying to get comfortable. She reaches out and touches my hip, tracing her finger over the fabric of my waistband.

'I really do like this.'

'Thanks.'

'You look good in a suit.'

Her fingers slip over my waistband onto my bare skin and I stop breathing altogether. She flips her hand over and presses the back of it to my waist as if taking my temperature.

'You feel like you're boiling up.'

I reach down and touch the small of my back. Sticky.

'I know. I think this suit is essentially made out of plastic.'

She nods, her hand still lingering on my waist. I'm hoping she's going to draw me towards her but instead she pulls her hand away and sits up.

'Let's go for a swim.'

'Absolutely not.'

I sit up too, slowly so as not to get too dizzy.

'Absolutely not,' she echoes.

She does a terrible impression of me, like someone off *The Crown*, emphasising all the 't's.

'Come on, it'll be fun.'

She's already standing up and pulling her T-shirt over her head. She's wearing a white bra underneath and I wonder for a second if she's going to take that off too. She pauses, presumably thinking the same thing, and then decides against it. She has more tattoos on her ribcage. Tiny little symbols and words I can't make out.

She looks down at me and holds out her hand.

'Come on. I'm not taking no for an answer.'

I let her pull me up onto my feet. I have to admit, as I kick my trousers off, it's a relief to be free of them. As subtly as I can, I reach down to check what knickers I'm wearing. I almost audibly breathe a sigh of relief when I discover that I did not go for the hideous flesh-coloured seamless ones. They're black and lacy and very uncomfortable. Much better. I pull my T-shirt over my head. I'm pretty sure we're wearing the same bra. I pick up my clothes and hug them tight to my chest, covering as much of myself as possible as we make our way closer to the sea.

Margot walks in first. I see her seize up from the cold. She swears and balls her hands up into fists but she keeps going.

'You've got to just do it,' she yells once she's waist-deep. Maybe at me but mostly at herself, before plunging herself under the water. When her head comes up she spins around to face me. She wipes water and her stupid wet fringe off her face.

'Come on, it's not bad once you're in.' She tips herself up onto her back and floats around like she's on a lilo, as if to prove how warm and relaxing it is.

I put my clothes down, take a deep breath and step in. I yowl. It's freezing. I end up sort of half running and half hobbling in and eventually launch myself onto my front, mainly to avoid having to continue to walk on the pebbles which are hurting my feet.

'Fuck,' I exclaim as my shoulders go under. But she's right. After a few moments it's not so bad. It's actually a relief.

I swim out and stop just in front of her. The water comes up to my chest. I move my arms, swirling the water gently around me, and look up at the moon.

'This is pretty nice, right?' she says, quietly, watching me.

'It is. You were right.'

The other people on the beach feel very far away.

'You know I've never been swimming at night here before,' I say.

'Are you serious?'

'Yeah.' I turn to face away from the beach and out into the waves. It's hard to see where sky meets ocean in the dark. 'Swimming in the sea in general makes me nervous. It's all just so unknowable.'

I'm aware of her standing next to me, I can feel her leg brushing against mine.

'But you're not nervous now?'

I laugh.

'What?' She turns to face me. 'You're not out here swimming in the dark because you feel safe with me?'

I turn to face her.

'I don't feel safe with you.'

I can't read her expression, I wonder if I've hurt her feelings but then she breaks into a grin, reaches out, puts her arms around my waist and pulls me towards her. I let my arms hang loosely by my sides for a second, kidding myself that I might pull away before wrapping them around her neck and letting her draw me towards her. I feel her stomach against mine.

'Well you *should* feel safe,' she says. 'I've got you, don't worry.' She lifts me off the floor briefly and then sets me gently back down.

I look at her. Her hands are on my hips, I feel her slip her finger under the lace at the back of my waistband. I still have my arms around her neck and I trace my fingers down her spine. She parts her lips and exhales heavily, like she's been holding her breath. I lean forward so our lips are practically touching. I feel like I'm on the precipice of something I can't come back from but before I can think about it too hard she leans forward and kisses me. Tentatively at first and then, when she knows I'm not going to pull away, more deeply. Her tongue pushes against my lips and I open my mouth. She tastes like tequila and cigarettes. I move my hands down her body, the curve of her back, I trace over the parts of her covered with words it's too dark to read. I brush my hands over her breasts and she moans into my mouth, I reach around to undo her bra and, just as I squeeze the clasp together, I remember that we're in the middle of the ocean. Do I hold it once I've got it off? Let it be carried away by the waves? This little thought brings me crashing back down to earth. Well, back down to sea. I suddenly want to laugh at the absurdity of my evening.

She senses my hesitation and pulls back.

'What's wrong?'

'No, nothing's wrong. I just . . .' I look back towards the beach. We're further away than I thought. We've drifted.

'It's fine, we're fine,' she says, frowning. 'Look, we can still touch the bottom.'

She holds my waist and pushes me down gently so my feet are planted solidly on the ground rather than just my tiptoes, and the water comes up to my chin. I nod but I suddenly feel very sober.

'I'm sorry, I think we should go back.'

I realise my teeth are chattering although I don't feel the cold.

'OK,' she says reluctantly and then immediately righting herself she says, 'Of course, of course, yes we'll go back.'

She lets go of me and we set off, half swimming and half wading towards the shore.

When we clamber back onto dry land, we're both shivering.

'I'm sorry, I don't know what . . .'

I immediately feel ridiculous. Like a child who's had a tantrum and ruined their own party.

I watch her getting dressed, her white T-shirt clinging to her soaking wet body, and I can't believe what I've just done.

'You don't need to be sorry,' she says, pulling her jumper over her head. She gestures at the clothes I'm clutching in my hands. 'You need to get dressed, you're freezing.'

I put on my trousers, which is impossibly difficult with damp legs. While I'm struggling with the zip, Margot picks my T-shirt up off the ground, turns it the right way out, and I let her pull it gently over my head. She passes me my blazer and I wrap it over my shoulders like a shawl.

'I'm going to walk you home,' she says.

'Can't we get an Uber?'

She wrings her hair out onto the beach.

'I don't think anyone's going to want us in their car, do you?'

'Ah. No.'

We walk back along the beach in silence, stopping at the bottom of the stairs to put our shoes back on. I realise when we're around the corner from my flat that I've let her walk me all the way home.

I want to invite her in so much. To peel the wet clothes off her, to feel her skin against mine. As if she's reading my mind she says, 'Not tonight,' very gently. She looks tired.

I open my mouth to protest but she shakes her head.

'Not tonight.'

'OK.'

She turns to walk away and I say, 'Text me when you get home' to the back of her head.

'I will,' she says without turning around.

I put the key in the door and look over my shoulder to see her standing on the pavement staring back at me.

'You should come to one of my gigs.'

'Oh no, I'm not sure it's really . . .'

'Yes. There's one in a couple of weeks, I'll text you the details.'

'It's just that it isn't really my . . .'

She gestures at me.

'We did your thing. So it's only fair we do my thing next, right?'

I look down at myself. My suit is an entirely different shade of pink than it was when I put it on earlier.

'This isn't my *thing*.'

She grins.

'Night, Natasha.'

I head straight into the bathroom, peel off my wet clothes and step into the hot shower. It takes a long time to thaw out. I realise even once I'm dry and in clean pyjamas that I'm still shivering. I tell myself to get it together, I'm behaving like some tragic swooning woman from a period drama. Gets wet once and immediately gets consumption. Once I've drunk a large glass of water and crawled into bed I check my phone.

Home and dry.

Glad to hear it. Sorry about tonight. I don't know what happened.

Don't be sorry. Nothing hotter than being made to wait.

If you make me come to a gig, you'll be waiting a long time.

We both know that's not true.

I don't know how to respond. I tuck my phone under my pillow and think of her lying in bed wide awake too.

6

I'm coming to the end of my second session with the student who's struggling to cope with his first big break-up. He's on the bottom end of my sliding scale of fees. An amount which doesn't even cover the cost of the room for the fifty minutes. He is subsidised by the people who can afford it. This is usually my favourite work because these are the people who, like me when I was a teenager, would never be able to access talking therapy otherwise. However, today I can barely concentrate. All I can think about is how much I want to get my phone out of my bag and see if Margot has messaged me. It is taking every single ounce of self-control I have to keep my hand firmly on my lap, clutching my pen.

I am seeing her in fifteen minutes. She's meeting me on my break before I go to peer supervision. I don't need to see her messages. My stomach flips with nervous excitement. It has been a couple of weeks since our midnight sea tryst and we've seen each other most days since, although only to do things like get coffee and go for walks. All very chaste, as if the night after Georgia's party never happened.

Liam, my client, is breaking my heart. He's one of those nineteen-year-old boys who look like they could be fourteen, all gangly and rosy-cheeked and wearing ill-fitting clothes. He has very light blond hair which somehow makes him look even younger, like a sort of stretched out toddler. He's very nervous and I can tell he wants to please me, holding back almost as if he doesn't want to cause me any trouble.

Liam, I'd said to him in our first session. *You are paying to be here. This is your space to speak about whatever you want to.* He'd looked at me like a deer in headlights.

He's telling me about the girl who's broken up with him and how she seems fine without him.

'We were together all through college, all through first year of uni and now . . . just out of the blue . . . and then I see her on Instagram and she's fine.'

'How do you know she's fine?'

'She's just . . .' his knee is jiggling so much it's actually quite distracting, 'she's going out, she's happy, she's smiling.'

'How does that make you feel?'

'Like she never cared about me. Like she can just move on that quick.'

I nod.

'Do you think you can get a full picture from social media?'

He shakes his head immediately.

'Do you think there's a chance she's not as fine as you think she is?'

'Maybe.'

'But even if she is fine. Let's say she is fine. What would that mean for you?'

'Just . . . it just . . .' he shakes his head, struggling to finish his sentence, 'it just makes me feel like shit.'

'But why?'

'Because . . .' His face is almost screwed up in trying to concentrate on his own feelings, it's surprising how even people who consider themselves emotionally tuned in can struggle to pinpoint exactly *why* they feel something. 'Because I thought we were the same. I thought we felt the same. It makes me feel like I just don't understand. Like I missed something massive. Like I'm just a massive idiot.'

He puts his head in his hands.

'How can people seem so happy and then just move on?'

He looks at me like he really wants me to answer.

I shake my head.

'I don't know,' I say. 'I'm sorry. I can see this is really painful for you.'

I glance up at the clock behind his head.

'We're just about finished for this week, did you have anything else you want to say?'

Liam shakes his head sadly.

'Are you finding it helpful to talk, Liam?'

'Yes,' he says immediately. 'I don't talk to anyone. Ever.'

'Why's that?'

He shrugs.

'Just never have. Not that kind of family. I just sort of keep things . . .'

He touches his chest, as if to say, in here. I find myself mirroring him.

'Well, I'm glad you're talking to me.'

'Me too,' he says.

I breathe a sigh of relief when he leaves. I grab my phone and see that I have a message from Margot saying, *downstairs*. I stand by the door and jiggle about on the spot, trying to wait long enough for Liam to be far from the vicinity. I give him two minutes and then fly out of the door and down the stairs.

'Natasha.'

'Mmm,' I say, squinting into the sun.

'Tell me about your twin.'

Margot is strolling along next to me on the seafront, licking sour cherry ice cream off a tiny pink spoon. She's got a baseball cap on and she's wearing her hair down. It suits her. I've tried to look cool in a baseball cap but it just doesn't work for me. It doesn't look deliberate in the way it does on her, I just feel like someone a baseball cap has happened upon. If I touch the parting of my hair I can feel my scalp burning.

'What do you want to know?' I say, scooping my own ice cream into my mouth (vanilla cheesecake flavour, two scoops as it's technically my lunch) and wishing I'd got a cone. I feel short-changed with a cup but Margot got a cup and I found myself following her lead.

'Everything. Twins are fascinating. I've got an older sister but we're not close, I haven't seen her in a long time. Are you alike?'

'Um,' I have another bite of ice cream while I consider my answer, 'we are and we aren't. I think yes, we are. In all the important ways.'

'You get along?'

I nod before she can even finish speaking.

'She's like the other half of my brain. I don't function without her.'

'Huh.' Margot reaches over with her spoon and digs into my ice cream, leaving a dark pink streak through the middle of it. 'Do you think she'd like me?'

I laugh but Margot's being completely serious.

'Sure, I mean, Natalie is lovely. But she can be terrifying.'

'Like you,' Margot interrupts.

'No, not like me. Like, I wouldn't mess with her. She has two nearly teenagers and a full-time job. She has absolutely no time for bullshit. She can detect it a mile off.'

'So you think she might think I'm full of shit?'

'Possibly.'

'Do you think that?'

'Possibly.'

I smile at her and she rolls her eyes but she's clearly not in the least bit offended.

'She gets on with my mum really well,' I say.

'Right. Which you don't.'

'Right.'

'What about your dad?'

I'm quiet for a moment. My stomach flips. I veer off to put my empty ice-cream cup into a bin and she does the same.

'He's not around,' I say when we start walking again. 'I told you that.'

'Right. Where is he?'

She asks it so easily that instead of trying to evade the question I simply find myself answering.

'He lives in California now.'

'Aren't you going . . .'

'Yes.'

'Are you going to . . .'

'Maybe. Can we talk about something else?'

Without missing a beat she says,

'Yep. Tell me about your first ever girlfriend. Give me all the gory details. Leave nothing out."

I can't help but laugh as I slap her on the arm. She grabs my hand, kisses it and holds onto it. We walk all the way back to my office, our sticky hands intertwined.

'You don't have to go this afternoon, do you?' she says when we reach my office building.

'I do have to go,' I say. She's still holding my hand and keeps a tight grip as I make a half-hearted attempt to pull away.

'Won't it be really boring? Can't you just tell *me* all about your clients instead?'

'It might be a bit boring, yes. And no, absolutely not.'

She smiles, not ready to give up but I think also knowing she's not going to win.

'You have some time though, don't you?'

'I have an hour but I'm meeting Charlie before. We always walk together.'

'Could you maybe not? Just this once.'

'What would I do instead?'

'I could come up.'

I laugh.

'No.'

But even as I say no, I'm half composing the message to Charlie making my excuse. I could always get an Uber. And it might be nice to not get quizzed on my dad situation again.

'No, no, or like, no we shouldn't but we're going to?'

'No we shouldn't,' I say, reaching forward with my free hand and picking a stray thread from her shirt. 'It's not very professional.'

'It's fun though,' she says and I let her lead me up to the entrance to my building. When we get to my room I close the door behind me and expect to see her creeping around in all my stuff but she sits down on my chair, beckons me to join her and we make out like teenagers for a full hour instead.

We're in Louise's living room. Charlie and I have the sofa to ourselves and Louise and Philippa are in armchairs either side of us, giving the impression they are at the heads of a table. The sofa is mint green leather and it is impossible to assert yourself while sitting on it due to both the depth of it, which means your feet barely touch the floor when you lean back, and the fact that every time you move in the hot weather, it squeaks. There is a loud, ticking clock above her mantelpiece which creates an ominous atmosphere, as though we're on a permanent countdown to something that never comes. On a hot day like today Louise has the French doors open onto the patio. Her kids, under strict instructions not to disturb us, are shrieking their heads off on the trampoline outside.

'Who would like to share first?' she says.

She asks this at the beginning of every peer supervision session even though every single session since we began meeting over a year ago has started with her sharing first. I take a sip of my lemonade. Louise always offers Charlie and I fizzy drinks instead of tea and coffee as we're twenty years younger than her and therefore, in her eyes, children. The metal straw Louise gave me rests perfectly in the small gap in my front teeth. Natalie once told me somebody died using a metal straw and now I think about it every time I come to Louise's house and drink a lemonade. How I'm living life on the edge.

'You go first, Louise,' I say.

'Oh, well. As long as everyone's sure?'

We all murmur how sure we are and Louise proceeds to tell us about a client she's been seeing for a couple of years now and who she simply cannot seem to make any progress with. I know Louise well enough now to know that she is not looking for advice, she is merely looking for affirmations that her approach is correct and the client is somehow faulty and so I settle back into the sofa and lean into thirty minutes of making all the right noises and nodding thoughtfully.

I volunteer to speak last. Philippa and Louise have enough to say for about fifty people so the odd 'Oh interesting' here and 'That sounds like the best plan' there have got me through the past hour and a half, which is just as well because my mind is swimming with Margot. It's honestly a miracle that I'm here. I feel half smug and half completely stupid. I have the pathetic urge to boast about what I'm missing in order to be here with them.

I lean forward and put my empty lemonade can on the table.

'Today I want to talk about a new client I have. She's in her mid-forties probably so she's . . .' I glance at Louise and Philippa, trying to quickly guess their ages, 'not . . . old.'

Charlie raises their eyebrows at me, I can't tell if it's to say, 'nice save' or 'what are you doing?'

'Anyway, what I'm trying to say is, she has kids, she's married to a man, she's got this very established life. And from what she's told me, she's embarking on something with a woman from her child's school.'

'An affair?' Louise asks.

'No. I mean, possibly. She's quite cagey at the moment. I think what I wanted to discuss here was that I'm struggling to connect with her. And I think perhaps she might feel the same about me. I'm not sure.'

'Even though . . .' Louise gestures to me.

I close my eyes briefly. She's not trying to be annoying.

'Yes. Literally the only thing we have in common is that neither of us are straight. I'm not sure that's enough to create a great connection with someone.'

'But,' Charlie says, 'she has come to you to talk about discovering feelings for women, right?'

'Yes.'

'Which is something you also went through.'

'Well, yes.'

'Hmm.'

I glare at them. There's nothing more annoying than a therapist's contemplative 'Hmm.'

'What?' I say.

I lean forward to pluck the deadly weapon from my can. I tap it against the palm of my left hand.

'I just wonder if the reason you're struggling to connect with her is related to something going on with you rather than something about her specifically?'

'Is there something you have in mind, Charlie?'

I dig the middle of the straw into my hand and then inspect the deep ring it's left there.

'Well, I wonder if her being a parent who is apparently on the verge of embarking on an affair is the thing that's bothering you and stopping you from being able to forge a connection with her. You fundamentally disagree with what she's doing, even if that's something you're not conscious of.'

'I don't *disagree* with someone exploring their sexuality whatever their circumstances. I don't judge anyone who comes into my practice. You know that.'

'I did say, even if it's not conscious,' Charlie says gently.

Louise and Philippa are watching this interaction with wide eyes, absolutely loving it. Charlie and I do challenge each other occasionally but I know I'm making this all much more interesting by getting so wound up. I don't know why. I come here to be challenged, to get ideas and insights into why things are and aren't working.

'I just wonder,' Charlie says, 'if it's something worth exploring, that's all.'

'Are your parents still together?' Philippa asks. She knows that they're not. We all know that kind of thing about each other.

'No,' I say through gritted teeth.

Louise and Philippa do the therapist 'Hmm' in unison.

I look at Charlie and shake my head slightly. *Don't tell them about my dad*, I scream in my head, hoping they'll somehow telepathically hear me. They nod slightly. They won't say anything.

'Actually,' I say. 'I've just thought of something else that I'd much rather talk about. Philippa, I wonder if you have any thoughts about my student who's struggling with his first break-up. I know you have a son who's a teenager. Do you have any thoughts about working with someone that young?'

She smiles knowingly and then she's off explaining teenagers to the rest of us. Her specialist subject. I can relax again. As annoying as therapists can be, at least I can trust that they're

166

not going to push me on a subject I'm clearly trying to avoid. Boundaries strike again.

When we eventually leave the house with a can of Sprite for the road I wait until we're at the end of the drive and then turn to Charlie and hiss, 'What was all that for?'

'All what?' they say.

Charlie is wearing huge sunglasses and I can't see what their expression is.

'I feel like that was an attack.'

'That's a bit dramatic, isn't it?'

We set off walking down the street together. We would normally go to the pub after peer supervision but I haven't decided yet if I want to spend any more time in Charlie's company.

'I know you think I'm being annoying, but I think perhaps your dad is something you need to address. It's for your good, your client's good. The greater good!'

They're trying to lighten the mood but I am decidedly dark for the time being.

'Something to address? Are you kidding me? Do you not think I've been addressing it for the past eighteen fucking years?'

'Honestly, mate? Honestly? No. I don't think you've addressed it at all. I think it's all locked up. And do I think you've addressed your dad potentially coming back into your life now? Not even a bit.'

I laugh, I feel almost hysterical.

'I don't know what to say. I can't . . . I can't take this from you.'

'Natasha.'

'What?'

'Have you decided if you're going to see him yet?'

'No! No, I . . . Why do I need to explain myself to you?'

We start walking again.

'I'm just looking out for you. I don't think I'd be a good friend if I was just to act like I think it's fine when I think you're actually harming yourself. I know you're avoiding me because it's easier to spend time with people who don't care and aren't going to ask difficult questions.'

'I haven't been avoiding you.'

'OK.'

'I haven't! I've been busy.'

'Doing what?'

I smile, despite myself.

'Spending time with someone who doesn't care and doesn't ask me difficult questions.'

Charlie grins, relieved that we're still friends. They pull me in for a one-armed hug and I rest my head on their shoulder.

'Do you think I'm stupid and a terrible therapist?'

'I think you're really stupid,' they say, kissing the top of my head, 'but I love you. And no, you're not a terrible therapist, but you'd be a *better* one with this client if you were more in touch with yourself. That's the last of it. I'll leave it alone now.'

'Really?'

'I mean . . . for now. Look, if you feel fine about it then I feel fine about it, OK? Just . . . promise me you'll pay attention to what's going on.'

I agree, even though I'm not entirely sure what they mean.

We're quiet for a few minutes as we stroll along slowly. Charlie fishes their phone out of the pocket of their high-waisted jeans and so I get mine out too. I have a message from Georgia.

> *Super last minute but do you fancy a drink this evening? I had a work thing that got cancelled and I've got a rare free evening!*

A rare free evening means an evening when Zara has plans. They are one of those couples that only makes plans when the other one is busy so as not to spend even a moment of time away from each other unnecessarily. As disappointing as it is to be someone's back-up plan, I'm not going to pass up an evening with Georgia.

'Listen, Charlie, I can't do a drink this evening. I've already got plans.'

Charlie looks at me, eyebrows raised.

'With Georgia!'

'Oh God,' Charlie says, wearied by me, 'another story altogether.'

'What's that supposed to . . . never mind. I'm going to go and meet her now.'

We hug at the point where we part ways and I squeeze

Charlie extra tight, trying to convey something. That I appreciate them. That I'm sorry I'm being so disappointing.

'Love you, Charl.'

'Then stop avoiding me.'

'I will, I promise.'

Georgia is already at the pub when I arrive, sitting outside on
a picnic bench to herself, reading a book. I love this about her.
She doesn't treat her phone as a substitute for company like a
normal person, she is perfectly content to sit by herself and
read. She's wearing a white shirt with the sleeves rolled up
and tailored black trousers which must be unbearably hot.
She's wearing glasses that I don't recognise. Round and dark
tortoiseshell.

'New glasses?' I say, plonking myself down opposite her and
swinging my legs over the picnic bench.

'Yes!' she says, putting her book down and smiling. Even
when she's expecting you, Georgia has a way of making you
feel as though you're a delightful surprise. 'Do you like them?'

'Love them. Are they Ray-Bans?'

'Yeah,' she says, taking them off her face to inspect them
more closely, 'but I got them from this website for super cheap
so I feel like they might be Roy-Bans or something.'

'Well, your Roy-Bans look good.'

She smiles at me.

'Thanks! What are you drinking?'

Sometimes Georgia is on some kind of health kick which

involves no weekday drinking so when I tentatively suggest, 'Pint of lager?' and she says, 'Sounds good, I'll get the same actually', I'm thrilled.

She gets up to go to the bar and on her way past me stops to give me a kiss on the cheek.

'We haven't even said hello properly,' she says and walks into the pub.

She comes back with two pints of some local lager that cost £7.50 each. She is scandalised.

'Outrageous,' I say, tapping my glass to hers and taking a sip. 'It does taste nice though. Well,' I put my glass down, 'it tastes like beer.'

'I think this kind of thing is wasted on us. I know you'd have been happy with anything.'

'Correct,' I say, taking another sip. 'That's 50p right there,' I say, wiping my top lip.

'So,' she says. 'What's new with you? It feels like absolutely ages since we caught up. I haven't seen you since my birthday, I don't think. And it's not like we got a proper chance to catch up there. All a bit . . . mad.'

She glances down at her left hand and I nod and take another sip of my beer. We've texted a few times since then but it's just been niceties, weirdly formal. I texted her the day after the party (with a raging hangover) congratulating her again, she texted me to thank me for the gift. I asked if she wanted to get coffee soon and she said she did and neither of us ever followed up.

'It does feel like ages,' I say. 'Let's see, what's new?'

Margot, a voice in my head screams. *I went on a date with Margot. I called her in the middle of the night, took my clothes off and waded out to sea with her when I found out you were going to get married.*

'Not much,' I say. 'I already told you that Natalie's pregnant, didn't I?'

'Yes!' she says, beaming. 'You did! So wonderful.'

'So wonderful,' I say.

'How is she doing? I meant to text her.'

'Oh do, she'd love that. She's good! She's loving being pregnant this time. I think only having one in there is a relief.'

'I bet. Fuck. Imagine.'

'I know.'

We both take a sip of our drinks.

'Really, though,' she says. 'Not much going on? I thought you might be seeing someone, you've sort of dropped off the radar a bit.'

'No! I'm not. I actually haven't been on any dates in a while.'
Sort of true.

'Wow. Are you feeling all right?'

'I've just been really concentrating on work.'
Absolutely not true.

'Mmm,' she says, clearly not entirely convinced. 'And how is work?'

'Fine, yeah,' I say, hoping to portray the picture of calm, despite the internal screaming. 'Nothing to report. Anyway,' I say quickly, ready to change the subject. 'How about you? Are wedding plans all go, go, go? Where's Zara this evening?'

'Zara's at a birthday thing, someone from work.'

'Ah,' I smile, 'so you're allowed out.'

'Hey!' Georgia tries to look offended but ends up laughing. 'I'm always allowed out.'

'Sure.'

'I am!'

'OK! I just don't see much of you, that's all.'

She pauses a moment before replying.

'I know. It's very different. I mean . . . it's more different than I thought it would be.'

I nod. There are a lot of things I could say about how much I miss her but I don't know if she wants to hear them. I want to tell her about Margot just to see her reaction, to create some of the closeness we had before, or to see if it's still there lurking beneath the surface.

'What's it like living with Poppy?' she says. 'Is she driving you mad?'

'It's good, I like living with her.'

I wait for her to make some kind of comment, maybe 'I bet you do' but she doesn't.

'You know,' I continue, 'I barely see her.'

'Really?'

'Yeah she's always with Felix or saving the planet. She works a lot.'

'Woah, really?'

I smile.

'Yes! I know you think she's silly but she's not. You underestimate her. She's saving the world. She makes her own nut butter now.'

'I know, she gave me some.'

I grimace at her and she laughs.

'Felix is giving me driving lessons. Well, he gave me one driving lesson.'

'Oh god!'

'Yeah, it's like his community service. I feel like he thinks he might get some kind of tax relief from doing it.'

Georgia laughs again and I get such a kick out of it still. 'How was it?'

'Oh horrible, I'm probably never going to try again. To be fair he hasn't mentioned it since so perhaps once was enough for both of us.'

'Rubbish,' she says. 'So you're not going to be driving us about on holiday?'

'Ha. Absolutely not. I'll be the designated drinker.'

'I can't believe that it's so soon.'

She starts to pick a beer mat apart.

'I know! Are you excited?'

'Yeah I am. Did I tell you that Josh is coming?'

'No. Since when?'

'He claims he was always coming. I can't stop him if we're staying at Uncle Simon's. He said everyone was welcome.'

Uncle Simon is Georgia's mum's older brother who has a

lovely house in Santa Monica that has an open-door policy to all of Georgia's family and friends. I've never made it out there. 'So is Josh also coming out to Joshua Tree?'

'I doubt it. Let's make sure there's no room in the cars, eh?'

I shrug.

'I don't know, George. The more the merrier. He's not that bad.'

We're driving out to Joshua Tree for the last three days of our trip, returning straight to LAX from the desert for our flight home. Georgia's been several times before and is desperate for us to all experience it together. It sounds like a whole lot of hiking to me, but I've been promised lots of lazing about in the sun and drinking in a hot tub, which sounds like a pretty great way to spend my birthday.

I go inside to get us a couple of cheaper pints and end up coming back out with a pitcher of Pimm's.

'Natty!' Georgia exclaims. 'No, no, no I have work tomorrow.'

'Yeah so do I, it's fine though. It's mostly lemonade, isn't it,' I say as I pour her a glass and pick a piece of apple out. I realise I've not eaten dinner.

'I suppose.'

I take a deep breath. If I'm not going to talk to her about Margot there is something else I've got to get off my chest.

'George,' I say. 'Did I tell you about my dad?'

Her eyes widen behind her Roy-Bans.

'No, what about him?'

We haven't really talked much about my dad. I don't really talk to anyone about him, even Natalie. It occurs to me that in the past couple of weeks, the past couple of hours even, I've spoken about him more than in the past decade. To Charlie. And to Margot.

'Mum says he's living in California.'

'What? Where?'

'I don't know.'

'Well are you going to message him?'

'I don't know.'

'Or meet up with him?'

'I don't know.'

'Well what does Natalie think you should do?'

'I don't . . .'

'Natty!'

'What?'

'You've got to think about this, at least a bit.'

'Yeah, I will. I'm talking to you about it right now, aren't I? It's just really . . .' I feel around for the word and land on 'massive', which feels woefully inadequate.

Georgia sighs and shakes her head. I'm already regretting telling her. I fear I'm in for a lecture.

'I don't know how you can spend all day telling people how to be in touch with their feelings and aware of their emotions and all that stuff and be so detached from yourself.'

I open my mouth to object but she carries on.

'Honestly, you do this thing where you just compartmentalise to the point where things are so tidied away you can forget they even exist.'

'I don't know what . . .' I glance down at my phone to see I have a message from Margot and turn it face down on the table, 'you're talking about. I don't do that.'

'Come on,' she says, visibly frustrated now. 'You must be feeling something about potentially seeing your dad? How long has it been? Fifteen years? Longer? Or you must at least be feeling something just knowing he moved halfway across the world and didn't even mention it to you.'

'Well,' I say quietly, stirring the Pimm's, 'I think technically we were meant to find out from Auntie Linda in her Christmas email.'

She looks at me, clearly expecting more.

'Obviously I have feelings, George. I'm not a robot. Perhaps I haven't addressed them yet. Christ, I didn't tell you so you could have a go at me. I wish I hadn't said anything.'

That's not true. I'm glad she knows. I want her to know about me still. Georgia and I did properly talk about my dad once. I can't remember all of it. I was horribly drunk. I do remember sobbing into her shoulder. I remember saying she'd never know what it was like to feel unloved. I remember her telling me I would never be unloved. I spent the night curled up on our bathroom floor. She spent it beside me.

I pick up my drink and take a couple of large gulps. She does the same.

'Sorry. I'm sorry,' she says, taking off her glasses and rubbing her eyes, suddenly weary.

This routine is what we used to do all the time when we were together. She wants something from me, I don't give it, she tells me off, I retreat even more. It's terrible but I get a little thrill from knowing I can still elicit this response from her.

'It's OK.'

'It's not. It's not my business.' She puts her drink down and adds, 'Anymore.'

'Right.'

We're both quiet for a beat. Georgia refills our glasses. I watch her hand, her long fingers and short fingernails and the gold band.

'So how's wedding planning going?' I say, popping another piece of fizzy apple in my mouth.

She groans and puts her head in her hands.

'That bad?'

'No, it's not bad. It's just . . . I had no idea how much work goes into a wedding. There's just so much to think about.'

She waits a second, as though deciding whether to tell me something, and then leans forward.

'Zara has *binders* full of stuff. Like, not just a Pinterest board or a fucking . . . I don't know . . . folder on her laptop. Actual *binders* full of all this stuff printed out and handwritten notes.'

I can't help but laugh at her horror.

'I don't think that's abnormal, George. Some people are just wedding-people, aren't they? They love all that stuff.'

'Yeah I guess,' she stirs up her drink with her paper straw. 'I suppose I just didn't necessarily know that Zara was one of those people.'

'I didn't say I've never thought about the future, George. I said I've never thought about my wedding.'

'Right. But you never even for a moment, like, even fleetingly thought that you and I might end up together?'

This feels like an impossible question to answer because of course there was a time when I thought about that but it doesn't feel particularly helpful to say that now. I think about standing in the kitchen with Georgia a few weeks after we got together, she'd come in from work and wrapped her arms around my waist. She'd kissed me on the cheek and I had lifted my hand to touch the side of her face. Her head pressed into my shoulder, lips vibrating against my neck as she asked me about my day. I don't remember what I said but I remember feeling for the first time that I understood what people meant when they said a person felt like home. There it is, I thought, when she's here, I'm home.

I'm suddenly very warm. I tug at the neck of my T-shirt trying to let a little air in.

'I . . . I'm sure . . . it was such a long time ago now.'

She looks at me sadly.

'So, no then?'

'I mean . . . no, not really.'

She nods. I'm sure she's wishing she never asked the question.

'That doesn't mean I didn't feel . . . I really did . . .'

'Oh, I know. I know.' She waves me away and smiles broadly, deciding the moment's over. She's not going to make me tell her how much she means to me.

We chat a little while longer about work and about the weather and how much we can't wait for autumn to arrive and when we walk out of the pub together Georgia pulls me into a big hug.

'I'm sorry if I was weird, I'm a bit drunk and just sort of . . . overemotional. A lot going on.'

I pull back but hold onto her arms and look at her.

'You are very weird. But you never have to apologise to me. Let's see each other soon, OK? We've left it too long. That's why you were weird.'

'I know. We will. Well, we're seeing each other for a whole week soon!'

'And I can't wait,' I say, and I really mean it.

Once Georgia starts off home I pull my phone out of my back pocket to finally read Margot's message.

What are you doing on Saturday?

I'm seeing my sister. She's bringing the twins for the day. Why?

Want to come to my gig in the evening? You can cover your ears for everyone else apart from me.

A moment later another message follows it up.

We can leave early.

I can't help but smile.

Let me think about it.

Sure. Think about it and I'll see you there. It starts at 8pm, hang on I'll screenshot you the details.

It's actually in a venue I've heard of and her name is listed pretty near the top. I still haven't googled her. Maybe she's secretly famous. I don't reply but I know I'm going to go even though I'm sure nothing good is going to come of it.

When I get home, I'm surprised to see Poppy sitting at the kitchen table in front of her laptop. She's got her hair tied back and she's wearing what I would call a 'summer dressing gown' and what she would call 'a kimono! Isn't it fun?!' From the telltale ears popping up from under the table I see she has Diane sitting on her lap.

'No way,' I say and stand in the doorway, my hand clapped to my chest in shock.

She looks up and smiles. She rubs her eyes and blinks a few times, trying to adjust her focus now that she's not looking at the screen.

'I know, your eyes do not deceive you. I really am home before . . .' she picks up her phone to check the time, 'nine p.m.'

I open the fridge, desperately hungry and in search of something to eat. My body screams crisps but my mind says something with at least one vitamin in it. Poppy has leftover

stir fry which looks like it has tofu in it. Some sort of grey protein anyway. I pull it out of the fridge and wave it at her in its
Tupperware box.

'Can I eat this?'

'Of course!' she says. She looks genuinely delighted that
I've asked. I'm not normally super keen on ... 'Homemade
tempeh!' she trills and starts telling me the ins and outs of
making it.

'Wow,' I say and grab a fork, not bothering to heat it up or get
a plate. I take a huge bite and, actually, it's pretty good. Though
I think anything tastes good on an empty stomach after a litre
of Pimm's.

'Are you still working, Pops?' I say through a mouthful of
noodles.

'Yeah.' She frowns. 'I'm working on this campaign and I just
can't ... it's not right. And my boss isn't happy. I should have
stayed really but I just couldn't concentrate in the office. I actually have this splitting headache.'

She suddenly looks like she might cry, which is very rare for
her. I mean, she actually cries a lot but over things like pen-
guins losing their eggs or the ice caps melting or suddenly
feeling overwhelmingly very happy. Not about work or having
a headache.

'Hey,' I say, pausing the shovelling of stir fry into my mouth
to reach my hand across the table and give hers a squeeze.
'What is it?'

'Ugh!' She wipes under her eyes as if checking her mascara

hasn't run although she's not wearing any make-up. 'It's nothing, I'm just a bit overwhelmed.'

'Just with work?'

I pop a mangetout in my mouth and try to chew as quietly as possible.

'Yeah,' she says and looks back at the screen before sighing heavily and pushing it closed. 'And Felix.'

'Why? What's going on with Felix?'

I feel a pang of guilt. Although she's never here I also haven't really made any effort to find out what's going on with her. I've been so wrapped up in myself recently.

'It's just ever since he found out that Zara and George got engaged he's been hinting a lot about us getting married.' She adjusts Diane so that instead of being curled up on her lap, Poppy is holding her like a baby. She just falls right back to sleep.

I nod and chase the last noodles around the Tupperware, wondering if she'll be disgusted if I just pick them up with my fingers.

'And then last night, I was staying at his and when I got there he'd cooked this beautiful dinner and we had this lovely evening and all of a sudden he went, "Poppy, I want to talk to you about something quite serious for a moment" and I was like, *shit* he's either dying or breaking up with me or . . .'

'He's going to propose,' I finish her sentence for her.

'Exactly,' she says.

'So I obviously had this look of complete horror on my face and he goes on to tell me he's been promoted at work which is fantastic but does mean it'll involve a lot more travelling and for longer periods of time so he wanted to speak to me first before accepting anything.'

'Oh!' I say. 'Amazing!'

'Well,' she says, 'that's what I said. I said, 'Oh that's so amazing darling, you had me worried there for a moment.' And he said, "I know, you looked like you'd seen a ghost. Did you think I was going to tell you I'd met someone else or something?" and I was like, "No! I was worried you were going to ask me to marry you!" '

'Ah,' I say, grimacing slightly, 'and how did that go down?'

'Like a fucking lead balloon.'

'Yeah, I bet.'

'He was just silent for ages. It was actually awful because he'd made this amazing tarte au citron and he just sat there not eating it and I just kept thinking, *am I meant to leave this?* But like, I couldn't because it was so delicious and he'd gone to the effort of making it vegan. So I just sort of ate it in silence while he watched me.'

'Yikes.'

'I know. So then I was just going to get up and start clearing the plates away when he goes, 'Would it really be that awful?" And I was like, "No it wouldn't be *awful*, like, that is so dramatic, but I don't want to get married, definitely not now, maybe not ever." '

'And what did he say?'

She frowns.

'He was really upset. He says he can't see himself with anyone else and am I saying I don't know if I want to spend the rest of my life with someone? And I'm like,' she throws her Diane-free hand up in the air, 'I don't know. How can I answer that? I don't know.'

She sighs again and strokes Diane's tummy gently.

'And he was like,' she bites her lip and her eyes fill with tears, 'he was like, "Well that breaks my heart because I know I couldn't ever love someone as much as I love you."'

A tear spills down her cheek and she wipes it away with the back of her hand. I move so that I'm sitting next to her and wrap my arm around her. She rests her head on my shoulder. Her hair smells sweet, of the cherry conditioner she's using, and faintly of smoke. Diane glares up at me.

'And I didn't say that! I didn't say that I don't love him, I just . . . I can't say forever. It seems so unreasonable. *Forever.* Like . . . what? Until I'm literally dead!?'

She laughs like she's made a joke.

'I mean . . . yeah. I think that's written into the contract.'

She pulls away from me so she can look at me.

'You get what I mean, right?'

I nod.

'Like, you're not trying to be with anyone forever, are you?'

I laugh and rub my eyes, suddenly feeling exhausted. My stomach is full and the booze is wearing off.

'I'm not trying to be with anyone for five minutes.'

She nods at me.

'Exactly, and you're happy, aren't you?'

She doesn't pause to give me a chance to answer.

'You're happy living this fabulous life where you date all kinds of people and you're not tied to anything, you've got a new girl every week and that's just . . . maybe that makes more sense than just the same person every day.'

I look at her. I know she just wants me to affirm what she's saying. She wants me to be living the perfect antithesis to her life so she can point at it and say, 'look, the grass *is* greener'. I mean, I'm happy in a sort of vague way. I suppose it's more accurate to say that I'm not unhappy. What's happy? I can tell this is probably not the conversation she's looking to have.

'I am actually seeing someone new.'

Her eyes widen.

'Who?'

'This girl who showed up to one of my training days.'

'Ooh,' Poppy says, 'so like a teacher–student thing?'

'Well, no. Not really, I . . .'

'Hot,' she says, choosing to ignore me.

I can't help but laugh, I sit back in my chair.

'It's obviously not going to go anywhere.'

'Obviously,' she says, quickly, which I can't decide whether I should be offended by. 'But you're having fun?'

I know what she wants to hear. And I am having fun, aren't I?

'Yes,' I say. 'Loads of fun.'

Poppy smiles, reassured, and pushes herself up from the table.

'Thank you for listening to me, darling.' She kisses me on the cheek and I just want to pull her to me. Tell her not to go to bed. Tell her it's OK to not want to spend forever with Felix. To not want to spend forever with anyone.

'Anytime, Pops.'

'Everything will work itself out, won't it?'

She looks at me earnestly, like she is asking if in my professional opinion everything with Felix will work out.

'It will. Whatever happens, everything will be OK. It always is.'

That doesn't really mean anything but it does the trick. She nods and heads out of the room, Diane right behind her.

I leave the Tupperware in the sink to 'soak' and get myself a large glass of water to take to bed. I pause at the fridge where a dark floral card has been added to our collection of bills, photos and old shopping lists. I trace my finger over the swirly gold writing.

Zara & Georgia
Save the Date
Saturday 1st August
East Sussex

7

I wake up alone in the flat on Saturday morning. Poppy stayed at Felix's last night and won't be back until later this afternoon, maybe not even until tomorrow. They've been glued to each other ever since they made up from their fight earlier in the week. I'm not convinced they've resolved anything but they're stuck in that place of mad panic at the idea of losing each other and then utter relief of not making any decisions that would change anything. Even if the change would be good.

I'm not meeting Natalie and the twins until midday so I have the whole morning to myself. There are all sorts of practical things I could be doing – namely starting my packing for our trip the following week but also washing, cleaning the kitchen, going for a run, doing a food shop, but I don't know why I even bother to run through the list when I know I'm actually going to stay in bed, eat some of the banana bread that Poppy's been trying to force on me all week and catch up on what the various *Real Housewives* are up to. My addiction to the *Real House-wives* is something Georgia has always found fascinating.

'It just doesn't *fit* with what I'd expect from you,' she once said, standing in the doorway of the living room as I approached the fifth or sixth hour of my binge-watch. But when probed she couldn't explain what exactly it was that she expected or why a penchant for the *Real Housewives* might affect that in some way.

I used to be able to give the *Housewives* all of my attention. When I was a student especially, I would be able to sit for hours glued to my laptop, enthralled by the drama and the outfits and surgery. But now I can't do anything for five minutes without the overwhelming compulsion to pick up my phone. I can't even concentrate on something mind-numbing without needing a second mind-numbing activity to distract me from my own thoughts. I've read endlessly about attention span and how you can retrain your brain to be able to concentrate on one thing for longer. I speak to clients about it all the time, I've recommended books about mindfulness to them, listened as people tell me they're sure they used to be able to read a book. I think they believe they're talking to someone who is enlightened. Who knows all the answers. They must notice that I reply to emails on Sunday mornings or at 2 a.m. on a Wednesday. The time when I speak to them is the longest time I spend away from my phone. When it's not even in reach. And even then I find myself making mental notes of things I want to check when it's back in my hand again.

Today I find myself looking again at the event info Margot sent me while a blonde woman drunkenly berates another blonde woman on the screen in front of me.

I already know I'm going to go. I've had vague notions of doing something else. Of seeing if Poppy wants to do something. Of finding a date. But I don't want to do anything else. I want to go and sit in a hot room and watch Margot read a poem or tell a joke or whatever it is she's going to do. I go onto her Instagram, a page I'm now very familiar with. She has a few thousand followers. Not famous. But not *not* famous.

She doesn't post much. Her last post was three weeks ago and it's a black and white photo of her laughing with one hand covering the side of her face like she's embarrassed that someone is taking her picture. She looks impossibly beautiful. Film-star beautiful. I make a note to get more photos of myself in black and white. I wonder who made her laugh that much.

I scroll back further and there are a few more of her. Some with groups of people, I zoom in on their faces. I'm not sure what I'm hoping to see. What is anyone hoping to see on Instagram? I just want to understand her. Something tangible that allows me to think, 'I know you.'

I go on WhatsApp and open my conversation with Margot. We haven't spoken since she sent me the details and I type out a few messages and delete them before sending:

OK. I'll come. Drinks on you though. What am I getting myself into?

She reads it immediately. She must be sitting on her phone the same as me. The thought of her lazing about in bed doing something so ordinary is weirdly jarring. Every time I think about her she's doing something deep and artistic.

Of course you're coming. I promise we'll have fun.

And then.

I can't wait to see you.

A shiver goes down my spine. I don't know what to reply and in the end I don't. I look at the time and realise that after two full episodes and the start of another (I had to see if they showed up to the White Party or not) I now have to rush to get ready if I'm going to meet Natalie and the twins at the station. Natalie has been up since god knows what time organising twelve year olds to get on a train on a Saturday so I feel like she probably wouldn't appreciate my excuse of 'too much *Housewives*' or 'stalking people on Instagram'.

I get to the station with wet hair and three minutes to spare. I message Natalie immediately to tell her I'm waiting for them so she knows I was early and then try to catch my breath. It's still hot today but there's a breeze so I stand in the entrance and try to cool down. I spot them coming towards me before they see me. The twins are either side of Natalie and for a moment they could almost be little again, about to take a hand each. Natalie is suddenly, extremely pregnant and I wonder how I didn't notice before. She's wearing a tight black maxi-dress and she looks gorgeous. Super tanned. Obviously been putting a lot of sunlounger hours in.

'Ooh, clean hair,' Natalie says as she kisses me on the cheek. 'You shouldn't have.'

'It's not for you,' I say.

The twins give me rubbish, half-hearted hugs.

'What's wrong with you two?' I say.

'We're hungry,' Ella says just as Daniel says, 'We're thirsty.'

'God you poor things. No food, no drink. What a terrible mother you've got.'

'Mmm, horrible, aren't I?' Natalie says.

I place a hand on her bump.

'Weird.'

'I know,' she says. 'Little alien growing in there.'

'It's going to grow up to be a big, hungry, thirsty alien.'

'Ugh no,' she says as we set off down the hill into town, the twins in front of us, 'I'm keeping this one a baby forever.'

We have a routine whenever they come to visit me. We get fish and chips and eat them on the beach, pretty much what-ever the weather. This has so far resulted in two seagull attacks and one lost cod but they won't be persuaded that it's better to eat them elsewhere. They'd rather risk the birds so that's on them. Then we have a paddle in the sea, lose some 2ps in the slot machines and get an ice cream before they head home. It's the perfect seaside day, we've been doing it for years and we keep waiting for the twins to grow out of it but no signs of that so far, I don't know if it's just so ingrained it hasn't occurred to them that we could do something different. I hope we're still doing this when they're twenty.

Once we've finished eating (we only have to scream at one seagull) we send Ella and Daniel off to 'test how cold the water is' so we can have some time to ourselves.

'Are you not coming?' Ella says.

'No sorry, babe,' Natalie says, 'pregnant people can't get their feet wet.'

She says it so easily and so seriously that for a moment even I believe her . Ella just accepts it completely and she and Daniel clamber off, shrieking about the pebbles on their bare feet.

'Wow, that was masterful,' I tell her, sticking my legs out in front of me and resting back on my elbows.

'Thank you. Bless her, she's seen me getting in the bath and I was in the pool with her yesterday. She'll realise later.'

She shifts so she's sitting next to me facing the sea. She rests a hand absent-mindedly on her stomach.

'So, Natty.'

'Mmm.'

'Are you going to see Dad on your holiday or not?'

I groan and throw my head back as though this is the thousandth time she's asked me this question. We actually haven't discussed it since the day we found out.

'Come on, you're off next week and you haven't even got in touch with him yet.'

I turn to face her.

'How do you know I haven't been in touch with him?'

'Have you?' She holds my stare.

'No.'

She reaches into her bag and gets her phone out.

'Right, I've just sent you his number. It's a new one apparently. Linda says it's better to get him on WhatsApp because he never checks his email.'

'Right.'

For some reason the idea of my dad being on WhatsApp feels absurd.

'Have *you* messaged him then?' I feel something tighten in my chest, the idea of everybody being in touch with each other but me.

'No,' she says and shakes her head. 'But I might. And I definitely would if I was going to be in the same country as him.'

We're both quiet for a moment, watching the kids wade out until the water reaches their knees.

'I feel like I shouldn't have to,' I say eventually.

She nods.

'I know, babe.'

'It should be him. Why do I have to reach out?'

I know I sound like a child but I don't care. I am a child. He's my parent. It's his job.

Natalie shrugs.

'You don't have to. But you're not doing it for him. You're doing it for you.'

'Maybe I won't do it.'

'You will,' she says. And she's right.

'What if he doesn't want to see me?' I say quietly.

She leans over and rests her head on my shoulder. I rest mine on top of hers.

'Then that's his loss. But, Natty. I think he will.'

'He hasn't spoken to us for a long time.'

'We haven't spoken to him either.'

We're quiet again and Natalie sits back upright.

'You're all bony,' she says, rubbing the side of her head as if my shoulder has somehow bruised it. 'Mum thinks you should go.'

'I know,' I say.

'It would make her happy.'

'Oh, for fuck's sake.'

'What?'

'Well how can I not do it now?'

'Ha, exactly. Oh, she told me to give you this.'

She roots around in her bag and passes me a bottle of factor 50 kids' sunscreen (Mum thinks the kids' stuff is stronger and refuses to wear anything else) and a little pocket guide to Los Angeles.

'Does she know you can get all of this info,' I wave the book at Natalie, 'on your phone?'

'It's a nice thing, Natty,' she says.

'I know! I'm just saying.' It is nice. I don't know why I can't just be nice too. I think I'm mad at her for being happy if I see my dad. Very reasonable.

Ella and Daniel come running back up the beach, both of their shorts are wet and they're grumbling about it despite having spent the last twenty minutes in the sea splashing each other.

'By the time we've walked to the ice-cream place they'll have dried,' I say and we all heave Natalie up and make our way along the beach and up the steps.

We leave Natalie outside the shop to wait on a seat in the shade under strict instructions to buy her something 'massive and chocolatey' and not 'anything with fruit or weird shit in'. As soon as we step out of earshot I am loudly and expertly lobbied for two scoops.

'Please, please I have barely eaten anything today.'

'Please, please can we? You're our favourite auntie and we hardly ever get to come here and see you and this is literally the only time we get ice cream.'

'OK so, firstly, you don't need to pick favourite family members, we love each other equally, but I do still appreciate that so thank you. Secondly, I know that you eat ice cream every single day, your mum sends me pictures of you eating Cornettos in your pool.'

They look up at me, wide-eyed and somewhat shiftily. I take a deep breath and stare at the board behind the counter, pretending as though I'm really weighing it up.

'But,' I say, 'I think that just this once, two scoops is allowed.'

They both jump up and down and hug me like I've agreed to give them a million pounds. Absolutely worth it. Plus I don't have to deal with them later after the sugar crash. Natalie rolls her eyes at me when we come outside with our towers of ice cream but she doesn't say anything about it.

We head back to the seafront but instead of walking down to the beach we perch on a wall and face out to the sea. The twins sit about ten metres away from us asserting their independence, once Natalie has passed them a wad of tissues from her bag.

'Are you looking forward to your maternity leave?' I ask.

Natalie nods furiously as she chews on a bit of brownie from her ice cream.

'I can't bloody wait. I'd leave now if I could. One baby is going to be a fucking doddle.'

Natalie is an early years practitioner and manages a small nursery that used to have around twenty kids and now has close to double that. Kids *love* her. She talks to them like adults. She doesn't take any nonsense and she accidentally swears around them constantly. She's also the kindest person in the world so even when she's being strict she's never scary. She'd already started her training when she got pregnant with the twins and as soon as she had them she picked it right back up again. I was at university doing around three hours of lectures a week at that time. I distinctly remember sitting in the library, genuinely believing that having a full year to write a fifteen-thousand-word dissertation was as taxing as it got.

'How's Luke doing?'

Natalie rolls her eyes. It is almost physically impossible for her to say something nice about him.

'Oh fine, the same as always.'

She pauses, running her finger up the side of the cone to catch the stray drips of ice cream and then leaning over to wipe it on my shorts. I slap her hand but she doesn't even register it.

'Actually,' she says as if it's only just occurring to her. 'He's a bit stressed out. Business is going well but I think he's feeling a lot of pressure. Babies are pricey and the twins just seem to need more and more stuff. It's endless.'

Luke owns his own contracting company. Or is it a surveying company. Building company? Definitely something to do with houses and definitely something which means he works about seventy hours a week. Every time I see him he's exhausted.

'He'd be happy to give up work and be a house husband. He loves all that stuff. Cooking and making the house nice and playing with the kids.'

'Can't he do that then?'

Natalie laughs.

'Yeah, he can do that when the nursery starts paying me enough to keep a house of five people going.'

'Five people,' I say, shaking my head.

'I know. Mad, isn't it.'

'Mad.'

'Oh my god!' Natalie says suddenly. 'Look who it is!'

I realise she's not speaking to me but to the person approaching us with a huge smile on her face.

'Natalie!' Georgia says as she gets closer. 'No, no please don't get up.'

Georgia bends down to where Natalie's sitting to give her a hug.

'You look amazing,' she says, standing back again to look at Natalie properly. She lifts her sunglasses up onto her head. She turns to me and lifts a hand and then, almost as an afterthought, leans forward and kisses me on the cheek.

'Hi Natty.'

'Hi George,' I turn to the twins who are watching with interest from their spot a few metres away, 'you remember Ella and Daniel.'

'How could I forget? Hi guys,' Georgia says, waving at them.

They wave back and then get back to their ice creams, completely disinterested.

'Looks good,' Georgia says, gesturing to my own ice cream that I'm now halfway through.

I hold it out to her and after a moment of hesitation she takes it from me and licks all the way around the edges just where it was about to drip.

'Strawberry something?' she says, handing it back.

'Sour cherry.'

She wipes her mouth with the back of her hand.

'Delicious.'

'So what are you up to today?' Natalie says. She's pushed her sunglasses on top of her head too but is now shielding her eyes from the sun as she looks up at Georgia.

'Errands,' Georgia says and moves her body around to show us the bulging tote bag she's carrying. 'I've been sent out to collect confetti samples.'

Natalie laughs.

'Confetti samples? It's just bits of paper, isn't it?'

'Ah,' Georgia says. 'That's what I thought too, but no. Now it's dried flowers and there's a specialist place in town that apparently does the best stuff so,' she points to the bag again, 'bag full of dead flowers.'

'Mad,' Natalie says. 'Well, babe. Congratulations. I'm sure it's going to be gorgeous.'

Georgia looks at me for a moment and I'm sure she wants to say something. But then she turns back to Natalie, pulls her sunglasses back down onto her face and says, 'Well, I'd better head off. It was lovely to bump into you. Honestly, Natalie, you look amazing. And, Natty, I'll see you next week?'

She asks as if I might casually back out of the holiday we've had planned for months.

'You will, George! Say hi to Zara for me. Hope she likes the dead flowers!'

Once Georgia is out of earshot, albeit barely, Natalie turns to me and says, 'She is fit, isn't she?'

I roll my eyes.

'No, she is though, isn't she?' Natalie says. 'Like, I know you're just friends now but come on. She's just got that thing.'

'What thing?'

'I don't know. That thing. Some people have it. I bet everyone fancies her.'

'It's just confidence,' I say.

'No, that's not it. It's like . . . don't take this the wrong way all right?'

'What?'

'Well, she's like a boy. No, no!' she says immediately on seeing me roll my eyes and open my mouth to object. 'No, not like a boy. Like . . . she has an energy though, don't you think?'

'Boy energy?' I say.

'No! Ugh, fine. I'm not explaining myself. But you do know what I mean and you're just being annoying.'

I do know what she means. George does have this energy about her. It is confidence partly, it's knowing who she is. It's the way she stands, the way she moves. Natalie is right – everyone does fancy her. I remember going to a work party with her once and watching the way she interacted with her colleagues. I texted Charlie to tell them that I had competition, I believe my exact words were: *turns out that Georgia is a magnet for the straight girls*. I guess the not-so-straight girls would actually be more accurate.

'What I'm saying is,' Natalie continues, 'if I was going to go lez it would be for someone like Georgia.'

'Well that is just lovely to hear, thank you.'

'No problem,' she says, now bored of this conversation that she started and scrolling through her Instagram.

I look down at my own phone and see that Georgia's messaged me.

> *Sorry to dash off, I'm on a tight schedule! I forgot how much you and Natalie look alike. Weird to see you with a pregnant doppelganger.*

I smile and glance at Natalie, trying to imagine myself in her shoes. I shudder.

When it's time for them to go home we trudge slowly back up the hill to the station. Comically slowly to the point where people have to walk in the road to get around us. I see them turn around to glare and then clock Natalie's bump and look away quickly, chastised. Very useful.

'So what are you up to tonight?' Natalie says.

'Oh, you know. Not much. You?'

'Yeah obviously nothing,' she says, 'what do you mean, not much? Why have you washed your hair then?'

'Well, I'm going to a gig.'

'Who with?'

'No one.'

Sort of true.

Natalie rolls her eyes, too hot and tired to mine me for juicy details.

When I wave goodbye to them at the station, I squeeze Natalie extra hard. I suddenly quite desperately don't want her to go.

'Ugh,' I say into her hair, which is extra glossy from all the baby hormones, 'you're all sweaty.'

'Yeah, you are too,' she says and kisses me on my cheek which I immediately wipe off. 'Hey, call Mum before you go away. And make sure you do what we talked about.'

'Yes ma'am,' I say and do a little salute. She glares at me.

'Bye babies,' I say to the twins and they willingly hug me this time, they don't even tell me they're not babies. They kiss me on the cheek with their ice-creamy lips and I want to just cling to them forever but they have to go, probably to be sick on the train. And ultimately, I know that I will be grateful not to be with them.

Before I walk home, while I'm still surrounded by people and buoyed by the energy of Natalie and the twins, I open What-sApp, click on the number Natalie sent me and message my dad.

Hi, it's Natasha. Linda gave me your number. She told us that you're living in California now and I'm going to be there next week with some friends. I'll be in Los Angeles. Is that near you? Mum suggested I contact you because maybe you'd want to meet up with me. Let me know.

I struggle with how to sign off. I type out *Love Natasha* and then simply *Natasha* but in the end I leave it blank. As soon as I've sent it I archive the chat so I don't have to look at it again and try to put it out of my mind altogether. Maybe he'll reply, maybe he won't. I've done my bit.

I find myself struggling to know what to wear to meet Margot. I root through Poppy's wardrobe but don't come up with anything I feel like myself in. I actually get to the point, sitting on the bed in my underwear surrounded by discarded clothes, where I'm dangerously close to frustrated tears and have to give myself a stern talking to. *I have lots of clothes, I look nice in them. She has seen me before. She knows what I look like.*

I eventually settle on faded black high-waisted Levi's, which I found in a vintage store about five years ago and have now worn to death, and a plain white T-shirt, which is just the right amount of cropped – I can just about tuck it into my jeans but if I lift my arms up it untucks itself showing a little bit of stomach. I wear trainers as always. I make an effort with my make-up, wanting it to be the perfect level of no-make-up make-up, as if I woke up with eyeliner that takes me a full forty minutes to perfect.

When I go into the kitchen to make myself a gin and tonic before I leave, some Dutch courage, Poppy whistles at me from the sofa where she is sitting with her laptop on her knee and Diane beside her. She's still working at 7 p.m. on a Saturday.

'You look great,' she says and smiles at me. She's wearing a satin short-sleeved pyjama top and shorts which have her initials on them from when her sister got married, as well as Winnie the Pooh socks pulled halfway up her shins. It's a look.

'Where are you off to looking all nice?' she says. 'Your eyeliner is fab, I can never get mine like that.'

'I'm going to Margot's gig, the person I was telling you about,' I say, opening the fridge hunting for tonic and pulling out a half-empty bottle of definitely flat tonic.

'Oh yes,' she says, wiggling her eyebrows at me. 'Your new girlfriend!"

'Not my girlfriend.' I say, holding up the bottles of gin and flat tonic at her, 'Want one?'

'Yes please,' she says and closes her laptop. 'Lots of lime.'

'Oh, did you buy limes?' I say, reopening the fridge to inspect it.

'No,' she says. I roll my eyes and close it again. I don't know why she thinks I'm some kind of magic bartender.

'What kind of music is it?' Poppy says. 'I haven't been to a gig in ages.'

'Um, not music,' I say. 'It's more like . . . comedy or like reading?'

'Oh!' Poppy says, 'how . . . interesting.'

'I know.' I grimace. 'I won't be staying long but I don't know, maybe it'll surprise me. Maybe it'll be great.'

I pass Poppy her gin and tonic, no lime, and then stand at the kitchen table and drink most of mine, heavy on the gin and light on the tonic, in a few swift gulps. I feel instantly calmer.

'I saw Georgia earlier,' I say.

'Oh yeah?'

'She seemed stressed.'

'That's weddings for you,' Poppy says.

I realise I never replied to Georgia's message from earlier. I get my phone out to send one now.

Good to see you! Hope you found the dead flowers of your dreams.

'What's your plan for tonight, Pops? You're not going to work all evening, are you?' I say, swiping my phone off and putting it in my back pocket.

She sighs and takes a sip of her drink.

'No, I'll do another hour or so and then Felix is coming to pick me up. I'm going to stay at his again tonight.'

'Are you guys OK?'

'Fine!' she says brightly in a way that suggests she really doesn't want to talk about it. I suspect she wishes she'd never told me about it. That there wasn't now a witness to their problems.

It's a beautiful evening to walk and I have plenty of time. I'm aiming for 'so late that it's already started' so I can creep in and stand at the back. As much as I've made a fuss about going, really I've been looking forward to witnessing Margot's words, how she expresses her thoughts and observations to an audience. I keep replaying her saying, *I've spent a lot of time thinking about you.* I want to know what she means. I can barely let myself think about how it would feel for her to talk about me this evening. Or how it would feel if she didn't.

I order myself a large glass of white wine with extra ice cubes when I get to the pub. It's quiet, a contrast to the garden and the street outside where everybody has taken their drinks, wanting to soak up the last few drops of evening sun. A couple of people head up some stairs at the back of the room and I follow them. It's darker up here, and hotter. As I'd hoped, it's already started. There's a sweaty man on stage speaking with one hand gripping the microphone still in its stand. He seems to have about half the audience's attention. He's animated, telling a story about visiting his mother. Groups of people are sitting around tables chatting among themselves but there's laughter too, he's working hard to win them over. I survey the room from the doorway and instead of trying to find somewhere to sit I turn right and walk along until I'm in the back corner of the room. I lean against the wall and take a sip of my wine. The ice has already melted.

The set-up isn't what I was expecting. The stage looks like the kind of thing we used for productions in secondary school, individual blocks that get put away afterwards. It's dark up here, the shutters closed on all but one of the windows. There are fairy lights strung all over the ceiling and with the only other lights coming from the small bar the effect is really quite magical. I peer along the wall where I'm standing and there are lots of other people here alone sipping their drinks and checking their phones. I wonder if they're about to be brave enough to bare their souls on stage or if they're just here to witness someone else doing it.

There's a brief pause when the sweaty man gets off stage (to rapt applause; even the people who weren't listening to him are cheering) and the room erupts into loud chatter. A few people get up and move around and I think about maybe getting another drink but then Margot steps up onto the platform and people start clapping and cheering. She puts her drink down, looks out at the audience and a hush descends across the room. I'm not surprised to learn that with no introduction and without saying anything she can all but silence a room. I feel invisible in my dark corner but she looks up as she adjusts the microphone stand and smiles right at me as if she knew exactly where I'd be.

She's wearing a plain black T-shirt with the sleeves rolled up and black skinny jeans. She's not wearing any jewellery and her hair is tied back. I wonder if she always wears this on stage, like a uniform.

'Hello everyone,' she says in an exaggerated husky voice very close to the microphone. A gentle ripple of laughter flows through the audience. She smiles as easily as if she's speaking to a group of friends at a dinner party. 'Thank you for coming and sitting in this furnace on such a beautiful evening, I really appreciate it.'

There's a smattering of applause and a couple of whoops in the audience.

'Today I'm trying something new.'

Someone in the audience whistles and she raises her eyebrows and gives a knowing look to the laughing crowd.

'Well, trying something new is a really nice way to put it. I've been trying all week to work on new material for tonight since that's,' she waves her hand around the room, gesturing at all the other people there who are going to perform, 'the whole point of the evening. But I . . .'

She shakes her head, takes a sip of her beer and then changes track.

'OK, so I've been writing a novel. It's about a plucky young Kiwi who moves to the UK with nothing but the clothes on her back and a dream. By day she serves people overpriced coffee and by night she wows crowds with her razor-sharp wit and expert command of the English language. I have . . .' she pauses and takes another sip from the bottle of beer, 'a wild imagination.'

I smile at her, although she's no longer looking at me. I said that to her the first time we went out for a drink.

'The problem is,' she says, pausing for effect, 'that I'm stuck.'

She looks directly at me now and I feel all the blood in my body rush to my face. I'm momentarily unable to hear anything other than the sound of my own heart beating alarmingly fast, like a hammer in my ears. I feel certain everyone in the room is going to spin around and look at me, but of course they don't.

'I thought, this plucky young Kiwi needs someone to speak to. To talk about what's going on with her, to try and figure out why she's so fucked up. So I thought, she needs a therapist, right?'

She throws the question out to the audience and everyone is so totally enthralled with her that there are nods all around the room. She takes another sip of her drink.

'She needs a therapist. So I thought, fine, I'll do my due diligence, I'll go and see what it's all about so I go to this course to learn about it and you know what I've done? Instead of writing a therapist into my book, I've started dating a therapist.'

The audience laughs and I resist the urge to cover my face with my hands. I put my empty glass down on the ledge behind me and fold my arms over my chest instead. Trying to somehow shield myself from my own embarrassment.

'Great for inspiration, you'd think? Perfect! So much material there. Just a few minutes of new material. That's all I needed. But ...' Margot shakes her head to herself almost. She's unrehearsed. She's speaking off the cuff. She's relaxed up there though, just having a conversation with this room full of people.

'It's like I've hit a brick wall.' She holds her hand up in front of her as if pushing against something and then puts it back down again, playing instead with the foil around the top of her beer bottle.

'I don't know what's wrong with me. I mean usually ... usually I can mine an experience, you know? I'll mine it for the absolute truth of it, the absolute heart of it, and then I'll use that later. I'll put it away to write a joke or a story and then tell you all about it in some way or another. But this week I guess I've been struggling to find the truth of this experience. Of this person maybe. So what I'm trying to say is: I'm sorry guys, I haven't done my homework because I've got a crush on a girl.'

She laughs and throws her hands up in the air and everyone laughs with her.

'How pathetic is that?' she says.

She tips up the bottle of her drink and finishes it. Before she puts it down she holds it up in my direction and says, 'Same again please.' She grins.

I'm certain then that people are going to turn around and look at me then but they don't. They assume she's talking to a friend or a manager or one of the bar staff. I stay exactly where I am, not wanting to draw any attention to myself.

'So basically,' she says, 'I was going to read you a funny extract from my novel but, as yet, there isn't one, and then I was going to try out some new jokes, say about, oh I don't know . . . dating a therapist? But as yet, there are none so instead I'm here just treating this like . . . oh fuck . . . I mean I guess . . . is this therapy, guys? I mean, I'm just looking for someone to tell me I'm doing OK?'

Everyone laughs and she says, 'Love me' quietly into the microphone, which makes everyone laugh even harder.

A man in the audience shouts, 'I love you,' back at her and without hesitation she leans forward and says, 'Dad?' into the microphone.

She lifts her empty bottle up again to the audience and my heart sinks but this time she just says, 'Cheers guys, I'm sorry for being so shit. I love you all. I'll see you next time with a broken heart and loads of jokes about it, I swear.'

She hops down off the platform to rapturous applause and is immediately surrounded by a group of people wanting to talk to her. I walk to the bar and order her beer and another glass of wine for me. When I get out my card I realise my hands are shaking from the adrenaline. I don't know what I expected, for her to pull me up on stage or something like it was a pantomime.

There's no sign of Margot once I've got the drinks so I go back to my corner to lurk. I put them down and get my phone out.

I open Instagram and see a photo of Zara at the top of my feed. She's sitting cross-legged on the floor wearing one of Georgia's hoodies and she's surrounded by wedding planning paraphernalia including bags and bags of confetti. Georgia's captioned it, 'Is this my life now?' With the monkey with his head in his hands emoji. I double tap the photo. I don't know why. She hasn't replied to my message. I guess they found the dead flowers they always dreamed of.

I'm aware of a presence next to me and I look up to see Margot leaning against the wall next to me. She's grinning.

'Right,' she says, 'so I almost told you not to come.'

'Why?' I pass her the beer and she takes a sip from it straight away.

'Thank you. Erm, because.' She gestures towards the stage. 'Because that was *shocking*. Thank God people didn't pay to be here.'

'It wasn't shocking. I mean, I get that maybe you weren't as prepared as you wanted to be but it didn't matter.'

'It does matter,' she says. 'But thanks. Listen, let's get out of here, I'm desperate for a cigarette and it's so fucking hot.'

I nod and grab my drink. We're just about to make our way out when she turns back to me.

'You look good.'

'Oh,' I say, shaking my head automatically at the compliment. 'Thanks, I just . . .' I'm about to say 'threw it on' but there's nothing like using that phrase to confirm you actually spent a lot of time on your outfit.

'Really good.' She reaches out and takes my hand to lead me downstairs.

The beer garden is rammed so we end up just standing outside the front of the pub. I lean against the wall and Margot stands in front of me. It means that every time she wants her drink which we've set down on the ledge behind me, she has to reach over me.

'I don't know how you do it,' I say to her as she hands me her cigarette to hold while she pats herself down for a lighter.

She finds it in the back pocket of her jeans, lights her cigarette and inhales deeply, blowing the smoke up to the sky away from me.

'It's really not that special,' she says, 'once you get used to it, it's easy.'

I shake my head.

'Easy for someone like you maybe.'

'What's someone like me?'

'You don't mind sitting in discomfort. Yours. Someone else's. An entire room of people's.'

Margot nods and reaches over me to get her drink.

'No one's ever put it like that before.'

'So . . .' I smile at her, suddenly feeling weirdly shy, 'you're dating a therapist?'

She smiles back at me.

'You wouldn't call this dating?'

'I don't know. I hadn't thought about it.'

She shakes her head at me, wide-eyed.

'This is why I can't get any work done.'

'What? Because of me?'

'Because you keep me guessing. I'm so busy trying to figure you out I haven't got time to do anything else.'

I laugh and she hesitates but then she laughs too. If only you knew, I think to myself, if only you knew how I feel when I see you.

I take a sip of my wine.

'I'm here, aren't I?'

'You're here. That's true.'

She reaches over me again to stub out her cigarette. It's busy outside the pub and everyone's shouting. I think a lot of people will have been drinking since lunchtime and are now very dehydrated and potentially suffering from heatstroke. There are some very red faces.

'Do you want to go?' I say.

Margot looks at me, surprised.

'OK, like . . . somewhere else or home?'

'Home. I mean, sorry,' I can't help but laugh seeing her face fall, 'my home. Do you want to come and have a drink at mine instead? Poppy's out.'

'Ah, so you can sneak me in?'

'I thought you'd be happy that we'll have the place to ourselves.'

'I am. I am. Come on, let's go,' she says, downing the rest of her drink and grabbing my hand, 'before you change your mind.'

I'm relieved to find when we get back to Poppy's flat that she's taken Diane with her.

'No dog?' Margot says, disappointed, as she takes off her shoes.

'Sorry, but you're not really missing much. She wouldn't like you.'

'Everyone likes me.'

'OK, but not Diane. She's very particular.'

I open the fridge and peer into it while Margot sits down on the sofa, she kicks her feet up making herself comfortable. It's a thrill having her here, being alone with her.

'So the only thing in here to drink is some flat tonic. Do you want a gin and quite flat tonic?'

'That is literally what I was going to ask for.'

'Perfect.'

Margot is on her phone, frowning slightly at the screen and typing furiously.

'Are you hungry?' I say as I pour gin into tumblers. I realise I haven't eaten since my ice cream earlier.

'Um, sure. I could eat.'

Margot stares for a moment longer at her phone and then switches it off and puts it face down on the side table next to her. She looks up and smiles at me.

'I can offer you crisps for dinner?'

'That would be great.'

'Ooh,' I say, opening the fridge again, inspiration suddenly striking, 'and hummus which,' I lift the lid off the pot and sniff it, 'smells totally fine.'

'That's perfect.'

I turn around to look at her.

'Really?'

'Really. Honestly. Hummus that smells totally fine is my favourite.'

I go and sit down at the end of the sofa her feet are on and she shifts them up slightly for me.

'So,' I say, taking a crisp from the bag, 'is it true that you're stuck on your novel?'

'Completely stuck.'

She reaches forward and I pass the bag of crisps to her.

'The research,' she gestures at me, 'kind of took an unexpected turn.'

'Sorry.'

'It's fine, I mean … I could always like, read a book or something.'

'I can send you a reading list if you want,' I say.

She bursts out laughing.

'Sure. Thanks.'

'Can I read what you've already got?' I say, already knowing what the answer will be as she picks up her gin and tonic.

'No, absolutely not.'

'Maybe when it's finished?'

'Maybe.'

'I didn't have you down as the type to be shy about your work.'

Margot rolls her eyes at me and kicks me gently on the shin with her foot. She leaves it there, resting gently against my leg, and it feels like all the blood in my body rushes to that exact spot

'I'm not shy,' she says. 'I'm particular. I want it to be perfect.'

'I get that.'

'Tonight was a very bad example.'

I look down at her foot, her toenails are painted red but they're chipped and smudged. It looks like they might have been done weeks ago and not attended to since.

Margot puts her drink down and picks up a framed photograph from the table. It's a picture of Poppy, Georgia and me from a few years ago at one of Poppy's birthday parties. It was long before Georgia and I ever got together.

'You look so young,' Margot says, peering closely at the photo.

'I was so young.'

'Is one of these girls Georgia?' She points and I lean over to get a better look, I don't know why. I know that Georgia's in the photo.

'That's her.'

'Pretty.'

'Yep. She doesn't look like that now.'

'What, she's not pretty?'

'Oh no she is, she just,' I lift my hand up and touch the ends of my hair, 'her hair's shorter now. I don't know. We all look different now.'

'What's going on with that? Are things OK with you guys since she got engaged?'

'Oh yeah,' I say, still looking at the photo instead of at her. 'I mean, I'm literally going on holiday with them next week so . . .'

'Oh god yeah,' she says. 'Why?'

At first I'm at a loss as to how to answer the question. I take a sip of my drink.

'I . . . well . . . because it's been booked for ages. It's sort of my birthday present. I told you that.'

'I suppose I mean, why do you want to go? *Do* you even want to go?'

'I do want to go,' I say. 'Yes, I do want to go.'

She cocks her head to one side and sits up a bit, her foot no longer resting on my thigh.

'You really want to go on holiday with your ex-girlfriend and her fiancée?'

'Um, yes.'

Margot frowns slightly.

'Why? Honestly. I'm not trying to be difficult. I just don't get it.'

'Georgia's not just my ex-girlfriend, she's my friend. She's been my friend way longer than she was my . . .'

'But doesn't seeing them together make you feel like shit?' Margot interrupts. 'Didn't it bother you so much when they got engaged? Doesn't Zara hate you?'

'I'm not sure she . . . hate's a bit strong . . .'

'I'm just trying to work out what you get out of it.'

'I get . . . it's, it's a hard dynamic to explain. Poppy's going as well and Felix and Josh, it's not like I'm going as their third wheel.'

'Can I tell you what I think?' Margot says.

220

'Please.' I take a large sip of my gin, not actually particularly sure that I want to hear what she thinks.

'I think there's a part of you that likes to rub salt in the wound. You strike me as someone who punishes yourself.'

I don't say anything for a moment, taking in her assessment. Somewhere deep in the recesses of my brain I can acknowledge that she's right in many ways. It rings true even if it does sting a bit. If I was advising someone else who'd reacted the way I did to their ex getting engaged I would probably not encourage them to take a long-haul holiday together. However, I really don't want to engage in any kind of self-analysis tonight. Especially not with her.

'I think I just want a nice holiday in the sun.'

Margot smiles. She looks almost disappointed but she doesn't push it.

'And there's that.'

Over the course of the night we inch closer and closer together. At one point after much cajoling, Margot brings me a black Moleskine notebook from her backpack filled with her writing. She allows me to read a single poem. It's short, only a few lines, and it's about the promise of evenings in summertime. She wrote it last week.

'Oh,' I say, 'this is beautiful.' I trace my finger over the dent of the pen on the page as I re-read it.

'You sound surprised,' she says. She's sitting next to me, leaning over my shoulder looking at the notebook. She's so close I can feel her breath on my ear. I can barely think straight.

'I am a bit surprised. Not that you can write beautiful things. More that it's very earnest, which isn't the first thing I think of when I think of you.'

'I can be sincere.'

She pulls back from leaning over my shoulder and I turn to face her.

'I guess I just mean that you're hard to read, that's all. You have a wall up.'

I'm relieved when she breaks into a smile.

'Oh please,' she says. 'You can talk.'

I smile back at her and she reaches out to pull my head towards her and kisses me. She tastes like cigarette smoke which I normally hate but for some reason I love it on her. We kiss for a few minutes like teenagers, her hand in my hair, mine on her back reaching under her T-shirt to touch her bare skin. We kiss like that's all there is. Like kissing is the end.

Eventually Margot pulls away from me and says, 'I want to see your room.'

I pull her back to me.

'Poppy's gone all night, it's fine.'

'No. I want to see it!'

I roll my eyes but get up and pull her up with me and lead her away and into my small bedroom that still doesn't quite feel like my own.

I walk through in front of her and switch on the lamp by my bed. I open my window just in case there's a chance of a breeze and draw the curtains. Margot closes the door behind her.

'So this is . . .' I start to say but before I can finish speaking Margot crosses the room, pushes me up against the wall and kisses me again, harder this time. I run my hands over her body, down her spine, the gentle curves of her hips and her thighs, my fingers lingering at the hem of her shorts. She pulls back and lifts my top over my head and with one hand reaches behind me and unhooks my bra. She drops it to the floor and for a moment stands back and looks at me, taking me in. In other circumstances I might be embarrassed but, because it's her and because I've had so much to drink, it feels good to be looked at and seen and appreciated.

We remove the rest of our clothes quickly and she moves us over to the bed, pushing me back so my head is just underneath my pillow. I think she's going to kiss me again but instead she moves down my body, she kisses my stomach, the inside of my thighs and then I feel her tongue moving against me.

I hear myself say, 'Oh fuck' out loud but it's like an out-of-body experience. I push myself against her and, just when I think I can't take it anymore, I feel her push her fingers inside me and for a moment it's like everything goes black. When I re-enter my own body she's looking at me; of course she's an eye contact person. I wonder if she's ever felt self-conscious in her life. I pull her head up so I can kiss her and then shift my body, gently pushing her off me and onto the bed.

She lies down on her side and I nudge her so she rolls over onto her front. Her hair has nearly come out of the hair tie, I tug it gently to remove it completely and she makes a noise that makes me wrap the bottom of her hair around my fingers and tug it again, a little harder this time.

Her back is one place where she doesn't have any tattoos. It's still a blank canvas aside from a smattering of freckles across her shoulders. I trace my finger along her freckles and down her spine, landing in the dip at the bottom of her back. I lean down and kiss it gently. She turns around onto her back again and I stay where I am, kissing her stomach, her hips, she pushes my head down impatiently. She holds my head the entire time, manoeuvring me, directing me. Always needing to be in control until the last moment when she finally lets go of me and she moves her hands to her face instead, covering her eyes as if it would mean I somehow couldn't see her unravel.

Afterwards she gently pulls me up and, for a moment, I take her in before shifting over so I'm lying beside her. She pushes my hair back from my face tenderly.

'Your room's really nice,' she says and I burst out laughing.

'Thank you.'

She leans forward to kiss me.

'Am I staying?' she says quietly, her mouth so close to mine I can feel her lips vibrating.

'Yes,' I whisper. I stop and look at her for a moment.

'What?'

'I'm just taking you in.'

She smiles broadly.

'Have you gone all soppy? Is that all I needed to do to break down that wall?'

I laugh and she pulls me closer to her. I wrap my arms around her neck.

'Well now I know, I'll never stop.'

'You might have to stop sometimes,' I say as she kisses my neck, her hands travelling down my back, her leg pushing between my thighs.

'Why?'

'I'm going away, aren't I?'

'When's that?'

'Wednesday.'

'So I might not see you until you get back?'

'Probably not, no.'

'Ugh,' she groans, 'don't talk about it. As far as I'm concerned we're staying here in this bed forever.'

'OK,' I say.

'OK we'll stay here forever?'

I kiss her gently.

'OK, I won't talk about it.'

I have the kind of restless night where I can't quite tell when I'm awake or asleep but I'm aware at some point, very early in the morning, of Margot kissing me and telling me she has to go. I rub my eyes and shift to sit up but she pushes me back down gently and tells me to stay asleep, it's early.

'I'll see you soon,' she whispers and the next time I open my eyes the sun is streaming in through the curtains and one side of my bed is cold as though she'd never really been there at all.

8

We are flying premium economy to LA. I've never flown premium economy before so to me this is actually a first-class experience. Before we even take off I have a glass of prosecco in my hand and all future flights are ruined for me forever. How will I ever sit in regular economy again when I have known the pleasure of stretching out my legs and getting drunk while the safety video is showing?

I'm seated next to Josh, we're on our own in a row of two and I'm by the window. Zara and Georgia are sitting in front of us and Felix and Poppy behind. Even though he can be annoying I can't help but feel that Josh and I are probably going to have the most fun on this flight, him always being as up for excessive drinking and gossiping as I am. Zara and Georgia seem flat somehow, falling asleep into their Pret coffees as if we're flying in the middle of the night and not at three o'clock in the afternoon. They're tired, they say. From having a lot on at work and from wedding planning. It seems to me they were much happier before they decided to throw a lavish party celebrating their happiness but I'm not sure when or if there will be a good time to make that observation.

Poppy and Felix are the opposite of flat, they're on edge, bordering on manic. They've been tapping and twitching and snapping at each other all morning to the point where I consider asking them if they've taken something. It seems that each other's company is the main thing stressing them out. Absolutely ideal for an eleven-hour flight.

'We can all swap seats once we've taken off, can't we?' Poppy says when we get on the plane. 'We don't have to stay in our assigned seats for the entire flight?'

Zara and Georgia don't say anything, too consumed by whatever conversation they're having about what's packed in each suitcase.

'Of course,' I say. 'That's fine, isn't it Josh? We'll all swap. It's fine.'

She looks relieved as she slides into her window seat.

Once we've taken our shoes off, tucked ourselves up under blankets and accepted a top-up of fizz, Josh remembers an email he has to send urgently before we take off.

'Sorry, I'll be back in holiday mode in two secs but I'll be actually fired if I don't send this.'

'Please, do whatever you need to do. I am in my happy place.'

I pick up the in-flight magazine but end up just staring at the first page. I've already put my phone away telling myself it will be good for me to go a few hours without it. I've sent my good-bye messages to Natalie and my mum and switched into airplane mode. But more than anything in the world I want to message Margot. I just want to see what she's doing while I'm doing this. I want to tell her how ridiculous it is. I want her to laugh at me for going on this couples' holiday alone, well, with my ex-girlfriend's baby brother. I flick my phone back off airplane mode. Messages rush in from Natalie and my mum and then, almost as if I'd known it was there, one from Margot.

Safe travels. Don't do anything I wouldn't do.

And then in a second message right below it:

I miss you already.

My heart leaps.

Thanks. Just about to take off. I'll keep you in the loop about all my wild adventures.

I can't bring myself to tell her that I miss her already.

I'll let you know when I land.

Oh god. Somehow that's even worse. More intense. Is she someone I have to tell when I land?

Just as I'm about to switch off my phone again, ready to sink into a solid few hours of obsessing about that message, another one flashes up on WhatsApp from a number I don't recognise. A number I haven't been able to bring myself to save in my phone.

Natasha, I'm sorry it has taken such a long time to respond. I didn't know what to say. I'm absolutely amazed that you got in touch. And thrilled. And in shock I think. I'm surprised that you want to see me but of course I want to see you. I will come to wherever you are. Just name a time and a place. I think about you all the time. And about Natalie. And believe it or not, about your mum. I really do hope to see you soon. Dad.

I stare at the message for a long time, reading and re-reading until I'm interrupted by Josh saying,

'Phew, finally finished. Holiday mode back *on*.'

I turn to him and smile. I forward the message to Natalie and flip my phone back onto airplane mode. I'll deal with that after a few more glasses of free booze.

Six hours into the flight Josh and I have drunk at least a bottle of Sauvignon Blanc each, eaten every single snack they've brought around (including, at a low point, just dry bread rolls), watched *Moana* together and cried copiously.

'Fucking hell,' Josh says, wiping his eyes. 'We just like . . . we have to respect the earth.'

I nod, dabbing my nose with a tissue and then applying my new plane-issued lip balm.

'A hundred per cent.' I say, 'It's just . . . we can't just take, take, take, you know?'

Josh shakes his head and unwraps a mini Mars Bar that they handed out earlier.

'You've got to be true to yourself,' he says.

'Ugh yes,' I say. 'Follow your heart.'

A face appears in between the seats in front of us. Georgia has a sleep mask pushed up on top of her head and is rubbing her eyes.

'What are you two idiots up to?'

'Um, learning,' I say, indignantly. 'About the *planet*.'

'Were you watching *Moana*?' Georgia says.

'Yes.'

'Josh, swap with me a minute, I want to talk to Natasha.' Georgia gets up, she is wrapped in her blanket like it's a towel tucked under her arms with her hoodie on underneath. The air con is unnecessarily aggressive.

'No,' Josh whines, wriggling down in his seat. 'I'm so comfy. I can't be bothered to get up.'

'You should get up,' she says and tries to drag him up by his arm. 'You'll get DVT. Have you even gone to the loo once? I swear you've been drinking non-stop.'

'Ughhhh,' he snatches his arm away but gets up, a shower of crumbs falling off him and onto the floor. He shuffles his feet into his new plane slippers and slips out and off towards the toilet at the front of the cabin.

George slides into the seat next to me, faces towards me and leans her head against the back of the seat, briefly closing her eyes.

'Are you not even going to try and get any sleep?' she says.

'I'm not tired,' I say, shifting so I'm facing her too, 'and what even is the time? I just feel like if I can stay awake until whenever bedtime is in LA I'll be fine. What time do we land?'

'Seven p.m.'

'See? That's fine. Just enough time for a house tour, food and bed. I'll be completely adjusted by first thing tomorrow morning. That's just science.'

I tap the side of my head. I'm only half joking. I do sort of believe I can beat jet lag and even, on some level, that jet lag is just a myth.

'I know you think jet lag is just a myth,' Georgia says, taking a sip from Josh's mini bottle of water, 'but that's just because you haven't done a long-haul flight since you were a teenager.'

'Um, OK, well I don't think my body has changed *that* much since I went to Thailand . . .'

I distinctly remember stepping off the plane with my group of friends the summer after sixth form, heading straight to a bar and feeling absolutely fine.

Georgia laughs in my face.

'Shut up. It hasn't. I'm as young and fit as ever. My body is a temple.'

'OK, you seem like you might be *quite* drunk right now, though . . .'

I reach into the bag at my feet and pull out a Pret mango and lime pot to wave at her.

'Oh shit yeah, sorry. I didn't realise you had some uneaten fruit in your bag.'

'Well yeah, I do. So there. I'm the picture of health, thank you very much.'

She laughs again and I can't help but smile. She's so annoying.

'Why did you kick Josh out of his seat then?' I say, nudging her leg with my foot. 'What's this urgent plane chat we have to have?'

'I want to know if you organised going to see your dad.'

'Right.'

'Why? What did you think it was going to be?'

'I was hoping this was going to be about joining the mile high club.'

'Shut *up*.'

She slaps my leg but I can't feel anything through the many layers of joggers and blanket.

'What? Zara's asleep, isn't she?'

'You're bad.'

She tries to look serious but she's still smiling at me.

'Sorry.'

'So, are you going to?'

'Join it?'

'Natty.'

'Yeah, probably. He just messaged me before we took off.'

Her face lights up.

'That's amazing news!'

'Yeah I don't know, is it?'

She frowns slightly, not quite able to read my mood.

'Yes,' she says, 'of course it is.'

'We'll see. I mean, we'll see if he even shows up or if he bails on me, or if he's nice. We don't know what he's like now, do we?'

Georgia is quiet for a moment.

'No, I guess we don't. But I know what you're like. And if he's anything like you then he's going to be great.'

'I hope we're nothing alike,' I say quickly.

'No, well. I didn't mean . . .'

'It's OK. I know. I know what you mean.'

I suddenly feel exhausted and a bit sick. I have no idea when I last drank any water.

A head pops through the seat behind us.

'What are we talking about, girls?' Poppy has her glasses on and the hood up on her special 'flight pyjamas'. A cream, fleece tracksuit she bought especially for the occasion.

'Got any water?' I say.

She disappears for a moment and then reappears with an enormous reusable water bottle. It weighs a tonne.

'Oh my god thank you,' I say as she manoeuvres it through the gap, 'you're an angel.'

'Keep it, I bought six litres.'

'Six litres?' Georgia says. 'Why? They serve water on the plane!'

'You have to keep hydrated! Flying's so terrible for you and of course . . .'

'For the planet,' I say. 'Yes we know.'

'I'm so bored,' she says. 'Felix has been asleep since we took off.'

'We'll be there soon,' I say.

'Georgie, swap with me. I want to sit next to Natasha.'

'No!' Georgia says. 'I don't want to go back to my seat. Zara's snoring.'

'Don't fight over sitting next to me, I just want you both to be quiet so I can watch *Up* and cry for two hours.'

We all end up putting *Up* on at exactly the same time so we can cry together but when I turn to Georgia after the first ten minutes she's fallen asleep. I peer through the gap behind me and Poppy is leaning on Felix's shoulder, her eyes closed.

I stay awake and watch it by myself but eventually I drift off, just in time for our descent.

Georgia's uncle's house is only a thirty-minute drive away from the airport. Georgia has hired a huge car to ferry us all around in. It's a big white 4x4 with extra room in the back where, surprise, surprise, Josh and I end up sitting with everyone's luggage piled up all around us and squashed onto our knees.

'Are you sure you can drive this, George?' I say from underneath a pile of suitcases. 'It's like a bus.'

'Yes I can drive it,' Georgia snaps into the windscreen mirror at me. 'I've been here before, remember?'

'Of course you can drive it, baby,' Zara says soothingly and pats her on the knee. Zara's just finished applying moisturiser and she looks annoyingly well rested. I have felt like something died in my mouth since the last meal I ate which I believe was some kind of breakfast/dinner hybrid involving egg and potato. It was disgusting even if it was served with actual cutlery. I ate the lot.

We all stay silent until Georgia manages to negotiate getting us out of LAX and onto the freeway, which is tense to say the least but once we're on the move she relaxes and so we all do. She puts the radio on and turns it up high, it's some country music station, and we all gaze out of the window at the pink skies as the sun goes down. Poppy turns around and squeezes my leg. I think she's going to say something but she doesn't, she just smiles at me and then turns back around and rests her head against the window.

We make it to Uncle Simon's house in what Josh declares is 'record time' and we stumble out of the car and onto the driveway which is behind a gate with a keycode. I've seen photos of the house before from when Georgia's visited but they don't do it justice. It's all on one level, I hesitate to say it's a bungalow because that's what my nan lives in and this could not be further from my nan's house. It's not big but it has three bedrooms and enough living space for us all to throw ourselves down into various chairs the moment we get through the door. Everything is painted white and the walls are covered in framed photographs. I squint at the one nearest me and Georgia as a toddler grins back at me, a saucepan on her head.

'Quickly, I know everyone's shattered but you've got to come and see this,' Georgia says and opens the sliding door off the living room and onto a patio. She gestures for us all to follow her out and we all groan and do as we're told. There's a long wooden table in the middle of the patio that looks handmade, but in a good way. The tiles on the ground are all mismatched, bright colours, and there are potted plants everywhere. There's the faint sound of music and chattering from a nearby house. Georgia bends down and flicks a switch which makes a string of bulbs light up above our heads. We all ooh and aah and then laugh at ourselves but really, it feels quite magical.

'Si's left us some wine, Georgia,' Josh calls from the kitchen, his head inside the fridge. And on hearing that, we all shuffle back inside.

'It's such a shame he won't be here,' Georgia says, taking the bottle of white wine from Josh and pulling a drawer open to find a corkscrew. 'Although, there wouldn't be room, would there?'

I look around at the group and, as the possible sleeping arrangements dawn on me, a ball of panic swells in my chest.

'Um, George . . . did you say there are three bedrooms?'

'Mmm-hmm,' she says, concentrating on getting the cork out of the bottle. 'I'll show you all round the place in a minute, I just wanted to do a quick toast to celebrate us being here if I can get this bastard cork out.'

'Right so, that's one for you and Zara, one for Poppy and Felix and then . . .'

Josh winks at me from the kitchen, his hand inside a bag of peanut-butter-filled pretzels, another gift from Simon.

'You and me baby,' he says.

Georgia finally pops the cork and swings around to whack him in the stomach all in one swift move.

'No, not you and her *baby*,' she says, silently passing the bottle to Zara who is on pouring duty. 'Natasha, you have a bedroom all to yourself. Josh, you're *obviously* on the couch.'

'Fuck off,' he says. 'You're kidding? Come on.' He looks at her pleadingly, a pretzel in his hand still, suspended in front of his mouth. 'But,' he looks around, 'there aren't even any blinds in here. Is there even any spare bedding?'

'You chose to gate-crash my trip, so all the beds are taken by people who were *invited*,' Georgia says. She passes a glass of wine to Poppy who jabs Felix in the side to wake him up. They both look like zombies.

Josh changes tack, turning to me instead.

'Natasha. Come on. The bed is huge. We can share a bed, can't we? We're practically family.'

I look up at Zara in the kitchen to see that she is glaring at Josh. Georgia doesn't seem to notice.

'Come on please,' he kneels down in front of me and hands me the pretzel he was about to eat. 'Come on. No funny business.'

I burst out laughing.

'Obviously no funny business.'

'Ouch!' he says, getting back up and perching on the edge of my chair instead.

I groan.

'Fine. Fine!'

'Natasha, no,' Georgia says from the kitchen as if I've just volunteered to go to battle on the front line.

'It's fine,' I say. 'I literally don't even care at this point. I'm so tired. I want to drink this and go to bed and I don't care if Josh is there or not.'

'Yes!'

Josh holds out his hand to high five me. He's all sticky.

'Right,' Zara says, her lips are pursed. 'Are we doing this toast so we can all go to bed?'

By the looks of it she hears herself, how irritated and uptight she sounds, and she smiles, shaking her head a bit. She reaches out for Georgia's hand, Georgia takes hers and kisses it.

'Yes!' Poppy says. 'Let's toast and get to bed.'

We all lift up our glasses.

'To being here all together,' Georgia says.

'And to you,' Zara says, 'happy birthday again.'

'Happy birthday,' we all say.

Just as we're all about to drink, Georgia says, 'And to Natasha! Happy birthday to you too.'

There's a brief pause and then Zara says, 'Of course. And to Natasha.'

I smile at her in what I hope is a gracious way but she looks away. We all finally drink the tiny glasses of wine and hug each other goodnight.

Thankfully the bed that Josh and I are sharing is enormous. One of those ones you get in a hotel room where you can't even feel the other person move. Josh agrees that he will sleep with a T-shirt and boxers on at all times even if he starts to boil to death.

'Fair,' he says.

We both scroll through our phones in bed despite unpacking

books onto our bedside tables. We each have a beautiful, brand-new hardback with an unbent spine. I am full of the best intentions. I really will open it.

I'm too tired to be properly annoyed about sharing a bed with Josh but there's something about it in the back of my head that's bothering me. I'm agitated. It doesn't sit right but that's not Josh's fault. It's my fault for being on a couples' holiday. I can't tell if I'm annoyed at myself or annoyed with Georgia or whether it's a bit of both.

It's 10 p.m. LA time which means it's 6 a.m. in the UK. On autopilot I go to check my work emails but stop myself. My out-of-office is on for you as much as my clients, I tell myself, parroting the same lines I give to them when they tell me they worked a full eight hours a day on their beach holidays. I've set a boundary and now I have to respect the boundary.

Margot's voice pops into my head.

You love boundaries.

I've already sent Mum and Natalie a message telling them that I'm still alive but I couldn't quite bring myself to send the same thing to Margot. I open WhatsApp.

> *Guess who I'm sharing a bed with? I'll give you a clue.*
> *Different from my usual type.*

She reads it immediately which is very satisfying.

> *Oh my god. Not the brother.*

The brother!

Jesus. Well, happy birthday to you? I wish I was there.

I hesitate a moment.

I do too.

Even though I obviously don't. I mean, I wish she was here in this bed with me, but not on this trip. I can't even imagine what that would look like.

I flick over onto Instagram and like a selfie that Natalie's posted. She's got her hair in a mermaid plait. She was just born knowing how to do them. I like a photo of Charlie's too. They're away for the weekend in one of those shepherd's huts that looks great on Instagram but in reality smells like the chemical toilet that's one foot away from the bed. We haven't really spoken much still and I feel a pang of guilt. I hope the 'like' conveys much more.

I go into my archived chats in WhatsApp and, before I can change my mind, I reply to my dad.

OK yes, let's do it. Just let me know a time and place. I'm in LA for the next 4 days. N.

Josh yawns and switches off the light on his side of the bed. He rolls over onto his side, right on the edge of the bed, facing away from me. I'm pleased to see that there's at least three feet between us.

'Get off your bloody phone,' he mumbles, already half asleep. 'We've been awake for like . . . thirty hours.'

I am about to protest, given he's literally only just stopped staring at his own phone, but I'm too sleepy and I know he's right.

'I know,' I say, putting it down on my bedside table, looking briefly at my unopened book and then mentally agreeing with myself that I'll pick it up tomorrow. I'll finish it tomorrow even. I'll probably race through it. 'Night, Josh.'

He's already asleep. My ex-girlfriend's little brother gently snoring beside me. Perfect.

I only manage to sleep for a couple of hours at a time throughout the night, my brain jolting me awake at random intervals which means that when I do eventually get up, bleary-eyed and desperate for caffeine, I am in a total fog of sleep deprivation and what I have to begrudgingly admit may very well be jet lag.

Georgia is very kind to me when I walk into the kitchen like a zombie. She doesn't gloat about being right, she just brings me a bottle of kombucha.

I take a sip and nearly spit it out.

'Where did you get this?'

'Um, the shop?' Zara says, smiling up at me from the sofa like I am very slow.

'When did you go to the shop?'

'Some of us have been up since seven,' she says.

'It tastes like vinegar,' I say, squinting at the bottle. It spuriously claims to be 'peach flavour'.

'It's good for you,' Georgia says. She's gone to lie down on the sofa with her feet up on Zara. They're both on their phones.

'Yes,' Zara says, looking up at me again, 'and it cost, like, ten dollars, so if you don't want it I'll have it.'

'No, I want it,' I say, clutching my peach vinegar to my chest. 'I'll take anything that's going to make me feel better. Where are the others?' I say. 'Josh was gone when I woke up.'

'Oh god,' Georgia says. 'I can't believe you're sharing a bed with him. I'm so sorry.'

'It's fine, honestly. I didn't even know he was there.'

'He went out for a walk ages ago, he's probably getting a coffee or something. Poppy and Felix haven't woken up yet. In fact . . .'

Georgia looks down at her Apple watch.

'They probably should get up soon, it's midday. They'll feel like shit if they don't try and get in the right time zone.'

'I'll get them,' I say. I get up to go and then remember my kombucha, pointedly taking it with me to show how grateful I am.

I knock gently on Poppy and Felix's door and then push it open and peer in, prepared to snap my eyes shut in case I see something I don't want to.

There's a stream of light coming through the bottom of the blinds where they haven't closed them properly but Poppy and Felix both have sleeping masks on. I pause for a moment before going to wake Poppy. They're both sleeping curled up on their sides facing each other. They're close. So close they must be able to feel each other's breath.

I creep in and walk over to Poppy's side of the bed and gently touch her shoulder. She stirs slightly.

'Pops, it's time to wake up. George says you'll feel like shit if you don't get up now.'

She grimaces and pushes her mask up over her eyes, squinting at the light. She looks up at me, frowning as if trying to place me.

'No,' she says eventually and turns away from me.

'Yes,' I say. 'Felix,' I say louder, 'you have to wake up.'

He responds by shuffling down the bed and pulling the duvet up over his head.

'Guys!'

I walk over to the blinds and open them and they both groan but Poppy sits up in bed, rubbing her eyes. I perch on the end and take a sip of my kombucha and shudder.

Poppy reaches out for it and takes a sip.

'Keep it,' I say.

She nods.

'I think we're going to go to the beach,' I say. 'So you just have to get up, put some clothes on, walk for, like, ten minutes and then you can just sleep on the beach instead.'

'OK fine,' Poppy says. 'How was sleeping with Josh?'

'Great.'

'We can make Felix sleep with him tonight if you want? And you can stay in here with me?'

I look at the Felix-shaped lump under the duvet, his hair poking out the top which Poppy is absent-mindedly stroking.

'Thanks, but honestly. It's fine.'

'Do you wish Margot was here?' She whispers this as if she hasn't told Felix about it already which I don't believe for a second.

'No,' I say. 'Well, maybe I wish she was here but that all of you lot weren't.'

Poppy smiles.

'We're not that bad, are we?'

Felix pulls the duvet down so his face is peeking out.

'What's all this?'

'Nothing,' I say, 'we're going to the beach, get dressed.'

We spend the afternoon taking it in turns walking into the sea, screaming and then running back out and drying off on the white sand. It's not busy but there are groups of people hanging out and lots of people jogging up and down the shore just at the point where water meets sand. They make it look so easy but I was exhausted just walking down onto the sand from the street.

Both Josh and I bring our books down to the beach with us but they sit untouched, getting sandy inside our tote bags. I mostly doze and listen to the others chatting. At one point I lie on my side and watch Georgia applying sunscreen to Zara's back while Zara sits in front of her, her knees pulled to her chest. When she's done she leans forwards and kisses the nape of Zara's neck. I close my eyes, my hand wrapped around my overheating phone.

We stay long enough to watch the sun setting, orange rays dancing on the waves, before making our way to the Mexican place that Josh and Georgia insist do the best margaritas in the city.

We sit outside on a terrace where all the walls are painted different colours and strings of bulb lights hang over the canopy. I'm sticky from being in the sea and I can feel that my cheeks are sunburnt. I'm so tired that I feel I ought to be grouchy but it's impossible to be grouchy when I have a salty margarita in my hand, so strong and with so much lime it makes me grimace. We order enough food for twenty people and then pretty much eat it all. Every kind of taco you can imagine, literally hundreds of tortilla chips. It feels restorative. I decide that LA could be the place for me.

I'm sitting next to Zara, who's drinking sparkling water, claiming to be too tired and dehydrated from the sun for any alcohol. But when I offer her a sip of my drink, after a moment of hesitation she accepts.

'Strong,' she says, shaking her head slightly as she swallows. 'Thanks.'

Georgia is sitting opposite us and I can see out of the corner of my eye that she's watching this interaction with glee. Just as I'm starting to feel bad for not making more of an effort with Zara for Georgia's sake, Zara opens her mouth.

'Everyone! Georgia and I were thinking about the plan for

tomorrow. We're all going to get up super early and do a hike up to the Hollywood sign *together*.'

I look over at Josh and he rolls his eyes. I suspect that he also hasn't made much of an effort with Zara.

'Now I know it's, like, a super touristy thing to do but we thought it would be fun for everyone who hasn't been here before,' she smiles at me in a way that I think is meant to be kind. I know for a fact that she has also never been here before. I guess she considers herself a local by proxy of being engaged to Georgia.

'I mean I'm happy to do super touristy things,' I say, 'because we are all tourists, aren't we?'

Georgia opens her mouth to say something but I interrupt her.

'So with that in mind, I want to go to the Walk of Fame tomorrow, too.'

'The place where all the stars are?' Poppy says, scooping up guacamole with a tortilla chip. Felix is on his phone next to her, his arm resting on the back of her chair.

'Yes. On Hollywood Boulevard.'

I wave my mum's pocket guide at them. It's actually come in handy. It might end up being the only book I read this holiday. I must remember to tell her.

Georgia groans.

'Natty, really? It's so tacky up there. It's just full of tourists.'

What is with these two?

'But I *am* a tourist. And I want to see the stars. I'm not saying you have to come with me. I'm just saying that's where I'd like to go.'

Georgia nods.

'Well,' she says, 'I suppose we could all go our separate ways in the afternoon.'

'I'll come and do touristy stuff with you.' Josh looks up from his phone; he's been editing a photo of himself in front of one of the painted walls for the past ten minutes. 'I've actually never been.'

'See?' I say to Georgia, pointedly. 'I know what the people want!'

I want to stay busy tomorrow to keep my mind off seeing my dad. So I don't have the chance to get too worked up about it or text him and cancel.

When Josh and I get into bed, weirdly at the same time as though we're a couple and this is our nightly routine, he turns onto his side and watches me while I'm staring at my phone thinking about what to message Margot. He's not wearing a T-shirt, just his boxers. Already breaking the contract of him being allowed to sleep in this bed.

'What?' I glare at him. 'Why are you staring at me? Also, why are you topless?'

'What do you think of Zara?' he asks innocently but there's a hint of a smile playing on his lips.

I put my phone down on the bedside table.

'Why?'

'Just interested. She's got a very different vibe to you.'

'She's nice,' I say.

'Nice?'

'Yes! I don't know. She's fine. I don't know her very well. She makes Georgia happy by the looks of it.'

Josh nods.

'Yeah, I guess so.'

'Why? What do you think of her?'

'Yeah same. Nice. Don't really know her. It's all happened quickly, hasn't it?'

I nod and move my phone slightly on my bedside table so I can see if I have any messages. None.

'I just always thought George would end up with someone a bit more . . . or just a bit less . . .'

He doesn't finish his sentence.

'I know what you mean,' I say.

'I thought she'd end up with someone different,' he says. 'I guess I'm just trying to work them out, that's all.'

'Maybe we'll get to know her more over the next few days and it'll all make sense.'

'Maybe. Right. Night Natty.'

Josh rolls over to face the other way and switches out his light. I don't bother to make him put his T-shirt on.

I pick my phone up again and message Margot.

> *You're probably still asleep but I'm going to bed with my boyfriend. It's gorgeous here. You'd love it.*

I press send and then:

> *I wish I was in bed with you instead.*

I quickly flip my phone on to Do Not Disturb so I don't have to see whether she replies or not. I switch my light off and lie awake for hours. My body not yet adjusted to the new time zone, my mind, which I hoped would be numbed by the tequila, racing at a hundred miles an hour.

We pile into the car at 6 a.m. for our Hollywood sign hike. I fall in love with Josh very briefly at 5:45 when he shakes me awake and passes me a freshly brewed cup of coffee. I fall out of love with Josh at 5:46 when he says to me, with a wink,

'How'd you sleep babe? Not too distracting being next to me?'

I am forced to throw my unopened hardback at him.

It's a forty-minute drive to the start of the trail and I initially plan to use that time to nap but instead I stare out of the window at this new city which feels too sprawling to get any kind of grip on in only a few days. Everything looks beautiful and hazy and full of possibility in the early morning light. I think about my dad waking up to this every day. I wonder if he's done this drive before. Done this hike before. If he's looking at these same streets right now.

The trail is quiet and it feels like we have the whole place to ourselves. It's hard to believe that we're only a few miles away from the metropolis below when it's all greenery and orange dust and million-dollar views. We decide to do the longer hike – around four miles as a round trip – but it doesn't feel too strenuous. There's the odd steep incline but it's mostly very gentle. Despite this, and despite the fact they insisted we all do this walk 'together', Georgia and Zara take off at top speed in their hiking boots and wraparound sunglasses and before long are just little, athletic dots in the distance.

The boys walk together a few feet ahead of Poppy and me who end up lagging behind because we're stopping to take photos approximately every twenty steps.

'I want to be in the moment,' Poppy says, as I get some 'candid' photos of her staring out at the view, 'but also, I really want the moment recorded forever, especially when I think my hair looks really good this morning.'

Her hair does look really good. She just has half of it tied up on top of her head in a messy bun but for some reason today it looks better than normal.

'You don't have to make excuses to me,' I say, putting one hand on my hip as nonchalantly as possible and taking a sip from my water bottle as Poppy directs me to find my best angles.

She gasps as she looks back at the photos.

'Honestly, these are gorgeous. The light is amazing. It was worth the early start.'

By the time we've finished our photoshoot, Josh and Felix are way up ahead. We walk quickly for a couple of minutes with the aim of catching up to them but it feels as though it's getting hotter by the minute and there's no shade. We admit defeat and decide to hang back at our more comfortable pace of barely moving.

'They'll wait for us,' Poppy says confidently. 'Plus, we'll catch them up. They'll have to stop for a break, won't they?'

'Maybe.'

'Felix will need a break at least. He hasn't done anything more strenuous than opening a bottle of wine in about ten years.'

'How are you guys doing?' I say. An image of them asleep, breathing in each other's faces, pops into my mind.

She sighs.

'We're great. I mean, we're good. We're always good though.'

We step aside to let a woman and her huge dog go past us down the trail.

'We're good,' she continues, 'as long as we don't talk about the fight. Or about marriage. Or about the future in general.'

'Ah.'

'So we're good right now.'

'How are you feeling about everything?'

'I don't know to be honest. I feel the same way. I don't want to get married. But I don't want to lose him either. Or hurt him. We have so much fun.'

'But . . .' I say, grabbing her forearm just as she stumbles on a bit of uneven path, trying to take a photo of the trail ahead.

'But,' she says, not even pausing to acknowledge her nearly falling flat on her face, 'I know I can't just keep living in the now. It's not fair on him.'

'I don't know,' I say carefully, not wanting to insert myself too much. And also not quite sure why I'm about to bat for Felix. 'Maybe living in the right now is fine if you guys are making each other happy. But I suppose it's whether Felix can live with that.'

'I also think that I need to . . .' she pauses as if waiting for the words to come to her and when they don't she takes a sip of water instead. 'I think I need to work out why, even if I love him, I can't say that I want to be with him past say . . . next week.'

'What would you want instead?' I ask. I look up ahead. I can't even see Josh and Felix anymore. I decide to pick up the pace, and Poppy falls in line with me as we start to march along.

'That's the thing. I don't know. There's not a thing or . . . or a person that's in place of Felix, it's just sort of . . . blank.'

'And the blank is more appealing?'

'No!'

She pauses.

'I see what you mean. Yes, maybe. Sometimes. Yes. I suppose the blank is more appealing.'

I nod.

'And when you think about the reality of if Felix left next week – we get home from holiday and you go your separate ways from the airport. How do you feel?'

I'm aware I'm straying into 'full therapy session' territory here.

'I feel . . . well, I don't know.'

She turns to me.

'When, in this hypothetical situation, am I allowed to see him again? Like – coffee at the weekend?'

'Poppy. No.'

'Well, when? I need to know so it feels realistic.'

I roll my eyes, exasperated.

'Fine. You're allowed to see him in three months' time, when he comes to pick up some stuff he's left behind at yours.'

'Three months?! That's a bit excessive, isn't it?'

'It's quite normal.'

'When you and George broke up, you saw each other every day.'

'True. But that was an . . . exceptional circumstance.'

'Why? How is it different? Maybe Felix and I could be best friends. We could see each other all the time, maybe not that much would have to change . . .'

'It's different, Pops. Felix loves you so much, it would break his heart. He couldn't be your friend.'

Poppy is quiet for a moment.

'George's heart was broken and she managed it.'

'What?'

'Nothing.'

'Her heart wasn't broken. She was fine.'

As I'm saying it a memory flashes through my mind of a few weeks after Georgia and I had broken up. How I got home from work and stood at the bottom of the stairs leading up to her room and listened to her on the phone to someone, maybe it was even Poppy. I couldn't make out what she was saying. I could just hear that she was crying. I stood in the hallway for a while, my forehead resting against the wall, not wanting to leave, as if somehow the act of secretly, silently standing nearby could be of some comfort to her. When I heard her hang up, I crept down the hall and out of the door.

Poppy looks at me and opens her mouth then closes it again, deciding against saying whatever it was she was planning to say. Instead she says,

'Ugh, I can't talk about this anymore. I'll cry. It's all too bleak. Maybe I'm being an idiot and I'll just stay with him and this is just cold feet. The seven-year itch.'

I don't remind her that they've only been together for two.

'Tell me what's going on with you instead. Let me live vicariously through you. How are things with Margot?'

My stomach flips hearing Poppy say her name, bringing her to life on this trail on the other side of the world.

'Oh, you know. It's nothing serious. Fun though.'

I say this like I'm on autopilot. I'm not sure why I feel I have to clarify that. Or if it's even true.

'Of course.'

'What?'

'Nothing serious,' she repeats. 'What happened? You're bored of her already?'

I laugh at the very idea.

'No, I'm not bored of her. Did I not just say we're having fun? I'm not sure I could ever get bored of her. I think she might tire of me pretty quickly though.'

'Why?'

'I just have a feeling.'

A wave of uneasiness washes through my stomach, I think of the morning I last saw her. Or the night. She was already gone by the morning.

She feels fleeting, I want to say. But I'm not sure that will make sense to Poppy and I don't want to answer a barrage of questions about it.

'Have you been texting her on this trip?'

'I mean. Yes.'

She laughs and shakes her head.

'OK, enough about me. Hey,' I say as casually as I can, not sure if I should be bringing this up or not. 'What do you make of Zara and Georgia at the moment?'

'What do you mean?'

'I mean, they're always bickering, there's a bit of a bad vibe, don't you think?'

'Hmm.'

Poppy looks at her phone, trying to see the photo she's just taken but the sun's too bright. She gives up and puts it in her bumbag instead.

'Actually yeah, Felix was saying something about this yesterday.'

'What was he saying?'

'That they don't seem very happy. He heard them arguing in their room. Just sort of very loudly whispering at each other. He put his ear against the wall, obviously.'

'Do you think it's just wedding stuff?'

Poppy shrugs. She's not really one for gossiping about other people. It's one of my favourite and least favourite things about her. I make a mental note to relay this information to Josh later.

'I'm sure it is,' she says. 'They love each other so much. It's been the ultimate whirlwind romance.'

'Yeah. I guess that's what worries me.'

'Sometimes whirlwind romances work out. My parents only knew each other a few months before they got married and they're still together now.'

'No, I know. I'm just looking out for Georgia.'

'Oh, she's fine,' Poppy says. 'Although actually I think she's going to be super annoyed with us, isn't she? Do you think they're all there already?'

When we arrive at the end of the trail everyone claims to have been there for 'hours', which is very dramatic. The view is spectacular. We all get plenty of Instagram content. Zara and Georgia don't fly off in front of us on the way back down, which feels as though it takes half the time, although when we make it back to the car my calves are aching. I feel almost deliriously tired.

When we get to the house we decide to order breakfast from the diner around the corner to eat outside on the patio. We've obviously already extensively reviewed the diner's tagged photos on Instagram so we can see exactly what we should be getting. Georgia has the app on her phone, going around the group taking orders. She starts with Zara who is getting an egg-white omelette with spinach, a side of grilled chicken and a green juice with kale and collagen in it.

'I'm getting banana, chocolate and walnut pancakes,' I announce. 'And an iced coffee please.'

'Oh god,' Felix looks at me. 'I was going to get eggs but actually that sounds . . . fuck it, I'll do the same.'

'Yeah, me too,' Josh says. 'I'll do the ones with blueberry in, what's that?'

Georgia looks at him.

'Blueberry pancakes?'

'Yeah, those.'

Poppy orders vegan waffles and some kind of almond butter smoothie.

'What are you having, babe?' Zara asks, and sips from her water bottle. I swear she has filled it up at least ten times since we arrived home. I almost want to tell her to slow down lest she actually over-hydrate and we all end up spending the day in the ER with her.

'Um,' Georgia says, frowning at the app and then looking up at Zara, 'I think also pancakes actually.'

Zara raises her eyebrows but doesn't say anything. She just takes another sip of water.

'Yes, Georgia,' Poppy says. 'Live a little, you're on holiday!'

'Yeah, I will,' she says. 'It's fine,' she says, turning to Zara. 'It sounds really good, are you sure you don't want something more fun?'

Zara shakes her head and smiles.

'I ordered what I *want*. I think an omelette *is* fun.' The smile is fixed on her face and the exchange seems completely cordial on the surface but I can't help but feel they'll be talking about this later. More loud whispering, no doubt.

When the food arrives and we all decamp to the garden, Zara stays indoors saying she's too hot to eat in the sun.

'I'll stay inside too then,' Georgia says, hovering in the doorway clutching her polystyrene box of pancakes, one foot outside in the sun.

'No, don't,' Zara says. 'Really, I'm fine in here.'

Georgia opens her mouth to protest but Zara just says, 'Really. I'm fine.'

Georgia comes outside and pulls the sliding door closed behind her so that the air conditioning continues to work inside.

'George,' Poppy says, her mouth full of waffle. 'You should really have just sat down with her.'

'What? Are you kidding me? She said she didn't want me to!'

'Mmm,' Josh says. 'But you're not meant to ask, you're just meant to do it.'

Georgia snorts indignantly.

'Shut up. What do you know?'

'I'm just saying . . .'

'Seriously, Josh,' she says, 'shut up.'

We eat our pancakes in silence for a few minutes. They really are exceptionally nice. Without a doubt the nicest pancakes I've ever had. I send a photo of them to Natalie.

'Maybe I'll come to the Walk of Fame this afternoon after all,' Georgia says, stuffing an enormous piece of pancake in her mouth.

'Really? I thought you hated that stuff?' I say.

She shrugs.

'It'll be fun. I'm just being a snob about it. I want to come.'

I look at Poppy and raise my eyebrows. She shakes her head in return and gets back to her waffles.

It turns out that to describe the Hollywood Walk of Fame as 'full of tourists' was an understatement. Georgia, Josh and I make our way along the street slowly, eyes fixed to the pavement looking mostly at names we don't recognise. The others were talking about some exhibition at LACMA that they might go to but when we left no one seemed in any particular rush to go. I wouldn't be surprised if they just ended up at the beach. As we were walking out of the door Georgia checked with Zara for a final time that she was sure she didn't want to come. Zara had given her a tight smile. *I'm fine*, she said, *you enjoy yourself*.

Hollywood Boulevard sounds like it might be a glamorous place but it's actually lined with sex shops and stores selling things like fridge magnets and hoodies emblazoned with the Hollywood sign.

'OK, I was right,' Georgia says as we almost slam into a group of people who've stopped abruptly in front of us to take a photo of Mariah Carey's star. I get my phone out too.

'What?' I say, angling my phone through the group of people.

'This is not fun. This is shit. Natty put your phone away, it'll get stolen.'

'It won't, she's fine,' Josh says, rolling his eyes. 'Although George is right,' he says to me, 'this is shit.'

They're absolutely right, it is very shit.

'Oh come on, it's not that bad, is it?'

'Yes,' they both say.

'OK, well what do you want to do instead?'

'Drink,' Josh says.

'We could get an Uber into West Hollywood, that could be fun,' Georgia says.

Georgia and Josh choose a bar they've been to before and because it's 5 p.m., it's not too busy and it's happy hour. We get a table in the corner of the garden so we can people-watch and order spicy margaritas. When I take a sip my eyes water.

'Fuck me,' Josh says, wiping his nose with a napkin. 'They weren't joking, were they?'

We all scroll through our phones for a while showing each other photos we've taken and talking through which ones are Instagram appropriate. Once it's been decided and we're most of the way through our drinks, Georgia puts her phone down and sits back in her chair. She closes her eyes and exhales dramatically.

'It's really good to have you here, Natty,' she says.

'Mate,' Josh says, 'so good. I can't believe it's taken this long for you to come out here.'

'I'm so happy to be here,' I say, 'I love it.'

I do. I could get used to the sunshine and the daily margaritas. I imagine my life here would be like one big holiday. I can see why my dad came here.

'So, is everything sorted with you and Zara?' I say.

'Oh yeah,' Georgia says quickly, stirring her drink with her straw, 'totally fine. She was just tired. We . . . we were just tired.'

Josh looks down at his drink and raises his eyebrows. Georgia catches him.

'What? I don't know why you've got anything to say about it. How are things with *your* girlfriend? Oh yeah, you haven't got one!'

'Maybe I have, maybe I haven't,' Josh says. He smiles at her serenely, which winds her up even more.

'You haven't,' she says, but she doesn't sound convinced.

'Sure,' he says.

'Josh! You haven't!'

'OK!'

'Ugh, what? Have you actually?'

'Might be seeing someone,' he says, catching the eye of the barman and gesturing for another round.

'Who?' Georgia says.

'No one you know, it's low-key for now. Seeing where it goes.'

'How come you didn't bring her, Josh?' I say, pushing my sunglasses off my face and onto the top of my head.

He smiles at me.

'How come you didn't bring *your* girlfriend?'

I widen my eyes at him.

'What girlfriend?' Georgia whips around and glares at me.

'I don't have a girlfriend. Josh is making stuff up.'

'If you don't have a girlfriend then who are you messaging literally every night? Honestly George, we'll have just got into bed and I'll be trying to make conversation before we go to sleep, maybe have a little cuddle . . .'

Georgia kicks him under the table.

'But she just ignores me. She has her phone over her face and she just grins all stupidly at it.'

He does an impression of me looking lovingly at my phone. I mean, it's probably entirely accurate.

'She's not my girlfriend,' I say as the waiter sets down our drinks. I thank him and take a large gulp. My throat burns.

'There is someone though?' Georgia says.

'Oh my god, yes! Fine! I'm sort of vaguely seeing someone at home.'

'Why didn't I know that?' Georgia says.

'I don't know. I've not really talked about it, I guess. It's not a big deal.'

'How long for?'

'I don't know . . . a few weeks maybe.'

'Weeks? Weeks? And you haven't said anything?'

'No . . . I . . . am I in trouble here?'

'No!' she says, catching herself and smiling at me. 'No, of course not, I'm just surprised. I just thought . . .'

'What?'

'Nothing!'

Josh shakes his head, obviously thrilled with the drama he's created.

'She thought you might have told her, Natasha. I think Georgia's saying she's hurt that you . . .'

'Shut *up*, Josh.'

'Yeah,' I say, 'shut up Josh. Or you actually will be sleeping on the sofa. He broke the contract last night,' I say to Georgia, hoping she'll look at me, that we're OK.

'How?' she says.

'No T-shirt.'

'Disgusting,' she says and smiles but she doesn't quite meet my eyes.

We're OK, I think. She doesn't really have a right to be mad although I can't help but feel that she is. Maybe not mad, but something. A small part of me, a horrible part of me, is secretly pleased. *Interesting*, the therapist that lives in my head says. *That doesn't seem very healthy.* I drown her out with tequila.

When we get home that night, later than we anticipated after another round of margaritas and lots of cheese fries, Poppy and Felix are sitting outside on the patio drinking wine. They're sitting next to each other on a bench and Poppy is leaning against him. They look so happy and peaceful, we decide not to go out and disturb them. Zara is sitting on the sofa in front of the TV but when we get in she switches it off and stands up. She announces she was just heading to bed and leaves the room without looking at any of us.

'Oooh, trouble in paradise,' Josh says at top volume as he walks into the kitchen and opens the fridge, 'again.'

Georgia ignores him.

'Night Natty,' she says and leans forward to kiss me on the cheek. She pauses for a moment, her eyes closed as if psyching herself up, and then follows Zara up the hall and into their room.

I head into the bedroom despite Josh's protestations that it's too early and 'I'm boring' and that we're 'drifting apart'.

I perch on the edge of the bed, clutching my phone. My heart is thumping. Keeping busy and slightly too much alcohol is not enough to numb the anxiety about tomorrow. I want to call Natalie but it's only 6 a.m., she won't be up. I briefly consider calling Margot but I don't know what to say. I don't want to talk to her. I want her here, to reach out to me and hold me and kiss me and transport me somewhere else.

God, I miss you

I type it out and stare at it and delete it. I'd regret it tomorrow.

9

I've arranged to meet my dad at Salt and Straw, an ice-cream place in Venice that's mentioned in my mum's guidebook and heavily featured on even the most cursory Instagram search for things to eat in LA. I've got my eye on birthday cake flavour, vanilla ice cream speckled with hundreds and thousands and with jam swirling through it. I might get some satisfaction from asking my dad to buy me birthday cake after missing the last eighteen years. It feels like it could be cathartic, although I'm sure if a client was telling me this was their plan, I'd question their motives. *What do you hope to achieve by doing that?* I might ask. *How might that make you feel?* I hope to achieve my dad acknowledging that he abandoned me, I think that would feel bloody great.

We're meeting at midday so I spend the morning nervously buzzing around the house. I drink a glass of ginger-flavoured kombucha which I hope will help my swirling stomach but all it actually does is rev up my anxiety, the caffeine giving it that extra boost. The others are going to get a 'wanky' breakfast at Cafe Gratitude and then go to the beach but, although I do technically have time, I tell them no. I have to get ready. To mentally prepare. I try to tone down how huge this is, what this means to me, but I'm not sure if I do a very good job. Everyone gives me a look on their way out as if I'm going in for major surgery and they don't know if they'll ever see me again. Felix ruffles my hair as he walks past where I'm sitting on the sofa and Poppy and Georgia come over to hug me.

'Ring me if you need me,' Poppy whispers and kisses the side of my head.

They all file out with Josh bringing up the rear.

'Have fun with your dad!' he shouts behind him, somehow blissfully unaware of how loaded this meeting is, which is oddly comforting.

I'd woken up to a long voice note from Natalie which I play now the others have gone and I can listen in peace.

'Morning Natty. Well it will be morning when you listen to this any-way, unless you're up in the middle of the night in which case put your phone away and try and go back to sleep! Big day today. Fuck. I mean, I can't really believe you're going to see him, can you? I sort of don't believe he's really out there living a life just like we are.

'What do you think he looks like? I guess he'll be all tanned. Do you think he's got veneers? Doesn't everyone in LA have veneers? He might look like Simon Cowell. Probably not though. Maybe he's had Botox. You'll take a photo, won't you? It's weird, isn't it, because it's not like we *couldn't have just asked Auntie Linda for a photo. Like, we could have seen what he looked like already but I'm not sure I wanted to know. I'm not even sure I want to know now actually, but I do if you've seen him. I feel sort of jealous actually. Jealous but also, like, really grateful it's you rather than me. I feel like I might just cry the whole time, or punch him in the face. Or both. I wish we could be doing this together. That would be the best.*

'Anyway, I'm rambling but I really just wanted you to wake up today and know that I think you're really brave and you're doing the right thing. And we love you so much, me and Mum. So if he's disappointing or unkind or whatever, it doesn't matter. Just us three matter, really. And the twins, obviously. And Luke, I suppose. At a push. Ugh, listen to me. The pregnancy hormones are making me all mushy. Love you, Natty. Ring me later, OK?'

I don't have the capacity to process what she's said properly. Not on a day where I'm trying to gear myself up for a casual ice cream with my estranged parent in a foreign country. It's too much emotional work for one day. I quickly type out a reply.

Ew. What has this baby done to you?!

And then I send a row of hearts, wipe away a stray tear and go and get dressed to meet my dad.

Deciding what to wear turns out to be a bigger challenge than I had anticipated. I want my outfit to both say, 'I just threw this on because I don't care' but also 'I'm very together and everything I

do is deliberate.' Having only brought carry-on luggage with me
my options for this very specific look are severely limited. I consider having a rummage through Poppy's clothes but in the end
I settle for the same stonewash denim Levi's shorts I've worn
every day since we got here and a white shirt tucked in with the
sleeves rolled up past my elbows. I put on a gold necklace with a
tiny anchor on it which Natalie gave me a couple of birthdays
ago. I'm wearing Birkenstocks. I feel it's a look that strikes the
smart casual balance perfectly. I leave my hair down but put a
hair tie around my wrist so that inevitably in ten minutes when
I can't stand to feel it on my neck anymore I can tie it up.

The summer of great weather at home means I'm looking
more tanned than usual and when I check myself out in the
mirror before heading out I decide that I look pretty good. Like,
if he says to me, 'You're looking well', he'll be telling the truth.
I do. I am well. I take a deep breath and head out of the front
door and into the sunshine.

I'm so anxious about not being late that I leave myself an hour
to do the forty-five minute walk. It's another beautiful day,
there's not a cloud in the sky but it's not ferociously hot yet. I
walk down to the beach and along the boardwalk so I can people-
watch and be near the water, which I tell people all the time is
very calming. Despite the blue ocean sparkling in the Califor-
nian sunshine being a world away from the choppy, freezing
waters of England's south coast, the effect is the same. I feel more
balanced, less frantic. As I walk along I try to let the feeling of
being a tiny, insignificant speck on this massive, unknowable

planet wash over me. Existentially terrifying to some, supremely comforting to me. I am a blip, I tell myself. I am a blip and this meeting is a blip and it all means nothing and the world is chaos so just see what happens and try to have a nice time. At the very least, I'll get an ice cream.

I get distracted when I arrive at the Venice boardwalk by hordes of people shouting over booming music coming from every direction. There's a man with his eyes closed dancing with a snake around his neck and a tiny dog with candyfloss pink fur being pushed in a pram. I consult Citymapper and turn off onto a side street with no pavements but lots of houses which look just like Georgia's uncle's house – blue and white one-storey houses with a veranda. They all look kind of run-down, like over-sized beach huts, but I know they're probably worth millions. I've got my eyes permanently peeled for celebrities.

When I eventually make my way onto Abbot Kinney Boulevard the sidewalks are packed with people and their dogs all walking very slowly. Normally I might have huffed and puffed my way around them but, knowing I have lots of time, I let myself stroll so that I can look into the windows of all the fancy shops and cafes. Halfway up the street there's a store which looks like an Apple shop but somehow even more high-tech, which, upon closer inspection, is actually a weed dispensary. I wonder about popping in to get something to take the edge off today but decide against it. I shouldn't need to medicate to have a meeting with a parent. Perhaps afterwards, as a reward.

It's easy to spot Salt and Straw by the queue of people lining up around the block to get in there as soon as it opens. I'm standing on the other side of the street waiting to dart across the road, trying to decide whether to join the queue or stand out the front, when I spot him.

He's standing to the left of the shopfront in the shade in front of the fancy-looking clothing store next door. He's not looking at his phone like all of the other people hanging around on the sidewalk. He's got his hands in his pockets, shoulders back, and he's staring up and down the street, looking out for me. My heart begins to race and I fight the urge to run across the road and into his arms. I'm surprised that that's my impulse. Instead I stay where I am, take a few deep breaths and take him in, wanting to have a moment to gather myself before he spots me. He looks exactly the same apart from now he has a deep tan and silver hair instead of dark brown like it used to be, the same as mine and Natalie's. He has on what look like linen trousers in off-white and a white T-shirt. His sunglasses are the same as mine. Black Ray-Ban Wayfarers. I wonder if he agonised as much as I did over what to wear. What impression he hoped to make with this outfit.

When the traffic is at a standstill, I nip across the road. He still doesn't see me and I realise I could probably walk right past him now and he'd never even know. Instead I take a deep breath and start walking towards him just as he turns his head to survey this end of the street. I know when he's seen me because he immediately takes his sunglasses off and blinks a few times as if checking to see if his eyes are deceiving him, if I'm a trick of the light.

'Hi,' I say, stopping a couple of feet in front of him. I leave my sunglasses on.

'Hi!' He lifts his arms as if he might hug me and then hesitates and ends up holding them out to his side as if to say, 'ta-da'. 'Here you are!'

I nod.

'Here I am.'

We're both silent for a moment, unsure of what to say now. The moment for a hug has definitely passed and I wonder if we'll touch at all. Whether we'll manage this entire encounter from a distance.

I look up the street behind me.

'I guess if we're going to . . .' I point to the line of people, 'we should probably . . .'

'Sure, yes. Yes, let's get in line.'

His accent is different. Not quite American, not quite English. That sort of odd hybrid people get when they've lived away from home for a long time. I wonder how long he's been here.

We walk in silence to the back of the queue and stand behind at least twenty other people.

'This line will go down really quick,' he says, his sunglasses now back on. 'It's always crazy busy but they move fast in there.'

'Have you been here a lot?' I say, trying to imagine him coming here with his partner, or their friends. His whole life that I know nothing about.

'Um, yeah, a few times. I really love it. I've got such a sweet tooth, it's terrible. I'd eat ice cream for every meal if I could.'

'Me too,' I say. It's not even really true, it's just something to say.

'You always did have such a sweet tooth. Natalie never did. You would always be there with your hand in a bag of sweets and Natalie would have hers in a bag of crisps.'

'She has a sweet tooth now,' I say, suddenly irritated. How dare he try and tell me something about myself, about my sister.

'Right, of course,' he says. 'Of course.'

We stand mostly in silence while we queue. It feels impossible to do small talk and wrong to have any kind of serious conversation standing with a bunch of people waiting for an ice cream. He's right though, the queue does move quickly. Once we reach the front and can see all the flavours, I feel quite overwhelmed. I want the birthday cake flavour but the version of me in my head who could request it in a sassy way doesn't exist in real life. She never does when it comes down to it. I order one scoop of birthday cake and one scoop of caramel sea salt and my dad says, 'Ooh that sounds good, I'll do the same.'

I pay. My card is in my hand and tapping the machine before he can even protest. He thanks me quietly and I almost feel sorry for him. We both go for cones rather than cups and they are the biggest ice creams I've ever seen. As soon as we get outside into the sunshine, which is much fiercer now than when I left the house, it's a full-time occupation simply keeping the ice cream from dripping down the cones and onto our arms. We walk as quickly as we can down to the beach and settle on the sand a few feet back from the sea. We sit next to each other looking out at the waves and attend to our melting ice creams.

'This is really good,' I say.

He beams as if he has personally made the ice cream for me.

'It is, right? Just perfect on a day like today.' He gestures up at the cloudless sky.

'Is it always like this?' I say.

'Mostly. It gets cooler in winter. And we get the June Gloom but yeah, it's pretty much just this. Sunshine and blue skies.'

'Heaven,' I say. I'm halfway through my ice cream now; I've reached the sea salt caramel scoop. It's the nicest thing I've ever tasted. I want to tell someone about it but I resist the urge to get my phone out and take a photo.

'Linda says you live in Brighton now?' Dad poses this as a question as if he isn't sure, even though I'm pretty certain Linda will have filled him in on as much as she knows before my arrival. Not that she knows much. I don't do a great job, or indeed any job at all of keeping in touch.

'I've lived in Brighton for a long time now.'

'I love Brighton,' he says. 'A great city.'

I nod.

'I like it.'

'And do you live with a . . . Linda didn't mention a . . .'

I look at him but he's staring resolutely ahead.

'I live with my friend Poppy.'

'Ah lovely,' he says. 'And you're a therapist.'

He knows that one then, for a fact.

'Yes I am.'

He shakes his head.

'It only feels like yesterday that . . . I just can't believe that you're old enough to do a job like that, but of course you're . . .' he shakes his head again, 'of course. That's amazing, Natasha,' he says to the ocean. 'That really is something.'

'Thank you.'

'And how is Natalie?'

'She's great. The twins are great. You know she's pregnant again?'

He finally whips around to look at me.

'No,' he says. 'I didn't know that. How wonderful.'

'It is. It is wonderful,' I say. I feel on edge talking about Natalie. Ready to be deeply defensive. Protective, although I'm not sure what I'm expecting him to say about her. I almost don't want him to speak about her at all.

We're quiet again for a while. Once the ice cream is gone I wipe my sticky hands on my shorts. Without something to do, the quiet feels more stressful. I feel an overwhelming need to fill the silence but I don't know what to say. Or I do, but I don't know where to start.

'Natasha,' Dad says eventually. 'There are a few things that I feel I have to say.'

'You feel you *have* to say?'

He pauses and then nods.

'OK, that I need to say. That I want to say to you.'

'OK.' My voice is steady but I can feel my jaw shaking. I lift my hand to the side of my face and place it there. My hand is shaking too.

He turns his whole body around to face me, but I stay where I am.

'I don't even know where to begin. I don't even . . . I never imagined when I saw you again it would be like this.'

'Did you think you'd see me again?' I say.

'Of course.'

'How?'

'What do you mean?'

'How did you think you'd see me again? Us again. You've never once tried to get in touch with us.'

'Well I . . . that's fair . . . I just. Yes, that's fair.'

He wipes his forehead with the back of his hand.

'I suppose I just want you to know how sorry I am, from the bottom of my heart, I'm sorry. Leaving you girls is the biggest regret of my life. I think about you constantly, but I thought . . . the longer it was since we saw each other, the harder it's been to imagine . . . I thought you must hate me.'

'I do hate you.'

I surprise us both. He sits completely still and eventually I turn to face him.

'I hate you. And I love you, obviously,' I say. My voice starts cracking and I swallow a few times, desperate not to cry.

'I just thought you wouldn't want to hear from me. You would have just told me to fuck off,' he says.

I smile despite myself. At the surprise of hearing him swear.

'I would have. But then you should have tried again and again.'

'I know.'

'That's what a parent does.'

'I know.'

I think of my mum and I feel suddenly sick. She's texted me every day since I arrived and at the end of every message she says, *Please message back just to let me know you're OK.* Even when I'm on the other side of the world, she can't rest until she knows I'm safe.

'You don't know.'

He nods again and, as if he's reading my mind, says,

'How's your mum?'

'She's OK,' I say.

'Did she ever meet . . .'

'No.'

'Are you close?'

I don't think I've ever been asked that question before.

'No,' I say.

'How come?'

'Because I remind her of you, I think.'

My dad puts his head in his hands and then rubs his eyes. Not like he's crying, more like he's trying to process what I'm telling him.

'I should have handled it all better. I know that. I just . . . you have to understand when I was growing up it was a different time and I was just . . . I still am . . . there's just so much shame.'

'I know about shame.'

'I know you do . . . I was just . . .'

'Don't you think I felt your shame? Your shame about who you were, your shame about who you loved and what you did? Your shame about us?'

'No, no I was never . . .'

'You were, Dad, you were. Please be honest. Please.'

He shakes his head vehemently.

'I was never ashamed of you.'

'You made us feel like it would be easier for you if we didn't exist.'

'No! That's not . . .'

'I'm telling you how you made us feel.'

'OK.'

I take a deep breath.

'And the way you felt about yourself, bloody hell.'

'I've done a lot of work on that.'

I laugh and shake my head.

'What? I know it sounds . . . I've had a lot of therapy.'

'You and me both.'

'Has it helped?' he says.

I nod.

'Sometimes. You?'

'Sometimes.'

We're both quiet for a while trying to take everything in. I become mesmerised by a woman in a sports bra and the shortest of shorts running along the sand barefoot and at an unbelievably fast pace. I watch her until she becomes a speck in the distance.

Eventually my dad speaks.

'I'm sorry that you've felt shame about who you are. I hope that you don't feel that way anymore.'

I can't tell him what he wants to hear, so I don't say anything.

'I don't think you're like me,' he carries on. 'You seem much braver than me.'

'I think that's true,' I say.

'You'd never abandon your family,' he says.

I want to tell him that's it. That after eighteen years apart he's tapped into my biggest fear in a matter of minutes. Pressed a finger into it like a bruise. We're that alike, that connected. Surely he knows better than anyone all the ways that I might let people down.

I take a deep breath.

'Where do you live?' I say.

He looks surprised at the sudden change of track.

'Um, do you know LA well?'

I shake my head.

'OK, well I live about forty-five minutes away from here. In good traffic. Up in the hills. Out in the sticks.'

'Nice place?'

He nods.

'I love it. It's small but . . . we have an incredible view and it's so peaceful.'

I nod, trying to imagine what it would be like to describe life as peaceful.

'What does your partner do?'

'Rick, he's an artist.'

I raise my eyebrows. I wonder if he's anything like the artist I've currently got on my mind.

'What sort of art?'

'Sculpture. He makes these big, beautiful stone sculptures.'

'What happened to Carl?'

My dad laughs.

'Oh, Carl and I ended a long time ago. It wasn't meant to be in the end. He's a lovely man though. We're still in touch. He stayed in France.'

I nod, trying to build a timeline in my head of my dad's life since I last saw him.

'So how long have you been out here?'

'Oh, must be ten years now.'

I raise my eyebrows but don't say anything. Ten years he's been living on the other side of the world. For some reason that feels like a punch in the stomach. I think of myself ten years ago. Just out of university, flailing. Twenty-one and wild with sadness, unable to quite pinpoint where it came from. Trying hopelessly, recklessly to find something or someone who could soothe me.

'And what do you do out here?'

'Well I don't technically work out here . . .'

'So you're a house husband?'

He chuckles at the idea.

'Oh, I don't know about that. I volunteer. I do a little painting. I cook . . . I guess yeah, I am a house husband. I hadn't thought about it like that.'

'It sounds like you got really lucky, Dad.'

He looks at me sadly and I smile at him.

'What about you?'

'Well, I'm not a house husband.'

He laughs.

'I mean, do you . . . have someone special?'

I shake my head.

'Was there someone?'

I pause.

'Yes.'

'What happened?'

'Oh,' I laugh, more bitterly than I intended, 'what always happens.'

He doesn't seem to need any further explanation.

'You deserve to be happy, Natasha. All I want is for you and Natalie to be happy.'

I can't believe that's true. He wants a lot more than that, clearly, or we wouldn't be sitting here as strangers to one another. But what's the point in arguing? I'm suddenly exhausted.

'I'm going to go, I think.'

My dad looks panicked; he looks around us as if searching for something exciting enough to keep me there.

'No, really? I . . . we could go and get a drink or some lunch or something? I want to hear all about Natalie's kids and . . . about everything.'

I shake my head.

'I'm sorry, I can't do this all at once.'

'Of course,' he says. 'Of course.'

'You know,' I say as I get up and dust the sand off my shorts. 'You should ring Natalie and she can tell you herself.'

He stands up too.

'She won't hang up on me?'

'Oh, she might. But if you want to talk to her that's what you need to do.'

He nods, he's looking at me desperately. I know he wants me to say something to make him feel better but I can't.

'I'll do it,' he says. 'I will.'

I decide to believe him.

'Are you?' I point back towards the boardwalk.

'No, I'll stay here for a little while.'

Before we can do the awkward dance around hugging, I lean forward and wrap my arms around his neck. He pulls me close and squeezes me. I can feel him smelling my hair. He puts his hand on the back of my head.

When we pull away, I say, 'I really hope I hear from you soon, Dad.'

'You will,' he says hoarsely. 'I promise.'

I nod and walk away quickly, the tears I've been holding back finally spilling down my cheeks.

I turn back after a minute or so and see he has sat back down on the beach, facing away from me and out to the ocean. I feel a pang of sadness for him. He's suddenly so small.

I walk around the canals for a bit. They are busy with people stopping to get photos for Instagram or pulling out big maps like the one at the back of my pocket guide but no one seems to care that I'm strolling aimlessly. I said I'd call Natalie as soon as it was over but I haven't had time to analyse it yet, to even begin to process what just happened. I stop and stand on a bridge, leaning over the edge, letting people mill around me. My heart is racing. I feel guilty for leaving him sitting there on the beach and I find myself for the second time in a day wanting to run to him. But I know that guilt is a common feeling among children of parents who abandoned them and I don't need to feel guilty. I haven't abandoned him. I take a deep breath. I haven't abandoned him. I haven't abandoned anybody.

I know what will make me feel better. I walk slowly back towards Santa Monica, ignoring messages coming up on my phone from Georgia and Poppy. I head up away from the beach and make my way to Gelson's. The air con is immediately soothing. There is quiet music playing and the aisles are so huge that although it's relatively busy, I have all the space I want to myself. I walk slowly, methodically up and down every single aisle looking at all the strange things you can't get at home. At the hundreds of different varieties of almond milk, the bags of salad that cost $9, I stop at the in-store bakery and pick up a box of soft chocolate chip cookies. They're $16. I walk around the shop holding them as I look at American pet food and laundry detergent and four hundred different flavours of crisps. Once I've paid for my cookies as well as a bottle of tequila which I think I'll require later and a bag of ranch-flavour crisps, I head outside and sit on the end of a long picnic bench. I am surrounded by people wearing clothes that they must be way too hot in, talking very loudly into their phones, picking at salad leaves. I open the box of cookies but find that I can't eat them. The small bite I take sticks to the roof of my mouth. The lump in my throat is still there.

I walk around the corner away from the noise and into the shade, get out my phone and open WhatsApp. I hold my phone up to my mouth and speak quietly into it.

'*Charl, you were right. Thank you. I love you.*'

I send it, take a deep breath and start recording another message.

'*Hi Mum. Don't worry, I'm fine. I know it's late there so I hope this doesn't wake you up. I just wanted to say . . . I just wanted to say . . .*'

I pause. I think about just deleting the voice note and starting again but I'm not sure I'll be able to articulate myself any better in thirty seconds' time.

'*I had to tell you that the guidebook you gave me is really coming in handy. I never would have thought of it. And so . . . I really appreciate that you did. I've used it a lot. So . . .*'

I take a deep breath. If I cry she'll think I've lost my mind. I can't remember the last time I cried around her.

'*Yeah that's it. Just . . . thanks . . . for the guidebook.*'

I finish recording and send it before I can change my mind and then forward it to Natalie.

'Just sent this to Mum – listen to it, it is EVIDENCE that I'm not a complete monster to her. See? Please reassure her that I'm fine and that it's not some kind of coded message telling her I've been kidnapped. Saw Dad. It was weird. He was very tanned. He looks rich. His boyfriend might be rich, he's an artist. He has a nice life. Not really sure how I feel yet other than I wish you were here so much. He's going to call you, or he said he would. I think he's really sad, even though he's kind of got everything. I feel sorry for him which I know, I know I shouldn't. But I do. I bought him an ice cream. How weird is that? Today I bought Dad an ice cream. Anyway. Love you. Love the babies. Love Luke. I'll speak to you later. Tell me if he calls you. I believe him that he will.'

10

The others are still out when I get home so I spend the afternoon in bed eating cookies and watching YouTube videos of
people doing their hair and make-up. I find it infinitely relaxing, my mind being slowly numbed, the bright voices and
product placement gently teasing out all the difficult parts of
the day. I message Georgia to tell her that I'm fine but exhausted
and going to 'head to bed and read'. She sends me back the crying laughing emoji. And a heart, in case I'm feeling too sensitive
for the crying laughing emoji, I guess, which I appreciate
because I kind of am.

I hear people chatting in the living room but they don't come
and disturb me until around 6 p.m. when there's a knock on
the door and Georgia's face appears.

'Natty, are you OK?'

I pause my video and put my phone and the cookies on the
bedside table. The girl I'm watching is halfway through a

forty-five-minute video where all she does is curl her hair. I'll pick it up again later.

'I'm OK.'

'Can I come in?'

'Of course.'

I pat the bed next to me and she closes the door behind her and gets in, pulling the covers up to her waist.

'Enjoying the book?' she says, grinning.

'It's excellent, thank you.'

I pick up the box of cookies again and offer them to her. She shakes her head as if on autopilot and then reconsiders and takes one.

'These are amazing,' she says, her mouth full.

'I know. I think I've eaten about a hundred of them.'

She takes another bite and looks at me while she chews. She has her Roy-Bans on, I wonder if she's actually been reading her book.

'How did it go today?' she says.

'It was good,' I say. 'It was good to see him, I mean.'

Georgia nods. She's looking at me so intently, with so much kindness, that I'm horrified to find my bottom lip start to wobble. I swallow a few times to get rid of the lump in my throat that's reappeared.

'It was . . .' I say, swallowing again, 'very sad too. For him and . . . for me.'

Georgia reaches over and takes my hand, she holds it between both of hers, squeezing it tightly. I let her for a moment but I don't want to cry so I pull it away.

'Where's everyone else?' I say.

'They're in the living room waiting for me to tell them whether they can come in or not.'

'You can send them the signal.'

Georgia nods.

'Guys, you can come in!' she yells at the top of her voice.

'Jesus, George. I could have done that.'

Poppy opens the door first and jumps onto the bed, crawling in between Georgia and I. She wraps her arms around my neck and hugs me tightly. Josh perches on the end of the bed near my feet and Felix sits down next to him and squeezes my foot through the duvet.

'You all right, mate?' Felix says.

'I'm all right.'

'Tough day.'

'Tough day,' I agree.

Zara stands at the end of the bed and she looks so uncomfortable that Georgia gets out of bed and goes to stand with her, briefly resting her head on her shoulder and then kissing it lightly. Josh immediately takes Georgia's place in the bed. He sniffs the pillow and rears his head back like he's been stung by something.

'It stinks of your horrible perfume, Georgia!'

'I'm not wearing any perfume.'

'Ugh, then what is it?'

Josh picks up the pillow and throws it at her.

'Maybe it's my perfume,' Zara says, smiling sickeningly at Georgia.

'Rough,' Josh says, not even bothering to lower his voice.

'Right guys,' Poppy says brightly. 'Let's all go down to the beach. We need to be quick if we want to catch the sunset.'

She turns to me.

'We thought that would be a nice way to spend our last evening here. And a nice thing for you to do after your difficult day.'

'That's perfect,' I say, smiling at her and then at everyone, 'thank you, that's perfect.'

We make it to the beach just in time. On warm summer evenings in Brighton the beach is packed with people wanting to catch the pink skies and the sun sinking into the sea but here there's more space, or maybe people are more used to it. I guess it's always a warm summer evening.

We sit in a row. I'm wedged between Josh and Georgia. Everyone chatters around me, someone was meant to bring crisps, someone's got blisters from their shoes. I sit with my knees pulled up to my chest and stare out at the sea. My mind is filled with the image of my dad sitting alone on the beach when I left him today and it's too painful, it's so vivid and the urge to run to him is so strong that I close my eyes, I grit my teeth to push it out. I try to focus on something else instead: Margot. What she's doing, when I'll see her. Whether she's awake like I am staring up at the sky thinking about me, waiting for the sun.

Even though we've only been in LA for a few days I'm surprisingly ready to get out of the city and do something different. I'm keen to shake off the meeting with my dad rather than sitting around trying to process it while walking around on the same streets as him. I want to be so far away that even if he rings me and wants to see me again before I leave, I'm not able to. Joshua Tree, LAX, home. No room for unscheduled visits with unfamiliar parents. It feels comforting to be in control. He hasn't texted me yet.

'I'm so happy that Joshua Tree is where we're going to spend your birthday,' Georgia says as we load our suitcases back into the car. I never bothered to unpack mine properly. Josh hung everything up on a hanger as though he was moving in. I know that Georgia will have done the same thing.

'So long as we're only doing a medium amount of hiking, I'm happy,' I say.

'Medium hikes only,' Georgia assures me. 'Maximum lazing around in the sun.'

'Perfect.'

Joshua Tree is a two-and-a-half-hour drive out of Los Angeles. We're all so used to each other's company by now that no one feels the need to force conversation or fill silences. I scroll through my phone for a while but end up feeling carsick, so I put it away and stare out of the window instead. The further we get out of the city the traffic thins out and the bleak urban landscape gives way to red sand, blue skies and incredible views in every direction.

'Guys,' I say, intermittently, 'look!' and everyone says, 'Yeah, I know, we're looking.'

We stop off at a huge supermarket for supplies. Georgia and

Zara have a list of all the sensible things we need and the rest of us split up around the shop grabbing whatever we want and then making our way back to their trolley to plead our case like children.

'I'm really not sure we need *this* many crisps,' Georgia says, staring at the mountain being presented to her.

'We do,' I say. 'Look at all these flavours. Dill pickle, ranch, hot sauce – how do you expect me to choose?' And when she still doesn't look convinced, 'George,' I say seriously. 'It's my birthday tomorrow.'

She sighs and gestures for me to put them in the trolley. You just can't argue with birthdays.

The roads around the house we're staying in are barely roads at all, more like huge, dusty craters. There are signs bearing the names of what look like makeshift streets, but everything looks the same. A red expanse. The satnav doesn't work around here. It doesn't even register the address as real. We drive around for a long time, giving Georgia deeply unhelpful advice.

'From the photo it looks like it's green, everyone look for a green house.'

'It looks like there might be a tree right by it, a sort of funny, bush-looking tree.'

'Yeah, that would be a *Joshua tree*.'

We wonder about finding someone to ask but we realise we haven't seen another car in a very long time. Eventually, we drive up the first road we came to an hour earlier and dismissed because it 'didn't look right'. We find our green house with the

Joshua tree right by it and absolutely nothing else for miles. The heat is dry and intense, it hits us like a wall as soon as we step out of the air-conditioned car. My phone tells me it's thirty-eight degrees but it feels hotter.

'This is fucking *sick*,' Josh says, leaping out of the car and immediately running around to the side of the house. We hear him whoop with joy and then he jogs back into view. 'Hot tub! There's a massive hot tub!'

Georgia gets out of the driver's seat and slams the door behind her. She looks very hot and very flustered.

'We know there's a hot tub, we booked it because there's a hot tub. We paid extra for the fucking hot tub.'

She's talking to herself really and I don't think anyone else can hear her apart from me.

'Hey, George,' I say quietly and grin at her, 'deep breaths. We're here. You did a great job.'

I pass her a bottle of water.

She smiles back at me and leans against the car, taking in the house and the expanse of desert behind it. She takes a deep breath and exhales slowly.

'It is pretty amazing, isn't it?'

'I love it already. Honestly, Georgia. Thank you for bringing me here.'

She takes a swig of water from the bottle and then hands it back to me.

'Thank you for coming,' she says, 'now let's get these bags in and unpack and then I can relax.'

'Not until we've unpacked?'

'No. No relaxing until we've unpacked.'

'Happy birthday to me . . .' I start singing and she laughs and wraps her arm around my shoulders and gives me a squeeze.

'Babe!' Zara says from the back of the car. 'Babe, when you've got a minute could you help me bring these bags in, there's stuff that needs to be in the fridge ASAP.'

'Coming!' Georgia says, letting me go.

I am thrilled to learn that there's enough room in this house for us all to have our own rooms. Josh's room is tiny with a single bed but he doesn't even complain.

'I'll miss you,' he says to me, 'but you know where I am if you get lonely.'

The house is beautiful. It has white walls with bright accents, beautiful rustic wooden furniture and huge plants everywhere. There is, very excitingly for all us English people, a massive fridge. And I mean massive, it's the size of my wardrobe at home. Once we've unpacked all our shopping and filled the shelves with booze and cheese and an unreasonable amount (in my opinion) of fruit and vegetables we just keep opening it again to stare at its vast insides.

'I mean, just look at this fridge,' one of us will say and someone will always reply, 'Don't, it's amazing.'

It might be the highlight of the trip so far.

That afternoon Zara and Georgia want to go for a proper hike in Joshua Tree National Park and I'm surprised when Felix says he'll go with them.

'Give me two secs, girls, I'll get my new hiking boots on.'

Poppy rolls her eyes.

'He spent a fortune on those boots,' she says to me as she fills her glass with ice from the fridge just because she can. 'And he hasn't worn them yet. I'm not going walking in this heat with him while he breaks them in.'

'Well I'm not going,' I say. 'I'm going to sit outside and read my book.'

'Yeah, same,' Josh says. 'It's too hot for a hike.'

Once the other three have set off with backpacks full of water and trail mix, Josh and Poppy and I settle down on the sunbeds outside. We're each wearing one of the ridiculously oversized straw hats which were hanging on hooks by the door when we arrived. We laughed at first but sitting outside for longer than a minute is impossible without one. We've all left our phones inside, safe in the air-conditioned house.

'It'll force me to read,' I say. 'Not that I need forcing, I really love reading, obviously.'

I lie back, sunglasses on, book resting on my stomach and close my eyes. All I can hear is Josh slapping sun cream on his legs and Poppy trying to adjust her sunbed. Everything else is quiet, an unfamiliar sort of quiet. The rustle of plants and shrubs I've never seen before. The shuffle of insects and animals I can't see and absolutely don't want to know about.

I pick my book up and flick through the first few pages to find Chapter One. I crack the spine, hugely satisfying, feels like I've really started now. As I do, a piece of paper folded in half falls out and lands on my chest. There is just one sentence scrawled across the middle.

You're hot and I miss you.

'Why are you smiling?' Poppy says. She pushes her sunglasses up and squints at me. 'What is it? You're all red.'

'Yeah it's a thousand degrees.' I touch my face – roasting – absolutely nothing to do with the heat.

'What is it?' she says. Her own book is placed underneath her sunbed, she's not even pretending to read.

'Margot wrote me a note.'

Poppy reaches over and grabs it out of my hand.

'Oh my god! I can't remember the last time Felix did something like this.'

I reach out to take it back from her but she just passes it to Josh instead.

'Ooh, a handwritten note,' he says, 'old school. Very romantic.'

They pass it back along the row until it's in my hands again and I stare at it, tracing my finger over the words.

'It's so romantic,' Poppy says. 'Boys just don't do things like that.'

'Hey! We can be romantic,' Josh says.

'Would you ever think to put a note inside a book for your girlfriend to find on holiday?' Poppy says.

'Oh Christ no, never.'

Josh lies back and pulls the front of his floppy hat over his eyes.

'If I had a girlfriend I bet she'd do stuff like this for me all the time,' Poppy says wistfully.

'Not your thing, Pops?' Josh says.

'No, unfortunately. Never has been.'

'Um,' I say, turning to face her. 'That's not strictly true, is it?'

'Oooh,' Josh says, but he doesn't move. Too hot and relaxed to properly lean into the gossip.

'You know what I mean,' she says matter of factly. 'Not in a relationship way.'

'I don't know what you mean,' Josh says from under his hat. 'What do you mean?'

I look at Poppy, eyebrows raised.

'Well . . . once or twice . . .'

'Once or twice!' I say indignantly.

'Fine! A few times when we were at uni so literally, like, a thousand years ago, Natasha and I just . . . kissed. Not a big deal. Just a few drunken kisses.'

She looks at me for back-up.

'Wasn't it? Just being stupid.'

I nod.

'She did it for the boys mainly,' I say.

'Savage!' Josh says, still not moving. 'Didn't have you down as the type, Pops. To use your friend like that.'

'I'm not the type! I was eighteen, completely stupid. You didn't mind anyway, did you, Natasha?'

I shake my head.

'Nope. I did not mind. I was equally stupid. It's fine.'

I'm surprised to find as I say it that I really don't mind now, whether I did then or not. I feel surprisingly tenderly towards eighteen-year-old us as though we were big, drunk babies which, in a way, we were.

'*Anyway!*' Poppy says. 'Margot must really like you.'

'Yeah maybe, it's like . . . five words.'

'No,' she says. 'It's the thought. She thinks about you.'

'She does, that's true.'

I put the note back where I found it for safekeeping.

After about thirty minutes of gently cooking on our sunbeds we collectively decide that the heat is unbearable. We head back into the house, switch the TV on and all immediately fall asleep. Our books remain untouched.

We're woken up by the sound of the others getting back from their hike. I glance at my phone and it's earlier than we'd expected them although the light is starting to fade.

'Fucking boots,' Felix says.

He hobbles in his socks over to where Poppy's curled up on the sofa. He sits down next to her with a thud.

'Where are they?' she says, rubbing her eyes and then looking blearily at his feet.

'I left them outside, I hope a fucking wolf takes them.'

'There aren't any wolves here,' Georgia says.

I glance at her and it's clear she's had quite enough boots talk for the day.

'Whatever then, a coyote, a fox, a fucking *bear.* Whatever is out there, I hope they take them and I never have to see them again.'

'Good hike then?' I say.

'Cut a bit short,' Zara says, a thin smile on her face as she gets an apple out of the fridge and takes a large bite out of it. She immediately freezes; it's obviously very cold and has hurt her teeth but she just carries on chewing and swallows without changing her expression at all.

'Well, it's good you're back really,' Poppy says, as Felix lifts his feet to rest them on her legs. She reaches out a hand to touch a sock and then pulls it away very quickly. 'It's getting dark. There's always tomorrow.'

We spend the evening getting in and out of the hot tub and try-ing to capture on our phones just how beautiful the night sky is. I've never in my life seen so many stars. A blanket of stars. More stars than sky. Enough to make your head spin.

We've also had enough drink to make our heads spin but everyone's in great spirits.

'What on earth is that?' I say.

Somewhere, probably miles away, there are people banging gongs and chanting but because of the sparseness of the land-scape it sounds like it's happening next door.

'Ayahuasca ceremony,' Josh says. 'Loads of people do them out here.'

'What, like drinking that tea and then throwing up?'

'Exactly. Purging all your demons. Getting to the heart of your deepest, truest self.'

'Ugh,' I shudder and sip my wine, 'sounds awful.'

I end up sitting next to Felix for a lot of the evening. He claims he is never getting out of the hot tub because it's the only thing that makes his feet feel better. I try not to think too hard about sharing the water with his blisters.

'Felix,' I say.

'Yes, Natasha.'

'Are we ever going to talk about the driving lessons?'

He bursts out laughing and shakes his head at me.

'Do you want to do another lesson?' he says.

'No!' I laugh too. 'Why? Would you want to teach me again?'

'God, no,' he says. 'It was terrifying.'

'What? You were so calm, weirdly calm!'

'I wasn't, mate. I thought I was going to die. I don't know what came over me. I mean, now I guess I know how I'd react in a crisis.'

'A crisis?'

'You know what I mean. When you think you only have minutes to live.'

'Brilliant. Thanks.'

'You can still borrow the car,' he says, 'just . . . maybe I'll also be in it. Doing the driving.'

When we head to bed that night, early because we're exhausted from the travelling and the heat, we have a soggy group hug, carefree in our swimsuits and towels and traipsing wet feet on the beautiful fluffy rug in the living room.

'Love you guys!' Poppy says.

'Love you!' we all say back.

'And Natasha,' she says, 'at home you're officially thirty-one!'

Everyone whoops and cheers.

'But here, I'm still thirty!' I say quickly. 'Just! For one more hour.'

'Enjoy it darling.'

I wake in the middle of the night to Georgia looming over me, a wild look in her eyes. In the state between dreaming and consciousness I briefly wonder if she's going to murder me, a theory immediately supported by her covering my mouth with her hand as soon as I try to speak.

'Shhh. You'll wake everyone up,' she hisses as she climbs into bed next to me.

'How am I . . . you're the one who . . . what's going on?' I whisper back.

She grins and passes me an earbud. As I put it in she shows me her phone screen. Magic FM is playing, it's an advert for a windscreen repair company.

She looks at me expectantly.

'I . . . don't need a windscreen . . .'

'Shhh.' She rolls her eyes. 'Wait.'

We lie next to each other listening to the adverts. I yawn and she glares at me as if that's entirely inappropriate. Eventually the jingle plays.

'*Good afternoon folks, you're back with Magic. Joan from Battle is listening on her phone while she's washing her car. Careful there Joan! We don't want any phones near any buckets of water, do we?*'

The presenter chuckles and I turn to Georgia to roll my eyes but she's staring resolutely up at the ceiling, grinning.

'And we've got Natasha tuning in all the way from California . . . and it says here it's her birthday! Happy birthday Natasha! Your friend Georgia requested we play something special for you on your special day so here we go . . .'

'Here Comes the Sun' starts playing. I cover my mouth so I don't squeal and wake everyone up. I roll over onto my side to face her and shake my head.

'Happy birthday,' she whispers. 'I wanted to do something special, with you being away from your family and everything.'

'Thank you,' I whisper back. My hand finds hers under the covers. I mean to just give it a squeeze and let go but find myself holding on while we listen together. When it's done we take out our headphones and I stare at her in disbelief. She smiles at me and kisses me softly on the cheek. She slips out of the bed and out of my room.

I stay awake for a long time after that.

When I wake up to the sound of the coffee machine starting up in the kitchen it feels as though last night was a dream. I've been sleeping curled up on the right-hand side of the bed. I turn to my left and reach out to touch the sheets as if I might find some evidence that Georgia had really been there clutching my hand under the covers.

The only thing in bed with me is my phone and when I pick it up the screen lights up with messages. Nearly all of them are from Natalie. She's been bombarding me overnight with photos from our birthdays over the years. The final one is from today at lunch, while I was still fast asleep. She's sitting down at a table with a huge homemade chocolate cake (definitely a Mum special) in front of her and a big candle in the middle – one of those ones that's a sparkler and is meant to be fun but is actually terrifying. She's smiling broadly and has her hands together mid-clap. The twins are standing behind her, eyes wide at the sparkler and the prospect of cake, and my mum is sitting next to her, watching her and smiling. Luke must be behind the camera on Instagram boyfriend duties. I press play on the voice note she's sent and immediately burst into tears when the twins start singing 'Happy Birthday'.

'Love you Auntie Natty. Love you!'

There's a rustle while Natalie takes the phone off them.

'Happy birthday twinnie! Thirty-one! Can you believe it? Fucking hell. I'm going to start taking collagen. You have to as well. Look it up. Anyway I hope you have a lovely day, how weird that yours hasn't started yet. Send me photos of everything. Have an extra wine for me. Love you. I'm passing Mum on, hang on. Mum? Yeah, no just talk into it. No . . . you don't need to press anything. Yeah a voice note. You've done it before!'

I roll my eyes. My mum's voice comes on extra loud, presumably she actually has her mouth pressed up against the phone.

'Hello Natasha, happy birthday! Don't forget to put sunscreen on today. I put Joshua Tree into my weather app and it says it's going to be thirty-eight degrees. Put a hat on as well and don't go on any walks without telling anyone. I was reading about someone who . . .'

I hear Natalie in the background telling her not to be dramatic.

'*I'm not being dramatic! Someone died Natalie! Because two litres of water wasn't enough on their hike. So take three, Natasha OK? Right, that's all from me. Oh. Well. Also . . . I just wanted to . . . I got your message the other day and I just . . . I'm glad you're getting use out of the guidebook. That's great news. All right well, bye for now.*'

I send a row of hearts to Natalie and tell her she made me cry. She'll love that.

I have a message from Charlie too.

> *HAPPY BIRTHDAY BABE! I hope you're having an amazing time. I'm so jealous. I love you and I'm proud of you and I can't wait to hear all about your trip xxx*

I send them the row of hearts too. I have one more message which makes my heart leap, or contract – there's certainly some sort of cardiovascular event going on in my chest.

> *Happy birthday darling girl. I hope you have a wonderful day with your friends. Speak soon. Dad xxx*

I close down WhatsApp and then open it up again just in case. Nothing from Margot. I chew on the inside of my mouth while I scroll through Instagram, kidding myself I'm not on there specifically to see if she's posted. I'm relieved that she hasn't. Why am I relieved though? What does her not posting on Instagram prove? That she's not looking at her phone? That she's lost her phone? That she's dead? Would all of those be preferable to her having forgotten my birthday?

It's early days, I tell myself. Why would she remember my birthday? I'm disappointed in myself for caring so much.

I almost start crying again when I get up and make my way into the kitchen. The table is scattered with foil confetti in the shape of balloons and they've got me a big pink badge that says 'Birthday Girl' on it. I pin it to the front of my pyjamas.

'How does it feel?' Georgia says, passing me a cup of coffee. She comes and sits down next to me at the table.

'Um,' I say, taking a sip gratefully, 'good! Not really like it's my birthday to be honest. Aside from all this obviously.'

I pick up a piece of confetti and squash it between my fingers.

'Yeah, it's weird to be away from Natalie, huh?' Georgia says.

'Really weird. Hey,' I say. 'My dad texted me.'

Georgia's face lights up.

'That's great.'

'Well,' I say, 'it's the least he can do, isn't it? The bare minimum really.'

'True,' she says. 'But are you happy he did?'

I nod but don't say anything else as Poppy and Felix finally finish faffing about in the kitchen and come and join us.

'You need to go and get dressed, birthday girl,' Poppy says, grinning. 'We're taking you out for breakfast.'

We drive to a diner on the strip at the side of the highway. It's mercifully cool inside and there's a menu longer than my arm full of things designed to feed hikers covering vast distances. The waitress brings us huge glasses of sweet iced tea and I eat what I think could accurately be described as a loaf of French toast. It comes out of the kitchen with a candle on it and everyone sings 'Happy Birthday' to me, which is excruciating but I do kind of love it. The novelty of hearing *'happy birthday to Natasha'* instead of simply *'and Natasha'* as a rushed addendum to *'happy birthday to Natalie'* is always thrilling. I take a photo before I blow my candle out and send it to her.

'You're glued to your phone, Natty,' Georgia says on the way back to the car. The next stop on my birthday day out is a gentle hike in the national park. Zara is still in the diner with Poppy, filling up water bottles.

'Hmm?'

She actually tuts at me.

'You're glued to your phone! It's driving me mad.'

I look at her and she's staring straight ahead, the car key gripped in her hands already pointing it as if to unlock it even though we're too far away.

'Sorry, George. I don't even notice I'm doing it. I'm just chatting to Natalie.'

'You're not waiting for a message from someone?'

She still doesn't look at me.

'No!' I lie, although I'm not sure why. 'I'm just an addict. I'll leave it in the car on our walk. It'll be good for me.'

I immediately regret saying it. I know this means I'll spend the entire hike thinking about whether or not Margot has remembered my birthday.

Georgia sighs.

'No, you don't have to. I just really want us all to be present, you know?'

She shakes her head, more at herself than at me. When we get to the car she unlocks it but just leans on the bonnet instead of letting us in.

'Sorry, I don't know why I'm being so grumpy. You're allowed to be on your phone. It's easy for me to be present, isn't it? My person is here.'

We both look at Zara, marching alongside Poppy carrying an enormous pink water bottle.

'I really hate that,' I say.

'What?' She looks at me, surprised.

'When people say, "my person".'

'Oh.'

Georgia looks away again and then smiles as Zara and Poppy get to the car.

'The boys will be here in a sec,' Zara says walking straight past me and opening the passenger side door. I have the overwhelming and very childish urge to yell, 'Shotgun.'

'They're getting smoothies,' Poppy says. 'I think they're doing anything to put off this walk, Felix's feet are a state.'

'It's a really short one,' Georgia says, catching me frowning, 'I promise.'

*

Georgia's 'really short' hike takes three and a half hours. It's all fun and games at first. The landscape is spectacular. Red dust and blue skies and nothing for miles. By the second hour in we've all stopped speaking to each other. Not because we're irritated necessarily, more to preserve energy. I have never in my life been more aware that I am an animal who needs water to live. How useless and fragile we are in the face of the wilderness. A sure-fire way to fan the flames of an already burgeoning existential birthday crisis.

At home, once we're satisfied that we're no longer dangerously dehydrated and have refuelled sufficiently on trail mix (peanut M+Ms), we all slope off to our rooms to recover. I offer vague reassurances to Georgia as I head out of the kitchen that my birthday is definitely not ruined and that it was 'an experience!'

Instead of going with Felix, Poppy follows me into my room and lies across the foot of my bed like a dog might. A normal dog, Diane, obviously sleeps in the bed, head on pillow.

'Are you actually having a good day?' Poppy says, facing me, her arm under her cheek like a pillow.

'Apart from nearly cooking to death? Yeah, I am.'

I lie back and stretch my legs out. I don't know how I'll manage to get up again.

'Did you hear from your dad?' she says.

I nod.

'That's nice.'

'It is nice.'

I'm extremely glad not to be with Charlie who would probably be pressing me for a feeling deeper than 'nice'.

'And from Margot? I bet she can't wait to have you back.'

'Erm, nothing from her. Yet.'

Poppy frowns.

'But it's like . . .' She screws up her face, trying to work out the time difference and then gives up. 'It's the evening there! She's practically missed your birthday!'

I shrug.

'I know. But it's not a big deal, it's really not. We're very new. It's fine.'

'I don't think it's fine,' Poppy says.

We're both quiet for a moment. Poppy scrolls through her phone and then stops and raises her eyebrows.

'Well,' she says. 'Well, well, well.'

She doesn't elaborate. She goes quiet waiting for me to ask what she's found. I roll my eyes.

'What?' I ask.

Poppy hands me her phone. I actually already know what it's going to be. I saw it in the car on the way home. I've been trying not to think about it.

Margot's face looks back at me from the phone. Or rather it looks out into an audience. She's posted a photo from the gig the other night on Instagram. She's smiling slightly and biting her bottom lip. She has one hand on the microphone and another pushing her hair out of her face.

'So you found her on Instagram then?'

I wonder if they've all had a good look. If Georgia has. Poppy ignores my question.

'She had time to post that,' Poppy says indignantly.

'Right,' I say. 'But it might just be that she's forgotten my birthday. She's not posting that spitefully, Pops.'

'She shouldn't have forgotten your birthday,' she says, taking back her phone.

'OK. Well, she did.'

'I'm just saying,' Poppy says and then, more gently, 'I mean, she still has a few hours, I suppose.'

I nod and then somehow, like little kids at a sleepover who've been keeping themselves awake, we both fall asleep like someone flipped a switch. I dream that Margot is on stage about to tell all my deepest secrets to an audience of all my friends and family and I'm standing backstage but I can't get to her to stop her. When I wake up Poppy is still curled up at the end of the bed, my foot digging into her back.

By the time the evening rolls around and we're getting ready to go out for my birthday dinner I've managed to get to a point where I really believe that I don't care that Margot hasn't messaged me. I'm sort of just relieved to be alive. I decide that it's actually better that she hasn't messaged. I prefer that she's not bothered. I'm not bothered either, am I? It's all very casual.

That is until I'm just out of the shower and applying moisturiser to my sunburnt face when out of the corner of my eye I see my phone lighting up. It's too far away for me to properly read her name but I must recognise the shape on some subconscious level because my heart leaps in a way that it just wouldn't if it was Natalie or Charlie. I grab it.

Happy birthday! I can't wait to see you soon.

Relief floods through me and I immediately loathe myself for it. I don't let myself reply straight away even though I'd really like to tell her about the terrifying hike and the French toast and the place we're going for dinner and how much I want to see her.

Zara has volunteered to be our designated driver for this evening, which is very generous.

'It's my birthday gift to you,' she says as we're getting into the car. She looks gorgeous. I can't believe that she did the same hike I did today and doesn't look like a broken, pink husk of a human.

I'm just about to thank her for being so selfless when she adds, 'Plus I feel disgusting from drinking so much. I need a cleanse.'

The restaurant we're going to is in a place called Pioneer-town. It's not really a town or certainly not like any town I've ever seen before. It's essentially a main street in the middle of the desert lined with buildings that look like they're straight out of a Western movie.

'The whole place was built to be like a living movie set,' Georgia tells us as she parks, speaking into her rear-view mirror like a coach driver giving us a guided tour. 'So some of the places are real and some are fake.'

She turns around to look at us all before we get out of the car and she's grinning from ear to ear.

'I love it, it's so weird.'

We have a few minutes before our dinner reservations so we take a walk. The heat has finally died down and there's a gentle breeze. The sky is still deep blue but the clouds have just started to turn the palest, candyfloss pink, as if in preparation for the sunset. Josh insists on getting a photo of Georgia and me sitting on a bench outside a Wild-West-style saloon.

'The birthday girls only,' he says and ushers us into the chairs as soon as the couple ahead of us have got their selfie.

Zara turns the other way while we pose. She gets her phone out and takes a photograph of a tree.

I get Josh to send me the photo immediately. He's used an app that makes it look like he took it on a disposable camera so it's very flattering and we look about fifteen. Georgia has a huge smile on her face but is also midway through shouting instructions at Josh, I'm looking at her and laughing. I forward it to Natalie and my mum and then, as an afterthought, to my dad. I realise I haven't responded to his message from this morning.

Thanks Dad. Having a wonderful time as you can see!

The restaurant, Pappy and Harriet's, is like a huge dark barn lit by candles and fairy lights. The music is loud, the food smells incredible and the walls are lined with photos of bands that have played here.

'This used to be a biker bar!' Georgia says as we sit down at our table, her tour guide hat still firmly on.

I watch her as she picks up the cocktail list and then looks all around her, a huge smile plastered on her face. She's so pleased with herself for organising everything. It's very endearing. I try to catch her eye but Zara sits down next to her and immediately starts asking her questions about the menu. It's heavy on the Tex-Mex here and light on the salads so I'm sure she's deeply concerned.

I decide on a cocktail made with mezcal and jalapeños called a Highway Queen which just keeps being magically replaced when I finish it. Clearly one of the gang has given the waitress strict instructions to keep a full glass in my hand. We order nachos, quesadillas and, as a concession to Zara and our bodies crying out for a single vitamin, a couple of salads to share. There are more tortilla chips on the table than I think I've ever seen before in my life.

I'm sitting in between Josh and Poppy with Georgia opposite me and Felix and Zara either side of her. It's not a big table so everyone's squeezed in but it feels perfect in the dark with the music blaring. We're all having to speak very loudly to hear each other, I'm certain I'll have lost my voice by the morning.

We're finally all able to laugh about what Josh is now calling our 'near death experience' this afternoon.

'It was fun though, wasn't it?' Zara says and everyone at the table, apart from Georgia, groans.

'Or at least,' Georgia says, 'something you'll always remember about this holiday.'

'True,' I say, 'I will never forget the vultures circling overhead.'

'Natasha!'

'I'm joking. I loved it. It's given me a whole new appreciation for water. And for sitting down.'

Once we've nearly finished eating, a few of us still valiantly trying to make a dent in the mountains of fries and tortilla chips, Poppy taps her knife on the side of her glass. No one hears it.

'Everyone!' she bellows and then smiles beatifically once she has our attention. 'Since it's our last night I think we should go around the table and everyone has to say their favourite bit of the holiday. I'll start.'

We all lean in so we can hear her properly.

'My favourite bit of the holiday was when we all went to the beach on our last night in LA and watched the sunset. I know that will always be the thing I think about when I look back on this trip.'

'Oh yeah,' Felix says, taking a sip of his drink, 'same.'

'Josh, you go,' Poppy says.

'Well,' he says, 'probably sitting in the hot tub looking up at the stars.'

'Aww,' Poppy says, 'that's a lovely one.'

'Oh, and sharing a bed with Natasha, obviously.'

I smile sarcastically at him. He mouths, 'Miss you' at me.

'Mine is all the little walks we did alone around the neighbourhood, just us two,' Zara says to Georgia but loudly enough for us all to hear.

'Aw,' Georgia says, 'yeah, same.'

Josh rolls his eyes.

'What?' Georgia says.

'You can't even think of your own best bits? You have to share one?'

She glares at him.

'Fine. And I also loved the hike this afternoon. Some of us *enjoy* a challenge.'

'I'll go!' I say quickly before Josh can retort. 'Today is my favourite. I've had such a lovely birthday. Thank you all for making it so special.'

I raise my glass and everyone lifts theirs.

And eating ice cream with my dad, I think. I will never forget that.

We all start chatting among ourselves for a while. Poppy is telling me about the book she's reading. It sounds absolutely devastating but it's won a lot of prizes. Sort of high-brow misery lit.

'Literally,' she says to me, 'I am *sobbing* every night. It's amazing. I'll lend it to you.'

'Oh,' I say, 'no rush.'

In a lull, just when I'm thinking we should maybe ask for the cheque, I tune into Josh's voice. I think we all do on account of how loudly he's speaking.

'So,' Josh says, leaning back in his chair and taking a sip of his cocktail through a tiny straw, 'Felix, how did you guys meet?'

He gestures between Felix and Poppy, pointing at them with a French fry dipped in ketchup.

'Oh well, we got together after a mutual friend's birthday dinner, didn't we?' Felix says, beaming at Poppy. He always looks at her like he can't believe his luck.

'We did!' she says. 'We were sitting next to each other and hit it off.'

'Love at first sight,' Felix says.

Poppy smiles at him but doesn't reply. I distinctly remember when she met Felix. She said she'd met this 'lovely man' but that he was 'a bit ridiculous' and 'like the BFG'.

'Although of course,' Felix continues, 'we discovered that we'd probably already met at university, we were both at Durham. There's a chance we could have been in Klute at the same time. Like drunken ships in the night.'

He chuckles to himself and takes a sip of his beer.

'Oh,' Josh says, his eyes suddenly lighting up, 'you might have seen these two in action then?'

He winks at me and suddenly everything feels like it's gone into slow motion. I shake my head at him as if somehow I can get him to rewind but it's too late, obviously.

Felix laughs again, either not catching his drift or not caring.

'Oh probably, probably,' he says.

I take a sip of my drink and glance up at Georgia, hoping she might have missed what Josh said.

'What do you mean?' she says to Josh, frowning.

No such luck.

'These two,' he says, this time employing a fry to point between me and Poppy. '*Lovers!*'

'Lovers!' Felix says, and then bursts out laughing. 'No way?'

'No,' I say quickly to Josh and then to Felix, 'No, really no.'

I look at Poppy.

'Shut *up* Josh,' she says, rolling her eyes. She's smiling though, she doesn't know what this is going to mean to Georgia.

'Sorry,' Georgia says, looking around the table and then back at me, she puts down her fork. 'I'm not sure I understand.'

Georgia's voice is very quiet. It demands that everyone else be quiet too. Suddenly everyone's attention is focused on us.

'No, it was nothing. It was nothing, wasn't it, Poppy?'

'Literally nothing. I . . . sorry, this all happened years ago.'

Poppy frowns slightly at me, unsure what the problem is. I look away from her, worried it looks like she's trying to convey some sort of message.

'If it's nothing then what is he talking about?'

Georgia points at Josh who is leaning back in his chair, sipping from his tiny straw.

'I . . . it's so silly George,' I say.

I'm nervous for some reason. Why am I so nervous?

'Just once or twice at uni, Poppy and I sort of got together.'

I cringe. I sound like a teenager.

315

I look around everyone and smile, attempting to lighten the mood, but Georgia doesn't smile back and everyone else just drops their eyes down to their plates. Josh looks at me wide-eyed as it dawns on him that he's accidentally thrown a grenade into the middle of my birthday dinner.

Georgia picks up her drink and takes a few gulps of it. I wince watching her – it's strong. We got the same thing.

'Got together?' She spits the words out. 'Like how?'

'I . . .' I look at Poppy for help but she's suddenly very inter-ested in topping up her and Felix's water. He's frowning slightly. Not like he's cross, more like he has no idea what's going on.

'Like how?' Georgia repeats. 'Like you kissed her? You had sex with her?'

I'd been about to put a tortilla chip in my mouth, still trying to be nonchalant, but I put it back down on my plate. Nobody makes a sound.

'Georgia,' Zara says quietly, putting her hand on her arm. Georgia shakes it off.

'No it's fine, I'm just surprised,' she turns to face me again, 'I just feel like this is something I would know about. It feels like something you should have mentioned.'

Georgia looks around the table, as if she's only just noticed that everyone has gone quiet and is watching her intently.

'Does no one else think that?'

Everyone's silent for a couple of beats.

'Georgia,' Poppy says gently. 'I would understand you being upset if this was when you were together. But we're talking years ago. Before you guys even met! And like, no offence,' she looks at me and I prepare to be offended, 'but I'm straight! I like boys!'

She gestures at Felix and he nods, he's smiling in a way that makes me want to punch him in the face. I look away. I think that's probably the last thing this dinner needs.

'I don't think it's that much of a big deal . . .' Josh tries but doesn't seem to be able to finish his thought. He looks shell-shocked, unable to process the monumental shift in atmosphere of the past few minutes. I almost feel sorry for him. Almost.

Georgia shakes her head one last time, at me, at all of us, as if she doesn't recognise us at all. She removes her napkin from her knee, throws it down on the table and walks out of the res-taurant. Without even making a conscious decision to do so, I get up and follow her.

She heads straight out of the back door and around to the side of the outdoor seating area where people are smoking. Eve-rything is lit up with strings of fairy lights in the garden but, once you're away from the tables and the bar, it's suddenly much darker. You're very aware that you're in the middle of a desert.

'Georgia?'

'I just need a minute,' Georgia says, not directly to me but to the gloomy view in front of us.

'No. Georgia. What on earth is going on?'

'You can't just keep things from me,' Georgia says.

She turns to face me and I can see that she's furious. She

doesn't ever get like this so I don't know how to handle her. I know her upset. I know her stressed. I don't know her angry.

'I don't keep things from you! You didn't know this one tiny bit of information.'

'It's not tiny! It's not! It's my best friend and my . . . my . . .'

She looks at me, lost for words for a moment.

'My two best friends hooking up and not telling me.'

'I hadn't even met you George!'

'And you've got a girlfriend.'

'What?'

'You've met someone and you didn't tell me.'

'It's new!'

'It's not new. I asked Poppy. You've been seeing her for a while. She told me all about it. All about her.'

She looks down at her feet and I get a rush of righteous validation. I knew she'd been on her Instagram.

'I don't have to tell you everything. It's not serious! Why would I tell you?'

'What are you getting out of it then? If it's not serious, or whatever. What do you get out of it?'

I'm lost for words for a moment. This question feels like a trap.

'What do you mean? What do I get out of it? I like spending time with her.'

'No. I'll tell you what you get out of it. She's exciting and she's new. And it is *never, ever* going to go anywhere so you don't have to worry about it.'

'What the fuck? What the fuck are you talking about? What do you know about it?'

I take a deep breath.

'You're so angry with me, Georgia. Why? What's going on here?'

Georgia pauses. She wipes her mouth with the back of her hand. She's shaking.

'It's about you – It's about you –'

She's reaching around for whatever it is about me that's made her lose her shit tonight. 'It's about you not telling the truth,' she says eventually. It sounds so weak she can't even look at me.

'No, it's not. It's not even about me and Poppy. It's about me casually seeing someone. And that's bothering you. Why is that, Georgia?'

I don't even know exactly what it is I'm pressing her for. What it is I want to hear. She throws up her hands at me.

'Why do you fucking think? Why do you think, Natty?'

'I'm sorry,' I say quietly. 'I'm sorry that I couldn't be what you wanted.'

She shakes her head.

'I want you to be happy,' she says eventually but she shouts it, which sort of takes away from the sentiment. 'And I'm worried you're making yourself miserable.'

'I'm fine. I wish everybody would stop telling me they want me to be happy. I'm sick of it. Maybe *you* should try and be happy, because *you* don't seem very fucking happy either. Does a happy person walk out of a restaurant to yell at someone over a kiss that happened a decade ago?'

Georgia just looks at me steadily.

'You're not him, you know.'

Adrenaline pulses through me.

'Excuse me?'

She pauses but nods to herself, a reassurance that she's right.

'You're not like him. Your dad. You can let yourself be with someone. You might not let them down like you think you will.'

'Are you . . . who the fuck do you think you are right now? Where is this coming from? You want to talk about letting people down? You've known Zara for five fucking minutes and you turf me out of my home of three years.'

'What?'

She looks genuinely shocked.

'You just got rid of me.'

She shakes her head. 'How long did you think you could go on living there? Did you always just assume I was going to be your safety net?'

I look at her. My heart is pounding. I *had* thought she was always going to be my safety net.

I take a step towards her. 'You know what all this sounds like, George? It sounds like you're jealous. It sounds like you're still angry with me that I left you and you can't get over it.'

She moves towards me. 'You never left me, Natasha,' she hisses. 'That's the problem. You're everywhere. You're fucking everywhere.'

We're standing so close to each other now I could touch her. Just reach out and touch her.

'That's enough now.'

Zara is standing in the doorway, her arms folded across her chest.

We both spin around to look at her.

'Enough,' she repeats and walks back inside. Georgia looks at me, wide-eyed like she's just woken up from a dream, and then slowly turns and follows Zara back inside.

I stand there for what feels like a long time. I want to walk out into the unknown, across the empty, dusty road and into the darkness. But I don't. I stand with my hand on my chest, feeling my heart thump through my shirt and trying to catch my breath. Georgia's words echo around my brain, already beginning to warp so that I'm not sure whether I'm replaying what she said or what I felt or what I think about myself. After what feels like hours but might actually have only been a minute or two Poppy comes and stands beside me.

'Don't cry,' she says gently, a hand on my back. I put a hand up to my face and realise my cheeks are wet. 'Time to go home, I think.'

She takes my hand and leads me back through the bar. One more night. One more night and then I can go home.

11

It feels like it could be very early morning or very late at night, a time when I'm not meant to be awake. It's actually five o'clock in the afternoon and, having barely slept on the plane, I am deliriously tired. Poppy went straight to Felix's flat and I went home alone from the airport. I stood in the shower with the radio blasting just to drown myself out. That and the image of Georgia standing in front of me shaking and telling me I'm everywhere. *Fucking everywhere.* I can't stand being alone for longer than an hour.

I'd already messaged Margot on the way home from the airport saying I wanted to see her. Checking back now for her address to put into Uber I wince seeing that I actually wrote, *I need to see you.*

Margot lives in an area full of cute cafes and bars and Airbnbs hosting parties all weekend. Hers is the top-floor flat of a converted town house and, after she buzzes me in, I take my time walking up the flights of stairs inhaling deeply to alleviate my racing heart.

When I reach the top of the stairs Margot is standing in the doorway of her flat waiting for me. She's wearing red shorts with a stripe down the side and a loose white vest top. Somewhere between pyjamas and sportswear. She's wearing a gold necklace I've never seen before.

'You made it!' she says leaning in and kissing me. I can't tell whether she's commenting on me making it home or simply managing to get to the top of the stairs. I make an effort to appear not at all out of breath, like three flights of stairs is no trouble whatsoever.

'I made it,' I say and follow her inside. I kick off my shoes and add them to a basket filled with trainers next to the door. I hand her the wine I've brought with me. It's travelled all the way from LA – a bottle of Lisa Vanderpump rosé. Delightfully tacky and surprisingly expensive. I also bought a bottle for Natalie. Margot barely glances at the label – the name Lisa Vanderpump clearly means nothing to her. She needs an education.

As soon as the door is closed she pushes me against it and kisses me again, gently parting my lips with her tongue.

'I missed you,' she murmurs as she slips her hand under my T-shirt, tracing her finger down my spine.

I wrap my arms around her neck and feel some of my sadness slipping away.

'What did you miss?' I say.

'Everything,' she says, leading me by my hand down the hall

and into her bedroom. The hall is painted dark green. There's a huge framed Frida Kahlo print hanging on the wall which surprises me. I just can't imagine Margot choosing it for some reason.

'You missed everything? That's a cop-out,' I say, smiling despite myself.

'What did you miss about me?' she says.

I sit down on the bed.

She has music playing. It's Maggie Rogers. I would say on average fifty to seventy per cent of my dates with women involve Maggie Rogers playing in the background. It's dark in her room, blackout blinds drawn to keep the sun out.

'Did I say that I missed you?'

I smile at her and lie back on top of her duvet. It's thick and weighty, filled with feathers. My mind wanders briefly as I try to imagine how on earth she hasn't roasted to death underneath it over the summer but I'm soon brought back to reality when Margot climbs onto the bed, straddling my hips, her thighs either side of me.

'I know that you did,' she says and bends down to kiss me on each cheek.

I can't help but smile up at her.

'I did,' I confirm.

She nods, satisfied.

'Off,' she says and gently lifts my T-shirt over my head.

I do as she says and wriggle out of my jeans too. She moves so that she's next to me and does the same. She kisses me deeply and as her hands move over my body I feel myself relax, lighten, the heaviness of the past forty-eight hours shifting slightly. I sigh and pull her closer to me when her hand moves between my legs. I arch my back to meet her. Somehow nothing makes me feel like I can get close enough to her. Normally, I would probably have sat up, shifted positions, taken control, but I'm so tired and there's something about tonight where relinquishing it all to her is so appealing.

I can tell that she knows I'm feeling raw and vulnerable and for some reason today I don't mind. When I bury my head in her neck she bends down and kisses mine gently.

When she moves away or, more accurately, when I finally let her go, she frowns. Her leg is still between mine.

'You look exhausted,' she says, peering closely at my face.

'Thank you.'

'You do though.'

She reaches over and pushes a piece of hair out of my face and I rest my cheek against her hand briefly.

'God, I really did miss you.'

I say it before I even have a chance to think about it.

She smiles broadly.

'I like this jet-lagged you.'

'All helpless and pathetic?'

She kisses my neck, all the way down to my throat.

'Yes. You'll have to go away more often.'

'Maybe.'

She pulls back to look at me properly.

'Why are you so sad?'

'I'm not sad. I'm with you.'

I take hold of her arm to pull her down again but she stays put.

'You are.'

'I'm not sad.' I mean that, the sadness that started ebbing away when I got here feels as though it's almost dissipated entirely. 'I'm just . . . the trip had a weird ending.'

I tell her all about my fight with Georgia. How, even worse than not speaking to me, she's been speaking to me like a stranger ever since. Ultra-polite and distant. That when I thanked her for the trip she just said, 'You're welcome' without looking at me.

'That is really weird,' Margot says. 'I'm sorry that happened. I'm sorry you're so upset.'

'Thank you.'

'Why do you think she kicked off like that?'

'I don't know.'

Margot looks at me as if to say, 'come on.'

'I don't!'

'No theories?'

'I think she felt as though she was being kept out of the loop.'

'That's a disproportionate response though, no?'

'Maybe. We'd had a bit to drink so it was all quite heightened.'

'You don't think that it's because there's still some unfinished business there? That she might still have feelings for you?'

I'm quiet for a moment. It's too complicated to get into. I start to feel myself tense up again.

'Maybe.'

She nods. If she was a different kind of person she might be jealous or demand some more answers but she's not and she doesn't.

She gets up to go to the bathroom promising to be back in a second. As soon as she's gone I reach over and find the switch for the bedside lamp. I squint my eyes as I adjust to the light. It's only then that I properly take in that there are two bedside tables, one on each side of the bed, identical with the same copper lamps on top of them. Each one has a different pile of books on it, a hand cream, a lip balm and a phone charger coiled on top of it. I sit upright and swing my legs over one side of the bed. I pick up a photo frame from the bedside table closest to me and squint at it. It's Margot with a group of four other people. Two women and two men. They're all standing around a table piled high with food, maybe at Christmas time. It's an old photo, she looks really young. She has a full-on fringe.

Margot opens the door and smiles when she sees me holding the photograph.

'God that's from years ago,' she says and lies back down on the bed, pulling me back towards her. I let her.

'Um, Margot. I have to . . .'

I pause, deciding if I'm really going to do this. Do I really want to know?

'Did you once mention living with someone?'

'Maybe,' she says, lifting my hair up to kiss the back of my neck. I desperately don't want to probe any further. I want to lie there forever, I want to pull her hand down between my thighs and stay quiet but I know that I can't.

'Margot,' I say, speaking to the wall. Still not wanting to turn around. 'Does someone else live here?'

She pauses the neck-kissing but rests her lips against my skin so that when she talks she's muffled and I can feel them vibrating.

'Why are you asking that?'

'Because . . . I think this bedroom belongs to two people. And because you once said someone else lived here. There's two of everything.'

She sighs and pulls back so that her head is no longer next to mine, she unwraps her arm from around my waist but leaves it instead resting on my hip. I move my hand so that it's holding hers, stroking the tops of her fingers.

'No I mean, why are you asking? Do you really want to know?'

I close my eyes. I don't want to know.

'Yes. Tell me.'

She sighs and looks up at the ceiling.

'My girlfriend lives here.'

I snatch my hand back and cover my eyes for a second, inhaling deeply.

'For fuck's sake, Margot.'

I sit upright and grab for something to cover myself up, suddenly feeling horribly exposed. There's a throw on the bottom of the bed which I lift up and drape over myself.

'Does she know? Like, are you . . . allowed to?'

I gesture at myself. Are you allowed to have other women lie on your bed wrapped in your throws?

She doesn't move. She lies on her side watching me as if the atmosphere hasn't changed at all, as if I'm going to lie back down with her. She closes her eyes and then when she reopens them she shakes her head.

'Fuck. Fuck, Margot! Why didn't you say something? You know I would never have . . .'

She finally sits up, she arranges herself cross-legged but still doesn't make any moves to cover herself up.

'I think you would have.'

'If you think I would have, then why didn't you tell me?'

She's quiet, she raises her eyebrows, almost conceding I have a point.

'Things aren't good at the moment. We're just . . . she's staying with some friends, we're having a bit of space. She's so intense it's like she always wants me to . . .'

I hold my hand up to stop her.

'I'm not going to sit here, in your girlfriend's bed, and have you tell me what's wrong with her.'

'Fair enough. That's fair. But . . . listen, it's complicated. Everything's complicated, right? You know that. You know that more than anyone. It's not black and white.'

I don't say anything. I just get dressed as quickly as I can and then walk out of the bedroom to gather my stuff. I make my way down the narrow hall and into her tiny bathroom. It has cold black and white tiles on the floor. I look at myself in the small, copper-framed mirror above the sink while I'm washing my hands, I'm blurry and a bit pink. I wipe away smudges of black liner from under my eyes and push back my hair from my face. There are two toothbrushes in the cup on the sink. The bathroom smells a little of damp but mostly of the tobacco and vanilla candle perched on the edge of the bath. Before I leave I pick it up and breathe it in. Dark and sweet.

While I'm putting my shoes on Margot comes and hovers over me. She's put on an oversized T-shirt. Her arms are folded and she's biting her lip anxiously, something I've never seen her do before.

I stand up and look at her. I have one hand on the front door handle but make no moves to go.

'I'm not a bad person,' she says. 'I really do like you so much. That's why this . . . I know I haven't gone about this in the right way.'

'Gone about what? Cheating on your girlfriend? Lying to me?'

Margot closes her eyes, she looks as though she might be counting to ten, trying to gather herself.

'I'm going to break up with her.'

'No, no, no. Not on my account.'

'I was always going to break up with her.'

'It doesn't matter now, do what you want.'

'Please, Natasha,' she reaches out and holds my hand in both of hers, 'I know this looks bad, I know this makes me seem like an awful person, I know.'

I'm surprised to see tears in her eyes. She really is desperate.

'But I like you so much. I like this so much. I don't want it to end.'

She leans forward and kisses me gently. I let her and for a moment I start to feel all my resolve melting away. I could so easily let go of the door handle and we could pick up where we left off.

I pull away.

'I have to go,' I say.

She nods. A tear spills down her cheek and I look away before I change my mind.

I make my way down the three flights of stairs and walk the streets in a daze, a dizzy combination of jet lag and shock. Although it feels like I'm wandering aimlessly I find myself outside Charlie's flat. I knock gently.

'Oh my god,' Charlie says when they answer the door. They usher me in and close the door behind me. Their flat is cool and dark, it smells very sweet, like strawberry jam. I wonder if they've been vaping indoors. 'What happened, are you OK?'

I shake my head.

'No. I'm not OK.'

For the first time since my fight with Georgia I start to cry. Charlie pulls me in for a hug and I find myself sobbing. I realise that in all our years of friendship, Charlie has never seen me cry.

Charlie strokes my back gently until I calm down. I take a deep breath and pull away.

'I'm sorry, Charlie.'

'Don't be silly.'

'No I am, I'm sorry. Just turning up like this unannounced, ruining your evening. I just didn't know where else to go. I think I've made a mess of everything.'

'Oh, I don't doubt that.'

Charlie smiles at me and I can't help but laugh through my tears.

They hold me by my shoulders and look at me seriously.

'Cup of tea? Something stronger?'

'Tea please.'

Once Charlie returns from the kitchen we curl up on the sofa together. I pull a bright yellow cushion onto my knee and hug it to my chest. Charlie offers me a chocolate chip cookie from a nearly empty packet. I take one gratefully.

'So,' they grimace slightly, 'how bad is it?'

'I don't even know where to start.'

'At the beginning.'

I bite into my biscuit. My mouth is dry and it sticks to my gums.

'Actually,' Charlie says as I gulp down water trying to remember when I'd last had any, 'maybe just start with why you're here this evening.'

'OK.' I take a deep breath. 'I just found out that Margot has a girlfriend.'

The words don't sound as absurd out loud as they should. They sound inevitable. Margot has a girlfriend. Like puzzle pieces falling into place.

'Ah,' Charlie says, grimacing. 'I'm really sorry, Natty.'

'I don't even . . .' Fresh tears form and instead of swallowing them down I let them spill down my cheeks. I wipe them away with the back of my hand. 'I don't even think I've processed that properly. It's all too much and I'm just so tired.'

'What?' Charlie says gently. 'What's too much?'

Instead of just saying, 'Everything', which is what it feels like, I try to figure out exactly what it is that's making my stomach turn and my head throb but I can't quite do it.

As if they're reading my mind Charlie says gently, 'That's OK, sometimes it's everything.'

I nod.

'I feel like I'm . . .'

Charlie waits patiently for me while my exhausted brain whirs away trying to work out what I am. *You're not him*, the Georgia in my head says on repeat. *You're not him, you're not him, you're not him.* And then it comes to me.

'Freefalling.'

Charlie doesn't say anything. They just look at me steadily.

'And I don't know how to stop,' I say. 'So I just keep going.'

Charlie frowns.

'Like I'm just sort of flailing around while things happen around me. Moving in with Poppy, Margot, my dad, Georgia. It's just too much. My head is just constantly spinning and I can't stop it. Does that make sense?'

'It makes sense,' Charlie says. 'I know what you mean. What do you want instead?'

I answer straight away, in a moment of clarity, knowing exactly what I want.

'To be still.'

'Still,' Charlie echoes.

I nod.

'To be still for a while. For everything to just be quiet. So I can think.'

Charlie opens their mouth to suggest something but I already know what they're going to say.

'If you recommend that bloody Thai retreat to me, Charlie, I will scream.'

Charlie closes their mouth again and then starts laughing. I laugh too and whack them gently with the cushion I'm holding.

'You can do that, though,' Charlie says. 'Be still. Find quiet. You can do that anywhere. But it can be painful.'

'What do you mean?'

'Well, when it's finally quiet,' Charlie says, picking up the last cookie, breaking it in two and handing me my piece, 'you don't know what you might hear.'

12

December, four months later

For at least a decade, 9 a.m. on a Saturday has looked like one of a few bleak but familiar scenarios. A hangover would usually be involved. A painfully empty stomach from not eating dinner the night before, but one which I would not be able to feed for several hours due to the aforementioned hangover and the swells of nausea I'd experience until at least midday. I might be in my own bed which would be a bonus. I might be alone, even better. But both of those things were not guaranteed. A dark cloud of dread and paranoia would loom over my morning, a sense of something not quite right would sit on my chest. All of this with a smile on my face, a phone in my hand ready to numb the sensations, replace them with new ones. My head filled with knowledge of ways to combat the feelings of inadequacy, the hurt, the shame, the pain. Ways to talk about them, confront them, work through them, alleviate them. All locked in a box reserved for other people.

On this Saturday at 9 a.m., as I have been every Saturday at 9 a.m. for the past few weeks, I am sitting in an office in a woman's garden drinking a cup of coffee, eating a shortbread finger and in absolutely no danger whatsoever of throwing up.

It's one of those offices which are like glass shipping containers. Inside it's all wooden floors and panels and the smell is somewhere between a sauna and a hamster cage no matter how much the citrus-scented candle burns. There's a desk at one end of the office with a closed MacBook on it and a stack of books neatly piled up. There are two comfy armchairs facing each other, both have wooden side tables next to them. One has a notebook and pen on it alongside a cup of coffee. In the middle there is a very fluffy rug and on that rug is a very old, very tired black labrador who has gone grey around his eyebrows.

The first time I came here, Allison, my new therapist, asked me if I minded Alan sitting in on our sessions and I don't think I even let her finish the sentence before I told her that I would love it. He is completely silent and still unless he's having a dream in which case I become vaguely aware of him chasing rabbits in his sleep.

'How are you doing this week, Natasha?' Allison asks, her hands wrapped around her mug as if to warm them, even though the electric heater inside the office has made it so hot that I'm sweating underneath my jumper.

'Really well thank you, yeah,' I say, an automatic response but not entirely untrue.

I pause for a moment reflecting on what I might like to talk about this week. The first couple of times I came to see Allison everything poured out of me as though I hadn't spoken for months, years even. Which I suppose, in a way, I hadn't.

'I've had a great week at work, I have two new clients. I had a really useful peer supervision session. And I'm really excited today because it's my sister Natalie's baby shower.'

Allison smiles.

'How lovely,' she says. In a normal conversation one would probably follow this up with a question about the shower but of course this isn't a normal conversation. She's going to leave a pause now and wait for me to fill it with my thoughts and feelings, which of course, I do.

'When I found out she was pregnant, I don't think I really appreciated . . . I only thought about myself. I think I went through the motions of being happy for them. No, I *was* happy for them. I really was. But I could only see it through what it meant to me. Or what it meant in relation to my life. And now I just feel outside of everything that's going on with me, I just feel so happy there's going to be another baby. Another little person to love.'

Allison nods and cocks her head to one side. She takes her glasses off and rubs the lenses with the bottom of her shirt.

'I think it's quite common to view other people's big life events through what it means for you. I think that's a very human thing.'

I think for a moment.

'I suppose. I just mean . . . maybe I mean . . . I'm happier in general and so being happy for other people is easier than it was.'

Allison nods again and, when I don't elaborate, asks, 'What else have you been up to this week?'

'I went on a date.'

'And how was that?'

I shrug.

'It was fine. We didn't click so I probably won't see her again.'

I worry that Allison is judging me. I find myself wanting to say something to impress her, to prove I'm working on myself.

'I didn't get catastrophically drunk though! Or try to sleep with her knowing I wasn't bothered so that feels like . . . something.'

'What does that feel like?'

'Um . . . a step in the right direction?'

Allison just looks at me, refusing to confirm or deny whether she thinks it's a step in the right direction or not. Honestly, therapists are so annoying.

'Look,' I say. Ploughing on in the hopes of eliciting some kind of satisfying response from her, 'I like dating. I'm not doing anyone any harm by dating but I think perhaps the way I have a tendency . . . I really don't want to be careless with people. Or with myself. With anything. I want to take more care. That's what I'm trying to do.'

'What does that mean to you?'

'What do you mean?'

'What does not being careless mean to you?'

I pick up my coffee and take a sip. It's very strong. I make a face as if I've just had a shot of tequila.

'I know,' Allison says. 'It's these new pods I'm trying. Better for the environment but they're a bit intense.'

'No, no I like it. Bracing.'

She doesn't reply. She just looks at me waiting for me to answer her question. It's impossible to distract this woman.

'I think sometimes, in the past, I've used people without really meaning to. If I care then I'm worried I'll let someone down. Or they'll let me down. It's easier if I just . . . if everything's done at a distance.'

'Has that been easier for you?'

'In some ways.'

'And in others?'

'No. It hasn't been.'

'Why do you think you'll let people down?'

I sigh.

'I've just . . . it's always been that way. I don't really know why.'

'OK. So why do you think they'll let you down?'

'Well,' I say, looking at her like it's the most obvious thing in the world. 'Because my dad left, didn't he?'

'But what's that got to do with you?'

'Well . . . it's just that children tend to learn from their parents and they can end up replicating patterns of behaviour . . .'

Allison holds up her hand to stop me.

'I know. What I'm saying is, are you going to let your dad, a man who hasn't been a part of your life for the best part of twenty years, dictate what you're doing now? How you're treating people and letting people treat you?'

I don't say anything.

'Why do you think you'll end up doing to other people what he did to you and your family? Why don't you think you'll do what your mum did? Or your sister? Or your sister's partner?'

I pause before answering.

'Because . . . I think, I spent a lot of time as a child and as a teenager . . .' I start to cry, inevitable. Allison nods towards the box of tissues next to me and I take one. 'I spent a lot of time terrified that my being gay was going to mean . . . that I was more like him than I was everyone else.'

Allison nods. I think she's going to tell me that being gay has nothing to do with it. That people are people and they make mistakes and do things they're not proud of all the time. Things I've been telling myself. But she doesn't.

'Why did you think that?'

'I . . . I don't know. I think my mum thought that. She was so angry at him for such a long time. She still is angry. And I think I took a lot of that on. I felt a lot of that was aimed at me. I thought she was disgusted by me. That I was somehow betraying her too.'

'Is she angry with you now?'

I shake my head immediately.

'No. She's not.'

I'm surprised by my own answer. How sure I am of that fact.

'Are you angry with her?'

I nod.

'Yes I am. A bit. Not as angry as I used to be. But yeah, I think that's why I'm so cold with her because I'm afraid of getting into it all with her. That and, you know, she's really annoying.'

Allison ignores my throwaway comment, as usual.

'Why are you angry?'

'I wish she'd told me that it was OK. That I was OK. She made me feel like I was wrong. I just think she would look at me and see him.'

Allison nods.

I know we're running out of time for today's session.

'I'm seeing her today,' I say.

'How do you feel about that?'

'I feel good about it.'

Again, I surprise myself with my answer. It's true. I do feel good.

'She's going to be so happy today. She really loves us all even if she has a funny way of showing it.'

Alan twitches in his sleep, blissfully unaware of the human angst going on above his head.

'People often have a funny way of showing it,' Allison says and smiles at me kindly.

The 'surprise' baby shower is being thrown at Natalie and Luke's house. Supposedly she doesn't know about it but I don't believe that. She knows everything – she has eyes and ears everywhere in that way that mums just do. Plus I don't believe the twins have managed to act normally around her, they'll be too excited. Luke's driven her somewhere for a 'nice walk' which is suspicious enough. Even more suspicious is the fact that she hasn't complained about it and, by the looks of her Instagram story, has gone out on this walk with a full face of make-up and a blow-dry.

As soon as I finish therapy I race to the train to make it by midday in time to help set up. I have a book with me, it's a thriller and it works pretty well replacing all the adrenaline and endorphins I would normally get from sitting on my phone waiting for messages or wading through my emails. It allows me to leave my phone in my bag for almost the entire journey. Major progress. I take it out once to message Poppy and remind her I won't be home tonight. We've been spending more evenings together than usual while she and Felix are having some 'space' from one another. The 'space' is very undefined, however it is made much easier by the fact that he's spent the past two weeks working in Hong Kong. He comes back next week and every time I ask her what she's going to do she pretends she hasn't heard me.

I also do one quick scroll through Instagram. Charlie has posted a photo of themselves on a beach holding a white cocktail with a pink flower in it. The caption says, 'Take me back.' I leave a comment saying, *wait, did you go to Thailand?!* They have quite literally not shut up about it since they got back a week ago. I'm not sure they found themselves but they definitely found a tan and an annoying habit of looping every conversation back to their 'journey'. I follow my comment up with a heart. Charlie has been an angel to me for the past couple of months, the least I can do is appreciate their perfectly curated Instagram content.

In a rare moment of weakness I allow myself to look at Margot's Instagram. I mean, it's not hard to find. When I type 'M' she's still my first search result even though I've unfollowed her. We haven't spoken since the night I left her flat. She sent a long message apologising and explaining and trying to reason with me. I had intended to reply but I found that the idea of speaking to her was sending me into a tailspin. The opposite of the peace I was looking for. So the days turned into weeks into months and the message is still unanswered. She hasn't posted in a while but I watch her stories. A book she's been reading, the full moon last night. I hope when she sees my name there on the list of viewers she knows that I like seeing what she's up to. That I'm not hate-stalking her videos of the moon. I wish there was a way to subtly convey that to her without sending the heart eyes emoji.

As soon as I arrive at Natalie's house I run upstairs to change into my baby-shower outfit (the pink suit strikes again) and make myself look more presentable and less like a sweaty mess. My mum is in the kitchen with two of Natalie's friends and Luke's sister sorting out piles of tiny sandwiches and scones for our afternoon tea. When I get back downstairs I am very pleased to see that there are several bottles of prosecco in the fridge waiting to go. Just because she can't drink doesn't mean Natalie wouldn't want absolutely everybody else to. She's requested a glass of champagne be passed to her before the baby is after she's given birth which is, frankly, iconic.

'You look nice,' my mum says as I hover about looking for a job to do. She is carrying a plate with some of the most horrifying cupcakes I've ever seen on it. They have thick white icing shaped like a Moses basket with fondant babies wearing nappies on top. They're all bald with their eyes closed. They look like mole-rats. I'm not sure I'd be able to eat one.

'Thanks Mum,' I say, surprised. 'So do you.' She does, she's wearing a floral dress with long sleeves that I've never seen before. She's all pink in the face, excited about the day even though she'd probably never admit it. She looks tired. She's been working nights again recently. I know because we've been texting most days. I ask her to let me know when she gets home. She always does.

'Did you make these?' I gesture at the cakes.

'Oh no!' she says, horrified at the very idea. 'One of Natalie's friends did. They're very . . . um . . . unusual.'

I grimace and she smiles, almost shyly. I could cry at how little we know each other.

'Let me take them,' I say.

She nods and passes me the tray and then follows me into the living room where a table has been set up and covered with food. Mostly cake in various pastel colours. I'd be amazed if someone isn't horribly sick by the end of the afternoon. Because

Natalie and Luke are still claiming not to know if they're having a boy or a girl the decorations and banners covering the living room are equal parts blue and pink and, of course, the ultimate neutral baby colour – yellow. Almost everything has a duck on it. Combined with the Christmas decorations, which are already up, and the tree, which is way too big for the room, the overall effect is bonkers. I kind of love it.

Ella and Daniel are sitting cross-legged on the floor trying to blow up balloons filled with confetti inside. They have a lot to get through and are working at the speed of approximately one balloon per hour.

'Do you two want a hand?' I say.

'Yeah,' Daniel says. 'This is taking forever. I thought this would be the funnest job.'

'Yeah,' Ella says. 'It's the worst job. My *lungs* hurt.'

I sit down next to them on the floor and my mum heads back into the kitchen saying over her shoulder that she's going to bring us some drinks. She's gone before I can ask if there's any wine open.

I blow up a balloon as quickly as I can, tie the knot and then rub it against Ella's hair so she screams and runs over to sit on the sofa instead. Daniel laughs hysterically.

'Do you guys think your mum knows we're doing this?' I say, before taking a deep breath and getting started on balloon number two.

'Yeah definitely,' Ella says, sitting back on the sofa, not even bothering to pretend to carry on blowing up balloons now that

I'm on the case. 'She asked me this morning if she should do her hair. And I said I didn't know and she sat me down and was like,' she puts on a deadly serious face, ' "No El, *do I need* to *do my hair?*" So I was, like . . . yeah.'

I nod. That sounds about right.

'She'll still act surprised though,' I say.

'Yeah she will. And she doesn't know about the balloons,' Daniel says.

'True. Or all the cake.'

'Why is there so much cake?' he says, frowning at the heaving table.

'Not sure,' I say. 'Is the theme cake?'

Ella shrugs.

'You look nice,' she says to me after a couple more minutes of her observing my balloon-blowing.

'Oh thanks,' I say, looking down at myself. 'Yeah I like this suit now, I wasn't sure about it . . .'

'No,' she interrupts me. 'Not the suit.'

'Oh right.'

'Like . . . in your face.'

'Oh!'

'You just look nice.'

'Yeah,' Daniel chimes in, peering at me. 'Your face looks different.'

'I'm probably just not hungover,' I say.

'Yeah,' Ella says, already bored of this conversation, 'you don't look so old.'

'OK. Lovely. Thanks.'

Guests start arriving around ten minutes before Natalie and Luke are due back and we begin herding them around the house like sheepdogs until we finally have them all gathered in the living room. It's a tight squeeze and when we hear Natalie's car come up the drive we all fall silent. Well, we fall into fits of giggles and people shushing each other. I am standing next to Mum and when we hear the front door open she rests her hand on my forearm just for a second. I look at her and smile. She holds her finger up to her lips just in case I've forgotten to be quiet. Perfect.

'What a lovely walk!'

Natalie is performing very loudly in the hallway presumably while taking her shoes off, milking this moment for all it's worth. I can just imagine her saying everything while winking.

'Really Luke, thank you for such a lovely, long walk. Now I can't wait to go and put my feet up . . . in the living room.'

The fact that it's a performance is totally lost on Ella and Daniel who, despite wanting to be cool, are absolutely beside themselves with excitement. When she says 'living room' they start jumping up and down like they're going to explode with the effort of staying quiet for a moment longer. I get out my phone to film the moment she walks in.

'SURPRISE!'

Natalie does a blood-curdling scream when she opens the door. It's perhaps slight overkill but I think, even though she knew something was happening, she is genuinely overwhelmed with how many of the people she loves are stuffed into her house.

Once she's done hugging her friends and colleagues and loudly telling off Luke for keeping such a big secret from her (he rolls his eyes; I bet she's been asking him about it all morning) Natalie comes over to me, Mum and the twins and makes us all do a group hug.

'This is the best thing ever,' she tells the twins. 'Did you help do this?'

'We did all the balloons!' they say.

'They did,' I say. 'It's true.'

'Amazing, I knew you'd done them. The balloons are my favourite bit,' she says. She wraps one arm around my shoulder and whispers in my ear, 'Who is responsible for the dead baby cakes on my table?'

I burst out laughing and then cover my mouth quickly, not wanting to draw attention to the conversation.

'They're not dead,' I say. 'They're . . . resting.'

'I'm sorry,' she whispers and then beams at somebody walking by before hissing in my ear, 'they're dead and you need to get rid of them. They're cursing my house right now.'

I look at her trying to work out how serious she's being. It's completely serious.

'Yep,' I say. 'Got it. They're gone.'

She nods and then, just as she's about to go and speak to someone else, turns back to me.

'You look nice.'

'Yeah, that's what Ella said. She said I didn't look as old as usual.'

'No,' Natalie says, 'you do look old. Very old and haggard but it's something else.'

'The suit?'

'No.'

'OK.' Does everyone hate this suit?

'You seem . . . more yourself.'

'Than what?'

'Than . . .' Natalie throws her hands up in the air, 'than ever! Bloody hell, try and give a girl a compliment.'

Once everyone's said hello to each other and found out how we all know Natalie and downed a couple of mamamosas (Natalie's friends are very pleased with themselves for this one, they're also serving mamajitos), we're forced to play a game. Luke's sister wanted to do a whole load of them including stuff involving nappies and chocolate bars but fortunately my mum stepped in and insisted that Natalie 'absolutely hates games' which is true. Any kind of organised fun is torture for her. She won't even play Monopoly at Christmas.

After what seems like hours of faffing around with the laptop, so long in fact that I manage to drink another entire mamamosa and eat a fondant baby (delicious – though the rest of the cakes found themselves shoved under their bed upstairs while everyone was chatting), Luke's sister puts baby photos up on the TV screen and we all have to guess who they are. This is actually quite difficult because we don't all know each other very well and all babies look exactly the same but we give it a go. It's obvious who Natalie is because there are two of us. Little clones, all fat and happy sitting in the bath. When our photo comes on the screen my mum puts her hand on her chest and closes her eyes briefly. I think she'd like to say, 'Aren't you both lovely?' or 'There are my girls' but she doesn't, she'd never say that, but I decide to believe that's what she means. I lean over to her.

'We look so happy, Mum,' I say quietly and smile at her.

She looks surprised.

'Oh you were, such happy babies.'

She smiles back at me, properly.

When the baby guessing game is over and just as we're all about to go and top up our drinks and fetch yet another slice of cake, Luke coughs and stands up awkwardly in the doorway as if to stop us leaving. He tentatively taps a fork against the side of his glass.

'I just wanted to say a few words before we all . . . you know . . . get too drunk.'

One of Natalie's friends whoops and everyone laughs. Too late for some of us.

'I just wanted to thank everyone who did this for us today, it's so special to have you all in the same room. Our little family has had so much love and support from you all over the years because, let's face it . . . we didn't have a bloody clue what we were doing.'

'Still don't!' Natalie yells.

'Yeah,' Luke says, 'we still don't. But it's easier now because El and Dan can point us in the right direction when we're parenting them wrong.'

Everyone laughs again. Ella and Daniel are standing at the back of the room, their backs pressed against the wall, clearly absolutely horrified that their dad is making a speech and even more horrified that he's talking about them.

'Basically though,' Luke swallows, he looks extremely nervous, 'the main thing I wanted to say was, Nat, I really love you . . . so much.'

Natalie makes a face like she's going to cry and looks around at everyone, loving it. She won't actually cry because her make-up is too perfect.

'I love you so much even though you drive me mad. Really,' he says, as if getting distracted by his own thoughts for a second, 'you are so annoying.'

He shakes his head and gets back on track.

'What I'm trying to say is. You are my whole life. I'm lucky enough that you've been my whole life for the past fourteen years. I can't believe that our family is about to get bigger and there's going to be someone else to love as much as I love you,' he looks at Ella and Daniel and says, 'and you, and you!'

Despite themselves, there is giggling from the back of the room.

'Nat,' he says and takes a deep breath, 'I want you to marry me. Will you marry me?'

She is, for the first time today, genuinely shocked. Her jaw drops open. I fish my phone out of my pocket again to get a photo of her looking stunned. She'll love that for her story.

'Yes,' she says. I'm wrong about her make-up, she lets her perfect smoky eye slide down her cheeks as she bursts into tears and runs (as fast as a very pregnant person can) over to Luke.

I turn around to see the twins looking completely gob-smacked. They obviously weren't in on this one.

I look at my mum and mouth, 'Oh my god' at her. She smiles at me utterly calmly and nods. Luke had obviously told one person. I look back at Luke and Natalie, who have been accosted by Ella and Daniel. They look at each other over the twins' heads and smile. There is something magical about that private moment in a room full of people, they're just the two of them really, always. I don't realise I'm crying until my mum presses a tissue into my hand. She doesn't stop to chat; she's got snacks to urgently decant into bowls.

After the surprise proposal the baby shower takes a turn from being a fairly sedate get-together into a proper party. Natalie's friends do a booze run and by 5 p.m. everyone has switched to gin and tonics and abandoned all the small talk. I'm just speaking to my mum's friend Janine about her son's recent break-up (she's looking for some professional answers from me but I think a simple 'Don't cheat' would be a start) when Natalie comes up and says she's going to have to borrow me for a minute.

Once I've made my apologies and told Janine it'll all work out for the best, I whisper in Natalie's ear, 'Erm, thank you for that. I've been stuck there for a *while*.'

'No, I actually do need to talk to you. I need to show you something,' she says, tucking her hair ostentatiously behind her ear with her left hand.

'Yeah, I've seen the ring, Nat. You've literally been shoving it in everyone's face all afternoon,' I say.

She rolls her eyes. 'No, not that.' She grabs my hand and drags me upstairs.

We go into her box room. It's tiny, previously only used for shoving stuff into and then closing the door and hoping it doesn't all fall out. It has been transformed.

'Oh my god, Natalie,' I say, reaching out to touch the patterned wallpaper. Green stripes with little animals dotted all over it. 'This looks amazing.'

'Thanks, I know,' she says, taking a seat in the little armchair next to the white cot that's underneath the window. There are no other chairs in the room. She gestures for me to sit on the floor in front of her so I pull up the fluffy rug and lean with my back against the cot.

She has put some photos up on the wall behind her. Mostly of Ella and Daniel but also some of us when we were babies and some of Luke and his sister. There's a mobile made of felt hanging above the cot, the moon and stars.

'This really is special, thanks for showing me,' I say.

'No, not this,' Natalie says, rolling her eyes as if I'm somehow crazy for thinking she wanted to show me her baby's nursery.

'*This.*' She taps a box on the floor in front of her with her foot and sort of nudges it towards me, too pregnant to pick it up herself.

I lean forward to grab it. The box is shoebox-sized and white and has a lid on top, which I gently lift off. Inside, nestled in a lot of tissue paper, is a beautiful gold frame with a black and white photograph in it. The photo is of Natalie and me when we were about six or seven years old. We're dressed the same, in dungaree shorts and floppy hats. We have bare feet so we must have been in our garden. We're sitting on Dad's knees and he has an arm wrapped around us both holding us in place. In one of his hands he is clutching a pair of sunglasses, which it looks like he took off just before the picture was taken. I'm glad that he did because in this photo he is smiling from ear to ear. His eyes are all crinkled up until they've nearly disappeared like mine and Natalie's do when we really, really smile, not just Instagram smile.

I look up at Natalie and bite my lip, aware that drinking all the mamamosas earlier has put me in the emotional danger zone.

'This . . . this is from Dad?' I ask.

She nods. 'There's a card as well.'

I look in the box and sure enough there's a card nestled in the tissue paper. I pick it up.

'Can I read it?' I say.

She rolls her eyes.

'Obviously.'

Dearest Natalie,

Firstly and most importantly, congratulations to you and to Luke. I am so thrilled for you that you're going to have another beautiful baby in your family. There is so much to say that is too big for a card but I hope we will have many years to say all the things we want to. I know I cannot make up for lost time but I can use the time I do have wisely and I intend to do so. Thank you forever to you and Natasha for reaching out to me. I feel like I've been woken up from a deep sleep.

I treasure the photos you've sent, especially of Ella and Daniel. I can't believe how much they look like you. I hope that one day you can all come out and see me, you're always welcome. And I hope that one day I am able to come and see you too. Truly, just say the word and I will be there. I suspect you won't believe me but it is my job from now on to prove you wrong.

I hope you enjoy this photograph as much as I do. It has brought me immeasurable joy in the darkest of times. It has been hung in pride of place in every house I have ever lived in. And now I hope it will hang in yours.

Please also tell me if there's anything I can contribute towards financially. I know babies are expensive and you can't push them around in a photograph . . .

Speak to you soon.

All my love,

Dad

PS please pass on the card enclosed to Natasha.

I look up from reading and Natalie passes me a card. It's different to hers. A notecard tucked into an envelope. I turn it over and it's a vintage postcard from Venice Beach. I can't help but smile.

Dearest Natasha,

I found this postcard and couldn't resist. I have been to Venice Beach hundreds of times before but now it will always remind me of you. I can never thank you enough for coming to see me. I deeply regret that I did not previously give you the credit you and your sister deserve for being the kind of people who might give second chances. Of course you are kind and thoughtful and brave. I cannot wait to get to know you better.

Apologies, my writing is getting smaller and smaller, I fear I am running out of room. I have to tell you, I see so much of myself in you. You think deeply and you worry deeply and you care deeply and all of those things are wonderful qualities but I fear they are not serving you as they should.

This is easy to say from a great distance (in every possible way) but I wish someone had said it to me so, Natasha, my darling, please choose to be happy. What makes you happy? Who makes you happy? Choose that. You deserve that. I promise you do.

Speak soon.
All my love, Dad

I look up at Natalie and down the rest of my mamamosa. I am fully crying now and so is she. I pass it to her to read but she waves it away.

'I've already read it.'

I burst out laughing and whack her on the leg with it instead.

'Sorry, I couldn't resist.'

She starts laughing too.

'It's so nice. What he said.' She nods towards the card.

I take a couple of deep breaths but my heart continues to thump rapidly, so fast that it feels like a hum in my chest. I close my eyes. This is one of those moments, I realise. Clarity washes over me. One of those moments when all my thoughts and feelings align and jumbled words make sense and good advice slots into place like missing puzzle pieces.

'Oh my god, Natalie,' I say. 'I really do want to be happy.'

'I know you do.'

She looks at me earnestly. 'Do you know what makes you happy then?' she says. 'Or, who?'

I don't say anything but I nod and scramble to get up, knocking over the empty glass.

'What?' Natalie says. 'You're not actually going to run away without telling me, are you?'

I ignore her as I run out of the room and fly down the stairs in search of my phone. I nearly crash into my mum, who is walking around with cling film presumably trying to preserve dry cake and bowls of crisp crumbs.

'Ooh,' she says, 'careful, what's the hurry?'

'I have to quickly . . . I have to make a phone call,' I say as I grab my phone from the arm of the chair where Janine is now sitting, some poor other person is nodding at her, looking desperately for their getaway.

I squeeze Mum's arm as I go to shimmy past her down the hall and then, without even thinking about it, give her a kiss on the cheek.

'It's been amazing today, Mum,' I say.

She looks at me in shock but, as I wriggle past her, I feel her squeeze my hand.

The front door is on the latch so I duck outside, past the couple of girls smoking on the porch, and out of the front gate. The fresh air is a shock to the system. I suddenly feel incredibly sober and somehow even more drunk at the same time. My head is incredibly clear still, single-minded in what I need to do, but I feel wobbly like my legs might give way. I perch on the wall in front of the house, take a deep breath and press call.

There's no answer. Typical. I can't leave a voicemail, I just can't. It's not 2001.

I turn around and see that I'm alone now. The smokers have gone back inside. I decide to leave a much more socially acceptable voice note instead. My hands shake as I open WhatsApp and press record.

'Hi, it's me. Obviously it's me. God. OK. I might be a bit drunk on mamamosas. It's a baby cocktail. I'm drinking for two! Ha. No. I mean . . . no. Shit. I'm nervous. You make me really nervous. You've

always made me really nervous. Right, look. I've just. I've realised something. I've had an epiphany. A breakthrough moment. I really think I . . . I'm trying not to be careless, you see. I really want to care more. I do care. I care so much. It's . . . overwhelming. Fuck. OK. What am I trying to say? I'm trying to say that I want to be happy. I want to choose happiness. I know you can't choose happiness all the time and some-times things are going to be shit or get messed up and they won't work out but you can choose some happiness some of the time. So yes. I know what makes me happy. You make me happy. I love you. I'm in love with you. Fuck. That's so weird to say out loud. But it makes so much sense. It feels like a relief. Um, I hope . . . I hope this doesn't come as too much of a . . . shock? And I know I might not make you happy. It's a two-way . . . just . . . I had to tell you. In this moment, I just . . . you had to know. So um, call me . . . back? I guess? Or, um . . . block this number? Ha ha. No, no. I'm . . . don't do that. OK I'll go. Speak to you soon, hope-fully. Um, bye.'

The plan is to stay over at Natalie's but exactly eight minutes after I send the longest and most embarrassing message of my life (I watch my phone the entire time) I receive a message back. When my phone vibrates in my hand a pulse of adrenaline floods through my chest.

I think you should come over so we can talk in person.

When?

Right now.

I find Natalie and tell her I have to leave and thankfully she doesn't question it at all. She just gives me a hug and tells me she loves me and to ring her later. I kiss Luke on the cheek (although I'm not sure he'll remember tomorrow) and squeeze the twins, who are absolutely in their element, lapping up all the attention from the increasingly drunk adults.

Before I leave I have one last bit of sister business to attend to. I run upstairs with the tote bag I always carry with me, fish out the dead baby cakes from under the bed and chuck them inside so I can bin them on the way out. No curses in this house. We're choosing happiness today.

Just as I've grabbed my things and am pulling open the front door my mum comes up to me. Her coat is already on and she has her car keys in her hand.

'Natalie says you're off already so I'm giving you a lift to the station,' she says.

'Oh no, Mum, you really don't . . .'

'I've already got my coat on,' she says, as though that is an irreversible decision, and so I just nod and we head outside together.

When she starts the engine, Magic FM comes blaring on. Erasure, 'A Little Respect', is playing.

'I love this song,' I say.

'I do too,' she says and turns it up even louder.

We drive in silence for a while listening to the radio but as we get closer to the station she turns it down.

'You're all right?' she says, not taking her eyes off the road.

She grips the steering wheel in the ten and two position like her life depends on it. I wonder when she ever relaxes. *If* she ever relaxes.

'Yeah,' I say. 'I am all right. I will be all right.'

I think about my dad telling Natalie he feels like he's woken up from a deep sleep. I don't think I've ever felt that more deeply in my life. Everything feels brighter, louder, clearer.

'Mum,' I say. 'Thanks for suggesting I meet up with Dad. It's been sort of . . . a turning point for me. I didn't even necessarily realise it at the time but it has. I didn't realise how much I wanted that.'

She nods, still staring straight ahead at the road. Her knuckles are white.

'You know,' she says, after a moment, 'when I say you're like him I don't mean it the way you seem to take it. It's not meant to be an insult.'

'It's hard though, isn't it,' I say. 'Because I know that you really hate him . . . so it makes me feel like . . .'

'I don't hate him!' my mum says. I turn to her, she's shocked. She looks at me like I've said something so outlandish that she doesn't even recognise me. She reaches down and switches the radio off altogether. She's not messing about.

'I don't hate him, Natasha. I was very angry with him for a long time. I am still angry with him to be honest. Not for leaving. That's all . . . that was so long ago. That happens. I'm angry at him for not making an effort with you girls. I know you gave him a hard time but that's kids for you. Especially when they're hurt. They give you a hard time. You can't just opt out.'

We're both quiet for a minute. I can't remember the last time we had such an honest conversation. I can't remember the last time we had any kind of conversation at all.

'I really thought that you couldn't stand me because I was like him. I just felt like I'd let you down. And that I was going to keep letting you down.'

My mum takes a deep breath and exhales loudly.

'I'm sorry,' she says. 'I'm sorry because that is true to some extent and I didn't think you'd pick up on it but of course you did. I . . . you were a difficult teenager. And I was going through something very difficult. We all were. I can see why you felt like that. I can.'

She pulls up at the station drop-off point but I don't make any move to get out of the car.

'I wanted you to have an easy life,' she says eventually. 'And I was scared that you were going to have a difficult life because of . . . who you are. Your dad tortured himself. He was the first gay person I ever met, you know.'

She laughs but not bitterly. The sound of it is so unexpected that it cuts through the tension between us. I find myself laughing, too.

'He tortured himself, Natasha, and I desperately didn't want you to live a tortured life. I wanted you to have the perfect life.'

She looks at me like she might be about to cry. I reach over and hold her hand.

'I don't live a tortured life, Mum. I don't. I'm OK. Nothing's perfect. There is no perfect life, but I'm OK.'

She looks me deep in the eyes and something she sees there appears to satisfy her. She nods and squeezes my hand.

'You get to wherever it is you need to get to in such a hurry then.'

'Thanks for the lift, Mum.'

'Anytime. Will you . . . will you text me when you get home? I know you won't remember but . . .'

'I'll remember. I'll text you.'

I stand in the cold and watch her drive away.

The journey back to Brighton is the longest of my life. I clutch my open book and don't turn a single page. I can't even look at my phone. I don't want to know if she's changed her mind and doesn't want to see me. I just have to believe the last thing she said to me was to go to hers, right now. I sip on the litre bottle of water I bought at the station trying to cleanse my body of all traces of mamamosa, I want to be entirely sober when I arrive. I'm surrounded by groups of people being obnoxiously loud, travelling into town for their nights out. I look at them and instead of getting irritated with them I try to take comfort in their blissful ignorance. I am standing on the precipice of one of the biggest moments of my life so far and they have no idea.

When I arrive back in Brighton it's gone 8 p.m., it's dark and cold and it's drizzling. I could get a taxi but decide to walk instead, it doesn't take long and I feel like I could use the fresh air. I regret that decision five minutes later when the drizzle becomes a downpour and my head-clearing walk turns into a soggy run with my coat pulled over my head and my phone tucked into my bra to protect it from the elements. By the time I arrive at the front door I am a mess but I gather myself before I knock, wiping under my eyes for stray mascara and pulling my soggy hair back into a bun rather than letting it hang limply against my face. I discard the gum I've been chewing in a bit of old receipt I have in my pocket, hopeful there might be a reason I won't want gum in my mouth in the next thirty seconds.

The second I pluck up the courage to knock she wrenches open the door so fast my hand is still hovering in mid-air. She's wearing her dressing gown and an expression that suggests I needn't have bothered with the gum at all.

'Are you serious?'

Absurdly, I worry I'm going to laugh. It's either that or be sick.

'Are you actually fucking serious?'

I realise she's expecting me to answer. She does not invite me in. Instead she keeps one hand on the door handle like she might slam it in my face at any moment.

'I think . . . I mean . . . yes?'

I wince as she spins on her heel and stalks upstairs. I think I'm meant to follow her. I step inside, close the door gently and follow her up and through to the kitchen, keeping a safe few paces behind, not wanting to incur any further wrath.

'I can't believe it. I really can't believe it. How long has . . .' she waves her hands in the air trying to find the word for it, 'how long has *this* been going on?'

She grabs a wine glass from the cupboard above her head and fills it without properly looking, red wine dribbles down the side of the glass and onto the counter. She does not offer me one, obviously. It's a real shame because I'm starting to regret deliberately sobering up on the way here. I've never needed a drink more in my life.

'I . . . look, this isn't really how I imagined you . . .'

'Oh OK, what did you think it would be like?'

'Honestly, I didn't think you *would* find out! It's not like I've been waiting to do some big reveal. I'm not sure I even properly knew myself until . . .'

'OK, so you're not even sure, this is just something you've blurted out?'

I go to sit down on one of the stools at the kitchen island, still facing her. It starts to sink slowly and I slide back off and stand upright again. She glares at me, waiting for her answer.

'No! I am sure, I am. I mean, I did blurt it out, yes. Look, it's been a very confusing . . .'

Her eyes open so wide they look like they might pop out.

'A confusing day for *you*?'

She waves her glass in the air, more wine spilling over the top and down her sleeve.

'I just. What I'm trying to say is that I am sure. I'm sure. It's just that before I just didn't really realise.'

It sounds pathetic. We're both quiet for a moment. She gulps down whatever wine she hasn't sloshed all over the kitchen.

'I don't want to ruin everything,' I say eventually.

'Well, it's ruined.'

She says this quietly, almost like I'm not meant to hear.

I don't believe her.

She moves towards me and I hold my breath.

She sits down on the stool next to me. It sinks very slowly to the ground. She stays put. I sit back down on my own stool and it sinks down to her level. I swivel slightly to face her.

'Even like this?'

She gestures at herself. Her dressing gown is covered in wine now and various other unidentifiable substances. Her hair is freshly washed, longer than I've seen it in a while. She never quite dries her hair enough, if at all. It leaves damp patches on her shoulders. Her face is slick with face oil. I'm amazed that when she lifts the wine glass to her lips it doesn't just slide right off.

'What do you mean?'

I resist the urge to lean forward and tuck some of that sopping wet hair behind her ear.

'You love me even like this?'

I take her in. It feels strange to look at her now. No need to pretend anymore.

'Yes.'

'In my disgusting dressing gown?'

'Yes.'

'Fuck.'

'I know. I'm sorry.'

She looks at me and I can't read her expression.

She shakes her head and downs the rest of her wine.

'Natasha,' she says.

It almost looks like a smile is playing on her lips against her will. She is trying to be serious. I want to reach out and touch her so badly.

'Yes, Georgia.'

'What did you think I was going to say?'

I sit back as far as the stool allows.

'Huh. I . . . I actually don't know. I don't know what I thought you'd say to be honest. I mean, I hoped you'd be happy obviously, not . . .' I try to decide what the best way to describe her current state is, 'furious?'

She ignores me.

'You didn't have an idea in your head of what this was going to be like?'

'Um, no.'

'Did you think I would tell you that I love you back?'

'Actually . . . no.'

'Then why . . .'

'I just . . . I had to get it off my chest. And I thought you'd like to know. It's nice to hear, right?'

She's quiet for a moment looking at me. A large droplet of water lands on the floor.

'I've wanted you to tell me that for a very long time,' she says eventually, very quietly. 'I've always wanted you to love me.'

'I have.'

I nearly lean forward to kiss her but sense that she would potentially push me off my stool so manage to hold myself back.

Georgia shakes her head sadly. I'm worried for a moment that she's going to cry.

'No, you haven't. Not in the way that I mean.'

I put my head in my hands. When I look up to face her she's staring right at me, unblinking.

'That's fair,' I say. 'I know it's too late to say it now.'

She stands back up and I'm scared she's going to ask me to leave but instead she says, 'I need to put some clothes on.'

I open my mouth to make a comment about how I don't mind but decide given I am walking on wafer-thin ice already to keep quiet.

'Do you want me to . . .' I make as if I'm going to get up and leave.

'Are you joking? Do you think you can just say something like this and leave? Do you want to leave?'

'No! I don't want to leave, it was just . . . I'm trying to be respectful.'

She snorts.

'You stay there.' She points down at me. 'Don't move. I'll be back in a second.'

I hold my hands up.

'I'm not going anywhere. I promise.'

As soon as I hear the thud of her footsteps on the stairs I

immediately move to sit on the sofa. I have a feeling we're not going anywhere for a while and I may as well be comfortable. I slip my socks off, both soaking wet, and when Georgia comes back into the room in joggers and a sweatshirt I'm perched on the edge of the sofa, holding my feet in my hands trying to warm them up.

She doesn't say anything but I must look pathetic because she doesn't seem angry that I moved. She sits on the other end of the sofa to me with her legs up, crossed underneath her.

'Do you need to get changed? Are you freezing?'

'No honestly, I'm fine.'

'Natty.'

'Yes please. I'm freezing.'

She sighs.

'Go and put something warm on.'

'Are you sure?'

'Yes, you look tragic and you're getting the sofa wet.'

I run upstairs to her room before she can change her mind, promising to be as quick as I can. Her room is immaculate as always. Her bed is made as if someone is going to come and inspect it. I open her wardrobe where she keeps jumpers folded at the bottom and pick out a hoodie. There's a jumper underneath it, baby pink and soft. It must be Zara's. I prod it cautiously as if it might suddenly come to life.

When I get back into the living room Georgia smiles when she sees me. I'm wearing her old university hoodie from when she went on tour with the football team.

'You're so annoying.'

'What? I just chose the one at the top of the pile.'

'Liar. That was buried deep.'

I go to answer her but something flashes over her face. Like she's remembered that we're not just joking around.

I cross my legs, mirroring her, and lean with my back against the arm of the sofa. If I reached my leg out I could touch her knee with my toes. We're not far apart but the middle sofa cushion feels like a gulf.

She nods at the table.

'I got you some wine.'

'Oh god,' I say, reaching out for it and taking a few grateful sips, 'thanks.'

She just looks at me like I'm a mirage, her brow furrowed.

'What were you doing before I messaged you?' I ask.

'Settling in for an evening of rubbish telly and an early night.'

'Ah, this is a bit of a change of plan then.'

'A bit.'

She reaches for her drink and then sits back with it, clutching it to her. The soft hum of something is playing on the radio in the kitchen but I can't make it out. I wonder if it was on when I got here or whether she switched it on while I was upstairs. The rain is still hammering against the windows.

'How was Natalie's baby shower?'

'It was lovely,' I say. 'She and Luke got engaged.'

'I know,' Georgia says. 'She's already done a post about it.'

I roll my eyes.

'She looks so happy,' she says.

'She is.'

We're quiet again for a minute.

'Listen George, I'm sorry for everything that happened with Zara . . .'

I don't know if mentioning her is a bad idea but it feels weird not to.

'Thanks. Yeah. It's been a rough couple of months. It was the right thing though. We weren't . . . it all happened too quickly.'

'When did she move out?'

'Second week of October.'

'Fuck. That's fresh.'

'Yeah.'

'This is the last thing you need.'

'What?'

'Me.'

She doesn't say anything for a moment and then she sighs deeply.

'What made you tell me today?'

'Um, I think sort of . . . a number of things.'

Georgia looks at me expectantly.

'Tell me them.'

'Right, yes. Well. I got this,' I reach into the zip-up compartment at the back of my bag, pull out the postcard from my dad and pass it to Georgia.

She puts down her wine so she can inspect it properly and she's quiet for a minute or two while she reads it.

'That's beautiful,' she says, when she looks up. She passes it back to me. 'So, I'm what makes you happy?'

'Yes.'

'I'm not just what makes you feel safe?'

'No! I don't feel safe, I feel like if you told me to leave I would quite literally die.'

She smiles, despite herself, and rolls her eyes at me.

'I'm not joking. I think I'd just expire.'

'Lucky you're staying then.'

'Am I?'

'For now.'

Once we've finished our wine Georgia goes into the kitchen to make us a cup of tea and when she comes back she sits down and relaxes into the sofa and closes her eyes briefly. She doesn't put her mug down, clutching it in front of her instead.

'We haven't really talked about what happened on the trip,,' Georgia says, staring resolutely into her tea.

'No,' I say. 'We haven't.'

We're both quiet for a moment.

'I'm really sorry,' she says quietly. She looks at me anxiously, biting the inside of her cheek.

'No, you don't . . .'

'I do. I'm so sorry. I was just so unhappy and I didn't even realise. It wasn't really about you. Well . . . it was. But it wasn't. I should never have said that stuff about your dad.'

'George. It's OK. It's OK. I think we needed something like that to happen. We needed to be that honest.'

'I should have called you though, afterwards.'

'I could have called you.'

She shakes her head.

'I wouldn't have answered. I just . . . when everything fell apart with Zara. I couldn't face it. I've just sort of hunkered down.'

'I know, Poppy says you've become a hermit.'

Georgia rolls her eyes but she's smiling.

'She keeps bringing me round these horrible "treats".'

'Oh god, yeah you need to tell her you've developed a sudden nut intolerance,' I say.

'Really?'

'Yeah, that's what I did. "Late onset nut intolerance", it covers coconut oil too.'

Georgia laughs.

'Maybe I'll do that.' She takes a sip of her tea. 'She's been amazing.'

'She's the best,' I say.

'She's been telling me about how you're "on a new journey",' Georgia says.

I roll my eyes.

'Oh yeah? What exactly has she said?'

'You're drinking less.'

I raise my cup of tea at her as if it's evidence. We'll forget the wine. And the mamamosas.

'That you're going to therapy.'

I nod.

'I have a great therapist.'

'That you're seeing more of your family. That you're speaking to your dad.'

Georgia nods her head towards the postcard.

'Well, yes. That's all true.'

'You're happy,' she says.

'I'm happier.'

We talk about Georgia's family for a while. How they were devastated about the break-up but mainly, Georgia thinks, because they were so excited about a wedding. She gives me a Josh update. He's doing well. He's going to spend Christmas with friends skiing in Austria, which means Georgia has to spend Christmas at home alone with her parents and their disappointment. At some point Georgia looks at her phone and tells me, shocked, that it's two in the morning.

'I had no idea it had got so late. Did you?'

I shake my head.

'Are you tired?' she asks.

'No,' I say. 'The opposite.' I mean it. I could sit at opposite ends of this sofa with her forever.

She nods.

'Although,' I say quickly, 'I can go . . . if you have something you need to . . . tomorrow.'

I reach for my phone.

'You don't need to go,' she says. 'You can stay.'

'Really?'

I hold onto my phone for a moment to show how serious I am about getting an Uber if she wants me to.

'Yes. Stay.'

I follow her upstairs and into the spare room, my room, where she switches on a lamp that I don't recognise. It has a pink light bulb in it emitting a warm glow. I wonder if Poppy brought it round for her. I have a pink light bulb in my bedside lamp too because Poppy says they're good for promoting relaxation and calm. Everyone in our flat always looks slightly feverish.

Georgia moves back from the bed and stands in the doorway. I don't know what to do with myself so I just stand a couple of feet in front of her, I rest my hand against the chest of drawers that used to have all my clothes in. My heart is thudding so loudly I feel sure that she can hear it. I won't be able to sleep for a second knowing she's upstairs.

We're both quiet for a moment. I don't want her to leave me here.

'I'm still so mad at you,' she says eventually.

'I know.'

'Why did it take you so long?'

I shake my head. I open my mouth and close it again. I have nothing to say that she'll want to hear.

'You mean it though?' Georgia says, biting her lip as if embarrassed by the question. Or afraid of the answer.

'I mean it.' My voice sounds strange, the words catching in the back of my throat.

Georgia takes a deep breath and nods.

'Say it.'

'Georgia. I love you.'

I take a step towards her.

'I loved you before and I love you now and I'm sorry I'm late but I'm here now. I'm not going anywhere.'

Georgia reaches out and places her hand on my waist, she pulls me gently towards her and when I step closer to her she sighs as if she's giving in. When she kisses me I reach up and put my hands on the back of her neck, in her hair. I don't want her to ever pull away. When I'm sure that if I move my hands she'll stay, I reach down and slip my hands under her sweatshirt. When I run my fingers along her hip bone she moans softly into my mouth and it's the best thing I've ever heard. I can't believe I was ever so stupid as to let her go.

I am slow and deliberate as we move onto the bed. Somehow I feel like we have all the time in the world. My instinct is to be gentle with her. I don't want to hold her too tightly in case she changes her mind, in case something I do tells her that this isn't a good idea. Her body is softer somehow than I remember. I dip to kiss her stomach and she squirms.

'What?' I pull back, afraid I've done something wrong.

'Nothing, nothing,' she says arching her back, pulling me back down.

And then, 'It tickles.'

I laugh and kiss her again, moving over her hips. She laughs too, still squirming.

'I forgot,' I say, my lips against the inside of her thigh. I pull myself back up, my hand where my mouth was.

Georgia's fingertips press into the small of my back and, when I push into her, she digs her nails in. She has clearly not decided that *she* needs to be gentle with me. I bury my face in her neck and take in every sound she makes, the thudding of her heart beneath me. She hooks her ankle over mine as if to hold me in place.

When she eventually lets me go I move to lie down beside her, my ankle still hooked around hers, my hand resting on her stomach. She looks up at the ceiling and pushes her hair out of her face. We're both quiet for a minute.

'I love you too by the way,' Georgia says, slightly out of breath, peering up at me from under the covers.

'Oh, thank god.'

She laughs and leans forward to kiss me.

'But I don't really know that things can go back to how they were,' she says when she pulls away. 'I don't think you should move back in.'

I turn around onto my side to face her, pulling the duvet up around me. I notice for the first time how cold the room is, as if no one's been in here for a while.

'Of course. Yes. That's fine. I'm happy living at Poppy's.'

'Are you really?'

'Yes! I love it. I'm getting there with Diane, she doesn't growl at me anymore when I get home. Poppy's always cooking things even if they are a bit weird. It's great.'

'So you're not going to move in here.'

'Right. No, that makes sense.'

'But you love me.'

'Correct.'

'And I love you.'

I take a deep breath and exhale slowly, letting those words wash over me.

'Yes.'

I take her hand, which is gripping the top of the duvet, and kiss it.

'So,' she says, moving her hand away and frowning. 'What are we then?'

'Um . . . seeing each other?'

She shakes her head firmly.

'No . . . Natasha, I don't want to be one of many people you're . . .'

'I'm not seeing anyone else. Obviously!'

'Right.'

She looks dubious.

'I'm not. I don't want anyone else. I'd move in here right now if you'd have me. Although I do recognise that is probably not a sensible decision. We should take it slow, make sure we do it right this time.'

'Let's go on a date,' Georgia says.

'OK. Just one date?'

She rolls her eyes.

'Some dates.'

'Fine. That makes sense. We'll go on some dates. I mean, if we could have all our dates here that would be totally fine by . . .'

'No,' she says, cutting me off. 'Proper dates. We're going to go out together.'

'Ugh,' I say. 'Fine.'

Georgia laughs and I pull her towards me so that she's wrapped around me, her head resting on my shoulder.

'So,' I say. 'Are we sleeping in my room tonight then?'

'It's not your room,' Georgia says, her voice muffled from speaking into my hair.

'OK then, shall we go upstairs to your room because,' I pause to yawn, 'I can't keep my eyes open and it's,' I reach over to the bedside table to grab my phone and then sit up so quickly that Georgia's head slips off my shoulder and hits the bed with a dull thud.

'What?' She sits up too and leans over, trying to look at my phone. 'What's wrong?'

'I've got like . . . twenty missed calls from Luke and my mum.'

My hands shake as I stab at my phone trying to read the messages I've missed over the past hour. I have a voice note from Natalie.

'*Natty the baby's coming. Fucking hell. Mum's coming over now to stay with the twins. Thank god that woman's got a landline because no other fucking person is answering their fucking PHONE. We're getting a taxi to the hospital now because Luke can't drive because he's been drinking since lunchtime. I haven't got any of my stuff together. I don't have a bag packed because we've got another two weeks to go. This was meant to be my Christmas baby. It's not Christmas yet. What are we on? The 7th? Sagittarius. Yes. Fine. That's good. It'll be OK, won't it?*

Promise it'll be OK? You can promise me that when you call me back. Please, please be sleeping with your phone under your pillow. Please please check this before the morning. Will you come straight away? I don't think I can do it without you.'

'No,' I say to my phone screen. 'No, it's too soon.' Then I turn to Georgia. 'It's too soon, George.'

'It's OK.' Georgia is somehow already up and pulling on the clothes that are abandoned at the end of the bed. 'It'll be OK, it's just a bit early. It's OK. Babies are a bit early all the time.'

'Really?'

I get out of bed too and then stand uselessly in the middle of the room until Georgia comes and hands me my clothes.

'All the time,' she says. 'Get dressed. Ring your mum. We'll drive.'

'No, you've been drinking.'

'Two small glasses about five hours ago. I'm fine. Let's go.'

'Fuck, I should have stayed over. Then I'd have been there with her. Fuck, fuck, fuck.'

'You're going to be there now,' Georgia says firmly. 'Come on.'

'Natalie. I'm on my way. It's going to be absolutely fine. I promise. I am going to be there as soon as I can. I love you. And yes, everyone loves a Sagittarius.'

I call my mum when we get in the car. She answers on the first ring.

'Natasha. Did you get Natalie's message?'

'I . . . yes of course! That's why I'm ringing!'

'They're at the hospital now.'

'I know, I'm on my way.'

'Good.'

She takes a deep breath.

'It'll be OK, won't it?' she says.

'Mum. It'll be OK.'

We drive in silence most of the way. It feels like forever even though it takes no time at all, the roads are empty and Georgia is driving as fast as possible. Just as we're approaching the hospital I realise I have to send one more message.

> *Dad, it's the middle of the night here and Natalie has gone into labour. I thought you'd want to know. I'll keep you updated.*

By the time we arrive my mum is already there with the twins.

'Oh my god,' I say rushing towards them. Both the twins get up to give me a hug and I kiss them both on their foreheads. They're all warm and sleepy and they seem so young all wrapped up in their coats under the fluorescent lights that tears spring to my eyes. I swallow them back quickly. I don't want to embarrass them. I need to hold it together, especially given that my mum looks like she's having a nervous breakdown.

'Mum,' I say, holding her hands and shaking them slightly, trying to get her to look at me and not straight down the corridor opposite us as if trying to see through all the doors and walls to where Natalie is. 'Mum, it's OK. Come on, it's going to be fine.'

My mum nods and I go to move away but she's got my hands in a vice-like grip. My mum is usually annoyingly calm to the point of uncaring about mine and Natalie's health. Being a nurse she's seen it all. There is no bodily secretion that can unnerve her. No angle of a limb she hasn't seen before. We learned early on that the answer to 'My leg hurts when I move it' is 'Then don't move it.' It's unsettling to see her like this. This is not something she can bandage up. This is not something she can have any control over whatsoever.

'Do you guys want me to get you anything?'

Georgia is standing a few feet away and my mum and the twins turn to her, only just noticing that she's here.

'Georgia drove me here,' I say, by way of explanation.

'Tea? Coffee?' Georgia says but, before anyone can answer, the doors swing open and Luke is standing there absolutely elated and perhaps still a little glassy-eyed.

'Baby girl,' he says. 'It's a baby girl.'

'Yes!' says Ella, shoving Daniel slightly so he has to steady himself on a chair.

'Are they?' My mum rushes towards him but stops just in front of him, leaving room for bad news.

'They're both OK. They're OK.' He bursts into tears and my mum opens her arms. He's at least a foot taller than her but somehow he looks very small with his head resting on her shoulder.

Mum and Luke go to be with Natalie while Georgia and I stay with the twins. They sit opposite us and while Daniel is on his phone, Ella looks up from hers and fixes us with a steely look.

'How come you were together in the middle of the night?'

'Um,' I say, glancing at Georgia who is also suddenly very interested in her phone, 'we were having a sleepover.'

'A sleepover?'

'Yes.'

She narrows her eyes.

'Was anyone else there?'

I see Georgia smiling out of the corner of my eye.

'No, it was a . . . private sleepover.'

Ella smirks, satisfied with the results of her sleuthing.

Thankfully Mum reappears to say that Natalie has requested my presence and that Georgia and I are allowed to visit.

'Oh no, no,' Georgia says, 'I don't want to intrude, I'll wait here.'

'Don't be silly,' I say and drag her up. We hold hands as we make our way down the corridor. When I let go she shakes her hand out a bit. There's a chance I might be just as tense as Mum.

Natalie is lying back in the bed, her hair in a perfect plait. She looks exhausted but beautiful as always. She does not have a glass of champagne in her hand but she does have a very tiny baby lying on her chest.

'Oh my god,' I whisper and rush forward to get a better look. Georgia stands back by the door.

'Is everything OK?' I say, sitting down in the chair next to her and pushing a stray hair out of her face. She must be exhausted because she doesn't bat me away.

'It's OK,' she says. 'They took her away at first,' her bottom lip starts to wobble, 'and it was horrible. I thought that . . . but they were just checking she was all right. And she is. She's OK. Just a bit early.'

The little alien in Natalie's arms squirms. She's all red and wrinkly. She looks extremely put out to be in this room full of harsh lights and loud noises, like she's been disturbed.

'She's beautiful,' I say and Natalie laughs, wiping a tear from her cheek.

'She looks like a gremlin,' she says, 'don't lie.'

'Natalie!'

'All babies do! A beautiful gremlin, but a gremlin nonetheless.'

Georgia laughs and Natalie looks up at her.

'Hi,' Georgia says shyly. 'I hope you don't mind that I'm . . .'

Natalie waves her hand.

'No, oh my god, are you kidding? Thank you for coming all this way. You don't have to hover in the doorway, you can come and sit down. Meet the gremlin.'

Georgia comes and sits next to me and cocks her head to one side, smiling at the baby.

'So do you have a name?' she says.

Natalie shakes her head.

'We haven't decided yet. We're going to get Ella and Dan's input.'

'Oh god,' I say.

'Input,' Natalie emphasises, 'just to make them feel involved. And then we'll choose whatever name we want.'

Natalie looks at Georgia, surveying her in a way she hasn't before. Georgia looks at me uncertainly.

'Georgia,' Natalie says, musing. 'Now that's a nice name, isn't it?'

'No,' I say. 'I mean it *is* a nice name, but no you're not naming your baby after Georgia.'

'Maybe I will,' Natalie says. 'You don't get to decide.'

There's a light tap on the door and then it flies open and Ella and Daniel run in with Mum behind them. I'm worried for a moment that they're going to launch themselves on Natalie but instead they stop very abruptly by her side and stare in awe at the baby.

'Woah,' Daniel whispers. 'It's tiny.'

'*She's* very tiny,' Natalie says, 'but she'll grow nice and quickly if she's anything like you two.'

'Can I touch her?' Ella says.

'Of course,' Natalie shifts slightly so the baby is closer to the twins, 'be very gentle.'

Ella and Daniel both reach out and stroke her head.

'She's soft,' Daniel looks up at Natalie and then around at everyone in the room, surprised. 'She looks like she's going to be all slimy and wrinkly but she's soft.'

'You looked slimy and wrinkly too,' I say.

'No I didn't!' he says but he's smiling. He goes back to being transfixed by the baby.

'Where's Dad?' Natalie asks them.

'Dunno,' Ella says.

My mum tuts.

'You do know! He's on the phone to his mum, isn't he? He's telling her she can come and visit first thing in the morning.'

'Oh yeah,' Ella says, 'he's on the phone . . . and he said we could name the baby.'

'No he didn't,' Natalie says quickly and then glances at my mum for confirmation, who shakes her head very firmly.

'We could call her Batman,' Daniel says.

'Right. Maybe.'

Natalie yawns and she suddenly looks shattered.

'Maybe we should give Mum some time to rest,' my mum says to the twins, 'let's go and get your dad, eh?'

They nod and each pat the baby very gently on the head by way of goodbye, as if she's a puppy.

Georgia and I get up to leave too. I lean in to kiss the baby and then kiss Natalie but she pulls me in close with her free arm and hugs me tight. I rest my head against hers, thinking how sweet this is and how nice she is when she's exhausted but then she whispers in my ear,

'You slept with Georgia.'

I pull back from her and she grins at me.

'Glad you found what makes you happy,' she says quietly, but loud enough that Mum hears her.

'What's that?' Mum says.

'Natty's happy,' she says and jerks her head at Georgia, who smiles awkwardly.

'Well we all are,' my mum says matter of factly.

As she ushers us all out of the room, she can't stop smiling.

Epilogue

One year later

It is pouring with rain. Not a gentle drizzle. Not a light shower. A torrential, terrible, stand-at-the-window-and-gawp-open-mouthed-at-it sort of downpour. This is not the plan.

Georgia joins me at the window. I can hear 'Driving Home for Christmas' playing on the radio in the kitchen, the station has been set to Magic Christmas for at least two weeks. Georgia has given up protesting and is embracing it. Well, tolerating it.

'Sorry darling,' she says and rests her head gently on my shoulder. 'It might stop.'

We jump at a crack of thunder. We're both quiet as it rumbles ominously.

'We're still going to have a lovely time,' she says. 'We just maybe need to reconsider . . .' she pauses, 'everything.'

'Should I just call them and cancel?' I say. I pull my dressing gown tighter around me and shiver.

'No,' Georgia pulls me away from the window and grabs

me by the shoulders, she gives me a little shake. 'Come on, there's no need to cancel just because of a bit of rain. Plus,' she looks at her fitness watch (some things never change), 'they'll probably have left by now. Just tell them to come here instead.'

'I wanted this to be perfect,' I say quietly.

'You can't control the weather,' Georgia says. 'Call them. I'm going to go and clear up and make it all lovely in here.'

She passes me my phone and heads out of the room, kissing me on the cheek on her way out. I sit on the edge of my bed and open the family WhatsApp group but, before I can send anything, a voice note pops up from Mum. She no longer sends any messages other than voice notes. She's hooked.

'Hi Natasha, it's your mum here. My app tells me it's going to be raining all day so we're all going to come to Georgia's . . . yours . . . to the flat instead. We can't be going for beach walks in this, I'm afraid.'

I roll my eyes; she says this as if I have suggested we take the baby out in the rain. Maybe I'll pop her in the sea as well. See if she fancies a swim.

'Tell me if we need to bring anything extra now you'll be catering for us all. They're picking me up in the car in about ten minutes so we'll see you around eleven. I'll keep you updated on our ETA. All right . . . bye for now.'

I resist the urge to message back saying, 'Please don't.' I'll be getting traffic updates now every ten minutes for their entire journey.

I walk into the kitchen and sit down at the table. I look

longingly at the coffee maker (Georgia) and she raises her eyebrows at me pretending she doesn't know what I want.

'Everything all right, love?'

My dad is sitting opposite me eating a piece of toast and reading the paper on his iPad. He holds it very far away from him even with his glasses on. 'Love' sounds funny in his accent, not quite English not quite American. He's been staying with us for the past week. The longest amount of time we've spent together in almost two decades.

'Yeah, this is just not how I wanted the day to turn out.'

I wave at the window just as Georgia puts a cup of coffee down in front of me. I grab her hand and kiss it.

'We're going to be cooped up in here all day now, I just thought maybe things might be easier if we could be out in the fresh air, you know? Lots to get distracted by.'

My dad smiles at me. He seems genuinely serene. I don't know how he's managing it.

'It's going to be absolutely fine. We don't need distractions. We've got the baby, we've got the twins. We can order in so you don't need to think about food.'

He says this last bit to Georgia, who is manically rooting through the contents of our fridge.

'Yeah, it's fine, isn't it?'

'It's fine.'

It's baby Grace's first birthday and I had a whole day planned. The twins and I were going to initiate Grace into our grand Brighton tradition – a walk on the beach, fish and chips and then back here for tea and cake since it's not ice-cream season. The weather forecast predicted that it would be crisp – blue skies and sunshine, *it said*. It was meant to be a perfect winter day and now it's going to be a disaster.

I'm meant to be showering and getting dressed but instead I lie down on the bed with my phone held at a dangerous angle above my head. Poppy and Charlie have both messaged me wishing me luck for today. We had them over for dinner last night so they could meet my dad and they did a very good job of being optimistic that the storm clouds, which were already brewing, would pass over.

I wish Poppy luck right back. She's seeing Felix today for the first time in six months. Earlier this year he agreed to the break she asked for and then in August he met someone new.

'*How are you feeling about it, Pops?*'

I see that she's recording a voice note, then she stops and calls me instead. I put her on speaker so I can potter around the room making the bed even though it will be remade later to Georgia's military-grade preference.

'How are you doing?' I ask.

'Ugh, well. I feel a bit sick about it to be honest but I think that's normal, isn't it? Not sick because I'm sad, just sick because it's weird and also because I might have had one glass too many last night. Ugh, I wish we were just doing a coffee. Why did I suggest lunch? How full-on.'

I peer into the mirror, smoothing out the lines on my forehead with my fingers. I must remember to ask Natalie later which face acid I should be buying.

'It's not full-on to eat lunch. You were together for two and a half years. It'll be nice to catch up, I promise.'

There's a long pause, I wonder if she is also inspecting herself in the mirror.

'Do you think he's going to tell me they're getting married or something? No. I mean, maybe. But that would be nice, wouldn't it? Nice for him. It's what he wanted. Quick though. No, but nice. I'd be happy. I would.'

Before I can interject she ploughs on, clearly having been obsessing over this all morning.

'And I just have to think that I'm happier now than I was. I'll keep saying that like a mantra all through lunch. *Happier now than I was.*'

'You are, Poppy. You're just more yourself. I'm very proud of you.'

She ignores me completely.

'Ooh so, I'm thinking. I was so inspired last night by Charlie talking about going on holiday alone last year and how they're going to go again and how they learned so much about themselves so I looked up the place in Thailand they went and it looks amazing and I think I should go. Like, I think it would be really good for me.'

She pauses to take a breath.

'Do you and George want to come?'

I sit down on the edge of the bed and laugh.

'Do we want to come on your holiday that you're going on alone?'

'Oh,' she says, 'I see what you mean. Well maybe you can just leave me alone for a couple of hours in the afternoon or something. I'll meditate, I expect. Something spiritual anyway. Maybe . . . pray?'

'Right. Let's see. Let me get through today first. Listen, I've got to go and get dressed. They'll all be here soon.'

'Eeek, good luck! Love you!'

'Love you.'

I message Charlie quickly while I shout to Georgia that I really am going to get in the shower now.

Poppy's coming on your next trip to find yourself.
Be warned!

Our buzzer goes just as Georgia is finishing hanging up the 'Happy Birthday' banner we had left over from her party this year.

'It's a bit wonky,' she says, climbing back onto the chair to fix it. I grab her arm and pull her down.

'She's one,' I say. 'She doesn't know what a sign is, let alone if it's wonky.'

I run out of the living room to answer the door and I just know that Georgia's going to climb back onto the chair to fix it.

My dad and I reach the top of the stairs at the same time. He's staying in my old room and has been getting ready in there for at least an hour. He looks very smart and I realise that he's nervous. Maybe even more nervous than I am.

'I'll get them,' I say.

He hovers at the top of the stairs.

'You look great, Dad,' I shout back up behind me. Before he has a chance to reply I open the door and the rest of my family descend upon me.

I stand to one side and let everyone run up the stairs. Luke races after Ella and Daniel, Natalie is behind them holding baby Grace. Natalie kisses me on the cheek. She is perfectly made-up but she looks completely exhausted.

'Bloody hell,' she says. 'I need a fucking drink.'

'Natalie!' I admonish.

'What?' She glances down at Grace who is peering up at me curiously, one chubby hand reaching out. I like to think it's so she can hold my hand but I know she likes the look of my hair, which is ideal pulling length.

'She doesn't know what I'm saying, does she?'

'I suppose not. Where's Mum?' I peer out of the open door behind her.

Natalie rolls her eyes.

'She's getting all her bits out of the car. I told her we'd just order lunch but she insisted on stopping off to buy all this food. And balloons.'

'For fuck's sake.'

'I know. She's nervous.'

I nod my head towards the top of the stairs.

'So's he.'

'Well they need to get over it. We're hardly parent-trapping them, are we?'

She honks with laughter at herself and pushes past me shouting for Ella and Daniel to take their shoes off.

I hear the front door of the building slam and my mum appears at the bottom of the stairs with two overflowing bags for life by her side. I reach out to take one and she looks at me gratefully.

'That took us no time at all,' my mum says.

'Yeah and I hear you had a stop-off?'

'Well I didn't know if you would have any food.'

I take a deep breath and decide not to react. She's nervous.

We take the food into the kitchen for Georgia to deal with. She is making six hundred cups of tea by the looks of it. My mum looks around the room nervously as though my dad might jump out from under the table and surprise her.

'They're all in the living room, Mum,' I say. 'Shall we go and say hello?'

'Oh well yes, we'd better, hadn't we?'

Without even thinking about it I reach out my hand and she takes it. For a moment I wonder if I'm going to lead her in there but she just squeezes it quickly and gestures for me to go ahead. She follows close behind.

In the living room, Grace is sitting on my dad's lap being gently bounced up and down. Ella and Daniel are sitting cross-legged on the floor by his feet telling him all about Grace's particular likes, dislikes, hobbies, etc. He is nodding diligently, knowing instinctively that the only role required of him is one of a captive audience. Natalie and Luke are sitting on the sofa next to each other with their legs stretched out in front of them. They look like they are on the verge of dropping off. One of Grace's dislikes, according to the twins, is sleeping at night time.

'Nan,' Ella says the moment we walk into the room, totally unaware of any of the adult awkwardness. 'Nan, come over here, we're telling our *grandad*,' she says the word with relish, new on her lips, 'all about Grace.'

Mum dutifully walks over and stands behind the twins. She looks down at Grace who is screeching, delighted at this man who is jiggling her about.

'And what are you telling him?' Mum says, reaching down and touching Ella's hair gently. She does the same to Daniel.

'Oh,' says Dad, 'they're being very thorough. I know what she's hoping to get for her birthday, what she might like for Christmas, where she goes on the weekends for her nights out.'

Ella and Daniel squawk with laughter. Everything about my dad is cool to them, from his funny accent to his smart clothes. More importantly though, he is new. I can't wait for the day when he is handled with the same cool disinterest bordering on pity that the rest of us are subject to.

My mum smiles too.

'Hello Martin,' she says to my dad.

'Hi Sandy,' he says. I glance at Natalie and she looks as close to tears as I am. My mum is a Sandra to even her closest of friends but to him she is still Sandy. My dad lifts the baby towards her, asking if she wants to have a turn.

'Oh no,' Mum says. 'She's having a lovely time with you.'

'Well,' he says. 'We're new friends. Just getting to know each other, aren't we?'

He beams at Grace and then up at my mum.

'So you are,' my mum says.

'Come and sit here, Mum,' Natalie pats the space on the sofa next to her.

Georgia bustles in carrying a tray with mugs of tea for everyone, including Ella and Daniel who have apparently decided they now like it although, I notice as they start shovelling, not without at least five teaspoonfuls of sugar. They're going to be fun later.

'Sorry,' Georgia says, 'there's some weird mugs here, we're not usually making tea for this many people.'

She makes a face as she hands Natalie a mug in the shape of a badger's head. A Mum special.

Natalie rolls her eyes and gestures around her at the immaculate living room.

'Oh please,' she says. 'We're so tired and our place is so messy we're basically down to putting teabags in our mouths and drinking directly from the kettle.'

Luke nods wearily as he watches Daniel dipping the teaspoon into the pot of sugar and putting it straight into his mouth. He briefly looks like he might say something but then he just closes his eyes, resigned.

'It's so tough when they're this age,' my dad says, turning Grace around so she's facing the group rather than him. She beams at everyone. He looks at my mum. 'Do you remember with these two? For the first six months it was like a war zone.'

'I will never forget,' my mum says seriously. She lifts her hand to her chest and shakes her head, overcome with the terrible memories of Natalie and I joining them in the world.

We're all quiet for a moment. Georgia's leg is jiggling next to me where we're sitting cross-legged on the floor. I can tell she can't bear the silence, she opens her mouth to say something, but before she can my mum puts down her cup of tea and says,

'So Martin, how are you getting on? Being back here, I mean? Are you enjoying your visit?'

I grab Georgia's knee, partly to share the moment with her and partly to keep her still. To have them in the same room together and chatting is so surreal. I look at Natalie to catch her eye and she raises her eyebrows at me.

'I'm having such a wonderful time. We're having a good time, aren't we, Natasha?'

He smiles at me. It's a casual question but I can see how desperately he wants me to say yes.

'The best time,' I say. 'We've watched, like, two seasons of *The Crown*.'

'Natasha!' my mum says.

'What?'

'Your father has not come all the way here just to sit and watch TV with you.'

'He wanted to! Dad, you wanted to! Tell her!'

My dad laughs.

'It's true, I did. And the weather hasn't allowed for too much else. All I did was come here to spend time with you all. I don't care what we do.'

'Yeah, see?' I say to Mum. 'He's having a *great* time.'

Before I can regress any further into my teenage self, Georgia interrupts to make everyone order lunch. There is a three-way battle of wills between my mum, dad and Georgia on who gets to pay. Natalie and I sit it out, more than happy to let them fight among themselves. In the end Georgia wins.

'I absolutely insist,' she says, holding her hand up at them both. 'You're our guests and it's my pleasure.'

We don't have enough room at our table for everyone, so the twins help me set up a picnic on the floor. Despite Mum's protestations that we ought to have plates and cutlery, everyone just eats their fish and chips straight from the boxes. I open a bottle of Sauvignon Blanc for the grown-ups, which is extremely well received. The twins each try a bit and are absolutely disgusted.

'Maybe it would be nicer with sugar in it,' I suggest and Luke glares at me.

'Please don't,' he says, quietly. A man truly on the edge. He necks his wine and I pour him another glass immediately.

Once everyone's finished eating and Ella is sitting next to my dad taking selfies with him to show him all the filters on Instagram, my mum asks me to help her in the kitchen.

'I've brought a cake with me,' she says. 'Don't laugh, it's come out a bit funny.'

She lifts an enormous Tupperware box with a handle on the top out of one of her shopping bags. I lean against the counter and watch her. Magic Christmas is still on. We've walked in halfway through East 17's 'Stay Another Day'.

She lifts the lid off the box gingerly as though something might come out and bite her. I go and lean over her shoulder.

'Oh, Mum!'

'I know,' she says, 'I know, it's rubbish but I just wanted to . . .'

'It's not rubbish,' I say. 'It's perfect.'

My mum has made the kind of cake she used to make when Natalie and I were little. The kind we had to choose out of a book every year. This one is a princess castle cake. I recognise it. It's covered in silver balls and pink icing and has turrets made of ice-cream cones. I remember at the end of one birthday party standing in the kitchen doorway watching her and my dad chopping a pink castle up to put into party bags, giggling with each other, picking silver balls off the top of the icing and popping them in their mouths. They'd really been happy once.

'Do you think she'll like it?'

'Mum, she won't know what it is.'

'Natasha!'

'She won't!'

My mum looks at me and for a moment I'm worried she's going to burst into tears.

'Mum, she won't know what it is but she'll know that it's pink and sweet and that it's for her. And *we'll* know what it is. And it's perfect. I already said it's perfect, didn't I?'

'You did. Thank you. Now help me light these.'

My mum produces a packet of multicoloured birthday candles and a box of brand-new matches from her bag.

'Mum, we have matches here.'

'Oh well, I didn't know. I didn't want to presume.'

I look at the ceiling, praying for it to give me strength. When I look back down my mum has covered the cake in candles.

'She's only one! You just need one candle!'

'Oh,' my mum says, waving me away, 'I'm doing some more for Ella and Dan so they don't feel left out.'

'They're thirteen!'

'You still feel left out when Natalie gets something and you don't, don't you?'

She's got me there. When we've lit all the candles and I've shouted through for everyone to close the shutters and switch off the lights we take one end of the cake board each, which isn't really necessary but feels like the right thing to do. Before we leave the kitchen we pause for a moment as if we're gathering ourselves before stepping out on the stage.

'You're doing great, Mum,' I whisper.

'Am I?' she whispers back.

I nod and we take deep breaths making our big entrance.

The cake is, of course, a huge hit with everyone. And even better, once we've reopened the shutters we realise that it's stopped raining. There is even, if you really look for it, the tiniest hint of blue sky.

'You know,' Georgia says as she nibbles on a turret, a silver ball dropping off and rolling under the sofa, 'we should go for a little walk on the beach now that it's cleared up.'

She is met with a cacophony of groans.

'No come on,' I say to everyone, I look down at my phone to check the weather app, 'the sun sets in half an hour apparently and if it stays this clear it'll be beautiful.'

'Yeah all right, you do that. I'll stay here and sleep,' Natalie says, resting her head on Luke's shoulder. He has already fallen asleep, a piece of pink cake still on his fork.

'No, you're coming,' I say. 'We're doing everything together,' I say, looking very pointedly at her and nodding my head towards Dad, 'as a *family*.'

By the time we make it down to the beach the majority of the whining, even from Natalie, has stopped. I'd anticipated gale force winds but as we clamber down onto the pebbles it's remarkably still.

Aside from a couple of dog walkers we're the only ones on the beach and when the sky turns pink it feels as though it's just for us.

'This was a good idea,' Georgia says to me and reaches out her gloved hand to hold mine.

Natalie and Luke are walking ahead with Grace who is fast asleep strapped to Luke's chest. My mum is right behind them with the twins who keep picking up stones and lobbing them in the direction of the sea. They don't get anywhere close but I don't think that's really the point.

Georgia runs ahead, she would say it's to let me have some time with my dad but actually it's because she's clearly itching to join in with the pebble-chucking.

My dad and I walk very slowly together watching the sky changing colour. We're quiet for a while. It's a comfortable silence. We've very quickly grown more familiar with one another over the past year but this week has been like a crash course in learning to be around each other.

'How does this compare to your LA sunsets?' I say, smiling at him. I notice that his teeth are actually chattering with cold.

'Oh,' he says without missing a beat, 'it doesn't compare at all.'

'It could stand to be a few degrees warmer,' I say.

'Maybe,' he concedes. And then shakes his head. 'No, it's exactly right. Everything is how it's meant to be.'

I roll my eyes.

'Dad.'

'What?'

'That's so cheesy.'

'I can't be cheesy when I'm surrounded by my family? On a day like this?'

Everyone has stopped to stand and look at the setting sun. Natalie has her phone out, obviously. I've left mine at home specifically to be in the moment. Plus, I'll just steal her photos later. My dad and I stop a few metres away from everyone to take it all in. The sky turns orange above the water and the waves gently lap at the shore. Georgia cheers at herself for skimming a stone further than anyone else. She turns around to us and points at the sea as if to say, did you see it? We nod encouragingly and my dad chuckles softly.

'You're right,' I say to him as Georgia runs back up the beach to join us. 'Everything is how it's meant to be.'

Acknowledgements

Firstly, thank you, Emma Finn, for your unwavering support. Your positivity and enthusiasm are infectious. I am so very lucky to have you in my corner.

Thank you to my wonderful editor Emma Capron for understanding and loving these characters as I do and for working your magic. Also, thank you for the notes which make tweets go viral.

Thank you also to Ajebowale Roberts for working so hard on this book and for your meticulous and insightful edits.

Thank you to Milly Reid, Lipfon Tang and Abbi-Jean Reid.

Thank you to everyone behind the scenes at Quercus who made this book happen, David Murphy, Isobel Smith, Chris Keith-Wright, James Buswell, Frances Doyle, Hannah Cawse, Sinead White, Rhian McKay and Nicola Howell Hawley.

Thank you, Beth Frees, for the beautiful cover illustration.

Thank you, Elizabeth Jollimore, for your generous bid and to Allison Hunt for having the perfect name for a therapist.

Thank you to all my friends for being so supportive. Special thanks to Susie for being my Brighton correspondent, to Katy and Cleo for the walks and the Mr Whippys and to Ashley for coming up with the title, and for providing much wine and gossip – my lifeblood.

Also, thanks to brilliant authors Emma Hughes and Emmett de Monterey for all your support. May our voice notes and DMs never see the light of day. Thank you, Dàvid Darvasi, for insisting every bookshop you enter orders copies of my books. I promise I will do the same.

Thank you, Grace, for providing me with a great character name. Reggie, you'll be in the next one. And not as a hamster.

Thank you, Mum and Dad. I would never have thought I could write stories for a living if it weren't for your steadfast belief in me. Thank you for being my biggest fans.

Thank you, Sarah, for consistently being the funniest person I know. Writing about sisters is easy because of you.

Jen, thank you for driving me around LA because I still can't. Thank you for your love, support and infinite kindness. Thank you for your ideas and for your gentle corrections of my appalling grammar. I'm sorry if I cursed our relationship by dedicating this book to you, but I think we can both agree, it was worth it.

Finally, thank you to everyone who has got in touch with me to say they want to read more uplifting stories about queer people. Everyone who tells me they wish they'd had these books when they were growing up, that they might have brought some joy or eased some pain – this story and all my stories are for you.

Laura Kay is an author and journalist. She has an MA in American History from the University of Sheffield, and now lives in East London. In 2018, Laura was selected as one of the ten PRH WriteNow mentees, where she developed her debut novel, *The Split*. *Tell Me Everything* is her second novel.